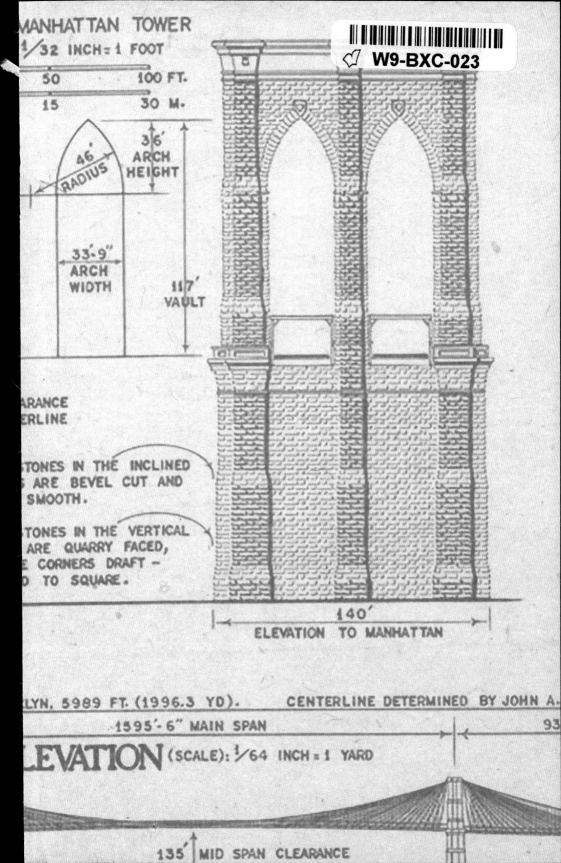

MANHATTAN TOWER

1/32 INCH = 1 FOOT

50 · · · · 100 FT.

15 · · · · 30 M.

46' RADIUS

36' ARCH HEIGHT

33'-9" ARCH WIDTH

117' VAULT

ARANCE
ERLINE

TONES IN THE INCLINED
ARE BEVEL CUT AND
SMOOTH.

TONES IN THE VERTICAL
ARE QUARRY FACED,
CORNERS DRAFT —
TO SQUARE.

140'
ELEVATION TO MANHATTAN

LYN, 5989 FT. (1996.3 YD).   CENTERLINE DETERMINED BY JOHN A.

1595'-6" MAIN SPAN   93

LEVATION (SCALE): 1/64 INCH = 1 YARD

135' MID SPAN CLEARANCE

Praise for

THE ENGINEER'S WIFE

"*The Engineer's Wife* is just the sort of novel I love and—I hope—write. Against all odds, a dynamic, historic woman builds a monument and changes history as she and her surrounding cast leap off the page. What a life, and what a beautifully written and inspiring story!"

—Karen Harper, *New York Times* bestselling author of *The Queen's Secret*

"Well-researched with great attention to detail, *The Engineer's Wife* is based on the true story about the exceptional woman who was tasked to build the Brooklyn Bridge. Though the great bridge would connect a city, it would also cause division and great loss for many. Tracey Enerson Wood delivers an absorbing and poignant tale of struggle, self-sacrifice, and the family transformed by the building of the legendary American landmark during the volatile time of women's suffrage, riots, and corruption. A triumphant debut not to be missed!"

—Kim Michele Richardson, bestselling author of *The Book Woman of Troublesome Creek*

"Who really built the Brooklyn Bridge? With its spunky, tough-minded heroine and vivid New York setting, *The Engineer's Wife* is a triumphant historical novel sure to please readers of the genre. Like Paula McLain, Tracey Enerson Wood spins a colorful and romantic tale of a storied era."

—Stewart O'Nan, author of *West of Sunset*

"*The Engineer's Wife* is historical fiction at its finest. Tracey Enerson Wood crafts the powerful and poignant story of Emily Warren Roebling, the compelling woman who played an instrumental role in the design and construction of the Brooklyn Bridge. This is necessary fiction for our time—paying tribute to women's overlooked contributions and reminding us of the true foundations of American history."

—Andrea Bobotis, author of *The Last List of Miss Judith Kratt*

"Tracey Enerson Wood raises Emily Warren Roebling from the historical depths, bringing to vivid life the story of the woman who saved the Brooklyn Bridge."

—Anne Lipton, MD, PhD, Harlequin Creator Fund Recipient
and author of *Putting the Science in Fiction*

the ENGINEER'S WIFE

TRACEY ENERSON WOOD

sourcebooks
landmark

Copyright © 2020 by Tracey Enerson Wood
Cover and internal design © 2020 by Sourcebooks
Cover design by Mumtaz Mustafa
Cover image © Ildiko Neer/Arcangel Images; National Archives and
Records Administration, New York and Brooklyn Bridge: Promenade.,
ca. 1898. Photograph. https://www.loc.gov/item/2002706694/

Sourcebooks and the colophon are registered trademarks of Sourcebooks.

Published by Sourcebooks Landmark, an imprint of Sourcebooks
P.O. Box 4410, Naperville, Illinois 60567-4410
(630) 961-3900
sourcebooks.com

Library of Congress Cataloging-in-Publication Data

Names: Wood, Tracey Enerson, author.
Title: The engineer's wife : a novel / Tracey Enerson Wood.
Description: Naperville, Illinois : Sourcebooks Landmark, [2020]
Identifiers: LCCN 2019032996 | (hardcover)
Subjects: LCSH: Roebling, Emily Warren, 1843-1903--Fiction. | Roebling,
    Washington Augustus, 1837-1926--Fiction. | Brooklyn Bridge (New York,
    N.Y.)--Fiction. | GSAFD: Biographical fiction.
Classification: LCC PS3623.O6455 E54 2020 | DDC 813/.6--dc23
LC record available at https://lccn.loc.gov/2019032996

Printed and bound in the United States of America.
WOZ 10 9 8 7 6 5 4 3 2 1

To all the readers and all the writers, without whom all is lost.

ONE

Washington, DC
February 1864

T he light, sweet honey scent of burning candles did not quite mask the odor of blood and sweat in the makeshift ballroom. Not far from the White House, the room was tucked inside a military hospital, itself a repurposed clothing factory. Noise echoed in the vast space, with cots, machinery, and great rolls of cotton neatly stacked against the walls. Tall windows let in slanted rectangles of light upon women in dark uniforms setting out flower arrangements. I too felt out of place. Dressed in a ball gown, I was like a fresh flower in a room meant for working men.

Double doors opened from an anteroom, and chattering guests tumbled in. An orchestra hummed, tuning up as men clad in sharp Union dress uniforms gathered in conversation groups with women in their finery. Nearer to me, a line of men on crutches and in rolling chairs aligned themselves along a wall, each of them missing a limb or two or otherwise too broken to join the healthier soldiers.

I nodded my greetings, hesitant at first. Like most young women in my small town of Cold Spring, New York, other than a glimpse of a few limping, bedraggled returned soldiers, I had been sheltered from the consequences of war. Here, the wounded men clambered over one another, some in hospital pajamas, some half in uniform, reaching out to me, seeking to be included despite their infirmities.

I ignored the bloody gauze wrapped around heads and the stench of healing flesh as I shook their hands, right or left, bandaged or missing fingers, making my way down the line. One after the other, they thanked me for coming and begged me to dance and enjoy myself.

In the letter that had accompanied the invitation to the event, my brother had been clear: *The ball is intended to be a celebration of life, a brief interlude for men who have seen too much, and the last frivolity for too many others.* It pained me to look into their eyes, wondering who amongst them were enjoying their last pleasure on this earth.

"So pleased to meet you. I'm Emily." I offered my hand to a soldier with one brown eye, his face cobbled by burns.

He held my hand in both of his. "Miss Emily, you remind me there is still some joy in life."

I smiled. "Will you find me when it is time to dance?"

The soldier laughed.

My face flushed. It was too forward for a lady to ask a gentleman to dance. And perhaps he was unable.

"You can't tell from my pajamas, but I've earned my sergeant's stripes." He tapped his upper arm. "I won't be joining the butter bars."

The term *butter bars* rather derogatorily referred to the insignia of newly minted lieutenants. Belatedly, I recalled my invitation was to the *Officers'* Ball, and the sergeant had apparently come to watch. My cheeks warmed. I had gaffed thrice with one sentence. Not an auspicious beginning, considering my goals for the evening.

More women filtered in, each on the arm of an officer. In contrast to the men against the wall, the exuberance and freshly scrubbed skin of these officers made me doubt they'd seen battle. I felt rather out to sea. I had insisted on arriving without a chaperone, as I had expected to be escorted by my brother, but he was nowhere to be seen.

His last letter had said the fighting had slowed during the winter months, but that could change at any moment. Even if it hadn't, he was a target. I shook the image of a sniper out of my head. Surely, if something terrible had happened, they wouldn't still be setting up for a ball.

The soldier still had a firm hold on my hand. I pasted a smile on my face and peeked about the room. Was it more awkward to mingle with the others, all in couples, or rude not to?

The sergeant jutted his jaw toward the center of the ballroom. "Go now. We'll be watching."

I nodded and slipped my hand from his, resisting a peek at my white silk gloves to see if they'd been soiled. My ball gown showcased the latest fashion: magenta silk, the skirt full in the back and more fitted in the front. My evening boots echoed the profile; with an open vamp and high heel, they reminded me of Saint Nicholas's sleigh. I smoothed the gown's travel creases and mulled its merits. *Comfort: adequate. Usefulness: very good, considering its purpose was to please the eyes of young men.* Mother had disapproved of the deeply scooped neckline, but she had sheltered me long enough. I was now twenty years old and craved amusement.

The handsome dress uniforms and elaborate gowns each guest wore suggested formality and elegance, but raucous laughter shattered the tranquility of the elegant piano music. Clusters of young men erupted in challenges and cheers, guzzling whiskey and fueling their spirits.

I stepped closer to a particularly animated group in which a tall, handsome captain held court among a dozen lieutenants. Perhaps he could advise me as to where I could find my brother.

"What will you do after the war?" someone asked.

"Rather the same thing as before. Build bridges. Blow them up." The captain raised his glass, and the others followed, laughing and cheering.

A bespectacled, earnest-looking young man asked, "Sir, why would you blow up bridges in times of peace?"

The captain's smile faded, and he leaned into the group as if sharing a great conspiracy. "There are only so many places to build a bridge, and sometimes we have to blow up an old, rickety bridge to make room for a new one."

I stepped back, feeling awkward for eavesdropping.

The captain continued his lesson. "I'll be helping the country to heal, connecting Kentucky and Ohio with a long-abandoned project. And then we'll be doing the impossible. Connecting New York and Brooklyn with an even grander bridge. It will become one enormous city. If you want a job after the war, boys, come see me."

I shook my head. The captain didn't lack for hubris. But just as I was about to approach to inquire about my brother, he excused himself and hurried off.

❧

Twilight had faded, and the candles and gas lamps burned brightly, as if the assembly's energy had leached out and lit the room. All the women seemed thoroughly engaged, so I wandered about, my worry for my brother steadily increasing. A tiny glass of golden liquid was thrust at me, and I took a sip, the burning in my throat a pleasant sensation.

The orchestra played a fanfare, and a deep voice rang out. "Ladies and gentlemen, the commander of Second Corps, Major General Gouverneur Kemble Warren—the hero of Little Round Top."

Relief ran through me like a cool breeze on a hot day. I should have known that the commander of thousands would need to make an entrance. Officers snapped to attention and saluted the colors as they passed, then held their position for my brother. My heart fluttered when I saw him, taller than most, shaking hands as he made his way through the crowd. Our family called him GK, as Gouverneur was a most awkward name. Thirteen years my senior, he was now in his thirties, with sleek black hair and a mustache that met the sides of his jaw.

After months of worry and cryptic letters from which I could only gather that his troops had won a major battle in northern Virginia, seeing my brother lifted me two feet off the ground. I waved as he scanned the room, his eyes finally finding me.

GK had been more surrogate father than older brother, our father having passed away several years previously. He was the closest to me amongst all our surviving siblings, no matter the time or distance that separated us. As he edged closer, my smile faded at the sight of his gaunt frame, the strain of war reflected in the streak of gray in his hair and the slump of his shoulders.

The young officer following behind my brother glanced my way. I looked, then looked again—GK's aide was the same captain who had been boasting about healing the country with bridges. His eyes landed on me for the briefest moment, then scanned the room as if the enemy might leap from the shadows.

I coughed to cover a laugh. While he tried to appear vigilant, his gaze returned to me again and again. Perhaps he had seen me eavesdropping.

I squeezed past the knots of guests toward GK, but the crowd was thick around him. He greeted the wounded men, exchanging a few words and shaking hands down the line. Next, he worked his way into the larger crowd, and I was pushed back by officers surging toward him as they jockeyed for his attention.

"Men of the Second Corps." GK's booming voice filled the room as if to assure them that he could be heard over the firing of cannons. "Let us welcome these fine ladies and thank them for honoring us with their presence."

He signaled the orchestra, and hundreds of young men in dark blue began to dance, their shoulders shimmering with gold-fringed epaulets, like an oasis after years in the desert. I danced with one handsome lieutenant, then another and another, each spinning me into the arms of the next in line. When at last I paused, gasping for breath, the officers gathered around me, helping me to tuck back the long ribbons that were losing the battle to contain my curls. While the other women sniffed their disdain at my exuberant dancing and frequent change of partners, the men laughed and vied for me. No matter about the women. I meant to keep my promise to my brother by providing amusement for his men.

A lieutenant came by with a tray of drinks, whiskey for the men, tea for the ladies, he said, although it was difficult to tell them apart. The guests emptied the tray save two. The lieutenant handed one of the glasses, filled nearly to the brim, to me. "For you, Miss...?"

"Just Emily." He needn't know I shared a surname with the general.

"For you, Miss Just Emily," he said, loudly enough to elicit chuckles from the crowd.

I took the glass and sipped. It was whiskey.

"No, all wrong." He took the last glass, swirled the amber liquid, and took a deep whiff of its aroma. Then he downed it in several gulps.

I poured the whiskey down my throat and held up my empty glass, pressing my lips together to stifle a cough. The group cheered and my spirits lifted, sailing on fumes of whiskey. I was no longer a fresh flower in an old factory. I was their queen.

The crowd grew louder, but this time, it wasn't me they were rooting for. A short, broadly built officer leaped into the air and landed with his legs split. The throng whistled and yelled "Just Emily!" for my response.

The group clapped a drumbeat, encouraging me. My competitive spirit outweighed my sense of decorum, and I spun, each step in synchrony with the clap, faster and faster until my dress lifted. Then I slid down into a split, one arm raised dramatically, my ball gown splaying in a circle of magenta folds around me.

As several officers helped me up, the crowd parted, revealing GK and his aide. My brother raised one eyebrow in warning, and the younger officer gaped at me. Heat rose in my face, but this time, it wasn't the whiskey.

"Moths to the flame." GK gave his aide a slap on the shoulder.

The aide then closed his mouth, his Adam's apple bobbing above his blue uniform collar. "Shall I escort the young lady from the dance, sir?"

My opinion of him matched that of the booing crowd.

GK rubbed his chin. "A generous offer."

The aide flashed a conspiratorial grin, but his smile faded when GK added, "But that won't be necessary."

Even though the captain had seemed a presumptuous young man, I was chagrined that GK was teasing him. GK slung his arm across my shoulders and led me away from the group.

"Emily, I trust you are enjoying yourself?" GK's face showed a mix of tenderness and disappointment. I wanted to curl up like a pill bug.

"Quite. It is my pleasure to offer a small bit of entertainment." I crossed my arms across my middle, feigning boldness. It had been a full year since I had seen my dear brother, and I wanted to show him how grown up I was and how much I cared about our soldiers. But despite my good intentions, I was a bit late to realize that my actions might reflect poorly on him.

One of the men called out, "Aww, let her stay and dance with us, sir."

"Not now. The lady needs a rest." GK maintained a grip on my arm, firm enough to tell me I was most certainly out of line.

The aide glanced wide-eyed from GK to me. His thick hair and neatly trimmed mustache were the color of honey, and his expressive eyes reminded me of the crystal water that filled the quarry at home.

"Miss Emily Warren, allow me to introduce Captain Washington Roebling." GK lifted my gloved right hand and offered it to his aide. "I owe my life to this captain and my sense of purpose to this charming sprite. It is only fitting the two of you meet."

The captain cleared his throat. "You—your wife? I thought she was unable to—"

"Gracious no." GK laughed. "My sister. She and my wife happen to share a name. Now then, will you be so kind as to guard the honor of *Miss Emily Warren?*"

I felt sorry for the poor man; his eyes took me in, from escaping curls to rumpled hem, as he reconciled my identity. Perhaps trying to oust his commander's sister from the event was only slightly less humiliating than ousting his wife. My presented hand hung awkwardly in the air until the captain regained his composure and took it in his own.

"It will be my pleasure, sir." Then his first words to me: "Miss Warren, Captain Roebling, at your service."

"Very well then." GK gave a last glance, a small tilt of the head to remind me to act with decorum. He went back to his hosting duties, signaling the orchestra to resume and coaxing the officers back to the dance floor.

My new guardian took my hand and kissed the air just above it, then regarded me for several uncomfortable moments. My hand warmed from his touch despite my silk glove. Sensible of his gaze, I smoothed my hair and adjusted my dress.

I was no delicate beauty. A lifetime of riding horses and chasing—and being chased by—my siblings had afforded me a robust constitution, so I appreciated a sturdy man. The captain certainly appeared stalwart; it was doubtful I could break his arm in a bit of horseplay, as had happened to one of my more unfortunate suitors.

Unlike most men, he towered several inches over me. Many accoutrements adorned his perfectly kept uniform: a sword and scabbard, red sash, gold braid, and the gold epaulets. GK had taught me to read a uniform: *Branch: Engineers; Rank: Captain; Position: Aide de camp; Appearance: Outstanding.* That last observation would be considered quite unofficial.

Still, I needed no honor guard, and this man had seemed insufferable.

"You don't need to escort me all evening," I said. "I'm afraid my brother has put you in a rather unrewarding position."

"There are worse duties."

Biting my tongue at his inelegant reply, I caught the eye of an officer behind him. "It was lovely to meet you, Captain Roebling, but I'll make my own way."

His jaw dropped—in surprise, relief, or panic, I wasn't sure which.

"Please don't concern yourself. I'll put in a good report for you with General Warren." I turned on my heel to flee, but the captain gently caught my elbow.

"Wait."

"Yes?" I wrinkled my brow at his offending hand, and he withdrew it.

The orchestra played a slow waltz.

"I believe the general expects us to set the example. May I have the honor of a dance, Miss Warren?"

I nodded my acceptance. It wouldn't be good form to refuse.

The captain led me to the dance floor where he was light on his feet, his hand gentle across my back, guiding me in graceful circles. "I'll let you in on a little secret."

"Oh?"

His eyes held mine; there was something quite endearing about them.

"The general caught me sneaking peeks at you."

A sympathetic soul—who admitted to watching *me*. The orchestra stopped, and other dancers retreated from the floor. Captain Roebling had a presence about him, a confidence I first took as hubris. Other officers called to him, but his eyes never left mine. Those ice-blue eyes seemed to see everything yet give nothing away.

The muscles knotting my neck softened as the shame from embarrassing my brother ebbed. My instinct to flee had disappeared, replaced with a desire to learn more about this curious man. "Why does the general say he owes his life to you?"

"Perhaps that's a story for another day. Or never." His hand went to his neck, and he absently fingered his collar.

The room grew quiet as couples dispersed for refreshments, and I worried I had spoiled the captain's mood, speaking of the war that GK was trying to put aside for just one evening.

The pianist played Liszt's "Liebestraum No. 3 (Love's Dream)." Candles flickered soft shadows into the golden light.

"May I have the pleasure of another dance, Miss Warren?" His hand, warm and firm, lifted mine.

"Please, just Emily."

He drew me close and whispered in my ear. "So I've heard. I am Washington. And for you only, just Wash."

We danced again, heedless of sustaining a respectable gap between us. The wool of his jacket smelled of earth, rubbing pleasantly against my cheek. I couldn't resist laughing at the other officers whistling and calling our names. That was, until Wash gently placed a finger under my chin and turned my face toward him as he swirled me around the ballroom. Had any other man done that, it would have felt disrespectful. But the way he held me—like a treasured gift—enchanted me.

All others faded away that night as we danced and talked, learning about each other's big families and bigger dreams. While I hoped to join in the effort to gain the right to vote for women, he was planning to forever change our nation's largest cities with the bridges he would build. His breath smelled like an exotic concoction of anise and cinnamon, and even as the light-headedness from the whiskey faded, I floated on a scented cloud, just listening to him. When it was time to go, I yearned to hold on to him and to the evening.

It seemed he felt the same. "It was my very great pleasure to meet you, Emily. I hope we will meet again soon."

"My pleasure as well, Captain Roebling. I mean, Just Wash."

TWO

I was staying in the District, near the Mall, with GK and his wife. Their small, run-down, brick town house seemed unworthy of a general officer, but of course, he was seldom there. He was to have a whole week of leave, and I was quite tickled to be spending it with him.

Just as we sat down for breakfast the next morning, GK answered a knock at the door. I peered around the corner. Captain Roebling, in a black wool coat and watch cap, presented a note. I counted on my fingers, not even seven hours since we had parted. Apparently, his definition of *soon* was rather shorter than mine. Then I chastised myself. Wash was GK's aide and had more than likely come to see my brother.

GK read, then folded the note and handed it back. "Captain, is this a ruse?"

"Yes, sir." Wash nudged a picnic hamper sitting on the stoop next to him with his foot.

"I see." GK turned and caught me eavesdropping. "Emily, will you kindly show Captain Roebling a proper way to spend a morning of leave?"

Having secured GK's blessing for an outing, Wash helped me into my coat. Bitter air gusted in when he opened the door.

"A picnic in February?" I asked.

"It's always a good day for a picnic if you choose your company wisely."

"I believe I have."

GK glanced outside where a carriage driver waited, stomping his feet and blowing breaths of cold-clouded air. "Find a good shelter so the three of you don't freeze."

Wash and I exchanged a smile. GK's concern was having a chaperone, at least the appearance of one, as well as the weather. Wash held my arm as we stepped off the porch toward his carriage. Snow had whitewashed the sooty streets, brightening the neighborhood.

Snowflakes fluttered about as we settled into the carriage, and Wash spread a red plaid blanket across our laps. He pulled the bell cord to signal the driver, and the horse pulled the roofed but otherwise open carriage into the street. Snow muffled the *clip-clop* of its hooves, creating stark stillness under the weak sun. Flurries gave way to pockets of gray-blue sky.

"I'm sorry. It's rather tight." He angled his long legs sideways to make room on the narrow leather seat. "Normally, it's only the general sitting here."

"And where do you sit?"

"I'm the driver." He grinned. "And sometimes cook." He tapped the covered basket on his lap.

"A good one, I hope. Where are we going?" I rubbed my ears, my bonnet offering little protection from the cold.

"Are you warm enough?" He extracted a brown fur lap robe from a supply box.

Heavy yet surprisingly soft, the robe chased the chill from my bones. "Bear?"

"Buffalo. The army has quite the treasure trove." He craned his neck for a view ahead. "There's a nice spot at the riverfront, sheltered from the wind. You can see across to Virginia."

"Virginia?" Images of stray Minié balls sailing around us made me shudder.

GK had explained how Wash had saved his life. Wash had heard incoming fire and pushed him out of the way, a bullet just grazing GK's neck.

"How close is the fighting?"

"Quite far, thank goodness. Two days' ride at least."

That didn't seem far enough.

His gloved hand squeezed mine under the lap robe. He was in a rather precarious position, courting the sister of his superior, although he didn't seem concerned, chatting jovially and playfully. He had yet to kiss me, and

I found myself imagining the feel of his lips against mine. The warmth of his body next to me caused alternating calm and excitement, like riding a horse at full gallop, then slowing to a walk through a sunny meadow.

The city had changed since I lived there during finishing school, transforming from a place to call home to a place to hold business. Dark shanties huddled next to marble buildings with Corinthian columns. Wide boulevards disintegrated into dirt roads with ruts and puddles, notorious for swallowing carriage wheels. In the distance, the Washington Monument rose to the sky in beautiful angled lines, only to be truncated at an awkward spot not quite halfway to the promised point.

True to Wash's word, we alighted in a small park on the banks of the Potomac, about two miles from the house. He sent the driver away with a scheduled return. My skin prickled in protest, both at the sight of the wide, unforgiving river and the departure of our chaperone. But if I wasn't safe with someone who had saved my brother's life, who could be trusted?

We spread the plaid blanket and huddled under the buffalo robe as we enjoyed the feast from the basket: scotch eggs, buttermilk biscuits, and jarred peaches—luxuries I had sorely missed in wartime.

I held out my hand for our shared jug of water. "How did you get all this?"

"I'm a good scrounger." He produced a flask from his coat pocket and waggled it in front of me. "Care for a wee nip?"

It was not yet nine in the morning. "An indecent hour for a nip." I accepted the flask and took a swig. *Hot. Hot.* It was coffee. I sputtered the burning liquid.

"I'm so sorry, I didn't think you would—" He grabbed back the flask and dabbed a napkin at the errant drips on my face.

I gulped down some water and laughed. "I'm fine, I assure you."

"Are you certain?"

I nodded. The concern in his eyes drew me toward his strong and beautiful face, making me want to circle my arms around him. Part of me pleaded for protection from future pain. He would, of course, soon return to the war, and I longed to wrap my heart in a layer of armor. But more powerful feelings were making their way through faster than I could keep them at bay.

He removed his glove and traced a finger across my lips, making them tingle. I took his hand in mine and squeezed.

Wash bent closer. "Em—"

I parted my lips, but half of me wanted to push away, to run, to let that suit of armor guard me from heartbreak. But the other half wouldn't budge from that blanket. An eternity of seconds ticked by until he grazed my cheek with his lips, and then found mine, waiting, wanting. The sweetness of peaches, the bitter of coffee, the soft brush of the tip of his tongue and tickle of mustache combined, overwhelming me and blotting out the world and all reason. The lap robe slipped off, and I closed my eyes and let his mouth, his soul, fill me with warmth while the chill air stung in counterpoint. His hand behind my head, he lowered us to the ground, his lips never leaving mine, his arms shielding me from the cold. At last, he rolled away, leaving me breathless and wanting more.

He groaned as he sat up, chugged some coffee, then gave my leg a few raps of his knuckles. "It appears all is in good working order."

I gave him a sultry look. "Are you speaking of you or me?"

He coughed. "You are most improper, Miss Warren. I shall have to report you to the general."

"And shall I report you for sending away our chaperone?" I sat up next to him.

He wrapped his arm across my shoulders. "They will surely jail us both."

Waves of the river lapped at the banks, reclaiming the snow. I had a sense of the water sucking me in, but it was the cold earth that seeped through the blanket and frosted my bottom.

He offered another opportunity to burn my tongue, then capped the coffee and pocketed the flask. "We had better take our leave before we become an unauthorized monument." Wash scrambled to his feet, then pulled me up, not a moment too soon before numbness set in.

I repacked the basket while he folded the blanket. "Have you thought about what you want to do after the war? Will you be staying with the army?"

"Don't tell me my whole 'uniting the country' speech was wasted on a bunch of butter bars."

"You saw me listening?" I tossed a napkin at him.

"Guilty. I'm not usually that much of a show-off. But when I saw you…"

"So I was eavesdropping and you were boasting and making up stories." I took his free hand as we headed along the river toward our meeting point with the driver. "Well, why don't you tell me more about these plans, if they're true, so we can determine who's the more guilty party?"

"Oh, they're true." He squinted at the river, the sun now reflected in it, then fumbled in his pocket for his timepiece. "The carriage should be here any moment." He placed the folded blanket on a nearby boulder. "A seat for my lady whilst she waits, and a story to keep her entertained."

"'My lady…she speaks yet she says nothing; what of that?'"

"Hamlet?"

"Romeo." Oh my. Had I just compared us to Romeo and Juliet? "Not that you…"

"Shakespeare has some big shoes to fill, but I'll do my best." Wash spread his arms wide and took a bow as if there were an audience of hundreds. "I was a young lad of ten years, on a ferry with my father." He picked up a flat pebble and skipped it across the ice-patched water. "We were heading from New York to Brooklyn on a January day so miserable, today is balmy in comparison.

"Passengers huddled with horses to keep warm on the open boat, with no roof to tuck under. Father paced, oblivious to the cold. I tried to keep up with him, slipping all over the icy deck. Sleet stung my eyes, and a fierce wind lifted my coat and sliced right up my back."

He pulled up his collar as if warding off the long-ago cold. "The river was clogged with ice. We were halfway across when the boat slowed. Rain came down harder, freezing on everything, crusting the paddle wheel. The bow hit a massive ice floe, and the boat jolted to a standstill."

Wash gazed across the river, his arm outstretched, beckoning the memory of a life-changing event. How uncanny that it conjured my own. But this was *his* story, and he certainly seemed to enjoy telling it. I forced my attention back on him.

Wash clapped his hands over his ears and winced. "The ice screeched against the hull. All around, seasick people leaned over the railings, groaning with each tilt of the boat. My father said, 'We must help.'

"The boat tilted in a wave, and a man slid across the deck, banging against the side rails. I grabbed Papa's arm, afraid of losing my footing. I was small enough to slip under the rail and into the water."

I cringed, my hands gripping the blanket as I pictured him being pulled to icy depths.

"At the bow, the crew shivered and stared at the ice, poking at it with a stake. My father grabbed the stake, leaned over the railing, and pushed against the ice with all his might, right at the point of the bow. The chunk of ice budged, and he guided it starboard.

"The sun was setting. We were running out of daylight. The men lined the rail at the bow with assorted tools. 'One, two, three,' they counted and pushed. After several shoves, a big chunk of river ice gave way, and the boat lurched forward.

"The paddle wheel creaked forward, its icy crust shattered like glass, and everyone cheered. We put blankets on the poor, frightened horses." He plopped down next to me and rested his hand on my knee. "I wanted to sneak under a blanket too."

My proper training warred with my sentiment as I at once welcomed his touch and the happy turn in his story, yet my mother's voice tsk-tsked in my head. I shifted away, worried the coachman or someone else would soon appear.

My hands and face were as frigid as if I had been on the ferry myself, and I was much relieved when the carriage approached. We climbed aboard and tucked under the robe. The carriage lurched forward, and I leaned my head on his shoulder, warm and solid. "Tell me what happened next."

"Papa said, 'No one should have to endure this. Let me show you something.' But I couldn't keep my teeth from chattering or get my legs to move, so he gave me his coat. I slipped into the sleeves, still warm from his arms, and he led me to the side rails. 'How much longer?' I asked him.

"'Ten years, *vielleicht*,' he said."

I cocked my head at the unfamiliar word.

"He's from Germany—it means 'perhaps.' Then Papa pointed toward the Brooklyn shoreline. 'You see that curve of land over there? I could build a bridge. Trains, carriages, mothers pushing baby buggies, all crossing safely and swiftly, any time of year.'"

Wash gazed out the side of the carriage, the Potomac disappearing in the distance. "Papa grabbed his journal and pencil from the coat pocket. Drew a roadway between two towers above a choppy waterline. He told me, 'When you're a grown man, ferries like this bucket of bolts will be rusting away in dry dock.'

"He gave me back the journal, and I drew a busted-up boat. I told him I'd help him, and when it was finished, we'd climb to the top of the tower and watch the buckets of bolts rusting away. Papa said, '*Sehr gut*, Son. We don't fight the river, we rise above it.'

"So that's the dream. It's why I became an engineer and build bridges."

"You'll build it when the war is done?"

"My father will, with my help. But it's proving quite a challenge, and first we must finish the bridge in Cincinnati." He stared at his fingers on the blanket while I wondered if I should ask him to explain. Then he twisted toward me, concern in his eyes. "Have I bored you, going on so?"

"Not at all." I cuddled closer, answering his real question with one of my own. "Will I hear more tomorrow?"

He squeezed my hand in promise.

✺

Wash and I spent as much time together as possible during his week of leave. We played chess and did word puzzles each evening, resting from our long walks and picnics during the day, always accompanied by a driver, GK, or his wife, whom we called Millie. My physical opposite, Millie was petite, even delicate. She wore the latest fashions with so much flair, I wanted to hate her for it. But her sweet nature prevented me from such a crass response.

Each morning, Wash arrived a bit earlier, and each evening, we prolonged our visit. The thought of him returning to war twisted my gut tighter as the days flew by. My dreams were plagued by visions of him running from an exploding bridge. On his last morning, dawn had barely broken and I was still slumped over my first cup of tea when I heard Millie answer a knock. Wash's deep voice lured me to the door in my morning gown.

"Captain Roebling," Millie tutted. "You want to squeeze more into a day than will fit."

"Exactly my philosophy." I beamed at him.

Pink bands lighting the sky framed Wash and his picnic basket in a rosy glow. "Sunrises are more beautiful than sunsets, wouldn't you agree?"

THREE

Cold Spring, New York

As abruptly as Wash came into my life, the war claimed him back. A letter arrived days after he departed, sharpening my longing for him.

My Darling Em,

GK and I have arrived safely, with one minor mishap. That foolish little stallion of mine fell down today, causing me to somersault over his head. But I was up long before he was and had to kick him to make him get up.

The next letter came a week later, just as I was entertaining notions of putting Wash out of my mind and starting a campaign to plead for women's right to vote. But I was torn, wondering if I might be more likely to see him in the District or by staying in Cold Spring as GK had meetings across the river at West Point.

He wrote:

I am able to attain only a few hours rest each night, stretched out across some chairs or curled up on the ground. When I return from this miserable place, I shall sleep, interrupted only for my attentions to you, for two years.

But Uncle Robert Lee isn't licked by a long shot, and if we are not mighty careful, he will beat us yet… I went up in an air balloon. I had a fine view of the battlefield, but unfortunately, the enemy had a fine view of me.

I read his letters each night before retiring, then tucked them under my pillow. My superstition was that he rested easier for it.

Sometimes he let on about more than fatigue and frustration: *The troops led by Useless Grant are tired and played out. I met with no mishap; one bullet intended for me went through my orderly's heart, killing him instantly.*

How does one answer such things? I wrote and tore up a dozen responses, offering support and sympathy, before deciding the only words coming from me should be sweet and hopeful. *I can only echo back times a hundred your own words: "My love for you I find is paramount to every other feeling, and the lapse of time and change of scene only deepens it."*

He did manage to make brief visits, but in the long stretches in between, I returned to my usual activities: visiting friends, riding, and following the progress of the suffragettes. It seemed like marking time, living with my mother, and waiting for my life to begin. At the same time, winds too strong to resist were leading me down a path that seemed more fate than choice. I was unsettled and short-tempered, my friends finding excuses to stay away. Indeed, I wasn't enjoying my own company.

Mother's neighbor and dear friend Eleanor White had invited me to tea at her home, purportedly to cheer her up after her own daughter had left the nest. I suspected the real reason was to divine my interests in a certain army captain.

Eleanor was plump and sweet, and I had known her my whole life. Her parlor was similar to Mother's, if somewhat smaller. A large green divan with a curving oak border flanked by two matching settees formed a cozy conversation nook. Walnut bookshelves framed a carved marble fireplace.

We sipped tea on the velvet divan. Between us, the morning paper declared "Is Suffrage a Lost Cause?" I squinted to read the smaller text: "Women Devote Energies to War Effort." My brief encounters with rolling bandages and packing boxes had demonstrated a distinct lack of energy for the tasks.

Eleanor followed my gaze to the newspaper. "The war won't last forever. What then?"

Visions of leading protests for the women's movement crossed my mind, quickening my heartbeat. Surely, there could be no more suitable activity for me.

"When the war is over, the suffragettes will become active again, and this time, I'll be done with schooling and able to help," I said.

Eleanor pulled her wrap closer. The fire had burned down, so I got up to add another log. I ran my fingers over the rough iron sculptures on the hearth and on the bookshelves.

Her family supplied iron to the foundry, and she made art from the castoffs. She had presented me with unusual gifts, such as the letter *N* on my bedroom wall. With help from a worker, she had constructed it by heating, then pounding a brick-sized iron remnant into shape and had given it to me upon my entrance into womanhood. Confused, I had reminded her I had no such initial in my name.

Eleanor had laughed. "No, dear. That is to put upon your wall so you will always know your true north." She had entertained me with her artwork on many childhood visits, showing me how they fit together and changed when viewed from different angles. They were certainly out of place in a traditional parlor, which pleased me all the more.

"What is it, darling? You're fussing about like a mama cat who's lost her kittens." Eleanor peered over her demiglasses, teacup at her lips.

"Not fussing. Studying." I tinkered with the perpetual motion machine, an iron, gear-shaped wheel with spokes that flopped over as they reached the top, continuing the circular action.

She suppressed a smile. "Have you developed a sudden interest in thermodynamics?"

"Perhaps. Would there be something wrong with that, Mrs. White?"

She shrugged. "Not at all. A good sign, I would say."

Her smirk was irritating me as much as the pinch of my corset stays. "Why don't you simply ask what you wish to ask?"

"That's not how it's done, my dear. You still have much to learn in the matter of polite conversation despite the fine example and mentoring of your mother." She set down the teacup and sighed. "But I understand today's young ladies see things differently."

"I didn't intend to be rude."

"Intention isn't as important as the words chosen, my dear." She twined her fingers. "How should I phrase it, then? What are your plans with your young gentleman?" She raised one eyebrow at me. "Or perhaps you prefer—are you engaged in activities best saved for marriage?"

Heat rose in my cheeks, and I cleared my throat, stalling to gather my wits. "I see how my question could lead a conversation in undesired ways. But let me try to answer." I tugged at the blouse collar squeezing my neck. "Captain Roebling is a very engaging gentleman who has favored me with attention and undeserved flattery."

"That much I've seen with my own eyes."

"Unfortunately, we've found each other at a most unsuitable time. He, of course, is in the throes of war, and I am just beginning to sort out who I am."

"My dear, timing is not something you can control. Neither is love."

"This is true. But there are things I must do—or try to do—before I can fall into another's world. One thing I have learned about the captain: his life is as focused and structured as mine is not, and if I were to fall into it, I would surely not be the same again. So I must resist, you see, as long as I can, with eyes wide open to all the possibilities."

An image of Wash with a bloodstain blooming on his chest stung my thoughts. "Included in those is the very real possibility that..." A sob threatened to choke out my words, so I reached out, placed my hand over hers, and moved on. "As for your second question..."

"Never mind." Her eyes lowered. "I think you've answered that."

❧

But as much as I tried to read about or engage in a world of possibilities, I found myself too often dreaming of a certain honey-haired captain with a deeply resonating voice that erased all others. On a day in late summer, I opened the door, expecting my mother's friends arriving for tea. Instead, there was Wash in full dress uniform. I flew into his arms as if lifted in a hot air balloon.

"Come," I beckoned, taking his hand and leading him to a private spot in our backyard. We sat on a double swing under a trellis. I wanted him all to myself, without the prying eyes of my mother and her gaggle of friends.

Grapevines and roses wove a fragrant nest for us, sheltering us from late afternoon sun. He gathered me into his arms. "You seem surprised to see me. Didn't you get my letter?"

"No, but you are a welcome surprise." We kissed, his touch tingling my lips.

He broke away from me much too soon, and I protested by grasping his wool-covered shoulders.

"There isn't much time," he said.

"How long do I have you?"

"I'm sorry, it was in the letter. Only an hour or so, I'm afraid." He brushed my cheek with the back of his hand, giving me a chill as he secured a wayward tendril of my hair behind my ear.

I wanted to yell at the unfair world, then sneak away with him to a faraway island, somewhere distant, deserted—except for us. I rearranged my face to hide my disappointment.

"I love you, Em." Wash slipped his hands into mine, then slid out of the swing, dropping to his knees in front of me. He gazed at me with wide and oh-so-blue eyes. "Perhaps this seems a bit hasty, but I know how I feel." He lifted my hand to brush the stubble of his cheek. "I want to be with you, only you, and time is not on our side."

"Wash? What—?"

"This is my clumsy attempt at asking an important question."

Heat ran up my chest to my face. My thrill at seeing him was being dampened by the armor trying to protect my heart. Yes, I wanted to see him, spend as much time together as possible. But there was still an enormous black obstacle before we could move on. I wanted to delay professions of love, delay thinking of a life together, because the war was all too likely to rip my soul to shreds. Mother had rather unkindly reminded me that as general officer, GK would be a target and his aides would give their own lives to protect him. The horror of losing my brother or Wash haunted my days and made sleepless my nights.

"We have plenty of time, Wash. I shall see no one else in your absence.

You can rest assured of that." I fought to control the tremor in my voice and patted the seat next to me. "Now come."

He shook his head with a laugh. "Emily, I am not down on my knee to ask you to be my inamorata. I am asking you to marry me."

"Oh," I squeaked. "Oh my." He had swiftly moved past professions of love without waiting for my response, driven past the uncertainty of surviving a war, and arrived, smiling and disconcertingly handsome, right where I longed but feared to be. I took a bit too long to gather my thoughts.

"That's not the answer I was hoping for." His grip on my hand loosened, his eyes clouded.

"Give me a moment, Wash. You've obviously thought through this, but it's all fresh and new to me."

"Forgive my presumption," he said stiffly. "I thought you felt as I did."

I had known this man for a mere six months. We had spent only a few days of that time together, yet I was already hopelessly in love. Still, I had imagined his proposal on some distant romantic evening after a proper and exciting courtship. This was too soon.

I brushed an errant rose petal from the folds of my dress. *Tell him no, we should wait, at least until war's end when we can spend more time with each other. We shouldn't act in haste but proceed with minds uncluttered by war and separation.* My thoughts ran to the wounded soldiers, the growing cemeteries that dotted every town. The heartbreak would be unbearable if I were to lose Wash—

"Yes," I said, ignoring my inner voice. I simply couldn't refuse him, look into those eyes, and then send him back to the fight. Especially when, deep inside, I knew he was right—I could no longer imagine my life without him. Whatever my world of possibilities was to contain, it must include him. "Yes, I will marry you."

He took my hand, and we stumbled across the grass and flower beds, my worries tucked away.

The next morning, I slipped on the engagement ring Wash had given me, delicate white gold with blue and crystal-clear stones arranged like a flower.

Although it brought me joy, it also evoked a deep sadness for a loss I had suffered years before.

I tucked those thoughts away and bounced down the stairs, humming "Love's Dream." Perhaps that was a giveaway. It took Mother about thirty seconds to notice my ring. She caught my hand as I headed to the dining room for breakfast, put on the spectacles that hung from a chain around her neck, and inspected the ring. "Something to tell me, Emily?"

"He proposed." I grinned, and she embraced me.

Mother took another peek at the ring. The gems cast stars on her face as she tilted my hand in the sunlight. "Good heavens, I believe those are diamonds. Your fiancé spared no expense. All of Cold Spring will be agog." She wrapped her hand around my wrist. "Come, let's talk."

Over breakfast, I reviewed with Mother what I knew of the Roeblings. "Washington's father is John Roebling. He was born in Germany but immigrated here for the opportunities. He—"

"So you've told me. Besides, I read. I probably know more about him than do you."

I looked at her through my eyelashes. I never read enough or the right things, in her judgment. "Wash plans to join his father in the family business after the war. He's built bridges for the army." Also blew them up, but I didn't think that improved his case.

Several months later, I harbored doubts about marrying a man I had known for such a short time. When I wrote to him with my concerns, he answered back:

You dread our growing cold after marriage; a short separation from my darling is the cure for that, but unfortunately the remedy is as severe as the disease. However, a little trouble in getting something always adds to the zest of it.

Our last visit before we were to be married was both glorious and heartrending. We reveled in each other's company while the clock ticked our precious hours away. For two days, we barely left each other's side, as if to prevent anything from wedging between us.

On the dreaded day of his departure, we lingered on the platform as the engine on the long, black snake of a train hissed its impatience. He hugged me tightly, and I closed my eyes to capture the security of being wrapped in his arms, the tickle of his mustache when we kissed, the piney scent of shaving soap on his neck. I wanted to preserve the moment like a rose pressed in a book.

A soldier appeared at his side. "Sir, it's time."

Wash whispered in my ear, "This is a mere blink of an eye in our life together. Stay strong, my love."

I stared at the toes of his boots so he wouldn't see the tears burning down my cheeks. He kissed my forehead, and his hand slipped from mine. He walked to the train, tall and straight and purposeful, chatting with the soldier. It must have been easier for him to close one door in his mind and open another, as if stepping from one compartment of the train to another. Perhaps he must in order to survive the brutal world of war. A final turn back to wave and Wash climbed into the railcar. I blew a kiss but too late. The black snake had swallowed him whole.

That year was horrific for the Army of the Potomac. I prayed for an end to the war. My brother and Wash wrote about having been in Petersburg and Spotsylvania, but their current location was usually reported as "somewhere in Virginia." The daily letters from Wash became weekly, then only a handful of letters through autumn. Although he tried to ease my nerves with lighthearted stories, the newspapers told a different one, that Virginia especially was a desperate place.

Wash and I traded letters about our families for months before we had the courage to let them meet. *Mother lost several children early on and protects the remaining six like a mama bear in a den of wolves*, I wrote. His letters gave me the impression his family was big, boisterous, and intense, softened by a wicked sense of humor. I was a bit intimidated to meet them. However, he showed no fear of his father meeting Mother for the first time. Perhaps my stories were not sufficiently detailed.

That autumn, we decided it would be best for our two surviving parents to meet, then leave the siblings to collide at the wedding. Neutral territory was selected. As Mother and I were coming from Cold Spring and Wash and his father from Trenton, we desired someplace in the middle. Upon my request, GK sent Wash to an iron foundry in Ringwood, New Jersey, to discuss munitions contracts.

Abram Hewitt, a business partner of Mr. Roebling's, offered to host our rendezvous at his estate near the iron mines. The Hewitts and their partners were the largest suppliers of iron on the East Coast, if not the country. As John Roebling was an inventor and manufacturer of iron rope, they were well acquainted.

The Hewitts' three-story mansion seemed a mix of styles: strong, boxy lines of Federalist, an Italianate cupola in the center of the roof, and bays with many windows. The gambrel roof and dormers reminded me of my own childhood home.

Mr. Hewitt, a tall, lean gentleman, showed us around the grounds. Acres and acres of formal gardens, ponds of all sizes reflecting their beauty, and well-kept lawns surrounded the mansion, as well as many curious structures made from iron. A giant chain, each link over two feet long, stretched across the front lawn.

"The iron was mined right here, and this chain was used to keep the British ships from sailing up the Hudson River," Hewitt explained.

"No, I believe the iron for the chain came from our side of the river, forged in Cold Spring," Mother said, her debate muscles already warmed up.

As the two of them seemed content to argue, I wandered into the garden a few steps away, admiring the fragrant blooms. Soon, the crunching of gravel announced that a carriage approached.

Wash hopped out first, holding the door for his father. I had seen a photograph, but it did not prepare me for the man in the flesh. John Roebling had slightly receding hair and Wash's ice-blue eyes, pierced by a frightful intensity. His salt-and-pepper beard came to a point at his shirt collar.

"Father, this is my beloved Emily."

I held out my hand in greeting, and Mr. Roebling squeezed it so hard, it was nearly painful. "Welcome to the family. You must be quite the young woman to so dazzle my son." Although he had a German accent, his English was rapid and nearly perfect.

Wash held out his arms to me. I was struck by how his usually well-fitted uniform hung away from him, and small lines had appeared on his face. We snuck in a quick kiss before following the others to a sitting area. Wash introduced Mother to his father.

Mr. Roebling greeted her with an outstretched hand. "Mrs. Warren, it is a pleasure."

A breath caught in my throat. He hadn't waited for her to first offer her hand. But Mother took Mr. Roebling's hand, appraising him from head to toe. "It's Phebe. We're to be family."

We settled into some intricate garden chairs, forged from iron, of course.

Mr. Hewitt opened a leather satchel he had at his feet and extracted a ledger. "If the ladies will excuse a bit of business, I've got the prices tabulated for you, Captain."

Mr. Roebling and Hewitt looked over the ledger, running their fingers down rows of numbers. Curiously, Wash paid scant attention, even though he was there on army orders. The distraction seemed so unlike my focused, mission-oriented fiancé.

The horses, which had been unfastened from the carriages and left a few yards away in a nearby paddock, suddenly jumped and brayed loudly. Wash shuddered and covered his face with his arms.

"What is it, son? You survive a war and you're frightened of a horse spooked by a rabbit?" Mr. Roebling chuckled, but my stomach clenched.

"Well then, as our business is complete, shall we go to the manor house for tea?" Hewitt said.

The others rose and headed for the manor house, but Wash remained seated, staring across the pond.

I lightly tapped his shoulder. "Wash, shall we go inside?"

"Hmm? I... We... No. We have only an hour or two...and a wedding to plan." He stared at his hands, alternately stretching his fingers, then balling them into fists.

"Should we take a stroll around the gardens?" I desperately wanted to get that faraway look out of his eyes. He had been quiet and withdrawn the entire afternoon. Was this what he was like around his father? Or was it something else?

Mr. Roebling had doubled back. "Washington, come."

"Yes, Father. I mean, no, we're..."

"We need a moment to ourselves if you wouldn't mind," I said.

"It's your fault." Mr. Roebling looked straight at me, his face tight.

"Pardon?" The blood ran out of my face at his glare.

"You've been like this the whole trip." He pointed at his son. "And ever since you met Miss Warren. Stumbling, indecisive, hardly the son I know. Is she doing this to you?"

Mother came to my rescue. "Come along, Mr. Roebling. Let the love-birds have a moment."

A chill ran through me, and I pulled my wrap tighter. Apparently, Wash being different around his father wasn't the issue. But it certainly wasn't me, was it?

The scent of a wood fire wisped from the manor chimneys. The thought of hot tea was very appealing, but time alone with Wash trumped the comfort of a warm room. As the others headed to the house, I guided Wash through the garden and toward the woods, dappled by the low autumn sun.

"I'm afraid your father doesn't think much of me."

Wash shrugged his shoulders. "He hardly knows you."

"That's all you have to say?"

He kicked the ground, sending a spray of leaves ahead of us. "Good God, Emily, we're trying to win a war. I should be at the front right now, helping to keep your brother alive. He should have sent his quartermaster for this task. But he sent me so that you and I could have a moment together."

Despite his harsh wards, relief flowed through me. He seemed to have snapped out of his queer mood, and I'd rather have a feisty man than a sullen one. A slight smile may have tugged at my lips.

He responded with a glare. "Don't you see what a difficult position this puts me in? I would never have asked for such a favor. But you did. So I came here only to fall into a situation that could compromise my and my family's reputation."

"Why did you come then, if it distressed you so much? Why not write to me about your reservations? And…that doesn't really explain…" I was hesitant to bring up the way he startled at a sudden noise, the way his hands shook, or that he appeared to have lost thirty pounds in a few months. It seemed we were already on unsteady ground. Knowing how worried I was would only add to his troubles.

He shrugged and broke off a dead tree branch as if the cracking sound were some sort of answer. I followed him down a narrow trail, then over rocks to cross a small stream. The chirping of cardinals and chickadees and the crunch of our shoes on fallen leaves soon replaced the echoes of our conversation.

He stopped so abruptly, I almost stumbled into him.

"Because I wanted to see you." His back still toward me, he tilted his head this way and that, searching for something.

"That's all I wanted to hear," I said softly. "It seemed otherwise."

He turned to me, his face an unreadable mix of emotions. "It will never be otherwise."

The heaviness in his demeanor rasped at my desire for a pleasant if all too brief visit. Yearning for his playful side, I pushed in another direction. "It seems you've been in these woods before. Am I one of a series of women brought into your lair?"

A smile slowly broke across his face. "A gentleman never tells."

After that rendezvous, I wrote Wash nearly every day but received only one letter in three months. I was beside myself with worry, all my worst fears hammering in my head. One morning before Christmas, a messenger in Union uniform appeared at our door. I had to grab the doorjamb as my knees gave way beneath me. I took a deep breath before opening the sealed envelope, my address hastily scrawled upon it in an unfamiliar hand. "A fine man," the Irish-accented messenger said, tipping his hat and turning back to the street.

Slipping out the letter, with relief, I recognized Wash's own handwriting. The short note said only:

My lips have fully recovered from your attacks and are in good fighting trim to receive you.

Your devoted Wash

Soon after, a note from GK provided at once a sense of relief and a nagging in my gut.

My dearest Emily,

With a happy heart, I tell you that I am releasing my true and faithful assistant to your attention. Although our battle is not yet done, the end is near enough that we can allow some of our best soldiers the rest they so sorely need and deserve. I assure you he is as strong and hale as could be expected after so great an effort.

After nearly four years at war, Wash left the service shortly after being promoted to colonel. He returned with his physical parts intact, although hollowness rounded his eyes, and I sensed a distance between him and the present world. It was the worst feeling to be unable to help the one you love, with no power to heal when it is the mind itself that is wounded. So I went about my business, filling journals with notes of wedding guests and party schedules, giving details to a man who feigned interest, then crept away to an empty room when no one was looking. All the while, I worried if the man who had returned from the war was the same man with whom I had fallen in love.

FOUR

Wash and I married in Cold Spring in January 1865, eager for our new life together. Mr. Roebling softened toward me, never repeating the accusations he had made at Ringwood. Indeed, it seemed Wash was becoming more able to keep his bearings or at least better at hiding it when he couldn't.

Mother conspired with Mr. Roebling—who insisted I call him Papa—to have two separate wedding cakes, one for each of us. They were connected by a sugar sculpture of what Wash described as a "remarkably accurate scale bridge." Lemon tickled our noses and buttercream coated our lips as we demolished every last bite, blissfully unaware of the prophecy held in the delicate spun sugar.

A few weeks after the wedding, we left for a weekend in Maine to be followed by a visit with the Roebling clan. At the train station, Mother adjusted my wrap, more out of parental habit than any real need. "Well, off you two go. My last baby to leave the nest." She erased an imaginary smudge from my cheek, then blew a kiss as we boarded the train.

I eyed the rows of seats crowded with chatty passengers. Wash bumped behind me, slowed by armloads of hand luggage he refused to let the porter carry.

"It's a long ride. You won't mind if I lay my head in your lap to get a bit of sleep?" I asked him.

His eyes twinkled. "Even better. Here we are."

At the rear of the railcar, thin sliding doors hung on either side of the aisle. Wash dropped the luggage and checked his ticket. "This one." He slid the door on the right, revealing a small compartment with a pull-down bed.

"How wonderful!" Relief at gaining a bit of space and privacy buoyed my spirits.

Giggling like ten-year-olds, we climbed in the berth and secured the door and a velvet curtain behind us. We weren't in there two minutes before he was unbuttoning my dress.

"Wash, they'll hear."

"Shh." He pulled off his trousers and shirt and slipped under the sheet. "Come here."

I leaned close.

He whispered in my ear. "We'll be very quiet." He slipped my dress down and kissed my shoulder. He placed a finger gently on my lips. "Can you do that?"

"Mm-hmm."

His hands pulled up my skirts and found my bottom. He kissed my neck, ran his tongue toward my breast.

I moaned.

"Control," he said.

"I'm trying." I laughed as I scooted under the sheet with him. It felt wicked, but I pressed my lips together while his lips and hands wandered. My skin sensed his touch more intensely through our enforced silence, his body warm against me, his scent of anise and cinnamon enveloping me like morning fog. He kissed me, deeply, hungrily, across to my ears and down my neck, tenderly cupping my breasts and making me shudder.

I ran my fingers over the powerful muscles of his chest and arms, skimming past his hips and scraping down his thighs. Yearning to be filled by him, I could wait no longer. I slipped my hands to his buttocks and drew him to me.

Wash glanced at the curtain. "We need to—"

"Shh." I closed my eyes, tilted my hips for him. With each rock of the train, we rode higher, his skin hot against my flesh. I rose up, up, up until I feared I would burst. We were as one—not two lovers on a train but a single spirit, bound for a destination that was ours alone. I bit his shoulder so my cries wouldn't give us away. With sweet release, we tumbled back to earth in each other's arms.

"Tickets." The conductor's voice seeped through our protective curtain as he made his way through the car. "Tickets."

Wash donned his shirt and trousers in a flash and slipped outside our berth.

He returned with a sheepish grin, and we laughed at our close call. It was a small bed for the two of us, but we didn't mind. We lay face-to-face, the rhythmic chugging of the train a drumbeat to the melody of our voices. As it grew dark, Wash lit the sconce over our heads. The warm light and shadows it threw heightened the handsome lines of his face: a broad forehead over widely set eyes, a strong, straight nose, and full lips peeking from his honeyed mustache.

Wash reached into his trouser pocket. "I have something for you."

"Let me help." I reached down, but he playfully slapped my hand away.

He opened a small velvet box to reveal a set of cameo earrings. "I got these in Fredericksburg." He brushed back my hair and fastened one on my ear. "Carried them with me, one in each pocket. Many times, my fingers came across them, and I would think of how lovely they would be on you."

In his palm, the silhouette of a woman in the cameo glowed in the candlelight. He pressed the earring into my hand, then clasped my hand in both of his. "Knowing this day would come, well—" He swallowed, his eyes hollow and unfocused.

"They're beautiful." I touched his cheek and brought him back. "I'll save them for a special occasion."

In fact, I would be loath to wear them. The change in his face was *not* what I wanted every time he saw them on me, and I couldn't countenance how they came into his possession during a devastating battle. I unclasped the one on my ear and tucked the pair back into the box. If they had somehow helped him get through the war, I was grateful for that. But now was the time to forget the horror and move on.

After an all-too-short weekend in Maine, we traveled to Papa's home in Trenton, along with several of Wash's siblings. Not exactly a honeymoon, but it was pleasant enough. The family was as busy as a hive of bees, Papa and Wash with preparations for their next project, the other sons running the wire company. The company, which Papa had founded, made iron and steel rope by machine-twisting long strands of wire into bundles called strands, then aligning those strands into cables of varying thicknesses. They were used in all sorts of industries, including bridge making.

Papa had hired Wash to help finish the Cincinnati-Covington Bridge, which had been long delayed by the war. Both men were eager to get to work. There was much excitement in the Midwest for the project to link Ohio and Kentucky, and Papa's name and picture appeared in national magazines. Headlines declared "Famous Engineer and War Hero Son to Bridge Ohio River!"

In the evening, the family left Wash and me alone in the study. Its high ceiling, crossed with rough wooden beams, gave the room an air of importance. A settee and a couple of small tables dwarfed by a weathered oak table occupied the space. Schematic drawings of a suspension bridge covered the table, along with pages and pages of detailed plans with careful notations of materials and measurements.

I enjoyed the drawings, artful renderings worthy of framing. The beautiful lines and symmetry of the bridge, cables strung like harp strings reaching for the sky, spoke to me. But a puzzling wall leading to the bridge detracted from its beauty.

"Why is this to be fashioned of stone?" I asked Wash.

"It's rather crucial, to keep people from falling into the river."

"What if it were made of iron cables so as not to block the view of the river and the bridge?" I drew a crude diagram. "More a fence than a wall. Wouldn't that make it more visually pleasing?"

He studied my diagram, then the schematics. "Interesting." He gave me a playful knock on the head. "Brains and beauty. Fabulous combination. Now if you learn to cook, I shall be able to retire in grand style."

I gave him my own playful knock on the head.

As our days in the Roebling household waned, Papa and Wash supervised a servant packing Wash's belongings in his spacious bedroom. They planned to leave that week on a three-day train trip, leaving me behind. In what had become a rather delicate issue, Wash had been evasive regarding when I would be able to join him in Cincinnati.

From my perch on the four-poster bed, I said as cheerily as I could muster, "My trunks will take some time to catch up with us."

Papa paced, hands on hips, muttering "these newfangled ideas." He ran fingers through his thinning hair. "There will be plenty of time for you to be together, but this is not the time. *Meine Frau* Johanna, *Gott segne sie*, understood this."

Arguing with John Roebling was akin to facing a bull with a red cape. I ignored my thundering heart. "My place is with my husband."

I hoped for validation from my husband, but he just nodded and handed an armful of uniforms to the servant packing his trunks. "Would you take these away, please?"

Papa waited until the servant exited. "Washington tells me you helped him with his schematic drawings."

"I made a tiny suggestion to enhance the view of the structure." I was getting rather accomplished at sounding calm.

The top of Papa's head grew red. "Ladies are not suited for this work. There are complex principles involved for which you have no training. You will be at best a distraction and at worst a danger."

I darted a look at my husband.

"My dear, this is between you and Papa. I won't be caught in the middle." Wash placed a pair of boots in a crate.

Papa and I glared at him from both sides.

Wash scrunched his face as if in pain. "Em, Papa is right. What we do is dangerous. Every day, I have to worry about a worker falling from a great height, a frayed wire snapping and slicing off someone's hand—or worse." He nodded toward Papa. "And it's deeply troubling to have my own father facing those same risks."

Papa rolled up some maps. "These risks are unavoidable, given what we do, and I have faced them for decades. And now, my son as well. My consolation is that I've given Washington the benefit of my experience and the best education in the field."

"I'm not proposing to follow you to work like a puppy," I said to Wash as he lifted textbooks from a shelf and handed them to me. "I have my own books to keep me company, and I'm not afraid of being alone, even in a strange city."

"Tell her how we live, Son."

"It's not the life you're accustomed to, Em. We live in dormitories, a stone's throw from the site. Meals in a mess hall, one step up from an army camp."

I tucked the books into a steamer trunk while digging my heels firmly in my position. "Surely, we can find private housing in a city the size of Cincinnati."

"Perhaps. But finding something as close to the work site as I need to be would be a challenge. And the riverfront stinks of slaughterhouses and factories. You would find it quite unsuitable."

"We can try at least. I'm willing to give up my creature comforts to be with you."

Papa cut in. "It's not only your comfort but your safety that worries us. *Liebe Gott*, it's not Cold Spring." He resumed his pacing. "And how would you manage a cook and a maid in a tiny flat? You can stay here with all you need. Or with your mother. If neither of those suit you, I will lease another home for you."

"You can visit monthly," Wash said. "We'll have a special weekend together, just the two of us." The men nodded at each other, pleased with their compromise. Wash laid his hand on my shoulder. "Of course I want you to accompany us, purely for my own selfish reasons. But your welfare is more important."

Papa opened his arms as if to include the whole world. "Emily, *mein Liebchen*, you have many talents. There are things we need you to do in New York. Then you can be with your mother, and it is safer this way."

"What would you have me do?" I shirked away from Wash's hand, closed the packed trunk, and latched the brass fittings.

"This bridge"—Papa pointed to a model of the Cincinnati bridge—"is just a prototype. The real challenge is the East River. That's what we're working up to."

"I'm afraid I'm not following."

"We need support in order to be able to build the New York bridge. Political, financial, social. That's where you come in."

"Me?" My eyes widened. Those didn't sound like tasks for which I was equipped. And most of all, I needed to be with Wash. "What would you have me do?"

Papa shrugged. "Speeches, meetings, dinner receptions, whatever necessary. We have to raise about seven million dollars."

My mouth fell open. They were responsible for funding the project as well as building it? And they were looking to me for help? And speeches! The mention of them steeled my resolve to not be left behind. "I don't care about living in a grand house or if I have to learn to cook on a campfire. I can survive without a maid. But I won't be a wife who's tucked away like a china doll."

The men mirrored each other, arms folded across their chests.

"Perhaps I can help raise the needed funds in New York when we all return from Ohio." I managed a weak smile. "What do you think, Wash?"

"I'm not opposed."

I gave him a *you-need-to-do-better-than-that* glare.

Wash chuckled. "You see, Papa, I've married not only the fairest but the feistiest of women. Emily's presence will not compromise my work. In fact, she is a gifted muse. And I can search for accommodations for both of us straightaway."

Papa uncrossed his arms, and I faced him. "With your permission, Papa, I will accompany Wash to Ohio. Upon our return, I promise to support the East River Bridge."

He took a long, appraising look at me, then with a nod, declared, "*Sehr gut.*"

FIVE

Cincinnati, Ohio

A fter Lincoln's assassination, the whole country was in mourning. Cincinnati paid homage in its customary veil of black. There was soot everywhere; one couldn't travel a block without bringing home enough coal dust to light a fire. Cinders from factory smokestacks and chimneys floated in the air like black snow.

Exploring the short distance from the river to our tiny flat, I followed a curious line curving through the dirt. After a few days of observing rats climb through cracks in our cellar door, I knew what had carved the path.

Somehow, rats in our cellar didn't bother me as much as the thought of thousands of them swimming in the river, riding the current, sleek and hidden. In the cellar, at least I could trap the vermin. A river was an uncontrollable beast. Long ago, one had taken away a part of me, never to be replaced. Now, it seemed, another had threatened to take me away from my new husband. I smiled at my victory in that argument.

Our neighborhood teemed with men who carried their lunch pails off to the slaughterhouses or shipyards, leaving their wives left behind to mind the children. Although I tried to engage the women, bringing muffins or a sampling of teas, it seemed no one had time for a temporarily displaced new bride. Although we were all—or mostly—Americans, it seemed we didn't speak the same language. I felt like an outsider, looking in at real lives while mine was only make-believe.

I read every book in my collection twice, as well as anything interesting the public library had to offer. In the tiny room that served as his study, Wash's textbooks stood in precise order, lined up like soldiers in every available space. Calculus. Trigonometry. Engineering. All subjects deemed unsuitable for women. Whether that was law or social expectation, I didn't know, but either way, the injustice—or perhaps sheer boredom—compelled me to investigate the forbidden fruit. I slid out a text with a deep yellow cover. A feather floating on its cover belied its weighty title: *A Treatise on the Calculus of Finite Differences*. I opened to a random page and was *treatised* with equations, Greek symbols, and seemingly Greek text.

The back of the book had keys explaining the symbols. I studied the keys, then flipped back to the first page. Eventually, the concepts began to make sense, and I was surprised by the ease with which I understood them.

I had never heard of a girl or woman being encouraged to study scientific or mathematical concepts. Papa believed that females had no mind for them, but how could they if they hadn't the proper preparation? Schools seemed to have no intention of changing education for women; it would take laws to force them to do it. All this reinforced the need for voting rights for women and for women to run for political office.

I tried to think of ways to support this cause, even while chasing a driven husband. New magazines were appearing with tales of marches and speeches, but it all seemed so far away and not practical at the moment. But perhaps my promised efforts to raise support and funds in New York for the bridge could somehow serve a dual purpose.

⁓

Late in summer, frustrated with repeatedly scrubbing the fifteen square feet of kitchen and my clothes sticking to me like a hot washrag, I snuck down to the construction site. After leaving a basket of fruit and bread for the workers, I settled into a hiding place amid six-foot-tall wooden spools of wire rope stored in a clearing above the work site. The location offered a spectacular vista while shielding me from view of the dozens of working men. A mechanical contraption of wheels and pulleys spun wire back and forth across the river over two monstrous stone towers.

Papa barked orders at his assistant engineers and numerous foremen, suppliers, and curious onlookers. It was quite the show, his fingers stabbing at the air or at someone's chest. I pitied an innocent passerby who seemed to be politely asking a question, only to be met with wild hand waving. Papa ripped off his hat and flung it to the ground. An assistant guided the hapless visitor outside the construction zone, pointing to the warning signs he had either missed or ignored.

With Wash's permission, I visited the site each day, sometimes bringing a meal to share with him but staying out of sight. One windless afternoon, the air crackled with explosives as men cleared the path for road approaches. Workers halted midtask, fingers in their ears. A ginger-haired mechanic, tools dangling from his wide leather belt, rushed across the site and knelt next to a worker who huddled on the ground, arms wrapped around his head. I squinted to see if the worker was injured. The mechanic helped him to his feet. I gasped. It was Wash.

He brushed himself off without a trace of injury. I breathed a sigh of relief, but it reminded me of similar behavior after the war. Something in him had not fully healed.

The mechanic remained at Wash's side, scratching his beard as they reviewed rolls of plans. Although he was probably forty years of age, he seemed boyish with his spritely movement and thin build.

Later, I munched a crisp pear, using the back of my hand to wipe the juice running off my chin, as I watched some John Roebling theater.

"Aha! This is what the boss has tucked away." An unfamiliar voice chortled behind me. "I wondered why he disappeared back here."

Startled, I dropped the pear.

The mechanic who had helped Wash minutes before grinned, showing off a lovely set of teeth and setting me at ease. He raised his bowler. "Sorry to spook you, ma'am. I'm Edmond Farrington." Plucking a handkerchief from his pocket, he dabbed his own chin in demonstration, then handed the pristine cloth to me. "You missed a spot."

"You won't tell on me, will you?" I glanced back to check on Papa and the other men, but none seemed be looking our way.

Farrington sat down on a pile of cut stones and propped his boots on another. "Well now, that depends on the contraband you bring me."

The mechanic made me laugh, and soon we fell into a routine, Farrington, Wash, and I. The two came to my hiding spot on breaks, updating me on progress while digging forks into the jars of preserved apples I smuggled in for them.

It occurred to me that I was much more comfortable in their company than with the aloof wives of Cincinnati. The steady progress of the wire cables and the hive of worker bees on the site held my interest much more than the pram-pushing ladies in the shopping district. In the evening, Wash would explain the work being done to help me make sense of what I saw during my visit.

Wash delighted in quizzing me in front of Farrington, and I always knew the answers from our dinner conversation the night before. "Better watch out," Wash teased Farrington. "You could be replaced by someone a lot better looking."

"Yup," Farrington replied, pointing a half-eaten apple at Wash. "*You* better watch out."

As summer turned to fall, the workload increased as deadlines loomed. Wash returned home each evening exhausted and irritable. I listened to his litany of difficulties and endeavored to make his home life comfortable. I tried to make a decent meal but never mastered the quirky cookstove. Far too often, Wash praised my attempts while sawing through charred meat. We desperately needed to hire a cook but were too stubborn to concede the point.

On a late autumn evening, father and son arrived together at our humble flat. Wash stalked through the door, bringing a blast of cold air and dust, followed by Papa, spouting a tirade in German. Upon seeing me sitting at our tiny kitchen table, he switched to English.

"It *is* necessary for me to return to Trenton." Papa waved his hat for emphasis.

"To check on your wire rope business despite choosing another supplier for the bridge," Wash retorted. "You overlook our own perfectly suitable product and give the contract to overseas competitors."

"Their wire is more suitable, with greater tensile strength. We must consider the integrity of the entire project, not merely what is convenient or profitable." Papa furrowed his brow and shook an accusing finger at Wash. "You shame me."

Wash faced his father chest to chest. "Importing wire from overseas makes no sense. The difference in strength is negligible, adding cost and delay for no good reason. There is no shame in being prudent *and* making a profit."

"I will not condone even the appearance that our work might be compromised by selfish gain. Our name, our reputation!" Papa pounded his fist on the table, rattling the place settings—and me. "They'll think us carpetbaggers!"

Wash didn't blink, his demeanor as calm as if they were discussing a visit to the park. "No one would ever suspect you of that. We have the means to produce what is needed, our factory mere hundreds rather than thousands of miles away. Furthermore, by bypassing our company, you prevent us from developing our wire products for new uses."

Papa fixed his eagle glare on Wash, an expression that had made lesser men cower. "Yet you complain that I return to Trenton." He leaned with fisted hands on the table, and his voice grew eerily quiet. "Be the man I have raised, or find your own work."

Horrified at the things Papa was saying, I attempted to exit. But without peeling his glare from Wash, Papa caught my arm. I froze in place, and the hairs on the back of my neck rose up as I steeled myself for his wrath. Earlier in the day, I suspected he had spotted me hiding among the wire spools.

Wash slumped into a chair, too tired to pull off his muddy boots. He wiped grime off his face with his shirt sleeve. "Go to Trenton, Papa. We'll manage without you. Perhaps while there, you'll find the best way to control a factory's output is to own it."

"We'll see." Papa focused his piercing gaze on me, my arm still in his grasp. But the crinkles at the corners of his eyes deepened as his face softened. "Thank you, *Liebchen*."

"Wh—what for?"

"For the bread and fruit. The men, they are most appreciative."

I blinked. "You're welcome."

Papa held out his arms wide. "You two have any hugs left for a crotchety old bridge builder?"

Bewildered by his change in tone, I gave him a tentative embrace. Wash rose to bear-hug him, and they slapped each other's backs as if they had never argued.

"Six a.m. tomorrow, Son." Papa put his hat on his balding head, and the door slammed behind him, his harsh words echoing in my head.

Wash groaned, holding one hand on his back as he bent to untie his boots.

I knelt to help him. "How do you change from harassed underling to beloved son in an instant?"

He shrugged. "When you grow up in a family business, you learn to straddle two worlds, always knowing which one you're in at the moment. Don't worry. He's just a stubborn son of a gun."

Despite the early workday and his constant fatigue, Wash labored long into the night, his drawings and schedules spread across every horizontal space. I tiptoed in, bringing him a fresh cup of tea every few hours. He gazed up with the faintest of smiles and that horrid emptiness in his eyes. When I left my soldier to his work and went to bed alone, guilt poked at the edges of my sleep.

I had attended a lecture at the Women's League about "soldier's heart," and I saw in Wash so many signs of the affliction suffered by his fellow veterans of the war, most recently the fall to the ground at the sound of the explosives. The doctor advised that the only cure was to be found in exertion followed by plenty of rest. Somehow, I had to keep his mind safe. He could no more do that for himself than he could keep the sun from casting a shadow. So I got up, wrapped my arms around his neck, and whispered, "Come to bed."

Having had my fill of construction-site peeping, I decided to take advantage of my location. Wearing all black clothes to match the coal dust was a helpful start. I joined local ladies' guilds, and accepting the need to do things on my own and without Wash opened many possibilities.

On a dark, clear night, I visited an observatory on a hill overlooking the city and peered through a giant telescope at an explosion of stars and planets. Across the river in Kentucky, I toured lovely ranches for sale with acres and acres of grassy pastures surrounded by white rail fences. Buying one was a far-off dream, but until then, I rode horses until my thighs burned and my heart galloped in rhythm.

SIX

1867

Champagne corks exploded skyward as a band played Sousa marches for a cheering crowd at the riverside. After years of torturous work, the Cincinnati-Covington Bridge was complete. Thousands attended the April dedication, climbing on chairs to toast the Roeblings.

Papa, Wash, and I were escorted to our seats in the front row—white wooden chairs stenciled with our names. A city official presented me with a bouquet of roses. It was certainly a lovely tradition, but my cheeks pinked, accepting honors for someone else's achievement. Papa popped up like a jack-in-the-box, shaking admirers' hands.

I perused the program, complete with likenesses of both Papa and Wash.

"Quite the show." Wash let his long legs sprawl in front of him, his face more relaxed than I had seen in two years.

"You have much to be proud of."

"I'm just glad it's done and Papa and I are still on speaking terms. We learned an awful lot." Wash folded his program into careful creases and tucked it into his jacket pocket.

"Yes, now the next bridge will go up lickety-split," I said.

Papa looked at me, his eyes twinkling with amusement. "Haven't you told her?"

Wash shrugged.

My heart sank. This did not sound promising.

Papa jutted his jaw at the new bridge in front of us. "The East River Bridge will be much more difficult than this one. A longer center span and higher for tall ships. It's not a serene river like the Ohio but deep and turbulent and tidal, changing direction twice each day, sometimes flowing at great speed."

He pulled note cards from his pocket and passed them to Wash. "Germany, France, and England are innovating underwater foundations. Go there. Study the latest technology."

Wash tried to hand the cards back. "Papa, I've told you, we—"

"You can take Emily." He caught my eye and winked. "Consider it a belated honeymoon, on me."

"And what of the fundraising for the East River Bridge?" I dreaded holding up my end of the bargain. Although throwing dinner parties would be amusing, I would rather swim upstream with rats than give a speech. A trip to Europe was much more to my liking.

"Enough time for that when you get back. I'm going to round up a bunch of bigwigs and take them on a tour of all my projects. Until the concept has a firm foundation of support, there won't be much you can do."

Despite the thousand or so onlookers, I leapt from my chair. Father and son rose in courtesy and confusion, and I nearly toppled them with hugs. "Thank you, Papa."

Wash gripped my upper arm, whispered in my ear, "We should talk about this."

After the ceremony, Wash and I packed our belongings, eager to escape our bleak little flat. "So you're excited about Europe?" His voice lacked inflection.

"Of course! Aren't you?" I tried to stuff the fancy dress I had worn to the bridge dedication into a trunk, but it popped back out. A real home with a maid and cook could not come soon enough.

"Do you understand what this means?" Wash sorted work clothes. Useable ones went into a crate, and those too frayed or soiled went into a heap on the floor. He moved sluggishly, taking too long for each simple decision.

I took a rotted set of trousers from his hands, tossed them aside, and wrapped his arms around me. "We'll have a whole year away from your father and the infernal schedule he keeps you on. You'll learn all sorts of new things, and we'll see places others only dream about."

Wash pushed away, holding me at arm's length. "I'll be signing up for another bridge project. This one is more dangerous and will take much longer to complete."

"Yes. That's what you do." I tried to read his eyes, but he avoided my gaze. "Have I complained too much?"

"Of course not."

"Then what is it, dear? I want to support you in any possible way."

"I know you do." His eyes finally met mine. "But what if I don't want to do it anymore? What if I want to live on the coast of Maine and paint the seagulls or buy land in Kentucky and raise racehorses?"

"Those are my dreams. You don't even like horses. Building the bridge has been your dream since forever."

"It's what Roeblings do."

"I knew that when I married you." I ran my fingers through his hair, still not sure what was bothering him. But the way he relaxed into my arms, it seemed he wanted what I did, to follow his dreams with me by his side. I contemplated sharing some exciting news, but the time was not quite right.

SEVEN

To Europe

I n port, the ship offered a new perspective of the New York skyline. The buildings in midtown crept ever higher, reminding me of children standing chin to nose, proclaiming *now I'm the tallest*. Trails of horse- and man-drawn carts, laden with merchandise, flowed back and forth from barges to warehouses squatting on the riverfront.

Hordes of people turned out to bid farewell to the steamship on the warm June day. I had been one of them many times, waving to the lucky passengers lining the decks. Now, we were the lucky ones, leaning against the rails of the RMS *Scotia*, blowing kisses, as the ship blew its farewell horn. Mother alternately waved a handkerchief and dabbed her eyes with it. GK, a head taller than the rest, waved an American flag.

The sight of GK especially tugged at my heart. During our time in Cincinnati, he had faced a terrible challenge. In order to cover their own poor judgment, Generals Grant and Sheridan had accused him of making cowardly decisions during the war. During the Battle of Five Forks, Grant had ordered GK to move his troops to support Sheridan. Grant had prom- ised Sheridan the reinforcements would arrive sooner than was humanly possible. In addition, GK had to disentangle his units from other skirmishes and cross a river after the bridges had been destroyed. But all Sheridan saw was that GK did not show up in time, and he accused him of dithering.

My dear General, I had begun a letter.

In his reply, he wrote, *I find I must once again provide guidance for you, dearest Em. The proper salutation is "My dear Major."*

Pangs of guilt tore at me for leaving on a grand adventure, helpless to ease his pain.

After a final wave goodbye, a porter led Wash and me on a tour through the ship, heading toward our stateroom. "She is the second largest and the fastest oceangoing ship in the world," he boasted above the chug of the engines and rush of water through the paddle wheel.

As we left the harbor, Wash and the porter argued about paddle wheels versus screws while I let the balmy salt air caress my cheeks.

In our stateroom, scale diagrams, models, and maps of New York Harbor crowded the cabin and walls. I waded through steamer trunks and piles of textbooks, shoving them aside to make order from the mayhem.

"Oh look, champagne." Wash nudged out the cork with a delightful pop, filled two glasses, and handed one to me. He lifted his for a toast. "To Europe." We clinked glasses, and he kissed me. "Darling, I've been terribly preoccupied, but I promise you'll have my undivided attention the entire voyage."

I eyed the room full of evidence against him. "No apology necessary. You'll study bridge building, and I'll see Europe—a fair trade, is it not?" I sipped, the cool bubbles tickling my nose. But despite his promise made mere seconds ago, his eyes fell upon the wooden models dominating the tiny table.

No, not again. A choice needed to be made: I needed to learn of his world or return to the familiar feeling of abandonment. It wasn't in me to settle for a life of domesticity—managing a household and having chats with my husband about the wallpaper or the rats in the cellar. In Cincinnati, we had drifted apart. I wanted to know his worries, help him think through difficult problems, be his partner in life. His work was so central to his being—I had to understand it.

I picked up a model labeled *Pneumatic Caisson*. It resembled a wooden shoebox without a lid, its exposed edges sharpened and several smaller boxes fastened within. "I will accept your undivided attention. Can you explain this contraption?"

He came up behind me, surprising me with an embrace. "Caissons can wait," he murmured in my ear. He pulled the ribbons that held up my hair and let it tumble. We kissed, and he led me toward the cabin bed with its crisp white sheets.

I stopped him with a palm to his chest, even though this was what I longed for on many lonely nights. "Just a short lesson. I'd like some understanding of what takes you away from me every waking hour."

He sighed. "As you wish, dear, a short lesson, under protest." He led me back to the table, and I picked up the model. "To begin, we build wooden caissons in the shape and size of the footprint of each bridge tower." Behind me, he pressed against my back, wrapping his arms around me.

"A huge, empty box?"

He nodded, clasped his hands over mine to turn over the model, open side down. "An open-bottom box about 100 by 170 feet—about a third the size of a city block."

"Hard to even imagine."

"Quite so. We caulk the seams with oakum and wrap it in iron to make it waterproof and airtight, then float it into place in the river, upside down, just like this. These caissons will be the foundations for the towers."

"Float? Seems it would be awfully heavy, wrapped in iron."

"About three thousand tons, but that won't matter. Compressed oxygen will be pumped in to keep it afloat as it moves into position. After that, we continue pumping in oxygen to keep the men working in the caisson alive." He kissed the back of my neck as one hand stealthily left the model and unfastened the buttons on the back of my dress.

"As we build a tower of stone on top, we dig out the unstable silt beneath and send it up a chute." He traced a path up my back, then ran it down my spine. His lips grazed my ear, making me shudder. "The bottom edges, or shoe, cut the path, and the caisson sinks far below the riverbed to bedrock." He pushed the model and my hands down.

I scooted the model back onto the table.

"Compressed air…keeps…while workers dig… No, I can't do this." He took a step back. "I have single-mission brain and body parts. I can speak of bridges or make love, not both."

I twisted around and poked his belly. "Ah, it would appear we have finally found your limitations."

"Indeed. Which shall it be? A lesson...or love?" He wrapped his arms around me, a decision made.

From the moment he dropped to one knee in a garden, Wash had been telling me to always choose love. When I pointed out that he often chose work, he would say, "My work is how I show my love. Would you rather I spent my time in pursuits that failed to support you?" But did he understand the heartbreak and fragility of love? Perhaps his emotional constitution was sturdier than I had presumed. It had to be, to go through war, to work under great pressure, with his own father, to love a woman who defied and rebelled, even when she wasn't sure what she was rebelling against.

As he dozed, the roll of the ship and queasiness in my stomach advised me the ship was in open seas. I could only hope the seasickness did not last the entire voyage—if it *was* seasickness. It wasn't right to delay any longer. I had to tell him.

"Sweetheart." I caressed his face with the back of my hand. "We have more to celebrate."

"Hmm?"

"I have the most exciting news." I rested my head on his chest, his strong heartbeat a comfort. "I'm with child."

He yawned and blinked. "What child?"

"Yours and mine."

He cocked his head.

"We're going to have a baby."

"You're not serious!" His eyes widened, his voice incredulous and not in a happy way.

I nodded, smiling with my good news. Wash pushed away and stumbled across the crowded cabin while donning his drawers.

"But we're on our way to Europe, for God's sake! You'll need doctors!" He grabbed bunches of his hair.

"Perhaps it's not the best of timing, but they have doctors in Europe, some of the best. And we have family there."

He paced, then threw my belongings back into their trunks. "You must get off the ship. We'll get the captain to turn around. What were you thinking?"

"My darling, the baby won't come for months! We'll be well settled by then." I took a pair of my shoes from his hands. My voice sounded shaky, so I took a few breaths. I did *not* want to cry. "I want us to be together."

He eyed the small but evident bulge of my belly. "Why did you keep this from me? Have you lost your mind?"

My hands went instinctively to the small mound that seemed to have appeared overnight. "A doctor is onboard. I inquired into the manifest." But in fact, I had not. Now I had done another awful thing. I had lied to him. Where did I start to go wrong? Is it so terrible to want to be with your husband so much that you keep important things from him? Indeed, the reality of a baby had not yet fully taken hold.

Wash slammed the steamer trunk closed. "You tricked me! You knew this…how long ago? And yet didn't tell me. Why, in God's name?"

"I thought the news would make you happy. We've talked of having children."

"You're getting off this ship at once, having the baby on American soil. Our child will not be an immigrant!"

"What happened to *always choose love*?"

He blinked, shook his head. Of course, that was my own interpretation of his thoughts.

"We are married. For better or worse. I fought your father to be with you. I picked up and moved my life to a rat-infested hole to be with you. This is our life. This is who we are."

"Understood." His tone softened, and he spoke evenly and directly as he did when counseling a worker who had made a misstep. "But now everything has changed. Your safety and that of our child must be our foremost concern. You must stay."

⁂

I didn't disembark and spent so much time huddled in bed and vomiting during the eight-day voyage that Wash didn't dare say anything to upset me. The ship landed in England, then on to Prussia, where we planned to reside in the village of Mühlhausen, Papa's birthplace and where many Roeblings still lived.

Located in the middle of Prussia, the small city had well-preserved medieval architecture, with spires of Gothic churches dominating the view on every street. From the surrounding hills, one could enjoy a lovely view of the farmland, the city center tucked inside a wall like a precious jewel. It was a peaceful place, even idyllic. Every sidewalk and street was scrubbed, every window spotless. Even the fields were precisely planted, not a stray weed to be found.

The German women were as industrious as they were kind. Each day, a neighbor would arrive at my door with a carefully wrapped wurst and a *Brötchen*—a crusty roll that looked like a tiny loaf of bread. As my pregnancy progressed, they fussed over me even more, making me feel lazy in comparison.

My immense belly got in the way of the simplest of things. Getting up from the divan required awkwardly rolling to the side, then down to the floor on all fours, then pulling and pushing myself to stand. Thankfully, we had a cook. All the *Brötchen*, schnitzel, and spaetzle was making me as big as a *Haus*. Wash's extended family helped by picking up and delivering our laundry. They spoke little English, and we got by with my few words of German and lots of pantomiming. It amused me that the German community worked much harder and took more interest in communicating with me than had the Americans in Cincinnati.

Our two-story boarding house was as overstuffed as I was. It bulged with our trunks and too much furniture. The baby was due in late October but nearly a month later had yet to appear. Wash asked me how I felt every two minutes and paced at all hours, making the wait even more unbearable. His pacing always set off alarm bells in my mind, and I got up to check on him. Upon seeing me, he startled, seeming not to know who I was for a moment. He didn't act as strangely as he had directly after the war, but still his behavior renewed my pangs of worry. I tried to conceal my own physical discomfort, hoping not to make him worse.

About the time I thought the child would never arrive, I received not the delivery I yearned for but more laundry. I was faced with a basket of clean clothes and a steep stairway to our bedroom. I considered leaving it for Wash to carry, but stubbornness reared its head. I climbed, holding the heavy basket at an awkward angle against my side. At the top, I stopped to catch my breath.

A sudden pain in my back caused me to drop the basket. I reached for the handrail to steady myself. I missed it, lost my balance, and tumbled down the entire flight, landing on the hard slate floor of the entry.

Pain sliced from my elbow to my hand, and my back ached like it had been kicked by a horse, but all I could think about was the baby. I held my belly, watching it rise and fall with my breathing. Minutes seemed like hours until I felt a kick. Then a few more kicks, the baby reassuring its terrified mama. Too shaken and achy to move, I waited on the cold stone until Wash came home.

With unearthly calm, he checked me and placed a pillow under my head. "I'm running next door to have them fetch the doctor. I'll be back in a moment."

He returned, and the doctor came quickly. He placed an ear horn on my belly while Wash stood close by, staring at his shoes. The doctor spoke to him in German, then nodded and smiled at me.

"He says the baby is fine and you have only a few bad bumps and bruises. Em, you shouldn't be—"

My answer was a groan as a sudden pain gripped my lower abdomen and my stomach tightened. Our baby was finally on the way.

Giving birth was by far the hardest thing I had ever done. How in God's creation had my mother endured it twelve times? The doctor said I was losing a prodigious amount of blood due to my fall and gave me an injection to ease the pain. But the sensation of a knife twisting in my gut pierced readily through the fog.

When it was over, the doctor handed me our son, wrapped in a cotton blanket. Exhaustion made my arms so heavy that I couldn't reach for him. The sharp tang of alcohol and the musk of blood filled the air and unsettled my stomach. The four bedposts formed horses on a carousel as the world spun around me. Unreal, as if I were dreaming. Or drowning.

For the past months, I had imagined the moment we would lay eyes on our tiny baby and revel in the wonder of creating a new human being. Instead, I was stunned by his enormity. He hung precariously from the small triangle of fabric attached to a hook on a scale. "Twelve pounds," the doctor announced. The baby had chubby legs and arms and puffy pink cheeks. And big lungs. We named him John, after his grandfather.

The next day, Wash paced helplessly as the baby wailed for my milk. I was too worn out to lift my head let alone Johnny to my breast.

"I can't—" I moaned, wanting nothing but sleep.

Wash arranged some pillows to prop the baby, and at last Johnny latched on and quieted.

"I have to leave for a few days, some important appointments, but the nurse is here to take care of you." He kissed my forehead through an encroaching darkness.

That was the last I remember until the sound of the nurse shrieking "*Der liebe Gott!*" pierced my slumber. I awoke on my side, the baby sleeping in a cradle next to me.

"What?" I tried to form the word with unresponsive lips. The nurse lifted crimson bedsheets from my wet legs as I drifted back into the deep, dark river.

⟿

My hand was lifted to a damp, scratchy cheek. I felt his presence more than seeing him.

"Wash."

"I'm here, my love."

I unglued my eyes a slit, and Wash's tortured face swam before me. A terrible dread entered my mind, and my heart raced. "The baby!"

"He's fine, dear." Wash placed a warm hand over mine and took in a deep, jagged breath. "But the doctor says you need an operation. We've got to let him do it."

"Mmm… Thass all right…" Even through the fog, I knew as long as the baby was fine, nothing else mattered.

"I'm so sorry for leaving you. I'll…I'll never forgive myself."

His face was wracked with anguish, and I tried to comfort him.

"I fine." I felt the skin of my forehead being tugged as he plucked matted hair from it.

"There's something else." He hung his head. "We can't have any more."

"More what?" I asked, already fading into a soft dream.

"More babies."

The surgery stemmed the bleeding, but I was very weak and unable to get out of bed for a month. My heart ached for the children we would never have. I pictured Johnny running through fields with the sisters that weren't meant to be. I recalled my own childhood with nearly a dozen siblings vying for the best swing, the most attention, the biggest piece of bread. But part of me was relieved to never have to repeat the painful experience of childbirth. Johnny would have friends and cousins and parents who could devote themselves to him.

Johnny brought us great joy, and Wash no longer harangued me about my decision to accompany him to Europe with a child on the way. Likewise, I bit my tongue back from lashing him once I realized he'd gone away, leaving me and his newborn son for days while I hung in a precarious state.

When I had regained my strength, I accompanied Wash on research trips, sometimes leaving Johnny with the Roebling clan. Words like "caisson" and "quoin" became as familiar to me as "cat" and "dog." Or *le chat* and *le chien*. When the opportunity to study a bridge over the Seine arose, I used my facility with French to worm my way into the visit.

We reveled in each other's company, making love frequently and passionately once I had recovered, as if to make up for the lonely nights filled with his work and my waiting. It was the honeymoon we had never had.

Wash's spells of soldier's heart occurred less frequently, and his sweetness and lively sense of humor returned along with our lovemaking. He surprised me with unusual gifts of questionable taste. Once, he paid a few francs for some eggs from a farm woman, then drew comical likenesses of her on the shells and presented them to me in a lovely basket.

He had a knack for analyzing building design and why the human eye might perceive it with pleasure, as when we visited Versailles. The formal gardens were breathtaking with the precision of their carved hedges, the romantic twists and turns of the paths between them.

Wash pointed out features of the wondrous palace, such as the two stories of tall Palladian windows, precisely offset from each other. "It's the symmetry and balance, two related but different things. The grandeur in size, restraint in design, and the consistency in the color of the stone taken together please the eye and soothe the mind."

Especially enjoyable was our visit to England to see the architecture of Sir Christopher Wren. At the Royal Navy Observatory in Greenwich, Wash and I admired the perfect balance of grace, symmetry, and utility in Wren's dome.

Windows and panels alternated in pleasing scale, and glorious carvings at the zenith drew my eyes toward the heavens. An enormous telescope protruded through an opening in the roof, similar to the Cincinnati Observatory. Once again, I was able to see beyond our world. How tiny and insignificant our lives seemed in comparison. We were living our lives as they were meant to be lived, our place in the universe ordained by a power greater than us. My perspective grew and my worries abated. I was physically as strong as I had been before the pregnancy and emotionally even stronger.

In a Scotland dry dock, Wash and I watched workers prepare the new clipper ship *Cutty Sark* for launch. Wash was eager to explore the innovative hull design. Her framework was designed for speed, with several types of wood fitted into a graceful curve. We were both awed by the waterproofing—a skin of brass, much more elegant than his plan for the caisson.

A wooden structure cradled the ship, and we ducked under the spectacular hull. The special type of flexible brass sheathing, called Muntz metal, was a precise mixture of corrosion-resistant copper and zinc. It was heated to a blazing 800 degrees, applied to the lower hull, then carefully cooled. I reached up and ran my hand across the golden surface's breathtaking curves. One couldn't see and feel that without wonder, without a sense of calm. It was a privilege to view this treasure of art and science before it was forever concealed beneath the waves.

We were in a remote part of France when I failed at the first chance I had to truly help Wash with his work. He planned to dive underwater to examine foundations and needed me to hold his rope line, which was tied about his waist in case he got into some trouble. Refusing to ask his father to pay for an assistant, when he needed an extra set of hands, he chose mine.

Wash was studying a small bridge, its several stone arches leaping across the water in perfect symmetry. It was as if we had stepped into a painting. Lilacs scented the spring air while apple and cherry trees bloomed with abandon.

I sat on the bank of the stream, a cool breeze blowing over my bare feet, a picture book of the French countryside in one hand, the coiled end of Wash's rope in the other. The rope tugged, and Wash popped out of the water.

"Em! You must come see this!" He waded over to me, his wet bathing costume clinging nicely to his broad chest. He pulled off the swim goggles he had fashioned with round pieces of glass and bits of rubber, leaving black rings around his eyes.

I laughed. "You look like a panda bear."

He growled and rubbed his face on my white gauzy skirt.

I pushed his head away. "*Mon Dieu*, this is the latest in French fashion."

"You're all dirty." He gave me a smile. "Now you have to come in." He offered his hand and guided me down the short bank. "It's not too cold."

He gently pulled me, but I dug my heels into the pebbled shallows.

"I'm quite content right here," I said, although I wasn't at all. I wanted to climb back up the riverbank. The thought of going deeper into the water sent a shiver of dread through my body.

"What is it? You told me you could swim."

"I can survive."

He tilted his head. "And what were you going to do if I needed help?"

"It's not that I can't, physically."

"Metaphorically, then?" Wash waved at the sinking sun. "I've got the rest of the day and all night. Tell me."

Perhaps I should have shared the story with him long ago. Memories tucked in a recess of my mind sometimes boiled to the surface, with or without provocation. If I shared them with my beloved, could I finally let go? A dull pain formed in the pit of my belly, convincing me to keep my secrets buried. It was so long ago, after all. I stared at the water rippling over my feet, screams of terror from the past echoing in my ears. He was right. It was time.

My memories begin, as everything begins, with water. Flowing serenely between cascading cliffs, the river appeared so gentle, so welcoming. My fifth spring had arrived, and we children were set free to explore the budding world.

My brother GK led my sister Elizabeth and me on a narrow path through the woods toward the river, bent branches snapping back into my face. We weren't allowed to swim in the river but often threw pebbles into it and watched boats go by.

GK pointed out poison ivy, and I slapped at mosquitoes as we hiked a good mile from home, climbing all the way.

"Wait up," Elizabeth called from behind. My parents favored her, the golden child, the sky-eyed angel among the rest of us with dark hair and dirt eyes. She was heavier and slower, although six years old to my five. We were always competing: who was braver, smarter, taller? Hearing her clomping behind me, I giggled and raced farther ahead.

White sunshine blinded us as we emerged from the woods. The dirt path ended at a smooth stone ledge. We scrambled up the rock to the top of the cliff, high above the water.

"You see that, Emily?" GK pointed across the river to a bald mountain, as pockmarked as his face. He was thirteen years older than me, therefore fascinating, and seemed to change with each day. We crept to the edge of the rock for a view of the iron foundry just upriver but far below us. "They shoot the cannons across the river to test them."

The woods rustled behind us as Elizabeth caught up. "Get back from there." She huffed, her shoulders rising and falling with each breath.

I ignored her, mesmerized by the river slithering through the rounded green mountains like a glittering snake.

"Here comes the train." GK pointed to the river's twin, a black snake running beside it.

Elizabeth pulled on his arm. "I mean it. Get back."

"Stop it." I pushed between them.

"You're too close." Elizabeth held her hands on her hips.

"Shut your mouth. You're not the boss. We got here first."

"Enough, you two." GK herded us back from the cliff, but I wasn't having any of it. I kicked the back of her knee.

She whirled around, reaching for my hair. "Stop it, you baby."

I punched at her face, and she blocked with an elbow. My brother pushed us both back toward the woods, but we escaped him, mindful only of unsettled rows and hurts of the past.

We tussled, a shoe hitting a knee, an elbow meeting a chin. GK grabbed her corn-silk hair and a wad of my brown curls and pulled us apart, our fists swirling in air. He let go of her first, the older, more sensible one. She backed away, her plump cheeks pinked, her hair wild.

"You look like a witch," I said.

She shoved me, or tried to anyway, arms stretched, hands ready to flatten across my chest. I dodged. She stumbled forward, and her momentum carried her the few steps toward the edge. She tried to stop but slid on loose gravel. I ran to catch her, but GK stiff-armed me back, reaching to grab Elizabeth.

But he missed.

She screamed as she tilted, then tumbled off our rock and crashed into a clump of trees below. She was safe there for a moment, the tender green branches nesting her body.

"Hold on!" GK yelled.

She scrambled, no baby bird but a little girl seeking solid earth. Branches gave way, and she fell out of sight, her voice echoing in the riverside canyon.

GK scooped me up and jumped down off our perch. He carried me, slipping and jerking, down a narrow, steep path, barely wide enough for a foothold. We zigzagged down the face of the gray rock mountain, and I hid my face in his shoulder. About halfway down the cliff, he put me down on a fallen tree. "Stay here. I'll be right back."

THE ENGINEER'S WIFE   61

"No, don't leave me!" I clung to him.

He hesitated. Elizabeth's cries for help were like a baby bear calling for its mama.

"You'll be safe here, Emily." He cupped my chin in his hand. "I've got to help our sister."

"No, no, no." I wrapped both arms around his leg.

Groaning in anguish, he picked me up and tossed me over his shoulder. I clasped his brown shirt as we bumped down, down, down. At the bottom of the ravine, he set me on a patch of pebbles at the edge of the water.

"Help me," Elizabeth cried. She was in the river, clinging to a branch, her face curtained with blood.

The water rushed by much more quickly than it appeared from above. Logs and branches swept by faster than I had ever run. Having no experience in the water, I stepped in to help. A shock of cold water captured me. I paddled madly to keep my head above the water. My head slipped under, and I arched my neck to get a breath.

The current dragged me under, sunlight wavering through a filter of water. Then strong arms scooped me up, and I sucked in a great breath of air. The river pulled against us, and GK stumbled, waist-deep and weighed down by me and our sopping clothes. When we reached the shore, he set me down, told me to stay put. I obeyed, wet and shivering, my sister's pleas filling my ears.

He jumped back in and swam to Elizabeth, still clinging to the branch. He reached her just as the current yanked her from it. She slapped at the water and clawed for him as he grasped her dress and pulled her toward him. He lost his grip on the branch.

I watched them float away, arms flailing, voices muffled, their heads bobbing under the water, until only one head popped back up.

I shared my darkest secret, about the most horrible day, of losing my sister and my fear of the water ever since.

He wrapped me in his arms, my head tucked under his chin. "I'm sorry, my love."

I raked my foot against the wet pebbles. "So GK was determined to teach me how to swim. For several months, he woke me before dawn, and we snuck out of the house to a small pond covered with lily pads. He would pick me up and wade into the water until it reached my feet. I screamed in terror when we went any deeper. Gradually, he helped me overcome my fears enough to separate from him and paddle around him like a puppy. My strokes grew stronger over time, but I was much relieved when he declared the lessons to be completed."

"Was that the last time you swam?"

"Once or twice since, but I'd be perfectly happy never to swim again. Every spring, we go back to the overlook and throw flowers down the cliff in her memory."

GK and I, the guilty survivors, had made a pact. We had taken a life. Whether we called it an accident or fate or irresponsibility or recklessness, it was just a name for our pain, not a way to live with it. We had told no one the full story of what happened that day. It was a secret that both bonded and haunted us.

I rested my hand on Wash's cool, wet chest. "Each year, we renew a pact: *to work twice as hard, be twice as good, and have twice as much fun*—for Elizabeth."

He caught my eye, his lips curled into a slight smile. "That explains so much." He lifted me up. "But this won't do for the wife of a bridge builder. We'll be around water our whole lives." He leaned close. "Come. You'll enjoy it with me."

"No, put me down!" I kicked my legs free.

"Emily, you are going to have to face this sooner or later."

"Not now." I stepped back. "Is that why you brought me here? Did GK tell you? Have you known all along?" My insides felt exposed like a freshly gutted trout.

"No, I wanted you here, thought we might enjoy the day together, and I could benefit from your assistance. But now I think you rather need help yourself." His fingers swirled the water, tinkling around us and smelling of yesterday's fish. "Nothing's going to hurt you."

"I'm not ready. You'll have to find another assistant." I stepped through the murk back to the riverbank. My feet slid on its slippery face; I grabbed tree roots for support.

He approached with sloshing steps, and his warm hand rested on my back. "Stop. Let me help you."

I hugged the steep bank, breathing the scent of mud and grass and worms. Tears flowed down my cheeks.

"It's all right." He gently tugged my shoulder.

When I could breathe without shuddering, I echoed him. "All right." He slid his hands down to make a seat for me, and I wrapped my arms around his neck. I raised my legs around his waist, and he slowly, slowly waded in. My arms clung tightly to him, my face tucked into his neck as he crept deeper, the water chilling my legs. Bile rose in my throat, and I struggled to breathe.

But I did breathe, in jerky gasps at first, smoothing and slowing as his musky smell calmed me. With the clutch of his hands under my bottom and the solid wall of his chest against me, I pushed thoughts of swirling, rapid river from my mind. "Are your arms getting tired? You can bring me back."

"I can hold you as long as you need."

Shivering, I inched my legs into the waist-deep river while wishing to be lifted away from the snake that stole my sister. But he rocked me with the current, repeating, "Don't worry. I've got you."

My trembling stopped, and the corset laces of fear and guilt that had long squeezed my chest loosened. We kissed, the stream gently flowing past. The sky darkened and the crickets chirped. I dipped my fingertips in the water, making peace with it.

"Good?" he asked.

I nodded, and he slipped his arms from around me, reached under the current, and brought up a muddy piece of junk. "Aha. This is what I wanted to show you."

I raised my eyebrows at his offering.

He swirled it in the water to rinse off the mud, revealing a white ceramic pitcher with beautiful lines and in good trim. He raised it like a trophy. "An artifact of an ancient culture."

I wiped my streaked face, trying to resemble a normal sort of person. "Or something that fell off someone's boat last week."

EIGHT

New York City, New York
1868

After returning to the States, we lived for a short while with GK, Millie, and their son in their Manhattan home. I took turns with Millie minding the children, which allowed me a bit of free time to explore New York.

The streets were quite congested, and the horse and buggy proved cumbersome to maneuver, as I favored driving myself. Still a country girl at heart, I longed to ride in the saddle. There was quite a kerfuffle when I raised the idea, with Millie aghast, Wash in favor, and GK bemused.

"Emily runs counter to the rules," GK said. He kindly lent me his horse and a sidesaddle, and I rode the streets, delighting in the sights and bustle of the growing city. If the people of New York were offended, they showed no sign. Indeed, there were smiles from the ladies and gentlemen tipping their hats. I guided the horse with precision—filthy water befouled the streets, carrying the debris of life toward the river. I had read in *Harper's* that a better system of sanitary waste disposal was to be established. It could not come soon enough.

New buildings shot up, and the city was becoming more crowded. Immigrants poured in, creating neighborhoods where only the mother tongue was spoken or English with lovely accents.

One of my favorite routes took me past a line of Chinese butcher shops. Plucked whole ducks and chickens were displayed in the windows, their sad heads drooping from nooses, their wrinkly feet dangling in midair. If I lingered too long, a shopkeeper would swipe a cleaver across its neck and present the bird to me for purchase.

The smells of frying garlic and onion along with melodic conversations and lively music pouring from the shops on the Italian streets were a treat. How bland my own culture seemed by comparison. I wandered into a market, enticed by a woman in the window, kneading pasta dough.

The shopkeeper waved me over with a floury towel and demonstrated rolling the dough into one-inch-thick logs on a butcher block. She dusted my hands with flour, then plopped a dense ball of dough into them. As I rolled it into a log with flattened palms, she sliced hers into thin chunks. Next, she curled my fingers and pressed my thumb into one small chunk. "Orecchiette." She tugged on her ear.

I looked at the squashed circle of dough, then at her, confused.

She laughed, lined up the pasta chunks, then pressed her thumb into each one with a flourish, creating little cups that resembled tiny ears. "Orecchiette, yes?"

"Yes!" I tried the maneuver, but mine remained more flat circles than sweet little ears. After thanking her for the lesson, I purchased a sack of dried orecchiette to bring home.

Wandering the fragrant and colorful streets, I fancied myself some sort of goodwill ambassador, bringing the cultures together, making the city better for everyone. So far, my diplomatic pouch contained one condemned chicken and a hundred little ears. Quite a start for a hopeful ambassador and abominable cook.

In Trenton, the Roebling family was nearly as foreign to me as the immigrants streaming in from Castle Garden. Wash was the eldest, and his seven siblings adored him, clambering all over him like barnacles on a ship the moment he walked in the door. Although my family was affectionate, the Roeblings made the Warrens seem positively prickly by comparison. I suspected that two of his sisters married men from Staten Island just so they could be near Wash.

Wash hugged his father, his sisters, his brothers, every day, any time of day. He was so given to hugging that I called him my Washbear. The little sisters giggled at that, and Wash advised that I was calling him a raccoon in German. A lump caught in my throat, remembering him emerging from the river, pulling off his goggles, revealing two black eyes.

❧

Wash purchased for us a three-story, redbrick home with a rooftop garden on Columbia Heights in Brooklyn. We had a magnificent view of the river and future site of the East River bridge.

As soon as he signed the papers, we raced over for a tour of the empty house. While Wash used field glasses to test his new perspective from every window, I gleefully let water flow out of the kitchen tap. No more running outside and manually pumping, nor barrels needing to be filled from the public tap—water came from city pipes buried deep underground. Our coal boiler produced steam to warm the house and powered water pumps, which filled a cistern on the rooftop. The previous owners had converted an upstairs bedroom into a bath. I was up there, imagining luxuriating in the large cast iron tub, when Wash called from below.

"Em, come see this."

With one arm cradling Johnny, the other firmly gripping the banister, I hurried down the long, curving staircase and found Wash in the parlor.

"Prepare for the unveiling." He unlatched the center panels of the back wall and pushed until they folded like a mahogany accordion, opening to the large dining room. "*Et voilà!*"

"How lovely!" I twirled into the empty space, my voice echoing on the bare walls and floors. "Imagine the entertaining we can do." The previous owners' cook, praise God, was staying on with us.

He took my hand and spun me around, humming a tune while Johnny sat on his quilt, clapping and cooing his approval. We danced and laughed and dreamed of all the joy we would have in our new home.

There was also an indoor privy. "We're darned lucky to have it," Wash said.

I was not convinced, as the sewer stench wafting through the house was most unpleasant. I refused to use it, preferring the outhouse instead. Wash muttered something about improper venting and had his brothers make custom iron pipe at the factory, tearing up walls and ceilings installing it. For months, our lovely new home gaped with exposed pipes.

Thankfully, our library was left intact. The floor-to-ceiling walnut bookshelves and the carved fireplace with a marble mantel made up for its small size. I envisioned curling up on an overstuffed divan with Wash, reading Dickens and Oliphant, or following Alice down the rabbit hole with Johnny.

But my husband got to it first. His favorite books and texts from Rensselaer Polytechnic Institute, carefully arranged by subject and year studied, took up three of the walls; his maps and plans filled every drawer. Conceding his need for office space, I created a reading nook in the parlor and lined every inch with my own books and favorite art. What I lost in privacy, I gained with my view of the comings and goings at the front door.

Wash had little time for social events, but I was invited to teas, needlepoint circles, and such. I soon grew weary of these gatherings. Endlessly pulling thread through muslin seemed pointless; I wanted to see more, *do* more. It was time to revisit my dream of joining the women's movement, time to meet people pushing in new directions.

One muggy day in late June, I hired a minder for Johnny, then accompanied Papa and Wash on the ferry to Manhattan. The men needed to sample the soil structure at the proposed bridge site, and I needed to sample some new adventures.

Upon arrival, Wash offered his arm as I disembarked, and the three of us gathered on the wharf. The air hung thick with humidity, so I removed my gloves and fanned myself with them.

Wash rummaged in his satchel and pulled out some rolled-up papers. "Em, please give these to GK and my regards to Millie."

"What is this?" Papa asked. He regarded the rolls with a furrowed brow as Wash tucked them into my day bag.

"The old plans."

"I told you to destroy them."

"They are pieces of art and history, Papa. GK may appreciate them or destroy them if he doesn't."

"As long as they are not around to remind me of that foolish committee."

"What committee?" I asked.

"The Bridge Committee that voted to scrap the trains on the bridge in an effort to save money," Wash said.

"Shortsighted fools," Papa grumbled.

"One more thing, Em." Wash extracted a folded note from his pocket. "Here's an address I want you to ride by. An elaborate building is going up. C. C. Martin tells me this fellow is creating quite the stir in social circles. He may be someone we want onboard."

"I've got my orders." I slipped the note in my bag and gave him a kiss.

"Be careful now. No talking to strangers." Wash waved a stick of his favorite cinnamon chewing gum at me before popping it into his mouth.

I laughed. "Who, me?"

"I mean it this time." He put his hands on my shoulders, the warm, spicy scent overriding the salty, fishy air. "This isn't Brooklyn. I had better walk you to the coach." He checked his timepiece.

"Why don't you come with me? GK and Millie would love to see you. And he will be heading back to Iowa soon. It's been forever since we've done something just for fun."

"As far as the coach is all I have time for, I'm afraid."

His answer didn't surprise me. Work time was precious to him. "It's only a few blocks. I'll be fine on my own."

I stepped up the hill as fast as I could without hiking up my dress, a bit disappointed Wash wouldn't join me but still gleeful for the freedom to explore.

Handing the carriage driver Wash's note, I said, "Take Park Avenue, please." It wasn't the shortest route, but I was in no hurry, and I wanted to see the beautiful homes that had escaped demolition. In the ever-changing city, commercial enterprises were sprouting up, replacing many residential neighborhoods.

The carriage halted at a large corner lot where an extraordinary building was under construction. Elaborate stone underpinnings nearly filled the parcel of land. Rounded arches reached skyward, similar to the ones in Papa's bridge towers in Cincinnati. Workmen swarmed the site, sawing and hammering and employing all sorts of steam-powered machinery. Although an iron fence surrounded the property, the gate was wide open.

Inside the gate, a tall man studied architectural drawings. His top hat, black coattails, and white cravat and gloves hardly befit the sweltering afternoon, yet not a drop of sweat formed on his brow as he provided instructions to a gaggle of workers.

The section closest to the street was nearly complete. A muscular mason carried hammers and chisels up a tall ladder, then gracefully leapt upon a stone ledge. The heavy tools seemed an extension of himself as he chipped at a gable. He mopped his sweat-beaded face with a rag and gestured toward his handiwork for my approval. I smiled and gave a wave of appreciation, which he rewarded with a hoot and a feigned kiss.

Instead of turning away as my mother had taught me a lady should, I walked straight toward him. He laughed, waggled his eyebrows, and made more kissing noises, then feigned losing his balance.

This tomfoolery alerted the gentleman in the coattails, who rolled up his drawings and started over to investigate. Perhaps fifteen years my senior, he was clean-shaven except for bushy sideburns, with slightly graying hair and an engaging smile.

"I'm off at six, *bella signora*," said the mason in a thick accent from high up on his ledge.

Both men's stares bore down on me as I walked to the heavy wooden ladder. With all my strength, I lifted and bumped it over three feet, just out of the mason's reach. My formerly pristine white cotton gloves now resembled a chimney sweep's, so I plucked them off, then turned away.

"*Ciao, bella*, you're a strong one. Put that back."

The elegantly dressed gentleman tucked the plans under his arm and adjusted the diamond pin on his puffy cravat before he approached me, obstructing a path of escape. He lifted his hat, which shone of fine silk.

"Well, now. Whom do we have here?" he shouted over the construction noise. "If you weren't such a fine specimen, I should have to charge you admission." He smiled, rubbing his thumb and fingers together for the phantom payment.

"Good afternoon, sir. This worker and I encountered a bit of a problem."

The well-dressed man side-eyed the ladder. "It seems you have solved it."

The mason above crossed his beefy arms and glared down at me.

"This is an extraordinary structure. Are you the architect?"

The gentleman guffawed, removed his hat, and bowed deeply. "Phineas Taylor Barnum, at your service. Entrepreneur, philosopher, and philanthropist. Master of ceremonies and entertainer of kings. I dream of grand mansions, hire architects to design them and scurrilous chaps like him to build them."

"Mrs. Washington Roebling." I offered my ungloved hand and glanced up at the stranded mason. "Forgive me. I have an eye for beauty but an intolerance for disrespect."

"Delighted to make your acquaintance." Mr. Barnum made a rather elaborate show of removing his right glove and bringing my hand to his lips. He held it a moment too long, making me squirm, but his twinkling gaze never left mine, drawing me in. "We are of a mind. You have earned my respect, as I rather enjoy a spunky woman.

"Allow me to be your tour guide to the magnificent new American Museum, madam." He placed his hand ever so lightly on the small of my back. "You shall be the first of many millions destined to cross its threshold."

His voice was soothing, low, and melodic, his face hypnotic with his earnest, deep-blue eyes and easy smile. I was entranced, as a schoolgirl might admire her instructor.

A thought edged into my trance, and I remembered Wash's stern warning. "While your offer is most generous, Mr. Barnum, perhaps I should make the tour while in the company of my husband?"

"Nonsense. You're quite safe with me, and we'll remain in clear view of all. Won't we, Luciano?" Mr. Barnum shouted this last bit up to the mason as he squired me toward the entrance.

My curiosity overwhelmed my sense of propriety; I accepted his arm and accompanied him, much to the distress of the marooned Luciano.

Mr. Barnum and I climbed the wide marble staircase to the flat roof, some five stories from the ground. I halted on the landing, breathless from the climb and dizzied by the height. My corset seemed to have shrunk two inches, pinching my waist and taking my air. I fished in my day bag for a fan.

A spectacular view of the river unfolded, but I kept my distance from the edge.

"Are you quite all right?" His eyes flicked to my heaving bosom.

"Fine, thank you." *If I could loosen my corset.* "Pray continue."

"It's still a shell of course, but when complete, there will be twenty rooms of exhibits. Astonishing flora and fauna from around the world, some living, some preserved." He bubbled with enthusiasm, all his gestures grander than necessary. "Researchers—anthropologists, biologists, historians—will come, along with the merely curious." He raised his arms to the sky. "New York will become a destination. The Paris of the Americas."

"*C'est magnifique*, Mr. Barnum."

"Ah, you speak French? Then I have something very special to show you. But you mustn't breathe a word of it." He dug his hand into his trouser pocket. "Do you promise?"

"I do."

"This is something never seen in this country, presented to me by King Louis Philippe."

I crossed my arms, my lips pouting with disbelief.

"Truly. He was quite entertained by my General Tom Thumb and bestowed this bauble in appreciation." Mr. Barnum held out his fist, then opened it to reveal a crystal sphere, about two inches in diameter. Inside the sphere was a tiny replica of Notre Dame de Paris Cathedral. "Would you like to hold it?"

Much heavier than it appeared, the crystal was flawless, the tiny cathedral suspended in solution, which magnified the model's exquisite detail.

"We've attempted to replicate it in my glass-blowing shop. Sadly, we've accomplished mostly gooey gobs, although we have managed a few wine glasses." He gestured toward the center of the rooftop. In between piles of lumber, a waiter was setting fine china and crystal on a small table with two chairs side by side.

"It seems you are expecting guests?" I handed back the bauble. "I should take my leave."

Two balding, Asian men strode up the stairs, arguing in a foreign language. Identical in every respect, including manner and formal dress, they marched past us to the table. My eyes widened; the men were attached to one another from chest to waist. The two sat side by side, arms crisscrossing their backs, adding the clatter of dishes and cutlery to their argument.

"No need to leave. They'll ignore us." Mr. Barnum's eyes twinkled with delight at my evident surprise. "You've not seen the Siamese twins Chang and Eng?"

I shook my head.

"You would have been very young during their working days."

"I believe my…um…husband has seen them," I stuttered.

"Ah yes, a husband. Such a shame I didn't find you first." He winked. It was an outrageous thing to say, but he said it with such impish charm, I could barely take offense.

"You tread the line of impropriety, sir. Do you not care what others think?"

"When I can control what people think, I shall truly be able to perform magic. My own wife wouldn't waste the bat of an eye, but it seems the opinions of others is of concern to you?"

"I wish I cared less, but it's something ingrained in me."

"Things ingrained sometimes have to be pried out, like a splinter." He waggled his eyebrows, making me laugh. "I do welcome your opinion, however."

My opinion was that he worked twice as hard and had twice as much fun in the bargain. Unlike my Wash, who seemed too often stumped by the second half of the equation.

Mr. Barnum conjured a lit match from thin air and held it to a cigar that appeared in the same fashion. "What calls you to me, Mrs. Roebling?"

I fumbled in my bag for Wash's note. "My husband and his father are to build a bridge to Brooklyn." I glanced toward the river. "They're taking soil samples this very moment. Word of your enterprise has spread and—"

"Excellent! Apart from enjoying your charms, I should like to know more about this bridge. Will be useful for my businesses." He popped the still-burning match into his mouth. "Now, let us dispense with this Mr. Barnum nonsense, shall we? Call me PT."

My throat constricted. "How do you do that?"

"Dispense with my surname?"

"No, eat a lit match."

He winked, tucked his cigar in his mouth, and hid both hands behind his back. Then he winged his arms to his front, fists forward. "Choose one," he mumbled past his cigar.

I tapped his right fist. He turned it over and flattened his palm to reveal the crystal sphere. But this time, it was snowing inside the globe. Tiny white flakes swirled around Notre Dame, transforming it into a breathtaking winter scene.

"The world is full of magic, my dear. You just have to know where to find it."

NINE

Niagara Falls, New York
1869

D espite the years of planning and great need for the bridge, there were naysayers. The East River was one of the busiest shipping lanes in the world; the bridge would need to be higher and longer than any other. Even so, there were sailing ships that would not fit under the planned bridge. The New York Council of Reform predicted the bridge would seriously damage commerce in the harbor, tax the financial abilities of the two cities, and be taken down by action of the courts, or demolished by the wind.

In order to raise funds and improve public relations, Papa arranged a series of meetings, then a two-month tour of his existing bridges for the rich and powerful. He included a core group of consultants: engineers, local political leaders, and the powerful contractor William Kingsley. Excluded was William M. "Boss" Tweed and many of his Tammany Hall cronies. Papa didn't want the negative publicity the corrupt politician would surely bring. Even so, Tweed bribed his way into holdings of private stock in the New York and Brooklyn Bridge Company after state officials received his financial incentives to approve the project. The state charter gave control of the project to the stockholders and therefore they became most of the bridge committee.

The final stop on the tour was Papa's crowning achievement: a double-decked suspension bridge spanning the swift and dangerous Niagara River.

Papa was eager for me to meet the committee there. "You'll charm the last dollar out of those turnips," he said.

Wash had been on the site tour for the past two months, and I longed to see him, so after leaving Johnny with Millie, I headed north. On the train to Buffalo, I paced the aisle in anticipation. The prospect of visiting the falls both thrilled and terrified me. They were magnificent in pictures, but I wasn't sure how I would react to the swiftness of the river or the roar of the falls. Panicking in front of so many people would be humiliating and certainly not helpful to Papa and Wash's cause. I slowed my pace and hugged my elbows to me, forcing my mind to calm, imagining the security of Wash's arms around me.

I changed trains in Buffalo, and Farrington met me at the station in Niagara Falls, then brought me by carriage to the bridge. As we stepped from the carriage, it seemed we were late. A dozen men held stovepipe hats to their heads as their overcoats whipped in the bitter wind. They gathered on the lower deck, high above the churning river, the falls thundering a short distance downriver. The sound assaulting my ears, the terrific height, and the sight of rushing water made me freeze in fright. Wash's broad smile erased my fears only enough to keep me from bolting.

"Gentlemen, please avail yourselves of the view, and take a moment to meet my lovely wife, Emily."

Some craned their necks at the train tracks above them while others peered into the great rapids below. A horse and buggy rushed by, and one of the men cleaved to the railing, his knuckles as white as the snow on the distant trees. Farrington and I traded a look. The deck rumbled, doing little to ease my jittery nerves. I approached the man, hoping to ease his discomfort while distracting myself from my own. Farrington introduced me.

"Benjamin Stone," the man said in a clipped English accent, tipping his hat. He was dressed in a natty three-piece suit, the chain of his pocket watch stretched across his broad belly. "Railroad engineer and consultant."

"Shall we move closer?" My hand guided him away from the edge. "It seems they are about to speak."

Papa and Wash gathered the investors with much hand shaking and shoulder slapping.

"This is a fiasco." Mr. Stone mopped his brow.

I blinked my surprise. "Pardon?"

Another large man waved his arms for attention, positioning himself front and center. Stone nodded in his direction. "That's William Kingsley, a building contractor. We can count on him to raise our concerns."

"Oh?"

Stone gave me an impatient glare. "It's his men who would be put at risk during the construction." His face softened. "Pardon me. I shouldn't expect a lady to be knowledgeable of such things."

Kingsley raised his voice, battling to be heard over the raging falls. "How can you compare this structure, a mere eight hundred feet long and secured between two solid rock cliffs, to a bridge spanning a much greater divide with no such support?"

Stone eyed the trusses supporting the railroad level above, a cold sweat collecting on his face even as I shivered.

"Did you work on this?" I asked, nodding toward the tracks above.

"Heavens, no. A foolhardy thing, and I predict a calamitous end to the practice of running trains over bridges."

"I understand that plan was scuttled for the East River Bridge."

"It took some persuading, but we prevailed on that one." Stone lowered his voice, ensuring his words were out of earshot of others. "There are some powerful influences scheming to reintroduce the trains. We must remain vigilant."

He spoke as if he'd quite forgotten who I was. He gazed into the churning waters below, his face frozen in horror.

My gut clenched in empathy. I wanted to guide him away.

"Eight hundred feet or eight thousand, what is the difference?" Papa waved dismissively. "I consider what a bridge must hold, then design it six times stronger than necessary."

The crowd turned toward the sound of a train whistling in the distance. Wash showed Papa his pocket watch and nodded toward the ties and tracks above.

C. C. Martin, Papa's second assistant engineer, approached. Tall and lanky, his elbows and knees seemed sharp enough to poke holes through his drooping suit. A dark, scraggly beard did little to improve his image. "Watch this, Mr. Stone." Martin pointed at the train tracks above. "A railroad expert like you will appreciate it."

But Stone held his top hat aloft as he elbowed his way to the front of the assembled crowd. "A bridge over the Ohio River recently collapsed in high winds. I suspect that engineer thought his bridge six times stronger than necessary as well."

The group shifted uneasily, shouting, "Hear, hear."

"It is we who will carry the guilt for any who perish on your bridge," Stone shouted above the grumbling of the men, the roaring of the falls, and the approaching engine. "Four workers perished in Wheeling. How are you going to prevent such tragedies on a much larger project?"

"Faulty design caused the failure of the Wheeling bridge—"

A train thundered above us, shaking timbers and sending a hail of dirt and gravel upon us.

Cheers went up, but Stone's eyes grew wide with terror as he held his arms and hands protectively over his head. He staggered from the crowd, crying, "No, no." The squeal of brakes covered his cries of anguish.

Stone stood apart from the group, quivering and gulping, pointing to Papa and Wash, who wore broad smiles. He set his jaw and puffed out his chest, and fire replaced the fear in his eyes. "You seem to think this some sort of joke." The group quieted as Stone's voice rang out. "What do you know of the perils of locomotives? Have you factored in the tremendous forces of weight, the dynamics of motion, the power of nature?"

"Gentlemen." Papa's calm demeanor was a contrast to the shuddering bridge, the clatter of the exiting train, and the strident words of Stone. "The East River Bridge is a necessity. It has been studied, planned, and argued about for decades." He flicked dirt from his lapel. "We must not be paralyzed by fear. Risks must be taken for progress to occur."

Wash stepped forward, his golden hair and beard in contrast to his black hat and coat, his eyes capturing the attention of all. It seemed even the falls hushed as his voice rang with passion. "We have toured my father's bridges, from strong and utilitarian like this one, to soaring works of art as we saw in Pittsburgh. Never have his designs failed, even with steam locomotives crossing a chasm as great as this. We have studied in Europe and refined what we learned there. We have no doubt of our facility. None. Gentlemen, the time is upon us. If we do not undertake building the East River Bridge, someone else will—perhaps with disastrous results." He scanned his audience. "And in that circumstance, we might indeed find ourselves culpable."

The committee cheered, perhaps because the train had faded into the distance. Farrington sidled up to Martin and me. "Don't worry. We'll prevail. The men know Stone's a bit—as they say in England—bonkers."

I suspected something personal caused Stone's trepidation. Fear had its reasons, and I could empathize with Stone. Rivers made me bonkers as well.

TEN

Manhattan

Papa's tour was a great success in gaining approval and seed money, but the work of fund-raising largely remained. Shortly after returning from Niagara, I pleaded the case with other possible benefactors. The first visit was to Phineas Barnum's American Museum (featuring Giants! Dwarfs! Industrious Fleas, Educated Dogs, and Man-Eating Tigers!).

Wash had built a three-foot-wide scale model of the bridge to pique the showman's interest, and I intended to surprise PT with the gift for his museum. I went alone, as Wash did not seem to enjoy his company.

"There's no competing with a showman," he had said.

I lugged the model on a cart by ferry, where it attracted much attention. After many curious looks and questions, I uncovered it for the passengers to see. They exclaimed in wonder and chortled at a comment regarding the irony of a bridge on a ferry. I took the opportunity to give them a quick explanation. After that, I had plenty of assistance getting the cumbersome cart and model into a carriage in Manhattan.

The smell of coal fires was especially strong, like a manufacturing plant, as the carriage rounded the corner to the American Museum. But I remembered no factory nearby.

The coachman opened my door. "Are you sure this is the place, ma'am?"

The wind shifted, and acrid smoke choked us. Through the ashen cloud, beyond the front gate, the museum appeared as a burnt-out shell. Gray wisps curled from heaps of rubble. I ran to the gate and pushed through, my eyes stinging from smoke. *Please, God, let everyone be safe.*

Several workers poked through the debris, their clothes and faces blackened with soot.

"Can you tell me where I might find Mr. Barnum?" I steadied my voice while the foul air scorched my lungs.

"Just around there." A worker pointed with a coal-colored board.

On what must have been the grand staircase, PT, in a black cape lined in red satin, perched like a giant red-winged blackbird over a charred forest, cradling a ball of fabric in his hands.

He answered the obvious question before I could ask. "A lantern, knocked over by a breeze." He shook his head. "A breeze."

I waited for a show of anger or his philosophical wit, but he was quietly grim, his eyes vacant, his movements slow and purposeless.

"I'm so sorry. Are you—is everyone—all right?"

"A few of my workers suffered some burns, I'm afraid. Thankfully, most of the animals escaped. Unlike this." He held up a scorched and tattered tailcoat, exposing his forearm, streaked with angry red burns and blisters.

I lightly tapped his uninjured arm. "It's only a coat. I'm more concerned about you."

He leaned close to me, narrowed his eyes, and growled, "I am the great P. T. Barnum. Creator of magnificent museums and things beyond imagination."

I took a step back, alarmed at his tone.

"Have no doubt about me. I will rise like a phoenix." He turned away with a theatrical flourish. It might have been comical if not for the circumstances.

A month or so later, PT wrote, *The task of rebuilding and finding accommodations in New York City for my collections have dominated my time, but I am eager to hear more about your bridge project.*

We met at his temporary headquarters near the Battery. I brought some plan drawings, reserving the scale model for a more permanent home. Spring was bursting with tulips and daffodils, so he put on his top hat, and we set out for some fresh air. We walked along the banks at the southern tip of Manhattan, extended like the toe of a ballerina where the Hudson meets the East River. I was grateful for my long stride to match his fast footing.

Although PT didn't mention the injuries and losses from the fire, neither did he show me his latest magic tricks. "What do you need?" he asked in a brusque, businesslike tone.

"We need all the support we can muster, on both sides of the river. Mr. Roebling estimates the bridge will cost six to seven million dollars to build."

"Husband or father-in-law?"

My bootheel caught in the coarse gravel, and I stumbled. "The latter."

He held an arm out to steady me. "Quite a challenge."

"My father-in-law?"

"The money."

I unfolded a map. "We're about eight blocks away from the site."

He offered his arm. "Shall we walk it?"

As we strolled, I blurted my memorized review of the plan.

PT drew a lit cigar from his jacket pocket. Apparently, he couldn't resist a small dose of magic. Taking a draw, his mouth curled into a one-sided smile.

My cheeks warmed despite the cool day. He had an uncanny ability to unsettle me.

He reached into his trouser pocket and pulled out a fistful of bread crumbs. Squealing seagulls and cooing pigeons appeared as if on cue, and he threw a great fan of food for them. He sprinkled some crumbs on the top of his hat, and a pigeon landed on it, pecking away.

Dodging an emboldened gull, I pressed on despite his effort at creating a tiny circus. "Imagine how exciting it would be. Uniting two great cities—the amenities of New York plus the lovely residential areas and charm of Brooklyn."

"A fine proposition," he said. "I believe my audience will double with the quicker transit. Fortune favors the brave and never helps a man who does not help himself."

"I've heard that. Who said it?"

"I did."

I twisted my wedding ring about my finger, contemplating financial negotiations with someone who spewed grand phrases but nothing substantial enough to report to Papa and Wash. He seemed to relish the edge of propriety. Perhaps that was the means to reach him. "You could move your headquarters to Brooklyn. I hear you have quite the following there. One woman in particular."

"Ah, you tempt me, fair lady, but I'm afraid my business keeps me here." He removed the cigar stub from his mouth and chuckled. "But I do have a mason I can lend you."

ELEVEN

Cold Spring, New York

O
n a warm afternoon a few weeks later, well-dressed women outnumbered the few men, including GK and PT, mingling on my mother's manicured lawn. Mother had never allowed widowhood to affect her station in life. Teas, garden parties, card games, all went on as usual, with or without a gentleman friend to accompany her. The sun, which would never have had the temerity to be absent from one of her events, shone high in a cloudless sky. Groundkeepers had set up one hundred small wooden chairs facing a makeshift stage.

From the window of my old upstairs bedroom, I spied Mother entering the back door. Her heels ticked across the oak floor from the hall to the formal dining room.

"Emily? Em-i-ly!"

I ignored her calls. Without my prior knowledge or consent, Mother had included a presentation by me in her event. She and Papa had become frequent correspondents and were likely colluding. He had asked her to spread the fund-raising word, and she was only too happy to volunteer me.

I had spent most of the morning writing my speech, and my mind weighed heavy with the dread of delivering it.

PT was so gifted at this. Indeed, his fame was much more widespread than I had known when we first met. Furthermore, he seemed to enjoy the attention of a crowd, lived for it in fact. Glancing out the window once more, I saw him holding court with the audience below. I could not make out his words, but his admirers stood in a semicircle around him, mouths agape in rapt attention.

I dawdled, sprawled across my old bed, flipping through an album of drawings and daguerreotypes. One was devoted to my mother's grandchildren, blurry images of smiling babies in white bonnets. I gasped. There were none of Johnny; I had yet to send one.

Another yellowed album had twelve pages, one for each of the children Mother had borne. She had lost five to childhood infirmities before I came along. And then we lost Elizabeth.

GK was quite gifted at portraits, and a quick glance at the album might tell even a stranger the story—sturdy, well-fed children with a vague unease or unhappiness about them. After the accident, strict rules were enforced in our home, as Mother was determined that none of her surviving children would be taken from her.

Pa had been my hero; I eagerly awaited his footfalls upon our front steps each evening. He would twist my curls around his finger and say, "You have eyes the color of money," eliciting a stern look from Mother and a laugh from the others. We would beg him to take us on a buggy ride or to dip a line in a nearby lake.

"Rowboats are no place for a child," Mother would say, instead directing us to our books or a chore left undone.

No longer could we run barefoot through the lush green lawn, as Mother thought we might get hookworms, while attending birthday parties threatened typhoid and consumption. Swinging on vines was strictly out-of-bounds.

The sound of cheering below drew me back to the window. A clump of people gathered near the wellhead. "Ooh, aah," they said in unison.

Long, giant bubbles floated above them, re-forming into great spheres that glistened in the sunshine. When the group parted, the source of the bubbles became apparent. PT dipped two sticks attached by loose strings into a bucket. He lifted the contraption out of the bucket and spread the dripping sticks in the breeze, creating the amazing bubbles. A tiny monkey in a red vest screeched and chased the bubbles or hid behind a guest in mock terror.

Mother's calls echoed up the stairs, and I scowled at my speech notes scattered across the desk, butterflies flitting in my stomach. My impulse was to flee, but instead I found solace by turning another album page— GK's drawing of me holding a long twig. That was the day, about a year after my sister's accident, when the same impulse to flee nearly took my life.

My classmates and siblings had teased me about my speech, for I had difficulty pronouncing the *s*, *z*, and *th* sounds. This earned no sympathy from Mother, who made me stand in front of ever-larger groups, repeating the most difficult words.

"E-nun-ci-ate," Mother said at the dinner table one day after I had stumbled through the prayer. My siblings, even my beloved father, were laughing at me. I could bear it no longer and ran out of the house and toward the dirt road. The woodland across the street was forbidden territory. Autumn had painted the trees with brilliant oranges, reds, and yellows. Soon, cold, clear nights would rob the forest, leaving the trees to face the winter stark and barren.

The Hudson River sparkled through the woods. I missed Elizabeth and longed to run down the hill to its banks to be closer to her. I wanted us to be together, to watch the steamboats ply the river's great width. But the memory of the swift current and several lashings to my bottom enforced my boundaries.

I found a long stick and broke it over my knee to make a sharp point. Then I drew a spiral in the dirt road, bigger and bigger, making a game I had played with Elizabeth. Lost in my design, I didn't hear a horse-drawn carriage until it was nearly upon me. I leapt out of the way barely in time to avoid the thundering hooves and carriage wheels. The shouts of the angry driver lingered as I stood in a cloud of dust.

The stairs squeaked as Mother ascended. She appeared in my doorframe, catching me in my chemise and petticoats, my dress tossed aside in the stifling room. I wasn't about to put on a fussy dress and itchy crinolines before it was absolutely necessary.

"Emily! What on earth? We're about to begin!"

"Why did I agree to this?" I muttered, mostly to myself. I had successfully avoided other speaking engagements, but it seemed my luck was running out.

"These are important people," she reminded me as she replaced an errant hairpin in her tightly wound and graying bun.

"I'm sure. But I'm not the expert they want to hear from."

"You learned plenty enough in Europe. And surely, you can explain the bridge's importance to those who will benefit from it."

"I'm so inept at public speaking, Mother. Can't you make an excuse for me?"

"Fine. I'll have GK do it. He's sure to enchant the audience. Of course, I'd have to introduce him as Major Warren, an engineer with nothing to do with this bridge." She wiped her reading spectacles with her handkerchief. "I'm sure he won't be disappointed in you."

"I'll be down in a moment." Effectively goaded, I dressed in a hurry, pulling off my petticoat and letting the crinoline caging stand alone, fashion conventions be darned.

Outside, I was pleased to spot Mother's friend Eleanor.

"Emily, so good to see you. How is our little Johnny?"

"Growing, one and a half years old, and expecting to be treated like a king. The reign of terror begins."

"Ah yes. God made toddlers adorable to make up for their swath of destruction. My goodness, we've hardly seen the little chap."

The little hairs on the back of my neck stood up, sensing judgment. I set it aside with a breezy "He's in Trenton with his father at the moment. We didn't think he would enjoy speeches."

"Who does?" Eleanor glanced around to ensure we didn't have an audience. Then she pulled out several small, thin slivers of iron. "I want you to try these—a new type of hairpin. You're the perfect test subject."

Her own hair hung in wisps gathered in a bun the size of a walnut. I could see why she needed my help.

The slivers, unlike regular hairpins, were doubled and connected at one end. She prized one open with her teeth and slid it into a lock of my hair. "I'm applying for a patent. What do you think?"

I rubbed a sore spot where she had raked the pin across my scalp. "It's rather scratchy."

Mother's eldest friend, Henrietta VanDrie, joined us, a mass of gray hair piled precariously on top of her head, her purple dress buttoned halfway up her neck. Her rather loose tongue probably eliminated her as Eleanor's "test subject."

"How's that Roebling clan?" she asked, her nasal accent belying her Brooklyn roots.

The arrival of Carrie Beebe spared me from recounting the antics of my large and complicated set of in-laws. Out of Carrie's earshot, Henrietta referred to her as "the mouse" due to her soft speech, drab hair color, and habit of scurrying in, unnoticed.

Carrie passed around copies of her manuscript-in-progress, entitled *Violets*. "I'd love your opinions, ladies. You're all in here somewhere."

A few eyebrows raised. I politely took a copy and feigned interest in page fifty-seven. More than her story, I was interested in the creation of the manuscripts themselves. Carrie had procured a prototype of a typing machine and was happily punching out her stories on it, reporting any issues back to the inventors.

A male voice boomed. "My, what a delightful collection of young ladies." The circle of women parted, giggling with hands over mouths, as P. T. Barnum joined us. He proceeded to delight them with card tricks until, catching my eye, he asked them to excuse the two of us.

"You've hardly said a word and ignored all my best tricks."

"My apologies. I'm rather preoccupied." I waved my notes, now droopy from the humidity and my moist gloves.

"Ah. Stage fright."

"Please take your seats." Mother herded everyone to rows of chairs. She stepped to the lectern in front of them, in full control as always. I fanned myself with my notes, my heart climbing into my throat.

"Ignore them." PT touched my cheek. "Look at me."

I did as he asked, his warm blue eyes showing a tenderness that allowed me to relax my shoulders from their rigid position.

"I will place myself in a middle seat. Seek me out. The audience will think you are addressing each one of them. Then, if you get stuck, make them all disappear." He lifted my chin. "Speak as if I were the only one listening."

After a few welcoming remarks, Mother said, "And so, it is with much pride that I introduce my daughter, Mrs. Washington Roebling."

A smattering of applause greeted me as I made my way to the front.

Taking a deep breath, I peeked at the audience, who stared back at me expectantly. Sweat dampened my brow, and a rivulet ran down my backbone. My hands shook as I fumbled with my notes. Sweat blurred my vision; the crowd swirled in front of me as if I were underwater. The hushed murmur flowed like water through my ears with bits of conversation popping through.

I tried to regain my composure, closing my eyes and opening them to see GK in the front row, nodding encouragement.

Clutching the lectern with each hand, I began. "A bridge connecting New York and Brooklyn is a necessity for progress in our state and our country. When complete, it will be a monument to—"

Hecklers shouted objections and questions.

"How much of our taxpayer money is going for this?"

"Another of Boss Tweed's scams."

My vision narrowed, and I wiped my hands on my dress and fanned my face with my notes. My eyes darted around the audience, seeking PT. "In the interest of everyone's time, please hold your questions until the end, and I promise to answer each one."

I finished my speech, stronger, more confident under PT's steady gaze. The audience clapped politely after I had conveyed my message, but whether it swayed anyone's opinion was another kettle of fish.

My relief at finishing was short-lived as I remembered my promise to Papa. The thought of repeating this speech over and over made my stomach churn anew. My mind spun toward a means to rid myself of this obligation. Perhaps I could find refuge in motherhood. Or magic.

TWELVE

Brooklyn

I was late. Wash had requested my presence at the waterfront at 9:00 a.m. sharp, but Johnny captivated me, squealing in delight as we sprawled on the floor in his room, bouncing a rubber ball between us. Now scampering about on two sturdy legs and beginning to talk, he was at the age when a mother falls in love with her baby all over again. His squeals made me laugh and squeal with him.

Mother snapped her fingers for our attention. "Emily, you have fifteen minutes to get down there." She made a grand wave toward the door. "Now shoo."

I picked up Johnny, gave him a squeeze, and kissed the top of his head, taking in his soapy baby scent. "Thank you, Mother."

"You really ought to procure a nanny." She pulled my squirming, protesting baby away.

"We're managing well without one." I spoke through clenched teeth. Inwardly, I agreed with her but felt obliged to support the opinion of Wash, who felt raising our son ourselves was the more modern approach. I kissed the soft pink hands Johnny held out to me.

Donning my hat and gloves, I hurried out the front door. The coachman paced the cobblestones in front of our carriage. A gust of wind stole the little green cap off my head, and he bent to retrieve it. Apparently, Eleanor's hairpins couldn't substitute for a proper hat pin.

The end of June in New York can be clammy and chilly or full of glorious sunshine, a harbinger of warm days to come. That particular day was of the former, unpleasant sort. The air was scented with the coal fires of winter, and I berated myself for not bringing a wrap.

The *clickety-clack* of the wheels seemed to tick off each maddening second during the brief ride to the waterfront. A deep fog had settled in overnight, but change was in the air as the wind picked up, breaking blue holes in the sky. On a ridge above the shoreline, swirling puffs of white gauze parted, revealing children wearing short coats as they played in the street. The muddy brown East River slowly reappeared, full of choppy whitecaps as it made its way toward the Narrows.

We stopped at the waterfront where small waves lapped sand and pebbles. The driver offered his arm as I stepped out, considerable relief on his face to have delivered his charge more or less on time. I made out my father-in-law's unmistakable frame and purposeful stride along the pier that ran beside the ferry slip and took in a deep breath to brace myself.

Years of meetings, speeches, and hard work had raised enough funds to get the project moving. I had expected a small crowd and reporters from the newspapers, but only Wash and a worker setting up a tripod were present on the narrow ribbon of shoreline.

"Ah, there you are, my lovely." Wash beamed at me as I stood above him on the pier. In some ways, he was so very much like his father: calm, calculated, methodical. But Papa lacked his son's warmth, the openness and playfulness that drew me in. When work went well, Wash was happy and engaging. Indeed, now he was engaged up to his shins in river muck, shoveling dirt into small mounds. "This is Mr. Young, Father's surveyor."

"Foreman, as of yesterday," Mr. Young corrected with a tip of his cap. He was of medium height and build, dishwater-brown hair, and cheeks scarred from youthful blemishes. Many men, including GK, hid them with beards, but Mr. Young had no such vanity. He pieced together his tripod, compass, and scope and fiddled with its settings.

"Please pardon my tardiness." I glanced around. There was no one but the seagulls, whose cries seemed to berate my absence for this special event. "Did I miss the ceremony? Johnny had just—"

Wash laughed. "It's a big moment for us, but not enough fanfare to interest the public." His eyes sought Papa, who was at the end of the pier, looking across the river through a spyglass. "Father wasn't interested in even this bit of ceremony." To Young, he said, "Even though he's been obsessed with building this bridge since I was ten."

"I know," Young said. "I've been with him almost that long. You made a wise choice, heading off to war."

"As it turns out, the escape was only temporary."

The fog was lifting, and I could make out a flash of red across the water on the Manhattan shore. Relief at not having disappointed them lifted within me as well.

Wash waved Young away from the tripod and peered through the scope. "Father has made contact." He turned to us and lifted his shovel. In an official tone, he pronounced, "And now, with two witnesses, I proclaim the New York and Brooklyn Bridge Project to be officially underway." He plunged his shovel deep into the muck, and I clapped at his proclamation.

"I better go tell Mr. Roebling." I glanced at the pier, but only a wisp of fog marked where Papa had stood. "Where—?"

"He probably went out on the rocks to get a better view." Wash shrugged, his boot pressing the shoulder of the shovel, scraping into the grit.

I hurried down the weathered gray boards of the pier, picking up my skirts to avoid tripping. I shuddered at the thought of having to leap into the brown water to save Papa. Despite my experience in Europe, I still loathed rivers. I pushed those thoughts away. A person shouldn't allow one tragedy to cause yet another.

As I approached the end of the pier, there was Papa, jumping from one to another unattached piling. My panic ebbed, relief washing over me. I called to him as he clambered among boulders, black and slick with river slime, jutting out of the water past the pilings, but my voice faded into the fog.

Busy with his footwork, he didn't see me. He carried a red signal flag, its staff about ten feet tall. A gust of wind made it snap sharply and caused him to teeter on the slippery rock. He knelt down to gain stability, waves lapping at his knees while he lifted the spyglass that hung from a strap around his neck and peered across the water.

As Papa lifted his signal flag, the ghostly image of a double-decked ferryboat appeared through the fog, blocking the view across the river. Trails of black soot streamed from its twin smokestacks, and commuters crowded the rails fore and aft of the paddle wheel. Papa checked his pocket watch and shook his head. The ferry probably didn't keep a schedule as precise as his own.

As Papa could neither see nor hear me, I turned back toward Wash. A gust of salty wind made me shiver, and I rubbed my arms, longing for the warmth of the nursery. If I returned home now, there was still time to play with Johnny before his nap.

Wash was drawing lines in the shoreline sand with the shovel and speaking to Young. "We drilled core samples in this area and hit bedrock at forty to fifty feet." He looked up at me with a grin. "You tell him?"

"No, he needs all his concentration to perform acrobatics on the pilings, and now he seems upset that the ferry is in his way."

Wash scratched his beard. "Ha! He hates ferries."

The ferry approached Papa's signal flag, the churn of its engines growing louder. But something was amiss. The ferry was travelling far too quickly, as if the land had popped out of the fog before it was expected.

I ran back down the pier. A moment later, Wash and Young's heavy boots pounded the boards behind me. The ferry made its turn toward the pier and once again blocked the view across the river.

"Late again, blasted ferryboat," Papa yelled from his perch atop a black boulder. "You'll soon be replaced by real engineering, you bucket of bolts!" He shook his fist at the boat, and passengers waved back.

I cupped my hands around my mouth and yelled, "Papa, get back here!" An aura of foreboding filled me, sensing a danger that Papa did not.

He waved to me, climbed off the rocks, and stepped across the pilings toward the pier. The boat barreled ahead, dangerously off course, heading for the pilings rather than the slip.

"Slow her down!" Papa yelled. The wind picked up, blowing hard off the water and drenching him in waves that smashed against the pilings.

Passengers cried out, thrust off their feet as the boat overcorrected its course in a rapid turn. The ferry came straight at Papa, blowing its horn. He tossed aside the signal flag and stepped quickly across the pilings. Climbing up iron struts on the corner post of the pier, his right boot became jammed between a strut and the ferryboat slip, leaving his foot hanging over the empty slip. A loud blare of the horn filled the air, longer this time. I froze in place, watching in horror and not knowing how to help without risking my own life.

Wash caught up with me. "Father! Get away from there!" To me, he hollered "Get back!" as he climbed down toward Papa.

I tried to follow him, thinking the two of us could safely move Papa out of danger, but Young grabbed my shoulders.

"Please, ma'am. Stay here." He rushed to help Wash.

"Papa! Move!" I stayed out of the way, frightened and useless as an ant under a falling tree.

The ferry horn blew long and loud, then was nearly drowned out by the gnashing of the engine's gears as they ground into reverse. The paddle wheel frothed the water as it strained to change direction. Passengers crowded the rails, yelling and gesturing frantically. Instead of an ant, I became a girl, struggling against a raging river current.

Papa struggled to pull his boot from the crevice, lost his balance, and nearly fell into the water. He tried to unlace his boot but was unable to untie the knot. The ferry slammed into the free-standing pilings and snapped them with a loud *CRACK*. The boat shifted sideways from the impact and slammed into the end of the pier, its boards shaking beneath me. Wooden planks heaved and crumpled from the force, pulling Papa toward the water and further entangling his foot. I screamed for Papa. I screamed for Elizabeth. *No! The river must not take another!*

The passengers screamed also as they toppled from the impact, as the ferry continued its uncontrolled landing. It smashed against the slip, now only a few yards from Papa, his legs dangling over the water and he still trapped in its path.

Climbing through the jagged, broken boards, Young reached him, grabbed him under the shoulders, and pulled him back from the water. Wash lay next to Papa, trying to pry out his foot. He was also in the path of the ferry. My mind went white. I saw nothing but a head of honey hair against the silver-and-gray one, a broad back in a dark shirt.

In addition to his trapped foot, the spyglass strap around Papa's neck was caught on a broken board. Ignoring Young's warning, I dropped to my hands and knees and crawled across the mangled pier, avoiding the holes and broken planks. Papa turned his head to me, his eyes strangely calm, and hooked a thumb under the strap tight against his neck. I pried the strap loose of the board.

"Get back," Papa gasped, and I scurried back to safety. Wash and Young pried away jagged boards quickly but calmly despite the screams of the passengers and the sound of wood and metal clashing.

"Wash!" I screamed, the ferry now inches away from his head. With a shout of anguish, he grabbed Papa's boot and pulled mightily, the boat narrowly missing Wash as he tumbled backward. He held up his empty hands, helpless, as the ferry crushed into his father.

Three weeks later, Papa lay in our guest bed, his swollen leg elevated on a mound of pillows. Over and over, I relived the moment, wondering if I had gotten there a moment sooner, had not frozen, statue-like, at the critical time, I could have made a difference. Were it Wash or Johnny, would I have hesitated?

Guilt squeezed my chest like a too-tight corset. I had failed Elizabeth. I had failed Papa. I sensed my own gentle father's presence, consoling me as he had so many years ago. I longed to have myself a good cry, to fall apart utterly and have someone else pick up the pieces as my father did then.

But I kept my qualms to myself; there was nothing to do about that. Only the task at hand, trying to save Papa's leg and possibly his life. So I sniffed back tears and literally rolled up my sleeves. Abiding his emphatic instructions, I poured water over his mangled, toeless foot, a task I had kept up night and day since the accident. Exhaustion gradually consumed me as I numbly poured my regrets and sorrow over the angry red stump of his foot.

"It does no good," Wash whispered in my ear as I refilled a pitcher at the kitchen tap. "But I adore you for doing it all the same." He wrapped his arms around my waist, rested his chin on the top of my head.

It would have been unkind to say *at least it keeps the stench of rotting flesh at bay*. Instead, I nodded, resting my arm over his for a moment of comfort.

Wash's sisters took Johnny to their home in Staten Island, and I was ever grateful for their help. Our home was not a fit place for a young child at the time. Workers visited, hats in hand, gathering instructions and assuring themselves that John Roebling was still in charge. While we worried we might lose Papa, they worried that the whole bridge project—and their jobs—were jeopardized. Every day, Dunn, a tall, ruddy laborer, came by to ask if he still had a job.

Mr. Young, tears streaming down his face, barely left Papa's side. He offered some comfort, a welcome relief from the selfishness of the others. "The old man's still got it, I tell you. Tough ol' coot was still barking orders as they hauled him away."

Dunn replied, "God, I hope so." I hoped Papa didn't hear when he added, possibly to disguise his anguish, "I need this job."

Wash, never one to enjoy a fuss, much less a crowd, shooed them down the hall. "All right, fellas. Conference is over. I'll see you at the work site shortly."

Papa's face was frozen in an unnatural grimace, his lips in an uncontrollable contraction away from his teeth. He hadn't uttered a word in two days. *Lockjaw*, the doctor had told us. While Papa was by nature overbearing, he had always been kinder to me than to most, and I would have given anything to hear him bark some orders.

I carefully parted and combed his hair, just as he would have, and held up a mirror for him. When I saw the startle in his eyes at the reflection of his contorted face, I quickly tucked away the mirror. How he must have felt, a man accustomed to being in control of many men and machines, reduced to having someone comb his hair.

Wash wiped the drool from his father's chin. "You don't have to meet the men here. I'll take your messages to them."

Papa was suffering from near total paralysis and groaned with pain, but his mind was clear, and with great difficulty, he could move one arm. Picking up a scrap of paper and clenching a pencil like a bird's foot around a branch, he wrote *You can do it*.

Wash read the note, still clenched in his father's hand, and assured him, "Of course, Papa. I'll keep you up-to-date. Every detail. I'll run back here a hundred times a day if I have to."

Papa added a word to the note.

"'No'? What do you mean?"

Papa underlined *you*, impatiently stabbing the pencil.

Wash paused, his face crinkling. "No, Papa, I can't do it without you."

Papa's eyes grew fierce, and he moaned. With his one good arm, he banged against the bed.

"Calm down. You'll give yourself another spell. Emily—help me!"

Papa moaned loudly through his grimace and grew more agitated, as if a convulsion was imminent. He grabbed my arm.

I stroked his hand and spoke quietly to him. "Papa, stop. We're listening."

He calmed and motioned toward a drawing of the bridge, which I gave him. He stared at it a long while, then planted it on Wash's chest, holding it in place with a stiff finger. Wash clasped his hands around Papa's, his head and shoulders sagging.

"Yes, Father. I'll build your bridge."

Papa rested peacefully for a few hours until he was hit by a seizure so violent, it knocked him to the floor. I helped Wash and Young put him back in bed, pillowing his rigid frame as best we could. At long last, his vast store of energy consumed, he slipped away.

Wash and I sat for hours, holding hands. I recounted memories of my own father, reliving boat trips and picnics and running through meadows, hoping to help Wash remember that his father would live in his heart forever. He shared memories of running around the farm as a small child and of later chasing his siblings around the wire rope factory. He told of working with his father, building aqueducts and bridges, all wonderful adventures now come to an end. When the tears finally came, he rested his head on my shoulder, and I held him, heaving and inconsolable as never before. The only thing I could do was be with him, my own tears a steady stream.

Later that evening, we stood arm in arm as undertakers carried out the sheet-covered body of his father. One of them came back and handed the bridge drawing to Wash, departing with a little salute of farewell.

"My orders from the general." Wash dabbed at his eyes with a handkerchief.

The room seemed as though a storm had whipped through and left us desolate. I couldn't imagine how I could hold my darling together while falling to pieces myself. I pushed the dark grief down into a gaping, swirling tunnel beneath me. I could address that later. For now, I had to be a sturdy rock for Wash to cling to.

"Can you build it without him?" I traced the lines on the drawing.

But I needn't have worried about Wash. While Papa's scent still lingered in the room, my husband held on to his father's presence by donning it like a mantle. "I made a promise I intend to keep." He took my hand, his lips caressed my fingers. "And I have you."

My insides somersaulted with grief and trepidation. He had just turned thirty-two, and I was but twenty-five years old and no replacement for his father. How would I be of any use? I twined my fingers with his. *"Sehr gut."*

THIRTEEN

Contrary to Wash's intimation that he would rely more heavily upon me, I found myself consigned to running our home, feeding him at odd hours, and patiently listening to the travails of a man possessed. He seemed to go through the motions of mourning Papa's death as if he had no place for his grief. Instead, he masked it with overwork and refused to speak of it. Did he have the same feeling of emptiness that I felt? Sometimes, it seemed I existed as an outer shell, my innards torn away like the horseshoe crabs stranded on the beach.

I longed for my life in Europe or even Cincinnati. There, Wash kept regular, even if long, hours. It had seemed I was of some use to him, and I enjoyed the role of travel companion. Of course, part of that longing was for Papa, for the time we were all together, father and son working, building, arguing.

But in New York, we fell into the same expectations I had always resented. For some women, the pleasures of home and hearth, the daily tasks of creating an atmosphere of domestic tranquility, are paramount. Although I adored little Johnny and enjoyed all my time with him, it shamed me to admit that it wasn't quite enough. I rankled at the thought that my sole purpose in life was to amuse a baby and keep a respectable home. How could I fully enjoy his sweet scent if I spent half the day changing and boiling diapers? Wasn't it better to seek fulfillment of my desire to make a difference in the world, however tiny, and then return to my beloved son, content with accomplishment?

But Mother was of a mind, and I agreed: Wash and I could both benefit from more domestic help.

"Do what you wish," Wash told me.

Those words echoed in my ears a few days later when a letter arrived from PT. He had agreed to financial support of the bridge project but insisted he be kept informed of its progress, a welcome task for me.

My heart skipped about at the sight of his elaborate script upon the missive. It was an invitation to a private tour of his latest adventure: the building of a circus in midtown Manhattan. If by "do what you wish" Wash meant to include visiting a man unaccompanied was a question I neglected to ask. After all, his mild contempt for PT was understood, and our son would love the excitement nearly as much as I needed it.

We traveled to Manhattan on the despised ferry, Johnny delighting in the spray on his face and fascinated by the action of the paddle wheel. A happy moment to cherish, even when it entwined tragedy like a green vine growing on a dead, hollowed tree. I turned my face to the wind and relished the salty spray on my own face. It was good to be out of Brooklyn.

I hired a hansom cab to take us to Barnum's Circus, a cluster of huge tents, animal housing, and some small buildings, nestled in the middle of Manhattan.

PT greeted us, opening the scrolled-iron gate himself, arms wide open, a look of elation on his face. I could feel my spirits rising as if a hot air balloon had captured me and was lifting me away from ordinary life. A capuchin monkey rode on his shoulder, sometimes hiding its tiny face in its master's hair, the salt-and-pepper coloring providing excellent camouflage.

Having four daughters of his own, PT fussed over Johnny with an ease I found charming. He bent low and inquired, "Do you want to see the elephants?"

At Johnny's shy nod, he hoisted him onto his shoulders as the monkey scrambled down and ran ahead.

We stopped at a supply bin and scooped peanuts into a big burlap sack.

The monkey screeched. PT tossed a peanut to quiet him. We made our way to a large animal barn, followed by a trail of chickens, ducks, and the occasional kitten.

The smell of hay and animal dung hit me first, ahead of trumpeting calls that announced we had reached the elephants. PT set Johnny down, and my little boy raced down the row of stalls as fast as his little legs could carry him. I smiled, and my sore heart felt some healing as joy leaked into it once again.

As we walked past each stall in turn, Johnny helped fill the troughs with peanuts for the enormous beasts. Johnny's eyes widened, and he covered his ears with chubby hands when they trumpeted their thanks. An elephant nudged me with its trunk. Johnny laughed, and I picked him up so he could pat its forehead.

"You know, they're quite delicious," PT said.

"The elephants?" I gasped.

He chuckled and pointed to the trough, bristling with peanuts.

"You eat the animals' feed?" Nothing surprised me about this man. I had seen my first peanut not long before, delivered for horse feed. They were a recent arrival from the southern states.

PT grabbed a handful and opened his palm to me. "Try one."

I scowled but bit into one, then promptly spit it out. It was horrid—powdery, dry, and tasteless. I grabbed the one Johnny was about to put in his mouth.

PT bellowed. "No, like this." He shelled the peanut and brushed the nutmeat across my clamped lips. "Mmm. Be brave."

Gooseflesh prickled my arms. It was hard to imagine PT doing such a thing if Wash were present, so it seemed we were teetering on the line of improper behavior. That, of course, was where he most enjoyed being, and I felt a tingle of excitement. I pinched the nut from his fingers, parted my lips, and popped it into my mouth, watching and enjoying the amusement on his face. He was right—it was tasty, chewy, and mellow.

We walked between tents, the corridor lined with posters of circus attractions: bearded ladies, dwarfs, and contortionists. I couldn't imagine making a living by being on public display. I'd had enough difficulty making a speech on my mother's lawn. "Do they choose this life, or do their circumstances offer no better choice?"

His eyes narrowed. "I've rescued them all, human and animal alike, from much worse fates."

My grip on Johnny's hand tightened instinctively at his tone. "Of course, I mean no offense to your work."

His face brightened, his mood changing with the quickness of lightning, and I struggled to keep up. "The noblest art is that of making others happy." He parted a sumptuous gold velvet curtain to reveal a circus ring. The high-topped tent was as big as a three-story house. Cabling, ropes, and swings hung from the ceiling like an enormous spiderweb. Acrobats practiced their routines, walking tightropes and swinging from trapezes. A man coaxed small, bouncy dogs through rings of fire. Johnny bounced with glee and clapped his hands.

A bucket of animal feed gave me an idea. "PT, why don't you sell peanuts to your audience? A new treat to enjoy while watching the show." I plucked a circus flyer from a stack, rolled it into a cone, filled it with peanuts, and handed it to PT with a flourish. "That will be five cents, please."

"Hmm. Excellent profit margin. You've quite the mind for business." His smile sent a warm rush up my face.

"Roast them like chestnuts and add some salt," I suggested as I helped myself to another nut.

He led us to a swing large enough for four adults. It consisted of a wooden platform suspended on four iron pistons. The pistons were attached to a twenty-foot-high circular iron frame. He gave the platform a push, and it traveled in an arc, remaining flat as the pistons did their work.

"My performers will take this full circle, but that may be a bit too high for the baby. At least his first time." He lifted Johnny onto the platform.

PT stepped on, then held out his hand to help me on as well. Johnny giggled as he wobbled on the unsteady floor. PT pumped higher and higher. I screamed and we all laughed heartily. With Johnny safely in the middle, I went to the opposite side from PT, and together, we pumped it into a great arc, reaching ten feet into the air. My spirits soared as we sailed high, then were sucked down by gravity, then up, breaking free again, like a bird on the wing.

"High enough?" he yelled over Johnny's squeals.

"Yes!" I laughed, and we stopped pumping. As the swing slowed to a lazy back-and-forth, an acrobat climbed a rope, catlike, all the way to the peak of the tent. He hung from one arm, securing a trapeze.

"Supple," PT said.

"He certainly is," I agreed.

"No, that's his name. Harry Supple. A ship rigger until I rescued him."

Johnny rolled on his belly, resisting PT's efforts to pull him off the swing.

"Sailors make wonderful performers, having no fear as they climb around masts and ropes a hundred feet in the air."

I remembered the dozens of cable spinners performing their own tight-rope act as they built the bridge in Cincinnati. We would need those skills, and there were several shipyards in New York City. A fine labor pool and untethered to the price-gouging of our current labor contractor, Kingsley.

He handed Johnny to me, squirming and kicking in protest.

"PT, you mentioned that you had a wonderful nanny in your employ?" I had written to him about my frustrations.

"Ah, yes. I believe you'll find Miss Mann an excellent candidate." PT produced a peanut from behind Johnny's ear and amused him by making it appear in his opposite hand, already shelled. "My children were quite fond of her. She's seeking a new position, as my youngest is no longer in need."

"Mr. Barnum, sir?" The disembodied voice of his assistant seemed to float in. "Mr. Otis is waiting to see you." I could see no one. Nothing was ever normal in his world.

"We should leave you to your work. Thank you for the tour." It saddened me to leave, and as I took Johnny's hand, he resisted, two feet planted firmly on the ground, just as I wished to do.

"What's this?" PT pulled a toy elephant from Johnny's collar and gave it to the wide-eyed child. He plucked a pink rose from his sleeve for me.

I nodded my appreciation as I sniffed its fragrance while Johnny stroked the tiny carved elephant.

"What do you say, Johnny?"

"Thank you," said my little cherub.

"The addition of Miss Mann to our household would be a godsend. The bridge construction requires all of Mr. Roebling's time—" I paused, cringing at my own criticism of my husband. "Perhaps I shall soon be able to assist him more directly. We are in your debt."

"Nonsense, Peanut. It's my pleasure."

Before I could work my first glove over my fingers, PT lifted my hand and kissed it full on, his lips hot against my skin. A shiver ran down my spine. He raised his eyes to mine, and I yearned to kiss him. I slipped my hand away from his. Slowly, too slowly. *What is wrong with me?* I loved my husband and would never intentionally hurt him. Yet I knew if he had a sense of what I was feeling at that moment, he would be most disturbed.

PT didn't play by the rules, so I had to be the one to set limits, and we were already flouting them. I was torn by opposing forces: my pleasure in his company and also needing his financial backing for the bridge, and society's rules—I shouldn't be visiting him without escort. Although I was fairly sure I could resist temptation to go any further, it seemed wrong to put myself in a delicate situation.

I had only my instincts to guide me, and it seemed my instincts were clouded by emotion. It seemed the answer then was to separate those emotions from any action. I could feel what I must feel; there was no controlling the yearnings of the body. The sin was only to act upon them, at least with someone other than one's husband. I was suddenly eager to get home to Wash.

"Where has the day gone? I must be getting home." I swooped up Johnny and hustled through the curtain, dropping one of my gloves in my haste.

FOURTEEN

Brooklyn, New York
1870

At dusk, our bedroom window offered a spectacular view of the riverfront, the play of the light and lengthening shadows changing throughout the day. The scene had vastly altered over the last days and weeks. A row of ramshackle houses on the ridge above the river had been demolished, affording a direct view when the caisson was floated into place in early spring.

Peering through the spotting scope Wash had set up to monitor the bridge construction from home, the number of workers I could see dwindled as the caisson sunk below the river surface, taking the workers with it. I panned past barges, heavy with stacks of stone, cranes, and generators, and focused on children playing king of the hill on the mountainous debris of their former homes. I would ask Wash how the families were being relocated. Perhaps I could be of some assistance to them.

Closer to home, workers filed up the street, empty dinner pails in hand. Some walked with a normal gait, others stiff and bent. I tried to spot Wash among them. A worker I recognized, O'Brien, was having a particularly difficult time. He had been a frequent messenger to our home, usually accompanied by several of his children. A muscular Irish laborer, it appeared he could carry twice his own weight. Tonight, he stumbled, dropping his dinner bucket and tools. He stooped, hands on his thighs, his breath coming in shuddering heaves.

His adolescent son, Patrick, and another man came running. They stretched O'Brien out on the ground, lifting and bending his legs for him. After a few more moments, he stood up on his own.

"Mama." Johnny, now two, tugged at my skirt, a picture book clasped to his chest. I scooped him up, and we nestled in a chair for story time.

I had just tucked Johnny in bed when Wash returned, his clothes filthy and smelling like a swamp. I asked him what had happened to O'Brien.

"Caisson disease. From working in high air pressure."

"Will he be all right?"

"He should be with some rest." He unbuttoned his shirt as I ran the bath.

I gaped at his holster and pistol. "Is that loaded?"

"Not anymore." He smirked.

I was still getting used to seeing his facial expressions, since he had shaved his mustache and beard because he was "tired of picking out grit."

His casual smirk and the sight of the weapon made my palms sweat. "Why are you carrying your gun, Wash?"

"I'd hoped we'd hit bedrock by now. But we're meeting more boulders than anticipated."

"You're shooting boulders?" I gathered soap and a washrag. An odor, reminding me of a river rat, permeated the air when he dropped his trousers. I tucked the soap bar under my nose for relief, wondering if working in those awful conditions could affect his judgment.

"Something like that." He patted the holster on his hip. "Going through the hatch today, I noticed how long the ladder was getting. Must be forty feet by now. So we have twenty or thirty feet to go." He removed his holster belt and set it on the pile of clothes.

My dirty, stinky husband relaxed into the tub, making silt soup of the water. "Workers are getting irritable down there. Fights break out, and I spend half my time settling them."

I widened my eyes and glanced at the gun.

"Ha. Don't worry. It's not for that. I hid it under my shirt, out of sight. The caisson is a strange place, and some people don't adapt well. It has a good high ceiling, but the shadows and dank smell give a feeling of being in a cave. The limelights cast an unworldly glow."

I tried to imagine working in the strange space. It was far from anywhere I wanted to be, but I was curious all the same. "How do you feel in there?"

"Well enough. One tries not to think about the weight of the water and ground pressing in on all sides, but a body senses it anyway." He scrubbed his face and arms with a rag. The soap slipped from his hands and leapt into the water over his lap. "Fetch that for me, will you?" he said with a playful grin.

I peered into the murky water. "Not on your life."

He splashed me, and I shrieked in protest, dabbing my face with a dry towel. "Tell me more about what it's like down there."

"Well, at the moment..." He looked down at his lap.

I threw the rag at his head, and it fell to his shoulder. "In the caisson. What's it sound like?"

"Ohhh." He recovered the errant soap and scrubbed the back of his neck. "Sounds are strange in compressed air—eerie, jumbled. Like this. Put a finger in your ear."

I did.

"Now jiggle it around a bit. That's what it sounds like. Imagine the clang of iron as men break down stones with pickaxes. Air compressors hiss, gears and pulleys squeal and grind, metal scraping metal." He cupped water in his hands and flung it onto his head.

"Here." I poured clean water from the French pitcher over his head.

He wrapped his finger with the chain to the drain plug and pulled. "I'm always listening for the hum of the generators and air pumps on the roof. Any change, and I'm topside immediately. Oxygen has to be pumped in at an ever-rising pressure to counteract the increasing pressure of water and earth on the outside walls...and to keep us alive."

I wrapped my arms around myself, imagining being trapped inside this open-bottomed box, far below the river. For the first time, my head buzzed not only with worry for his health and comfort but for his very life. "What happens if those compressors fail?"

He must have detected the tremor in my voice. "Don't worry. Four are on all the time. Two more available for backup. If something happened to all four, the walls would hold up long enough to get 'em started up again."

Deciding not to explore walls caving in to spare myself more nightmares, I took a different tack. "What do you walk upon?"

Wash stood up, his body dripping, his scent decidedly more pleasant. I started to rub him dry with a towel. He was so pleased about the events of the day, I grew excited for him, just like our early days together. His eagerness and bodily warmth comforted me. I felt I could melt into his very being, somehow making us both safe.

He grabbed the towel and wrapped it at his waist. "You're distracting me from my story."

"Clearly." I was ready to move on to the bedroom, but he was enjoying telling his story.

"There are walkways of wooden planks over the ground. Piles of rock and silt—like stalagmites. A shiny bit of metal might turn out to be a tea kettle, a pitchfork, or even a piece of jewelry buried in the riverbed. But we don't take too much time to hunt treasure. Mostly, we're clearing a path for the shoe."

"The shoe?"

"That's the layer of metal wrapped around the bottom of the outside walls and three feet up the inside walls." He made a V with his hands. "The walls come to a point—like a row of sharp teeth—to cut into the ground."

I dabbed at little puddles from his splashing. "How do they clear the path?"

"By digging ditches around the inner walls. Just like prison or the army." He chuckled. "They pry out the boulders with picks and shovel the rubble into the chute. The digger on the roof brings it up, and workers on top cart it away."

"And if the boulders are too large to fit in the chute?"

"That's where the gun comes in."

"You have yet to explain that."

"Yesterday, O'Brien and Dunn were taking turns, one holding an iron bar wedge, the other whacking a three-foot boulder with a sledgehammer. But the wedge kept slipping. So Dunn sat on the boulder with the bar between his legs, and O'Brien hammered away—until Dunn shrieked in pain." Wash laughed.

"Oh my, that's not funny."

"No, he was putting him on. Later, my foreman, Young, tells me O'Brien got sick the night before. And numb from the Grecian bends. He was worried about him smashing his foot or something.

"The air pressure was well above normal and rising. I went topside with O'Brien for a rest. I get a little shaky too when I first come out." Wash held up his hand.

I curled my fingers around his. They were warm and strong, as always, but I could feel a strange vibration within them. My eyes met his in concern.

"Don't worry about this tough old bear." He shook my hand off. "I decided we have to find a better way to evacuate the boulders—we're running out of time. In normal atmosphere, we could use powder to blow it up, but there's more oxygen down there and nowhere for the blast to go. It could cost us our eardrums…or worse.

"So I did an experiment." He picked up the holster, took out the revolver, clicked out the chamber, and gave it a spin. "The air could explode. And shooting a hole in the walls or ceiling would cause the air to whistle out. Nevertheless, a test—one careful shot—was in order."

"Young said it was too dangerous. He lit a match, and *whoosh*." He threw his arms into the air.

"Wash, the oxygen!" Why had my extraordinarily careful husband suddenly begun taking risks?

"I told him to evacuate the men. After the other men were out of the caisson, I loaded my revolver, aimed at the ground, and fired. I expected a huge *bang* and blowback, but the report was strangely muted, echoing like a shout down a well. We waited a bit, but nothing happened. I put a finger in my ear to check for blood, but no."

I gingerly picked up his soiled clothes. "Wash, do you think you need to take some time away from the site? You've been working without a break for so long. I'd hate for you to make unwise decisions…"

He threw his head back with laughter, and not in a way I was accustomed to. His recklessness, his strange, almost giddy reaction to my concern gnawed a pit in my stomach.

He looked at me, eyes dancing in amusement. "There needed to be one more test. I aimed for the boulder at an angle so the ricocheted bullet would land harmlessly. I fired, a rock fragment blew off, and the bullet zinged into a support beam. No explosion, no pressure wave, no problems." He grabbed both of my arms, blue eyes full of excitement. "I told Young to get me some dynamite."

The strength in his grip, the surety of his decision, eased some of my concern for his well-being. But my head reeled at the thought of explosives in that treacherous box. Even though Wash slyly dropped his wrapped towel and now smelled delicious, I could no longer be enticed into the bedroom.

***

A few weeks later, Millie brought her son, a bit older than Johnny, for a visit. She agreed to watch the boys so I could bring Wash the biscuits she had made.

Wash was thrilled with the rapid pace of caisson descent, now that he was blowing up all obstacles. I was less thrilled with this new danger to add to my worries. Wash said they had only about ten feet to go, less than a month at the new pace. The progress wasn't evident from the outside. As the foundation sank from the weight of each new layer of stone, the top of the tower remained just above the waterline.

I carried a dinner pail across the makeshift walkway from the shoreline and navigated around huge wooden boom derricks as they lifted stone blocks from a barge and placed them on the tower. The work site was bristling with activity, even as the sky grew purple with dusk. The huge metal jaws of a clamshell digger descended through an air lock into the caisson, coming back up dripping with rocks and sludge, causing me to dodge quickly past.

I headed toward the caisson entrance, a sealed hatch the size of a manhole cover inside a small shack. A sign read *DANGER. CONCENTRATED OXYGEN. No smoking.*

I greeted the burly guard with *EINAR* written across the front of his shirt. He crossed his considerable forearms over the letters. "I'm sorry, ma'am, I can't let you go down there." With his singsong accent and straight blond hair, I guessed him to be of Scandinavian descent. "I'll have that supper sent down next shift change. Probably minus a few things," he added with a chuckle.

Standing ramrod straight and clutching the warm pail to me, I fixed my face in a serious scowl. "I won't stay long. Visitors spending only a few minutes have shown no ill effects."

Einar tilted his head toward the edge of the tower, where men guided carts filled with boulders, muck, and unconscious workers down tracks to the shore. A few pale and sweaty men lay on stretchers, holding their heads. One struggled to a standing position, then collapsed in pain. Other workers retched.

"It's no place for a woman, even if you are the boss's wife." He appraised me head to toe. "Maybe especially."

"Is there a law against it?" I tried to maintain my stern look, but my scowl began to falter upon witnessing the sickened men.

"Probably."

I arched an eyebrow at him. "Is it your place to argue with the boss's wife?"

Einar shrugged. "Your funeral." He turned a wheel on the hatch, and we waited as air hissed out. Then he checked a gauge and left me to open the hatch myself. "Good practice. You'll have to open the one at the bottom of the chamber too."

Clenching my jaw, I struggled with the lock until the hatch flew open with a blast of warm air. What would I see down there, and how could I maintain my composure? I hadn't thought past this point. My eyes measured the small opening, comparing it to my full and stiff dress. It would be a tight fit. Setting down the pail, I attempted to squeeze through the portal, but the volume and stiffness of my skirts trapped me with one leg in and the other out. I was a poor bridge, spanning two worlds but going nowhere myself. How could I understand my husband if I could never take a step into his world? I yanked at the dress, so humiliated I didn't care if it tore to pieces. Seeing no way to go through, I held out a hand to Einar.

Chewing his lips and feigning a cough, Einar took my hand and pulled me free. "As I said, ma'am. You can't go down there. Now let me take that supper off your hands."

Later that night, I sat at my vanity, attacking my unruly curls with a hairbrush.

Wash lifted the French pitcher and poured water into the bowl. "I'm sorry, dear, but it's not a good idea for you to go into the caisson."

"I wanted to see you and bring Millie's biscuits," I told Wash's reflection. I wouldn't have mentioned my ordeal, but Einar had snitched.

He combed his hair, still wet from the tub, dried the new stubble of his beard, then walked slowly and stiffly to the bed.

"You're getting worse." I felt the familiar knot develop in my stomach. "Have you consulted the doctor?"

"Interestingly enough, Dr. Smith offered several treatments."

I had to help him into bed. He groaned as I tried to straighten his legs.

Wash glanced toward his whiskey and medicine bottle on the nightstand. "No one knows the cause exactly, but he is eager to prescribe the treatment, which amounts to little more than a dulling of the senses. A little backward, don't you think?"

"Dr. Smith is a bridge company physician, not specially trained for this." My mouth twisted. "Perhaps no one is." I poured whiskey in a glass, counted out the prescribed three white pills. "Even so, if no one knows the cause, he can observe which treatments work and which don't." I tucked a pillow under his bent knees.

"Ah yes," he said. "The good old trial-and-error method used by the so-called science of medicine. What happened when engineers employed that method? 'Let's see if this bridge will hold the weight of a person.'" He popped a pill and shrugged.

"A carriage." He popped a second pill. Shrugged.

"A train." He popped the third pill and gagged dramatically.

"Oops, not a train." He drained the whiskey.

"You're impossible."

"Forgive my lack of respect for doctors. They can chop off toes to save a man's foot but can't keep the tetanus from killing him anyway."

I climbed into bed, kicking the warming brick out of the way, then looped my arm around him. "Your father wouldn't want you to—"

"I feel fine when I'm down in the caisson, and I can handle the pain of being above ground."

"The pain of being alive without your father, being out of the caisson, or both?" I curled up next to him, soothed by his warm, soapy scent.

"Oh, my love, let's just enjoy each other." He kissed me, gathered my nightgown, and slipped his hand under it. "See? I'm starting to feel better already."

We made love, allowing me to forget all about caissons and their hazards. But after, while he drifted into sleep, knees tenting the bedcovers, images of men on stretchers floated in my mind, keeping me awake through many hourly chimes of the clock.

***

I hated being foiled by a stupid dress. By the next morning, I had devised a new plan. I rose before Wash and searched his armoire, scavenging for work clothes. Finding nothing remotely my size, I donned a shirt and trousers, a simple task compared with the complex assembly of my usual undergarments and dress. How lovely it would be to be dressed in a minute, ready to greet the day.

I was quite involved with adjusting the suspenders in hopes of keeping the pants from trailing the ground when I saw Wash's amused face in the mirror.

"Care to explain?" He gave me a peck on the cheek on his way to his washstand, where he used a badger brush to lather under his chin with shaving soap. I was happy he had decided to grow another but less expansive beard.

"I'm dressing for work. I can't lie about while you martyr yourself with too many responsibilities." My fingertips were the only things exposed in the much-too-long sleeves.

"I see. And what work is that?" He scraped his neck with a straight razor, then toweled off the remaining lather. "Hopefully nothing outside this bedroom. And that"—he pointed the razor toward my outfit—"fails to arouse this audience."

"Good news, you're feeling better. Bad news, you're quite the pig."

"Oink. What is this foolishness, Em?"

"I can't get around the work site in a big dress and delicate boots." I rolled up the offending sleeves. "Besides, you didn't seem to mind my help when we were under bridges in Europe."

"That was different."

I pushed bunches of shirt into the ill-fitting trousers. "How so?"

"It was risky, to be certain. But we were unknown, under cover of darkness. We could claim to be clueless foreigners." He cut a neat part into his hair. "You're my wife. You can't be parading around in men's clothing without comment or worse."

"I am dressing this way out of regard for safety and sanitation. Surely, no one would object. You are the chief engineer. Couldn't you issue a rule about suitable work attire?"

He stopped combing his hair and turned to me. "But, my darling, it *is* a rule. *All men shall report to work in proper work clothes and boots. Hair not to exceed chin length, beards no longer than...*"

"Then what—is—the—problem?" I said, jabbing my curls into a work hat with each word.

"Dear heart, I make the rules, not the law. You can be arrested for impersonating a man."

"Now that's absurd. If women can't wear prescribed work clothing, then they're shut out." I didn't want to argue with him, but the unreasonableness of this vexed me, and I wanted it to vex him too.

"Then I advise you to speak to your congressman post haste."

"You know darn well they won't listen to a woman. Good Lord, we can't even vote!"

"Don't point your daggers at me. I think women should be able to vote, dig wells, fight wars, run for office, do whatever they wish."

"Hah! Maybe I should do the unthinkable—wear men's clothing and get myself arrested." My curls sprang loose as I tossed the hat aside.

"Please don't. Your desire to help is admirable, and you *should* be able to wear trousers if you prefer. But it's not up to me, and I have other battles to fight."

"What do you suggest I do? Look at these." I opened my wardrobe and pulled out several fussy dresses, their hems soiled and shredded from my various misadventures. "It is complete insanity that women can't lawfully wear trousers."

"Do whatever you choose. But promise me you won't get arrested." He buttoned his perfectly tailored shirt.

"Getting arrested may be what it takes. If I can attract the attention of the newspapers—" My mind raced with possibilities.

"Emily, please, no arrests. It would be bad publicity for the bridge. Not to mention both of our reputations. We could lose everything. You must promise me."

"I'm not sure I can promise that."

He set his jaw and eyed me in such a way that I knew better than to continue arguing.

"Fine. But you have to help me find a way around this."

He rubbed his grizzled cheek, then poked around the dresses, fingering the frayed bottoms. Then his eyes lit up. "I've got it! Bloomers! You know, like the lady coal miners wear." He rifled through some old magazines to a picture of a cheerless woman dressed in a makeshift uniform, holding a shovel. Her simple, straight dress ended abruptly and unattractively at midthigh over baggy pantaloons that gathered at her ankles. The effect was rather unbecoming and somewhat comical.

"Dearest, no dressmaker would make this. It would ruin their reputation. And I've always been hopeless at sewing." I bit my lip, however, already envisioning myself photographed by the newspapers wearing a bloomer costume much finer than this.

He kissed my forehead. "And so, years later, I discover *your* limitations."

~❦~

My main limitation seemed to be a distinct lack of knowing my place. Or rather a lack of interest in my preordained place. I dutifully chatted with other young mothers but soon found my attention wandering from the conversations we struggled to sustain as our children played. I knew better than to visit PT without a strict schedule or accompaniment. And it was too long a ride to Cold Spring to visit my mother very frequently.

So I began writing to leaders of the women's movement, asking how I might become involved. But with Wash occupied night and day at the construction site, it became clear he needed to establish an office to coordinate the various suppliers, meet financial and political backers, and manage the finances. Suddenly, I was thrust into a new role.

After a thorough search of Brooklyn, I located space on the ground floor of a three-story brownstone. Many large windows provided ample light and a view of the street activities, while a back room could be used for storage. After securing the lease, we advertised for someone to manage the office. After several disastrous interviews, it occurred to Wash that I was the most qualified for the position.

Alas, what seemed logical to Wash and me did not seem so to the general public. I was expected to be at home and not out doing a man's job. My own mother sent a terse letter saying as much, and the women I had chatted with in the neighborhood all now had somewhere more important to be. Millie had gone to Iowa to spend time with GK, and I craved a visit with PT. That wouldn't lead to good things, so out of loneliness and boredom, I braced myself to withstand criticism and became an office worker.

One late summer day, two-year-old Johnny was with me at the office. He busied himself with a toy train, hardly taking notice of the steady procession of men as they came to conduct their business. A new contract had been signed, and I cleared my desk in preparation for an onslaught of questions and demands.

Late in the afternoon, the men started coming in faster than I could dispatch them. As they crushed into the small office on the muggy day, tempers flared. "Where is the chief engineer?" Followed by "He isn't here, but some lady is!"

This caused some pushing and shoving as men tried to make their way forward to see for themselves. Johnny was in a safe corner, so I ignored the jostling men. I dealt with a supplier who was incensed with the New York Bridge Company, the group of politicians and financiers who controlled the project.

"Tammany Hall greed!" the supplier spat. His anger further fueled the growing discontent. The ruckus was getting out of hand and too close to Johnny, who by now had picked up on the general unpleasantness and started to wail.

"What is this, a baby nursery?" The men began fighting with one another, hurling insults and accusations of profiteering.

"Scandalous! Kingsley is lining his pockets at our expense!" the supplier yelled.

Gathering my skirts, I climbed on top of my desk. "Gentlemen! I am here to keep this project moving ahead in a safe, legal, and timely manner."

"Why are we wasting time with a *lady*?" a man sneered.

"If you have a disagreement with city hall, I suggest you take it up there. Here, I act on the authority of the chief engineer, and my decisions are final. If you find dealing with a woman not to your liking, I suggest you march right out that door without a thought of returning, for I will be here tomorrow and every day thereafter. Have I made myself clear?"

There was much grumbling and jeering as some men reconciled themselves to the prospect of dealing with me while others put on their hats and headed for the door. Laughter erupted from a knot of men who passed around a note like schoolboys. One of them crumpled it up and launched it onto my desk. Rolling my eyes at their juvenile behavior, I picked up and smoothed out the wad. The crude drawing depicted a person in an elaborately bustled dress, the dress so cumbersome as to make the wearer lean over severely, using a cane. The bearded face of the figure was a striking likeness of Wash.

It felt as if someone had punched me in the gut, unfairly poking fun at Wash and finding me ridiculous, an impostor. Perhaps I was.

The bells on the outside door jingled, and a plainly dressed woman with light-brown skin entered. The men murmured and shook their heads but parted to clear the way for her. Johnny tugged on my skirt, and I climbed down to gather him into my arms.

My voice was clipped, as I was still hot with anger. "Yes, miss—how can I help you?"

"Miss Muriel Mann, referred by my former employer." Her eyes fell on Johnny as she handed me an envelope monogrammed with an elaborate letter *B*. "I'm available next week."

"Oh, yes. Mr. Barnum's nanny. Delighted to meet you, Miss Mann." I offered her my hand, but she did not take it, modestly inclining her head instead.

"Don't worry. I've not been known to bite." I cringed at her first impression of me. "This is my son, Johnny."

She bent down, holding her arms out to him. He looked back at me, and upon my nod, he ran to her, sending a twinge of sorrow through my heart.

At home in the library that evening, I slammed the crumpled drawing before Wash at his desk, expecting an irate response. He laughed.

I folded my arms and seethed. "They consider you a frail woman, sending me to do your work. Why is that funny?"

"No, it's not that." He carefully flattened the paper and tucked it into a book. "It's the Grecian bends."

"The what?"

"You know, the description of women in bustles. It's also a nickname for caisson disease. You see the resemblance between the familiar walk of the fashionable and the walk of the afflicted, don't you?" He took a few steps with an exaggerated, bent-over stance. He didn't have to exaggerate much.

"They're finding entertainment in your infirmity. It's disrespectful, and—"

"You're becoming far too serious, my sweet one. I must find where you have placed your sense of humor. And your bustle."

I playfully fought him off until we were half-undressed and he succeeded in making me laugh.

Some days later, I was enjoying a quiet morning in the office, Johnny happily occupied with several crates of hardware, when I was visited by the Metropolitan Police. "Now, I don't want to arrest you, seeing you've got a little one to attend to."

"Arrest me for what, Officer?"

The policeman, dressed in a sharp, dark-blue uniform, pulled a small book out of his pocket. "Impersonating a man." He flipped a page. "Improper supervision of a child." Another page turned. "Conduct unbecoming a woman. Woman working in excess of sixty hours per week." He slipped his book back into his pocket, rocked back on his heels, and took a long look around the room. The bell on the door jangled as a client stepped in but then quickly backed out.

The officer waved to Johnny. "Have you seen this?" He flipped his bobby stick end over end like a drum major's baton. Then he turned back to me, slapping the stick into his palm.

"Do you propose to club my child for these so-called offenses? Or only me?"

He tucked the stick under his arm and chuckled. "I'm following up on a complaint is all. This can all go away. *Pffft*." He flicked his fingers as if they were popping imaginary bubbles.

"How do you propose we make it all go away?"

"Some people find that a small donation to a certain charity makes the complainers stop complaining."

My blood rose, realizing his true goal, and I evaluated my choices, none of them good. I opened a desk drawer and pulled out a ledger.

He leaned over to watch me write the check. "A tenner once a month should do it."

The officer came back each month, and I paid him, the expected amount rising each time. My gut twisted in fear of being arrested for bribery of a public official. I desperately wanted to tell Wash or write to GK about it but was afraid doing so would make them guilty as accomplices. To my great dismay, I had become a criminal. Unwittingly, yes, but I saw no alternative. At least the men entering our office had suddenly become more courteous now that we had paid for police protection. Some of them practically tiptoed in.

I could afford these bribes. But what about those who couldn't? Tammany Hall was entrenched in city and state government. We needed fresh leadership, and half of our population wasn't even able to vote. Was I abandoning my true calling, women's suffrage, by helping to build the bridge?

FIFTEEN

Cold Spring, New York

Mother, her friends, and I sat at Henrietta VanDrie's massive oak table. The hot, sticky summer was finally giving way to fresh breezes, and cool, crisp apples filled baskets in every corner. Piles of newspapers and pamphlets fought for space amid teacups and sewing notions. Miss Mann had arrived just in time to help with Johnny, as my life was about to take yet another turn.

Henrietta refilled our cups. "Ladies, it's time we took a more active role in suffrage." She was something like a third cousin twice removed to a woman who had married into the Vanderbilts of railroad fame. This well-off cousin had taken up the cause, and Henrietta was astute to winds of change. "Providing bail for the brave women jailed for infractions against manhood is only masking the problem."

Mother folded pamphlets titled *Women Are Citizens Too*, *Allow Women the Vote*, and *Freedom for Women*. She adjusted her reading spectacles, read both sides of the page, and then waved it toward Carrie Beebe. "You did a brilliant job, writing this."

Carrie flushed. "It's nothing. Any of you could have done it."

Eleanor drew her needle and thread through a square of white fabric stretched in a wooden ring. "But any of us didn't. I may have a gift for bending metal, but you have a gift with words. And it is words, repeated emphatically, in the right places, to the right people, that will change things."

"Eventually." Mother collected the pamphlets into a neat pile, which I added to my own. "We still have a long road ahead."

My hands were busy and my heart happy, listening to these ladies dream of future victories and swapping stories of their encounters with the Astors, Carnegies, and, of course, the Vanderbilts. Through the years, they had shared births of children and grandchildren and the loss of them. They discussed the politics of the country and the problems next door, sharing a bond that made each of them stronger. With a pang, I realized I had no group of women my own age to cherish as we grew older together.

"I have some news," Henrietta said in a hushed tone. "But you must swear to secrecy."

Eleanor and Carrie crossed their hearts. Mother rolled her eyes, and I sucked in my cheeks, amused at Henrietta's way of keeping secrets.

"You know the train station at Madison and Twenty-Sixth? It's moving out, caboose and caboodle." Even though we were fifty miles away in Cold Spring, we all understood she was speaking of Manhattan. She considered it the center of the universe.

"Nooo," came the chorus of replies, although we glanced at one another with shrugged shoulders.

Henrietta shook her head at the collective ignorance. Her teaspoon pointed skyward. "Uptown. They're moving everything uptown! That's where we need to demonstrate—and buy real estate."

⁂

A few days later, I met the ladies in the streets of Manhattan. The chill in the air was softened by the aroma of chestnuts roasting on street carts, and the wind created funnels of dust as shopkeepers swept the cobblestones.

I slipped one of Eleanor's improved hairpins from the swirl of my bun and handed it to her. These were still our little secret, as she was in the midst of developing an identity as a man.

"Female inventors won't receive serious consideration," she had assured me.

"The softer material at the tips does prevent scratching," I said, "but the metal has gotten a bit brittle with rust."

Excited chatter ensued as we joined twenty or so other suffragists and exchanged pamphlets. We marched in lines down the street, our numbers growing block by block as dozens more joined us, carrying signs, waving pamphlets, or chanting in support of suffrage. I was jostled on both sides as bystanders joined the demonstrators and the neat lines dissolved. Shopkeepers came out and waved with enthusiasm or hooted their protest. The sides were lopsided but equally demonstrative.

A scuffle broke out, and a rock sailed over my head while more thumped as they met their mark. The street grew thick with pushing and shoving people. I gave my handkerchief to a woman with a nasty gash on her forehead.

Police beat back the crowds with bobby sticks, which only caused us to protest with more vigor. Women were escorted to paddy wagons, possibly for their own protection. They didn't seem to be arresting anyone. At least I didn't see any handcuffs. Some of the women threw down their pamphlets and fled.

Alarm bells sounded in my own head as the police closed in on our group. Wash would be furious if I pushed it too far. My dress grew damp with perspiration as I tallied up the charges they could level against me. I couldn't do that to him, especially not now.

The women who didn't flee or get pushed into paddy wagons were shooed off the streets by the police. Many stepped back as soon as the police went by. But my situation was more serious, as I was known to the police, or at least one in particular. I glanced around to see if I recognized his face under one of the blue flat-topped hats. We had an agreement of sorts—illegal, of course, but I was not in a position of strength. This was a critical cause, and I badly wanted to take part. It seemed I was *meant* to be part of it, maybe even to lead it.

I set back my shoulders and straightened my stack of pamphlets. This was an opportunity to capture the interest of the papers. If being arrested shed light on my bribery, was that such a bad thing? I swallowed hard, ready to push forward, when Wash's voice ghosted through my mind.

This is not the right time.

As much as I wanted to support this cause, as much as I believed it was the cause for which I was born to fight, there was simply too much at stake. It couldn't be me, not at this moment. My efforts had to align with my husband's work. Our livelihood, his dream, the city's future, all depended on the bridge, and its political and financial support could all come tumbling down.

Deflated, I handed over my remaining literature. "Mother, I can't—"

"I know. Go."

I embraced each of my friends and headed home, my ears ringing with the shouts and jeers of the crowd, regret and chestnut smoke stifling my lungs.

⁓

When I arrived back in Brooklyn, there was an unfamiliar horse tied up outside our home. Glistening from a careful brushing, the bay mare only flicked her ears as I approached. A small emblem embroidered on the saddle blanket caught my eye: Metropolitan Police.

I halted in the middle of the street, the relief at having escaped the protest in Manhattan melted away, and the familiar twirl in my stomach became accompanied by a weakness of the knees.

There was a quiet café down the street where I might secrete myself. It seemed a logical choice, but then I imagined Wash inside the house being blindsided by whatever news or threats the officer might be offering. I had to go in.

As I made my way up the few steps of our stoop, I considered what my answers would be to Wash's inevitable questions. I hadn't precisely gone against his wishes, hadn't gotten arrested, or captured the attention of the press. Taking a great breath, I steadied myself, for surely, he wouldn't see it quite that way.

As I reached for the knob, the door flew away from me. Filling the space was the police officer I was quite familiar with. Apparently, my bribes were no longer enough.

"Good afternoon, Officer." I managed what I hoped was a carefree smile. "Can I help—"

"Ma'am." The officer avoided my eyes, tipped his hat, and hurried down the stoop.

THE ENGINEER'S WIFE   123

It was tempting to try to gain a clue from him as to what had transpired inside, but I didn't want yet another confrontation. I pushed through the front door.

Smoke curled into the hallway from the library, the scent of cigar smoke soon hitting me. From one smoker? Two? More? No conversation could be heard, and certainly the smoke seemed to be from Wash's favorite tobacco.

Wash was alone, seated in his favorite leather chair. He lightly stubbed out a cigar, saving the rest for another day. I tried to read his countenance. He wasn't the pacing bear I had feared, but Wash's worst anger usually hid behind a veil of calm.

Without looking up, he said, "So, interesting day in the city?"

"One could say that."

"One could say many things." His voice was rising, giving the first hint of his emotional state.

"Why was that policeman here?" I set down my day bag.

"I'd rather hear your explanation first."

Of course he would. But I wasn't going to show my hand sooner than I had to. I wondered what, if anything, my bribed officer knew about the protest in Manhattan. Why conflate that with the more probable explanation of his visit, which was to increase his take? "A police officer just left the house without a word to me. I think I have a right to know why. Where is Johnny? Is he all right?"

"He's fine. But I'll respect your request. Sit down."

I resisted the temptation to pace, sat down, and picked up my knitting.

"It seems you've missed a payment."

"Oh?" The needles clicked. I counted stitches.

"Don't pretend to be ignorant of this."

"I'm not pretending any such thing. Perhaps you can advise me on the extent of your knowledge, and I'll fill in details of how I've managed to keep the project going and both of us out of jail."

"God damn it, Emily, I told you not to cross the line."

"What would you have me do? Would you care to battle the whole corrupt system?"

"You could have come to me."

"I thought it best to keep you out of it. They wouldn't hesitate to shut the operation down, throw you in jail for some made-up offense. But me? I didn't think they would risk the image of police brutality against a delicate, innocent woman. And it would have taken brutality to get me into custody."

He surprised me by laughing.

"So what of it, then?" I put down my knitting. "Do we continue the... um...payments?"

"No, Emily. I have friends in city hall. Your police protector will be replaced."

"That easily? Incredible. All this time..."

"Not so easily. There will be a cost."

My heart, having soared for the briefest moment, started to sail back to the murky depths. "I'm afraid to hear it."

"I'm not upset at you going to the protest, even if it was without my knowledge or consent."

Oh God. He knew about that as well. I counted the stitches on my knitting needle. Counted again, the numbers not taking hold in my brain. I was startled when I looked up and saw Wash looming over me. I rubbed my face, tears starting to well up. Now, more than fearing his anger at me, I feared his disappointment. "You told me not to get arrested. And I didn't. I left so that I wouldn't."

He held out a hand to me. "Come here, my love."

Could it be that he wasn't angry, or worse, disappointed? I stood and fell into his arms, tears now running down my cheeks. "I'm so sorry, Wash. I'm trying to do what is right, but I don't even know what that is."

"Listen. It will work itself out. No permanent damage was done. But there is one thing that will have to change, at least for now."

"I'm quite willing to step away from the project. We can surely hire a man for the office work now, it's running so smoothly."

"No." Wash lifted my chin as he had years ago at the ballroom dance. But this time, I didn't see stars dancing in crystal-blue eyes, didn't tingle everywhere he touched. Instead, I felt the strength in his arms, saw the earnest care in his face.

"What then?"

"The agreement is that the harassment and payments will stop. In return, you must refrain from participating in protests against the government."

"I don't see—do I have any say in this?"

"I suppose you do."

So I had to make a choice. Did I follow my heart and protest against this ridiculous agreement that made a mockery of my rights as an American? Or did I follow my brain, which told me to consider the greater good of quietly working behind the scenes in the bridge project in an effort that might far outweigh what I could otherwise accomplish? Which path would lead to the ultimate goal—women's right to vote?

Frustrated with my shortcomings as a suffragist, I threw myself into the bloomer costume project. One afternoon, Johnny played amid the pile of discarded lace and fabric in the parlor as I took scissors to an old cotton skirt. I had just slipped on pantaloons and the raggedy skirt when there was a thump at the front door as it opened.

"Emily?" Wash called in a weak voice. He waved his hat at the coat hook but missed, and it fell to the floor.

I rushed to him as he shuffled into the parlor, grabbing furniture for support. He swayed, and I wrapped his arm over my shoulders and guided him to the settee. Taking a breath to steel my nerves, I lifted his legs so he could recline. He'd be better once he rested, I reassured myself.

Johnny scrambled onto his lap, causing him to gasp in pain. I picked up our son, who kicked in protest, and enticed him with his toy elephant.

"Thank you." Wash held out his hand for mine.

"That was an awfully long day." With my fingertips, I assessed the amount of quiver in his hand. Was it worse than yesterday? Afraid he'd note my dampening palm, I pulled it away.

"Sartorial triumph." His mouth twisted into a smile.

"Pardon?"

He gestured toward the odd handiwork I wore.

I smoothed the rumpled skirt, smiled to conceal my concern. "*Mon Dieu*, this is the latest in Brooklyn fashion."

He patted the settee, and I sat next to him.

"Fascinating." He raised his arms, twisted and turned. "The numbness and weakness is gone, just like that. Now there's a sensation of pins and needles, like when you lie on your arm too long."

I only hoped it was that simple.

"Hold on to your petticoat. Or whatever that is you're wearing." He took some shallow breaths. "I have some news." He clapped his hand on mine with a weak squeeze. "The caisson has stopped dropping. We've hit bedrock."

"Thank God!" I threw my arms around Wash as Johnny grabbed our legs. I scooped him up as well, my eyes brimming with tears. Everything was going to be fine. Wash wouldn't have to be down in the caisson any longer. "Honestly, I don't think you can spend another day down there."

Johnny dabbed his finger on my wet cheek. "Mama crying?"

"Happy tears, darling."

Wash patted Johnny's curls. "Now we can start the Manhattan caisson while we build the rest of the Brooklyn tower."

It felt as if the floor had dropped from underneath me. Of course, they had the Manhattan side yet to do.

"The tower will grow quickly and will be more exciting above water. And the crowds will come to watch. It will be a show bigger than Barnum's old museum." He coughed, his voice as rough as sandpaper.

Wash traced his finger down my crooked button placket. "You'll need a more fashionable dress. We'll be on the front page of the *Brooklyn Eagle*."

"With this caisson finally at rest, will Johnny and I see more of you?"

"Haven't you had enough of me already?" He gave me a lopsided grin.

"I'm serious. Let's take Johnny to the menagerie in Central Park." Afraid Johnny's bouncing would would Wash discomfort, I set the boy down.

"I haven't really the time, Em. You and Miss Mann should take him."

"Again?" My face fell. "Wash, this can't be all there is to family life. There's a world out there to share with our son. He needs—"

"Whatever you say, dear." Wash eyed a stack of documents a messenger had brought over earlier, covering the tea table.

"Here." I slapped the stack of papers on his lap.

He picked them up and thumbed through them while I stood before him, hands on hips, waiting for him to acknowledge the existence of his wife and son. My first gray hair sprouted in the time it took him to notice.

"Oh yes, thank you." He tapped the papers, then waved absently. "Of course, take him to the menagerie. He'll enjoy that."

My insides crumbled. He devoted every moment to his father's dream, but what about mine? I wanted to share how this made me feel, but clearly, I had been dismissed. If there was one thing I had learned about marriage, it was to wait until a receptive moment to express feelings such as this if I wanted any action on his part.

I went to bed alone after Wash fell asleep with his paper wives.

SIXTEEN

Wash's joy upon hitting bedrock was premature. For the next few weeks, he still had to descend into the caisson as brick pilings were constructed to support the roof under the tremendous weight of the stones above. Not until that was done could concrete be poured down the chute and the caisson sealed.

Meanwhile, I was beginning to enjoy my bloomer project. Wash had presented me with a sewing machine, and operating the treadle with my feet gave me a sense of accomplishment, even if what I was producing was not in the least wearable. A few unladylike words slipped through the straight pins in my mouth as I tried to free the machine from a beehive of thread and fabric.

The first time I heard the alarm bells on the street outside, they barely broke my awareness. The leather belt on the machine had broken and was flapping like a serpent until the gears ground to a halt. My creation nearly finished, I donned the skirt. My feet negotiated through the leggings, the twisted seams making an awkward fit.

Twirling for Johnny's entertainment had turned into a game of ring-around-the-rosy until we were interrupted by outside commotion. Clanging bells and the galloping of horses drew me to the window. Horses pulled a fire wagon through swirling snow, heading toward the river. A crowd hastened behind the wagon, sending a shiver of dread down my spine.

"Miss Mann!" I yelled.

She hurried over and picked up Johnny as I grabbed my cloak and flew out the door.

A neighbor advised me there was a problem at the bridge site and offered a ride in his carriage. I was in no mood for small talk, and we rode in silence. Noting his occasional glances at the leggings peeking out from under my cloak, I tugged it closed.

When I arrived, firemen were running hoses from the river to pumps as soot-covered and coughing workers stumbled from the work site. I approached O'Brien, who occupied Einar's usual station at the caisson entrance, and asked him what had happened.

"A wee fire, that's all, ma'am. A few minor injuries." He brushed ash and snowflakes from his coat.

"And everyone is accounted for?"

"Colonel Roebling is fine."

Farrington joined us. Coatless, in clean and crisply pressed clothes, it was apparent he hadn't been inside the caisson.

"Good evening, Mr. Farrington. I'm told everything is well under control." The augers of varying lengths and other tools slung over his wiry shoulders suggested otherwise.

He tipped his hat. "A pleasure, Mrs. Roebling. Just need to drill a few holes." He smiled his toothy grin. "You got some fruit for me?"

The hatch opened, and Young stepped out.

"Are you all right, Mr. Young?" I asked. "How are conditions down there?"

Before he could answer, his eyes bulged and he bent over, gasping for air. Farrington and O'Brien helped him to the ground. Blood trickled from his ears, and I cradled his head, staring at his pale, pitted cheeks. O'Brien dashed off for a stretcher.

After Young was attended to and Farrington had descended, I peppered O'Brien with so many questions, he finally sent a messenger down to investigate. I had neither hat nor gloves, and I huddled into my cloak, pacing for what seemed like hours. The long wait gave me too much time to imagine fire resurging, the men with no means of escape.

It wasn't the messenger who appeared at the hatch opening but Farrington, bringing a waft of smoke. Brushing cinders from his shirt, he frowned at the black streaks they left. He cracked a half smile for me. "Mr. Roebling sends regrets for his tardiness."

"He's not coming up?"

"He says you should go home. He'll be along shortly."

A chill raced down my spine, but as my ears and fingers were already numb with cold, I trudged home through the snow to wait.

Hours later, a horse and carriage approached, and voices drifted in from the street. A blast of frigid air hit me as I opened the door. The light of the streetlamp fell on three men carrying Wash down the front walk on a stretcher. He was very pale but lifted his hand. The men—O'Brien, Luciano, and Dunn—struggled through several inches of fresh snow up the steps to the foyer. I had them take him to the parlor.

"I'm fine, dear. No pain this time," Wash rasped.

"Was it the smoke?"

"No. A bit of a problem with paralysis."

Dunn pulled off a woolen blanket covering Wash's legs. His legs, mottled white and gray with blotches of pink, were exposed by rolled-up trousers. The men massaged them with sea salts and whiskey.

"I tried to get him to leave earlier, ma'am," said O'Brien.

"That will be all, fellas." Wash dismissed them with a weak wave.

The workers stopped rubbing and met my eyes with question.

Dunn spoke. "He's got the Grecian bends real bad, ma'am. The doc told us to keep rubbing till he moves his legs."

"I know the procedure," Wash said. "You're dismissed."

I nodded in agreement and escorted the men to the door, giving each a bit of money, although they tried to refuse it, before sending them on their way. Despite their concern and good intentions, Wash couldn't tolerate anyone but me around him when he was feeling poorly.

O'Brien stopped and turned back before I closed the door. "Ma'am, I shouldn'a mean to add to your troubles, but..."

"What is it, Mr. O'Brien?"

He spoke softly. "There's been workers in the caisson who...uh... weren't nigh as bad off as the colonel."

"Go on."

"I mean, they didn't lose use of their legs or nothing. They had some problems taking a breath."

I glanced back at Wash, then nudged the door a bit more closed. "Well, please tell them I'm glad they're getting along. It's difficult work, I understand."

"No, ma'am, that's just it." He flattened his hand against the outside of the door. "They blame it on all sorts of things, spinal meningitis, bad kidneys, accidents. But these were all healthy men, working in the caisson. There's"—he rolled his eyes up—"five men now dead."

"Thank you, Mr. O'Brien. Good night." After closing the door, I leaned heavily upon it. The news hit me like a ton of boulders. Something should be done, *needed* to be done for these men. And Wash—he was apparently sicker than the others. What if he were to succumb?

I pushed these thoughts from my mind. Wash was doing everything possible to prevent further injuries and now, it seemed, deaths from the mysterious caisson disease.

I knelt next to him on the divan and vigorously massaged his legs.

"Ah, it doesn't do a bit of good," he grumbled. "Quit wasting whiskey on my legs and put some in a glass."

I did as he asked, pouring myself a finger of whiskey as well, then sat beside him, fatigue setting in and replacing some of the worry. "What caused the fire?"

"O'Brien has problems working in the caisson, as you know. So I swapped him with Einar, who had never been down there before. We hang dinner pails on pegs on ceiling beams to keep them out of the way, and Einar used a candle, trying to find his. He must have fallen asleep during the hazard briefing.

"Anyway, I was watching Young wolf down a third chicken leg, wondering how he could eat so much, when his face took on a strange yellow light. Behind me, a flame was licking up a seam to the ceiling."

"Dear God." I took Wash's empty glass.

"The workers formed a bucket brigade and manned the hoses. I turned the spigots full on, but the smoke and flames quickly engulfed the ceiling and a support beam." His eyes flicked, seeming to calculate how much to share. "Einar was filling a bucket when a ceiling beam cracked over his head, shooting out flames as if doused in kerosene. The beam collapsed and pinned him to the ground. Dunn and I wrapped rags around our hands and beat back the flames, then we lifted the beam off of him."

"Is Einar all right?"

"A few burns on his face and hands and his hair is pretty singed, but he'll be fine." Wash rubbed his temples. "Then there was a loud *bang* and air roared up the burn hole. The caisson walls bulged, creaking and moaning."

Bile rose in my throat. I recapped the salts with shaky hands and poured myself more whiskey.

"I sent a messenger up top to turn on all six compressors. We were losing pressure fast, and the ceiling started trembling. I ordered everyone out except four men on hoses. Bricks on the new support columns had shifted out of place, and I worried the whole thing would collapse. I climbed a ladder to inspect the hole and sprayed water into the roof infrastructure. Then we patched up the hole and things stabilized."

"Now we can add fireman to your duties."

"Good gracious, no."

"So is the caisson safe?" My own question seemed silly to me, my lips striving to be logical. There was nothing safe about that blasted caisson.

He paused, stretched his fingers, then balled them into fists. "We'll do inspections. Farrington already drilled some holes."

"I don't understand. You said you had to patch a hole to keep things stabilized."

"The roof is not a solid, flat structure. It's courses of timber, built at right angles, with space in between." He coughed and paused to catch his breath. "I'm worried that unseen above the ceiling, flames could be licking up the courses until they hit the metal barrier of the roof. Then they would spread laterally." He pressed his hands together as if in prayer, raising them up, then pulling them apart.

"I had Farrington drill small sight holes to monitor any flame-ups. We have all the compressors going to compensate until we can patch it all up. But enough of that." He eyed the bedraggled bloomer costume I still wore. "What in tarnation have you got on?"

"You like it?" Relief at a new topic washed over me. "It's my new bloomer costume. Made it myself. Still haven't found a willing seamstress."

"It has a few design flaws." He fingered the raw edge of the hem. "Why don't I make one for you? It probably won't be any worse." His laughter dissolved into a cough.

I frowned. "Please don't make light of my work. This is an important cause."

"I'm not joking. I'll make your bloomer costume. Learned how to sew in the army. Mostly saddles and patches, but it's all the same."

"Don't be absurd. When would you have the time?"

He picked up a journal and pencil from the tea table and sketched with a tremulous hand. "How is garment design any different from engineering? Analyze the problem, create a design to solve it. Choose your materials, build to specifications." He mumbled as he drew.

"You work eighteen hours a day. This isn't your problem to solve for me."

Waving away my concerns, Wash sketched, his hand regaining some steadiness. He outlined with broad, sure strokes. Pausing in thought, his eyes fell on Carrie's *Violets* manuscript, abandoned on my reading chair.

"Must incorporate something of beauty for my pretty lady." Flowers bloomed in his design. "I'll have the time. The site doctor has confined me to home."

He said it so casually, I almost missed it. Matching his composed tone, I asked, "What exactly did Dr. Smith say?" I surreptitiously gave his waxy leg a little poke. Could he feel anything? I pressed hard—too hard—until he moved his leg.

"I've got caisson disease, no surprise. He's forbidden me to go down in the caisson for a while. I need to rest my brain and joints in normal conditions to prevent permanent damage—or some such nonsense."

"Permanent damage? How can you be so calm? You're ruining your health!"

"Easy, dear girl. This will pass. It always does. But I must stay home for now. Well, for quite some time." His eyes avoided mine.

"How long, Wash?" I rubbed my pulsing temples.

"Isn't this what you wanted?" He bounced his eyebrows. "Four weeks—or forever. He doesn't really know."

"But there's another caisson to build. How will the project proceed without you? Will the board appoint another chief engineer?"

"No one else is qualified. I can work from here. In any event, sewing would be good therapy for my hands and legs. I'm sure the good doctor would approve."

I softened. He needed to hear of my love and support more than my concern. And I certainly didn't want him to think he wasn't welcome at home. "It will be nice to have you home for a change." I held his face in my hands and kissed his forehead.

He brought two fingers to his lips. "You missed."

I kissed him again, closing my eyes against tears, my mind spinning with the turn of events.

"Hey now, none of that." Wash wiped a tear that had managed to escape. He held up his sketch of the bloomer costume, far better than anything I could create. "This will prove quite useful. You'll see. I'll need you to take messages to the men for me."

So I became a messenger. I soon dispensed with the time-consuming carriage and rode horseback to and from the work site several times a day, bearing a journal with drawings, instructions, and not a few irate responses. I was grateful for what Wash had taught me, for understanding the basics made me a better interpreter. As the information grew more complicated and I proved a dependable translator, the men grew more comfortable with me and their language less guarded in my presence.

There were difficulties, with much at stake. One evening, I presented a list of complaints from the company building the Manhattan caisson off-site, but Wash dismissed my concerns, tossing aside my traveling journal. "The design is sound."

"But it doesn't take into account so many things." I stabbed my finger on the detail from his diagram of the redesigned supply chute. This one was to be round rather than square. "For example, *this* no longer matches up with *this*." I drew a crude diagram of the chute raising from the caisson and not quite matching the opening at the top.

"I see." Wash designed modifications for the wayward chute and numerous other details, considering improvements in materials and technology since his father's day. He had to stay many steps ahead of the construction so that preparations could be made for the proper mix of tradesmen, tools, and supplies.

These tasks were difficult on such a massive project even with continuous on-site supervision. They were immensely more difficult to conduct through a messenger. My mind reeled with new information, my dreams filled with numbers and diagrams and men pointing fingers and shouting at me.

Each day that passed with men working in the Brooklyn caisson ticked like a clockwork bomb. I badgered Young about speeding up the shifts, getting the men out as soon as possible. I made a firm rule of no more candles in the caisson, and we added more limelights.

No one wanted the caisson work done more than Young, as he suffered nausea and headaches every evening when he left the site. He and C. C. Martin, who filled Wash's role on-site, came to our home at shift's end. We sat in the parlor, and they shared the day's events with me while Wash remained upstairs.

One particular evening, I offered them a drink, and Martin gripped the glass with a steady hand.

"Mr. Martin, the work in the caisson doesn't seem to affect you," I said.

"Aw, he stays topside all day." Young held up a hand, refusing a drink, then tucked his hands into his armpits.

I wasn't fooled; they were trembling.

"We must take care, Mrs. Roebling, to enter the caisson only when absolutely necessary and then only for the amount of time called for. Mr. Young takes unnecessary risks and faces the consequences." Martin put down his glass and stood to leave, smoothing his trousers, somehow unblemished during the long work day.

"That's a load of donkey dung and you know it." Young lowered his eyes. "Beg your pardon, ma'am. He gets me riled up."

"Quite all right. So, Mr. Martin, is it your opinion that Mr. Roebling takes unnecessary risks?"

Martin's hat, halfway to his head, changed direction as he pressed it to his chest instead. "Why no, I would never say that."

"Good night, gentlemen." I escorted them to the door. The suffering and risk to all the workers weighed heavily on my mind. I vowed to visit them and speak to Wash and the doctor about any support we could provide. But still, O'Brien's words echoed in my ears. *Five dead. Five dead. Five dead.*

SEVENTEEN

1871

Setting stone on the tower halted for the winter, although work repairing the burnt infrastructure below continued. C. C. Martin had, for the most part, taken charge of daily operations, and I worked closely with him to ensure Wash's instructions were followed to the letter. Although a capable engineer, Martin lacked Wash's urgent drive and passion for the project.

In mid-January, Martin and I climbed among the granite blocks and equipment, trying to get a vantage point of the tower, now protruding nearly twenty feet above the water. Cranes lifted great blocks of stone from a barge to the tower in preparation for laying when the weather warmed.

"How much weight can the caisson bear?" Martin had to yell, though he was nearly beside me, the wind carrying away his words.

"Mr. Roebling said it'll hold."

Pride crept into my voice, and Martin tilted his head with what passed as a smile. Wash and I had spent hours calculating the strength and stresses on the foundation, factoring in the support piers, the walls, and the amount of roof structure known to be sound. I had made countless treks back and forth, confirming or refuting the stability of every last support beam. Two horses were kept saddled up for me so that one could rest between rides. These trips sometimes numbered as many as a dozen a day and often went long into the evening.

Satisfied, Martin opened his mouth with another question when we heard the booming voice of Benjamin Stone. I stiffened when the worker with him turned and pointed us out. He marched toward us, his purposeful stride and glaring face like an oncoming storm.

Taking the journal from my hands, Martin said, "Think I'd better talk to him myself."

Stone tipped his hat and handed an official document up to me on my granite perch. "Mrs. Roebling, Mr. Martin. I'll get right to the point. The committee is exceedingly displeased with this arrangement."

I briefly flipped through the document, another bridge committee screed concerning a lack of confidence in Wash's ability to manage the project. "I assure you, Mr. Roebling is still fully in charge."

Martin scrambled down from the stone block and held out a bony hand to assist me.

Stone snorted. Peering about for what seemed an eternity, he turned his gaze back to us. "Ahem. I haven't *seen* him in charge. This is an order from the bridge committee. If Mr. Roebling is not recovered and able to fully assume his duties in two weeks, construction will be ceased until we can find a suitable replacement."

When I returned home, Johnny and Miss Mann had long since gone to bed, but a comforting scent of pot roast greeted me as I slipped in the front door. Wash hunched over the sewing machine, surrounded by piles of golden-yellow fabric.

Hugging him from behind, his warmth soothed my frosty cheeks and hands. "I should be doing that."

"Not if you wish to appear in public in it." He held up a nicely tailored short skirt with embroidered flowers. "This shorter length is more practical. I added peonies and violets. What do you think?"

I traced the elegant needlework. "How do you know so much about flowers?"

"I studied botany at Rensselaer, quite enjoyed it." He tucked away needles and blue, purple, and green embroidery thread. "Try it on."

As I changed into the midthigh skirt, he made notations in his thick notebook. It seemed I couldn't muster the skill to cook or sew a garment, while Wash effortlessly shifted from one area of expertise to another.

"Now, for tomorrow, I've described in great detail—" He took in the sight of me in the short skirt and grinned. "Lovely. Especially without the pantaloons."

I waved him off, but inside, I beamed. "Now that would be a scandal. It's a lovely bloomer costume, dearest, but..."

"Peonies too much?"

"No, my sweet Washbear, they're quite nice." I collapsed onto the divan. "The calls for your return to the site haven't stopped. Benjamin Stone came by on behalf of the committee to issue an ultimatum."

"It's bluster. Stop worrying. Martin knows what he's doing, and I'm on top of every step."

I waved Stone's packet of papers. Wash put down the journal and came over to read them.

"I'm tired. I want to wear proper dresses and attend teas and have a bit of merriment again. I have no time with Johnny, and GK and Millie want us to visit them out west." I pulled a needlepoint pillow over my face. "This is not the life I imagined."

"I don't recall this fondness for proper dresses and tea." He handed the papers back, then lifted my legs so he could sit under them as I sprawled across the divan. "Merriment and adventure, yes. And this is all part of the adventure."

"It's your adventure. When will we have time for family and to work on causes that are important to *me*?"

Wash smiled mischievously, ran his hand up my leg under the short skirt. "Patience, dear one. A little trouble in getting something adds to the zest of it." He moved onto his side, squeezing into the small space next to me. His lips feathered my ear as he whispered, "Sorry. Did you say something about a proper dress?"

❧

The next day, I wore my new bloomer costume to the work site. Beautiful and more comfortable than a long dress and petticoats, my heart sang that

Wash had made it for me. The stares and laughter of the workers rolled off me like gnats in a windstorm.

Making my way around the huge stacks of stone and heavy equipment seeking Martin, I came upon Farrington embroiled in an argument with Luciano, the mason on loan from PT. "Listen, you big *guappo*." Farrington was nose to nose with the mason.

"You want a ten-ton brick in an eight-ton hole, you stupid mick," Luciano retorted.

"That's your goddamn job."

Sensing an imminent physical altercation, I went to sort it out, pausing as a huge boom derrick lifted, then swung a block of granite past me and into position. The two workers cranking the derrick gears slowed at the sight of me. One gear driver put his fingers to his mouth and whistled to call attention to me. I chuckled when the other one gave him a swift elbow to the ribs.

Finally, my path was clear, and I reached the contentious duo. "Is there a problem, Mr. Farrington?"

"No, ma'am. Perhaps you can remind Luciano here—"

"Now I listen to a lady telling me what to do? Go change your baby's *pannolino*." Luciano spat on the ground, unbuckled his leather belt, letting the assortment of tools fall with a clang, then stormed off.

I shrugged, remembering the rather testy way Luciano and I had met. "He's still vexed about the ladder."

"How's that?" But Farrington was off to supervise the stone movers before I could explain. The derrick workers were still watching me, distracted. They let the next stone swing too far, right into the walkway. Farrington raised his hands and yelled, "Stop!"

With much grinding and clanking, they reversed the gears, but it was too late. The huge stone's momentum caused it to swing straight into Luciano's path. It slammed into his body and sent him flying past me and across the site. His head cracked against a stone wall. All the workers, Farrington, and I ran to him. His mouth gaped open as if in surprise, his eyes staring at a place we couldn't see. I turned away, but the image of his broken body remained. I went behind a stack of stones and retched.

I crouched there as the body was tended to, wiping my nose and eyes with a trembling hand.

"Sign here," a brusque voice demanded, and papers were shoved at me.

"Not now." I buried my face in my hands, wishing to be somewhere, anywhere but here. A few workers were already telling stories of the irascible Luciano. I wanted to make them hush. In fact, I wanted to slap their faces. But this was their way of dealing with the shock and loss. A tap on my shoulder—above me was the kindly face of Farrington. He offered his hand for me to stand.

"Come." Farrington laid a gentle hand on my back and led me to Luciano's body, covered with a blanket, on a stretcher.

Farrington recounted the incident and asked if I had anything to add. I shook my head, dabbing my eyes with a handkerchief.

"Don't take it so hard, Mrs. Roebling. It was an accident, none of your doing."

I only wished I could believe him. I signed the papers and handed them to Martin. Workers, hats in hand, formed a circle in respect.

Martin pocketed the papers and confirmed my suspicions. "Your presence here, ma'am, is a hazard."

It was several days before I could discuss the accident with Wash. He'd gone to Trenton to discuss the wire rope business with his brothers. Keeping John A. Roebling's Sons Company running smoothly was an ongoing challenge for Wash and his brothers, Ferdinand and Charles—more so for Wash, as he had inherited the bridge project as well.

My relief at his return soon turned to concern and a bit of annoyance. He took short, shuffling steps through the front door and headed straight to his favorite spot in the library.

"Why are these here?" He flung a stack of papers to the floor before flopping into his leather armchair. Its tufted back was canted at a comfortable angle, and its padded arms offered cushioning for his palsies. He rubbed his hands over the walnut roundels that fronted each arm. More than a chair, it was a command post where he dictated orders for others to carry out.

"And I'm glad to see you too." I picked up after him.

"Sorry, dear. A bit out of sorts." He pulled up his trouser leg, exposing a red knee swollen to twice its normal size. "Doc said it's a recurrence of caisson disease."

I stifled a gasp. "But you haven't been in the caisson for months."

Johnny tumbled into the room. "Pa!"

Our toddler presented his favorite storybook, but Wash glanced at me for interference. I grabbed Johnny before he could climb onto Wash's lap.

"What can we do?" I tried to keep my voice steady while I poured him a glass of whiskey. The damage was so deep, his symptoms recurred without even stepping foot in the caisson. Guilt stabbed at me, as part of me didn't care how tired and grumpy he was or what difficulties were brewing at the factory. I wanted out of the impossible situation.

"Just rest."

As he recovered over the next few days, I thought about what needed to be said. It was late in the evening, and we were preparing for bed when I broached the subject. "This is no longer working. We have to make some changes."

"What exactly is it you want?" He unlaced the brace that kept his back pain under control.

I was prepared for this and would not yield when faced with his physical infirmity. Waving a newspaper with the headline "Death on the Bridge," which recounted the accident that killed Luciano, I answered, "Your support. I can't do this alone."

"Do you think I'm happy about this? Do you think it's easy for me to work at a distance and keep the rest of the family afloat while you build my bridge?"

"*Your* bridge? Do you realize how long it's been since you set foot on the site? Why don't you let Martin take over?"

"Look at me! I haven't a joint I can untwist. I'm living in the shell of a goddamn crab!"

We both turned at a knock on our bedroom door, falling silent as we realized our voices would have carried beyond our bedroom. "Come in."

Miss Mann poked her head in. "I'm sorry to disturb you. Johnny has had his bath and is ready for bed."

"Give us a moment, then bring him, please." After she departed, I softened my tone. "Please come to the site. I'll help you. Not the caisson, mind you, but up top. It would put so many minds at ease."

He sat on the bed, his back curled into a C, hands resting on still-swollen knees. "Do you really think it would ease minds to see this?" He scanned the newspaper article. "How did this happen?"

"So many things. I can't—I'm not trained for this, Wash. Decisions need to be made, right on the spot. Sometimes, I try to imagine what *you* would decide. If I'm wrong, someone gets killed. Dozens could get killed by one tiny misstep."

Miss Mann returned with Johnny, and I breathed in his freshly bathed scent. "Thank you, Miss Mann. I'll see him to bed." I took his hand and led him to the platform rocker. "I'm a hazard."

"What do you mean?" Wash got up and took the few halting steps over to us and kissed Johnny on the head.

"A B C." Johnny selected a book and climbed on my lap.

The rocker groaned, and its springs twanged under our weight. I ran my fingers through the silk of his curls, which were growing darker each day. I tried to memorize the heft of him, his scent, the softness of his cheeks. I had so little time with my baby, now three years old.

"I'm quite the odd sight at a construction site, and distractions are dangerous." I nodded toward the newspaper.

"Em, the men can't help but admire you. Give them time. They'll learn better. But no matter what you do, accidents will happen. Yes, even fatal ones. There's no guarantee of safety in anything in life." He brushed a wisp of hair from my face. "You both could have been killed falling down a staircase."

"That's not the same at all."

"It is. We take all precautions, but sometimes things happen, and it's not your fault." He rubbed his knuckles. "You are my eyes and ears for now. You'll have to make decisions the same as I. Sometimes quickly and with less information than we'd like. Listen to what your gut says, make the decision, and carry on."

"A B C, Mama."

"All right, darling. 'A is for alligator.'"

After we finished the picture book, we tucked Johnny into bed. Wash sang a song:

"The Star that watched you in your sleep
Has just put out his light.
'Good-day, to you on earth,' he said,
'Is here in heaven Good-night.

But tell the Baby when he wakes
To watch for my return;
For I'll hang out my lamp again
When his begins to burn.'"

Wash extinguished Johnny's lamp, and we tiptoed back to our room.

"Where did you learn that song?" My eyes heavy, I shrugged out of my dress.

"Oddly enough, from the Confederate prisoner who wrote the poem. I made up the tune myself." Wash assumed his crouched position on the bed and rubbed his knees.

"Is there anything I can do?" I lightly touched his shoulder.

He flinched as if my fingers had sparked him.

"No, dear. Just leave me be."

We hired a maid and help in the office as I struggled to run a home, supervise a work site, and attend to Wash's needs, all while managing the business side of the project. On the bright side, I spent less time riding back home for instructions, having learned to do most of the calculations myself. The science of the construction intrigued me, keeping my mind nimble and giving me a sense of accomplishment I had never before experienced.

As my expertise and interest in the project grew, Wash's waned. Many evenings, I returned home to find him painting landscapes—"therapy," he called it—or attending to his rock collection and growing menagerie of pets. Mostly dogs but the occasional cat or rabbit also wriggled its way into our household.

Johnny had developed a fascination with sailing ships, and together, they built several clippers inside bottles.

"He has the Roebling mind and more nimble fingers." Wash tapped his own temple.

I admired their handiwork. "Johnny, you built the *Cutty Sark*!"

Wash rarely left the house. Although walking had become less difficult, his legs would sometimes give way without warning, sending him crashing to the floor if he had nothing with which to steady himself. A cane, sometimes one for each hand, became his constant companion.

Consumed with work, I grew weary of his growing list of aches and pains. Sometimes, I wished he could take a good dose of laudanum and sleep for a week. He'd be ever so much better. I had to be careful not to startle him with a touch, sudden movement, or even by speaking without clearing my throat in warning. All of these made him flinch and become even more irritable. Living with him became a tightrope walk over a pit of alligators.

"Could I have your attention for a moment, dear?" I asked after a particularly difficult workday.

"Whatever it is, I'm sure you have the good sense to solve it." Wash searched on his hands and knees for the rat snake that had once again escaped its habitat. The creature was black as coal with yellow eyes that reminded me of the devil in my Sunday school books. Its unnerving habit of showing up in unusual places caused me no end of fright.

Later that evening, as I used my good sense to luxuriate in a warm bath, the creature's head suddenly appeared above the bubbles. My shrieks could undoubtedly be heard clear down the street as I clambered out of the tub, then slid clear across the slippery bathroom floor in an effort to escape. After a bit of research, Wash discovered the beast had been misidentified; it was a water snake, "attempting to find a proper home."

I learned that better than discussing a concern with my husband was to bring a drawing, map, or the actual object and place it in his lap for further inspection. He seemed to enjoy the puzzle of it more than my attempted explanation. He would then describe in great detail his analysis and the simplest solution to eliminate the problem. He didn't use this method when it came to the snake, unfortunately, as the snake remained.

After an extended countrywide tour of his show, PT expanded his circus and moved it to Brooklyn, gaining much needed space at a lower cost. This also placed him closer to his customers, including Johnny and me. Sometimes, I was able to escape for a few hours to enter his world of outrageousness: the curiosities of nature, contortionists, and acrobats. But still he came to see me, always bringing a little gift for Johnny. I didn't ponder other reasons for his interest in Brooklyn. Alas, wisdom is often gained after we first have need of it.

PT sauntered into my office as I worked against deadlines of all sorts with towers of paperwork obscuring my desk. I held up a forefinger, and he studied the maps and diagrams lining the walls. After I cleared the most pressing tasks, I called him over.

He helped himself to jelly beans from the jar on my desk. "Your timely tip on the Madison Avenue property has been acted upon."

With Henrietta's permission, I had let slip information on the impending departure of the train station.

"I'm going to lease the property from the Vanderbilts, and my grand hippodrome will soon entertain tens of thousands. You have given me wonderful inspiration, Peanut."

"How so?"

"I specialize in family entertainment. Nothing offensive to woman or child. So why not take measures to assure their comfort and safety should they wish to visit without their gentlemen?" He leaned forward in the chair. "I've hired a legion of guards, one for each doorway, hall, and room."

"That seems a bit overwhelming. Your patrons may feel they are suspected of thievery."

"Hmm. Perhaps some should be dressed as patrons and roam about, offering to open doors and such. Or waiters with trays of libations."

"I'd have no quarrel with that." My eyes drifted to the pile of unfinished paperwork. "Your hippodrome sounds wonderful, PT."

"I won't keep you but a moment more. I've a most interesting proposition for you." He grinned mischievously.

"If it entails you shepherding the bridge project, allowing me to resume some semblance of normalcy, then I eagerly await your plan."

"Heavens no! I couldn't fathom a more taxing endeavor. In fact, I believe it my duty to brighten your circumstances with more exciting activities." He held out two hands, palms down, "Choose one."

I tapped the left, and he turned it over, revealing a small ivory envelope. It contained a lovely engraved invitation.

"A little soiree my wife, Charity, is hosting for the women's temperance movement."

"Hmm, what's in your other hand?"

He laughed and showed his other hand—empty.

I opened the candy jar as he reached for it. "What on earth is a Wife Charity? It sounds perfectly scandalous."

He grabbed a fistful of the rainbow-colored jelly beans, tapped his fists together, then opened them to reveal dozens of only the yellow and purple beans. "My wife, *Charity*, insists you come."

My hand flew to my forehead in chagrin. "So sorry. Your wife, of course. Please give her my regrets." My pile of invoices was not growing smaller, and I tapped my pen on them. "PT, it's been lovely to see you. Perhaps the four of us can get together another time?"

"Oh, but it will be fun." He rose, emptying his stash of jelly beans on my desk in two neat piles: one yellow, the other purple, the colors of my dress. "Music? Dancing." He twirled around, waltzing with himself. "The soiree will follow a rambunctious temperance protest right outside my museum. Think of it, Peanut! All the excitement and hubbub!" PT rubbed his hands gleefully. "Lots of the elite will be there. Leaders of the women's movement, the Reverend Beecher, probably mayors, congressmen. This is your chance to—"

"I'm afraid my protesting days are over for now." I filled my ink pen, considering whether to advise my friend of the agreement Wash had made with the police.

PT stepped back as Mr. Stone barged in, followed by ten sycophantic men in oily suits.

"*Mrs.* Roebling." A snake couldn't have hissed any smoother. He planted two beefy palms on my desk, a star-shaped scar denting the back of his left hand. "And where might *Mr.* Roebling be?"

"Good morning, Mr. Stone, gentlemen." I smiled with gritted teeth.

Behind and between the men, PT smirked and tipped his hat as he headed for the door.

I wished I were going with him. "In what way may I be of assistance?"

"I thought our directive was clear. And so I ask you again, where is *Mr. Roebling?*"

Stone shot a suspicious glance after PT.

"As you know, he is following his physician's orders and working from home."

"Then I shall visit him there. I have news from the Society of Civil Engineers," he said, holding aloft a small parcel.

"He's not taking visitors. I will see that he is informed."

"The deadline has long expired, and yet the chief engineer has not returned to work."

"I disagree. He is very much at work. Have you not seen the recent progress?"

"Indeed. We will not be put off much longer, but I'll allow two more weeks." He leaned a little closer. Spittle collected in the corners of his thin lips. "The board has requested a written record of your credentials and certifications, young lady. See to it they are made available."

❧

Whatever else happened, I had always taken comfort in my relationship with my husband, both in and out of bed. That evening, I gave him a passionate good-night kiss and ran my finger down his chest. To my surprise, he pushed my hand away.

"I'm sorry," he said.

I tried to guess what was bothering him. "I've not been the best company." I caressed his cheek, his beard soft against my hand.

He clasped my wrist. "Please stop. If you don't mind."

I did mind. *When had he ever refused me?* Never. "Have I done something to anger you?"

"It's not that. Good night, dear." He gave me a chaste kiss on the cheek. His hand quaked as he reached to extinguish the lamp.

My hurt and worry made what I said next harsher than I intended. "There are rumors about your absence from the work site—as if you're not involved at all, or worse."

Wash sighed as he pulled back from the lamp, leaving it burning.

"Some say you're an invalid—that you've lost your mental faculties and that physically, you're ruined." My voice was controlled, as I was treading dangerous waters. I reached for his hand, but then retreated, unwanted. "Your instructions appear in my handwriting, giving them even more fodder for their imaginations. Why are you pulling away from them—and from me?"

"Physically, I am ruined. I can't even be a proper husband." He dismissively waved his hand across his body.

"That's not true."

"It is true. You're just too busy to notice."

❧

Our grand dining room, once predicted to entertain dozens, echoed with only our two strained voices the next morning.

Wash dipped his toast in a runny yolk. "I've decided I'll visit the site, not that it will do any good."

"A prestigious institution calls for you to be replaced." I tapped the large envelope on the table, which he had studiously ignored.

"Wouldn't be the first time."

I sipped my tea while trying to divine his true feelings on the seriousness of the issue. "It's from the American Society of Civil Engineers."

Wash opened it, scanned the papers, and tossed them aside. "It's not the society's fault—just a few jackasses on the board."

"Stone."

He nodded. "For one. He sits on the ASCE and the bridge boards. Seems to entertain a grudge against me."

"Why?"

He shrugged. "It makes sense to create doubt and cause delays. Stone and Kingsley are making huge profits."

"But it seems to me Stone is pushing to shutter the project altogether, not delay it."

"Don't worry. The society knows my credentials and that the design is sound." He picked up the newspaper.

"Then you need to remind them."

"I don't need to defend my work or reputation against those bastards!" He slammed the newspaper onto the table.

"Address the society, Wash. Tell them that you won't tolerate their campaign of propaganda and that we must go on because that's what the people of New York require us to do."

"Ah, I see the answer to your dilemma."

"Then you'll speak to them? Good." I exhaled and tucked the papers back into their envelope. "I don't think we have to give them an exact date for your return—"

"I'll visit, but I intend to follow doctor's orders and work from home as before. *You* will be chief consulting engineer."

"Preposterous. I'm *not* an engineer!"

"Eads has no formal engineering training, yet he's bridging the Mississippi. Did you know that?"

"Eads has no degree?" I reached around him to collect his plate, casually brushing against him. I wanted to talk about the night before.

Wash usually couldn't resist giving me a quick squeeze here or there, but he pushed his chair back and stroked his beard instead. "Correct. Eads is self-taught, like you. Furthermore, you shall use your feminine charms and the intelligence you possess in abundance in a speech to win over the society."

"No, I couldn't!"

"You can. And you will be far more engaging than I ever was."

He didn't realize what he was asking of me. My knees wobbled and my mouth tasted of ashes. Speak? To the board?

I had never shared my gut-wrenching fear of public speaking with him. And this speech could either save or ruin him.

If I told him how I ran away from the fear as a child, nearly being run over by a carriage, he would only smirk at such an untimely excuse. If I shared how PT had helped me overcome my jitters during the speech at Cold Spring, he would become irritated by my friend's involvement. How could I share with a man who feared nothing something that didn't seem far outside my normal duties? I couldn't explain it to myself.

EIGHTEEN

The new P. T. Barnum Grand Traveling Museum, Menagerie, Caravan, and Hippodrome in Brooklyn was a maze of curiosities and a delightful escape. Rows and rows bristled with jars of pickled animal parts, stuffed two-headed animals, and costumes, deflated and frightful without the clowns in them. What appeared to be a taxidermied mermaid slumped in a corner, beady brown eyes staring vacantly above a matted, hairy torso and fishy bottom.

I thanked Henri, the watchman, for letting me in after normal hours. Over six feet tall, he was soft-spoken and had a slight limp, developed during his decade as a slave.

"Mr. Barnum is in his office, ma'am." Henri nodded toward the eight-foot oak door, with PT's monogram in a fancy script carved into it. "He salvaged this from the old museum."

He pointed to a sculpture next to me. "Don't touch the giant," he said with a grin.

Guarding PT's office was a ten-foot-tall statue of a naked man. The statue's hands were crossed modestly over its private parts but failed miserably, as its large member presented at precisely my eye level. A placard proclaimed: *The Cardiff Giant—a mummy created by an ancient civilization.* Despite Henri's admonition, I touched a fingertip to its mottled gray surface. Chalk came off on my glove. It was clearly fashioned from plaster.

Henri leaned toward me conspiratorially. "A giant hoax is what it is."

I nodded. It was certainly imposing, but how anyone could believe it was a petrified mummy eluded me.

Henri knocked and opened the thick door to PT's muffled "Enter."

PT sat in a spectacular walnut and red velvet chair, rather like a throne for a king, behind a desk replete with carved lions and elephants. Somehow, anything less would have seemed out of place. Painted posters advertising his circus and museum plastered every inch of wall. Even the rug was alive with color, vibrant blues and reds and gold.

PT was engrossed in paperwork. "Are we all locked up for the evening, Henri?"

"Yes, sir." Henri's soft baritone was quickly followed by the click of the door as he closed it behind me.

I cleared my throat while slipping off my gloves. "Am I intruding?"

His face registered surprise, then widened into a smile as he looked up and took me in, head to toe. "Well, well, my dear Peanut. To what do I owe this extraordinary pleasure?" He tucked his pen in its ornate holder and donned his tailcoat before coming around his desk. "Have you reconsidered attending the soiree?" His lips brushed the top of my offered hand.

"I'm afraid not. But it's always a pleasure to see you, Phineas."

"Ugh. Phineas is so stiff and formal."

"PT." I slipped my hand from his. "I need to ask a great favor of you concerning a rather private matter."

"As always, I am at your disposal." He moved behind me to check the office door, making me a bit uncomfortable with my choice of words.

"I'm sorry. Where are my manners? Would you like something to drink?" He slid open the sideboard, and a well-stocked liquor bar appeared.

"So much for the temperance movement," I teased. "Maybe a wee taste."

"Don't confuse me with my public image. One is real, the other sells tickets." He chose two crystal snifters and poured a generous amount of whiskey.

"It's about the bridge. We've reached a critical point."

"Yes, indeed. I've heard." We touched glasses. "To success in this great endeavor." He sipped. "I know your devoted husband is still rather indisposed. And although gossip about you abounds, I'm sure you're not half as guilty as most would have us believe."

I could see his grin straight through his whiskey glass. "Ugh, rumors. You know I've been serving as the coordinator of the entire project."

"I've heard juicier bits."

I sniffed the heady aroma of the whiskey. Even better than the taste. I sucked in a hefty swig. "I have not usurped my husband's role nor taken on a lover if that's what you're implying. My works puts me around men all the time. Must that make the tongues wag?"

"Shocking, isn't it?" He chuckled.

"I wish to defend Mr. Roebling's honor and my own as well. I've come to you for help."

He swirled the amber liquid. "Perhaps you are entirely too devoted to your husband's honor and his bridge."

I finished my drink, a pleasant warmth rising up my throat to my face. "I am well aware you're not half the scoundrel you pretend to be."

He took my empty glass, tilted it, raised his eyebrows. "A full scoundrel is a more apt description. But I have been utterly beguiled by your charms from the first, since I sorely lack anything remotely resembling finesse. Now, what is this great favor?"

"It is quite simple and in line with your talents."

"Ah, you wish to have a show! Perhaps a circus on the riverbank? Think of the positive publicity! Why, General Tom Thumb could make an appearance, and the Cardiff Giant!"

"Well, no, that's not what I had in mind. I want you to teach me some of your skills."

His eyes twinkled. "There are so many. Animal training? Magic? Philanthropy?"

"No."

"Ah, dancing." He hummed a tune. "I'm quite light on my feet." He raised my arm for me to twirl under, but I stood my ground. "No? What then?"

"Your professional skills. Your showmanship."

He hammered one fist into the other. "You want to go into show business."

"Heavens, no!" I laughed. "I need to speak to the board, to vouch for my husband's competence. I suffer quite a fright at the thought of speaking in front of an audience."

"I remember," he said softly.

"And I must explain the delicate matter of his health."

"As it happens, I'm quite an expert in the field. Speaking in public, that is. I know little of health matters."

"You will help me?"

"I shall like nothing better. It has always been my pleasure to be with you, Peanut." He took both my hands in his and gazed intently into my eyes. "How could I not, when your very presence lights a room? A delight to the senses, a fresh breeze in my cluttered life."

I cleared my throat and my mind from his spell and drew back. "I am, of course, prepared to pay you."

"Of course. I am a professional." He rummaged through a humidor for a cigar and held it between his teeth, patting his pockets for a match. He fumbled with a blue glass contraption, producing a tiny flame that failed to light his cigar. "It seems you are the only light in this room."

"In that case, what do you believe is a reasonable fee?"

"Five hundred dollars. Cash up front."

"Five hundred!" I extracted several banknotes from between my blouse and bodice. "I am prepared to pay twenty-five dollars."

He took the cash, slowly passed it under his nose. "If my fee is too steep, I have an alternative."

My heart sank. *The bridge company.* PT was already a financial backer. "Do you want the bridge named after you?"

"Ha! A wonderful proposition. But no, dear Peanut. I will train you to be a convincing and eloquent speaker. And I wish no cash nor eponymous bridge in return."

"Am I about to be compromised?"

"I am a flawed but more or less moral man. As fate would have it, we both have spouses to consider. I ask only a kiss. A simple kiss to seal the agreement and privately cherish in my memory forever."

"A kiss. Or five hundred dollars." My lips tingled from the whiskey, and my increasingly foggy brain tried to make sense of the deal. But it made no sense. Of course it didn't. This was PT.

"That's the offer. Valid only today."

He poured us both another shot. I contemplated the deal while nosing the whiskey, then downed it in one swig. I shook my head when he held up the bottle for a refill. He wiped our glasses and set them back into the bar.

When he returned, I pointed to my cheek as if to inquire *Will this do?*

He shook his head, his offer clear.

I pried my blouse away from my chest, suddenly sticky from sweat. *What was the harm?* Give him a swift kiss, a token for his memory. No one would ever know. I twisted my wedding ring. What had Wash said? I fought the warm fog and remembered: *Listen to what your gut says, make the decision, then carry on.* The office door was closed. Henri wouldn't hear. And part of me, loosened by whiskey, pined for the press of forbidden lips against mine.

"You are a scoundrel."

He grunted and slid his cigar into the humidor. "Indeed. But I am foremost a businessman, and I know the value of my services. The choice is yours."

"And I am a businesswoman. Therefore, I accept your offer."

He smiled and rubbed the bills of cash together in one hand and held out the other, beckoning the exorbitant balance. I slipped the banknotes from his hand and returned them to their hiding place, scratchy on my chest. His eyes widened, and he took my hand. I closed my eyes and tilted my head, ready for a kiss. He gently brushed back my hair, kissed my forehead and cheeks. Then, the softest brush of his lips against mine.

My lips parted in surprise, and I heaved a sigh of relief, only for his lips to press harder, his tongue to seek mine, offering a mix of whiskey and clove. He kissed me again, one hand caressing my cheek, the other firm to the small of my back. I clung to his shoulders and answered him in kind, my hands delight-ing in the smooth silk of his jacket, my body tingling from hairline to boot laces. I needed him. I needed to stop. But my mind swirled powerlessly above me as he kissed me like Wash didn't, and his hand crept toward my breast.

His lips bussed my neck, his sideburns tickling me. I stepped back, but he moved forward, leaning me against the rolled top of his desk.

An alarm rang up my body, and I palmed his chest. "Please—"

But still he held me. I placed my hands against his chest and pushed gently. "Please stop, I mean."

He let go and stepped back. He shook his head. "I got carried away."

My own participation made me squirm. I wanted it as much as he did, my body reacting to a basic need, my mind enjoying the attraction of a forbidden other. The difficulties Wash and I faced kept me from physical pleasures I so craved, but that was no excuse.

My mind reeling with shame, my body a mix of heat and chills, I bolted. Using both hands, I yanked open the heavy office door and ran through the maze of creepy atrocities in the darkened museum. *Smash!* A jar hit the floor, and a two-headed fish spilled out. I sidestepped it and kept running. The exterior door was locked, and I banged my fists on it. Henri rushed over to let me out.

"Good night, Mrs. Roebling."

❧

The next day, a courier delivered a white box containing the gloves I had once again left behind. They were cleaned and spotless, nestled in a cloud of silk along with a sprig of violets upon Carrie Beebe's book. The card read: *In the language of flowers, you inspire me: "Violets for watchfulness, faithfulness, I'll always be there." Please allow me the honor of upholding my part in our business venture. —PTB*

I thought of the first time I had left a glove with him in a hurried exit after visiting the new circus. And now again. It seemed PT was aware of his effect on me and was willing to brush it aside in the name of business. Exactly what I wished to do.

❧

The museum was different in daytime as I returned for my first lesson in public speaking. Warm sunbeams cast the collections in a more playful light, no dark corners to offer cover for frightening creatures. Patrons milled about, including several unaccompanied women. Henri chatted with Miss Mann as she minded Johnny.

"Don't break anything." I kissed Johnny's sweet face. His big blue eyes blinked in puzzlement that I would anticipate such a thing. So much like his father.

Conflicting thoughts tumbled in my mind, the wisdom of coming back here, wondering if there were other ways to solve my dilemma. Questioning myself regarding my true motives, I determined our intrigue had been nothing more than weakness and whiskey. I set back my shoulders. To be successful in a man's world, I would be strong.

PT appeared at exactly the appointed time and escorted me to a quiet area but within view of others. "Am I forgiven?" His mouth curled into a sheepish grin.

"I'm not blameless." I opened my purse and pulled out my traveling ink jar, eyedropper, and fountain pen. Lastly, I slipped out the two bank notes and held them out to him. He cupped his hand over mine, but I wriggled my fingers from his grasp. "And this is a business arrangement." My hands shook as I filled the pen, spilling ink on the oak table.

He paced behind me. "Nervous?"

I nodded, tried wiping the ink with a rag, but created more of a mess.

"Do you feel blood rushing to your head? Are your hands clammy and your nerves playing a symphony from here"—he touched the back of my neck, then ran his finger down my backbone—"to parts unknown?" He leaned closer, close enough to whisper in my ear, "Are you remembering our kiss?"

"This was a bad idea." I scraped back my chair, but he stopped my progress with a firm hand on my shoulder.

His ringleader voice rang out. "It is well to remember. Those are the same sensations you will have before an audience. Consider this a dress rehearsal, and learn to accept the discomfort, embrace it even, as a sign of your passion."

I stayed put.

He clapped his hands, startling me with his transition. "You must own the stage."

Own the stage, I wrote in my journal.

"No, no, put that down." He flung my journal away. "It must come from here." He tapped his chest. "You must connect with the audience." He pointed two fingers at his eyes, then at mine.

I held his gaze, hoping to convey sincerity and strength of will.

His eyes clouded in confusion. Or hurt. Or perhaps indifference, as in a second, it was gone, and he moved away and circled around me. "One by one, eyeball to eyeball."

We met many more times over the next few weeks. PT demonstrated speaking techniques. Imitating his style, I would laugh and gesture grandly. He corrected my posture and hand movements until I found a style of my own, and he made me practice speeches with himself, Henri, and Miss Mann as my audience.

One of his techniques allowed me to test my strength against temptation.

"The Chinese acrobats taught me this." He had me sit while he stood behind me, then pressed his thumbs on various points on my neck and shoulders. Each time, he said, "Feel this muscle. Let it go." He made circles with his thumbs and dug them deeper as I relaxed the muscle, causing me to wish he'd never stop. It was somewhere between pain and pleasure, and my body responded with a glow I'd never known before.

When he stopped, I fought the urge to beg for more. That would be against the rules I had set up for myself. If only there were someone to discuss this with, I could perhaps have quieted the voices in my head that insisted I was doing something wrong. Then I could have fully embraced the experience, reveled in the attention and physical pleasures without a care for how it might look to others. But one of those voices, coming from deep inside me, knew there was no one with whom to discuss my situation, because no one would properly have advised me to continue, even under the watchful eyes of Henri and Miss Mann.

On the day I was to present my case—or rather Wash's—to the American Society of Civil Engineers, the auditorium bristled with life. Or rather death: row upon row of men in dark suits, as serious as undertakers. Standing in the stage wing, my heart beat too rapidly, and my throat choked with anxiety. I placed a clammy hand on my burning cheek to cool it. PT's instructions echoed in my ears: *Accept the discomfort, embrace it.*

The president of the academy introduced me, and I took my place on the podium. What seemed like a million faces stared back at me. Having practiced and imagined the moment so many times, I separated my terror from the various muscles that controlled my speech. First, I focused on my breathing. I had learned to concentrate on what can be controlled: one needs a steady breath to bring words to life. I saw the audience not as a mob bent on humiliating me but as individuals who I would converse with one by one.

I began the speech I had committed to memory. "Thank you for the honor of being the first woman to address this great organization. I hope to assuage your concerns—" The words rolled off my tongue too tightly. The men sat back in their chairs, regarded their fingernails, checked timepieces.

My cheeks warmed, and my insides tumbled. No matter. Let my face burn with the passion of my message. Let my gut protest. I sought out one member of the audience, captured his gaze, spoke to him directly. He responded with a nod. Then I moved to the man next to him, and behind, and just in front of me. I spoke words not memorized like a child's catechism but etched into my soul, given life by my work.

They leaned forward in their chairs, listening as I ticked off our accomplishments. I stood tall, as if lifted from the ground. Perhaps this victorious rush of excitement coursing through my veins was what PT so enjoyed about the stage.

"Therefore, gentlemen, you can rest assured in my husband's mental acuity and technical brilliance as an engineer. I am deeply grateful for your efforts and concern." I paused for effect, scanning the entire audience. "But if, despite the lack of any evidence of mechanical flaw or wrongdoing on my or my husband's part, you still believe in your minds and hearts that he should be removed from this great effort, then I shall see in it the hand of God, which all my care could neither direct nor change."

I closed my eyes and took a deep breath, then opened them to see the audience on its feet, applause filling the auditorium and my heart. And there, in the front row, was PT. He held up his arms, hands clenched together in victory. I nodded, forgiving him for extracting payment with my honor. But I could not absolve myself.

NINETEEN

After the speech to the American Society of Civil Engineers, there was still the matter of the bridge company and their threat to remove Wash from the project. That spring, Benjamin Stone made frequent and increasingly harassing visits to the office, demanding documentation of Wash's health and my qualifications.

After several weeks, Wash's symptoms had abated, and he was able to walk short distances using a cane. He agreed to make an appearance at the work site while I made a visit to Stone's office.

"One last time, to get Stone off our backs. You can check the fire damage yourself."

Wash, always a gentleman, had insisted on carrying one of the satchels full of documents. "It's unnecessary, but I'll do it for you, dear."

We stopped in front of Stone's brownstone office building. Wash handed me the satchel, then frowned at me struggling with the extra load. "I'll go in with you."

"No. It won't do any good for him to see you—" I stopped. "Stone needs to know you're at the work site."

He shifted his weight from one leg to the other.

A pang of guilt ran through me. I was pushing him too hard. We should have taken a carriage. "Do you understand the power he has?"

"He doesn't concern me." He gave me a peck on the cheek before limping down the street.

I couldn't say the same about my nemesis. "Don't stay in the caisson too long, no more than five minutes at a time," I yelled after Wash. Then I gripped the heavy bundles and climbed up the steps to Stone's office.

Benjamin Stone sat behind his massive desk in the elegantly appointed office. To his right were tall windows, columns of light slipping between the thick green velvet curtains. He faced an ornate marble fireplace across the large room, above which hung a painting in an elaborately carved and gilded frame. Volumes of books were stacked neatly on shelves that extended all the way to a fourteen-foot ceiling.

I ignored the imposing surroundings and used a bit of PT's showmanship as I emptied the two satchels into a foot-high pile of documents on his desk. They appeared most impressive, especially with the mote-filled beams of light that shone from the window on them like treasures. PT would be proud. "My credentials, sir. No doubt you will find a lack of explicit certifications. Regrettably, they are not available to women in this country."

Despite all his earlier caterwauling and threats, he seemed stricken with a sudden lethargy and ignored my comments as well as the pile of paper. Instead, he simply nodded, rubbing the curious deep scar on his palm while he stared at something behind me. I followed his gaze to a painting over the fireplace. A woman with brown curls graced the portrait, alongside a little girl with similar ringlets.

"You should be very happy to learn that you can find Mr. Roebling at the work site should you wish to consult him." I gathered back my satchels.

Again, he nodded, his gaze still upon the painting. "My wife and child."

"They're lovely. How old is your daughter?"

His eyes darted at me, his face twisted in anger. "Don't you know?"

"No, I—"

"Sit down."

It was more of a command than a request, so I took a seat on the green velvet chair facing his desk. I clasped my hands together in my lap and set my jaw to receive another lecture.

He paced the Persian rug, stopping at the large window. "I find it despicable that you come here, professing your knowledge and competence, when you don't know pertinent history. Does the River Dee mean anything to you?" He stomped toward me, his face beet red.

I squeezed my eyes shut, his bearlike body looming above me not helping my concentration.

"A bridge failed, twenty, thirty years ago," I said. "Quite a different sort of bridge if memory serves me." I looked at him, seeing a face contorted in not just anger but grief. I glanced back at the portrait. A hole opened inside me, and empathy settled in where my hubris had vanished. "I'm sorry. Was your family involved?"

"It was 1847." He wiped his eyes and spectacles with a handkerchief. "I was an inspector, and railroads were expanding all over the continent. England, Scotland, Wales—my team had to cover every inch of track, approve every new engine, ensure every bridge was sound.

"It was too much, too fast, I kept telling them. They approved changes in original plans without proper thought to safety. We had a new route, to Ruabon, Wales. I had my wife and daughter join me for the first passenger trip, having missed them so. It was a gray, drizzly spring day. Hmph. Jolly ol' England and all that. But the railcar was a delight. Carved mahogany walls, velvet seats." He made circle motions with his hand in the air. "My little girl wiped the window so her rag doll could see out. Then she held it up, saying, 'Kiss Gertrude for me,' and I feigned a smooch on the grotty thing."

"That was sweet of you." How on earth this pertained to my credentials was utterly lost on me. It seemed a warning, the distant thunder before a storm.

"Hmph. As we crossed the bridge, a vibration began and moved toward us, building to a tremble. Then a wave motion rippled across the bridge like an earthquake, the iron struts shaking violently, working loose from the pilings. I heard pings as the twisting force strained the fasteners and rivets ricocheted like bullets. One shot straight through my palm." He massaged his scar with his thumb.

"We were thrown forward, then across the car. A huge crack sounded as bridge timbers gave way. We were tossed apart, just as I wanted to cradle them in my arms and keep them safe."

"Did you get to them? Did everyone get out of the car safely?"

"I punched through the window, hoping to create an escape. But the railcar plunged into the river. A shock of cold, gray water blasted me away from the windows. I fought the torrent and the desperate need for air, trying to reach my family. But they were too far, and roaring water overcame me. Shock faded to numbness as I sank into dark, frigid water. I swirled down, crushed and useless." He leaned back in his chair, eyes closed, defeated and empty as a rubber balloon. "I awaited my final relief, to be carried away in the swift current with the others."

I wrapped my arms about myself, my own horror of near drowning returning like a rushing river. "But you survived. And your wife and daughter?"

He shook his head.

"What a tragedy. I know of sorrow." In the portrait over the fireplace, the young subjects seemed more real now, the young mother having some resemblance to myself. I told him briefly about the loss of my sister at a tender age. We had a moment of mutual respect for each other and for forces of nature that man could not always tame. But his tender side disappeared with the speed of lightning.

"I understand the bridge committee once again intends for trains to be accommodated," he barked. "Tell me, young lady, do you know the weight of a train?"

"Well, I'm not—" I stammered.

"You have no idea. What is the added tensile and compressive strength required? How will the approaches be configured so the trains don't collide with other vehicles?" Stone glared at me.

"We—"

My mind raced to come up with answers to his rapid-fire questions when he thundered, "Don't answer! Fools! You think this is some game you are playing? It's high time the board put a stop to this before we endanger the lives of everyone who steps foot on that colossal disaster!"

"You insult the fine minds of the engineers who designed this, the skill of the workmen who are building it." I breathed slowly, in control. "All schematics are available for your review. I will consult with the engineers if you have specific concerns. In the meantime, your threats have served only to hamper the vital work taking place. And it *will* take place, whether you choose to cooperate or not."

I gathered my satchels. Despite my confident words, the new plan to incorporate trains had blindsided me. Notice of that was probably amid the pile of correspondence on my desk. "I'm terribly sorry about the loss of your wife and daughter. But past accidents should inform the science of engineering, not impede the progress of today." With shoulders straight and my head held high, I marched out of his office. But my heart was breaking once again as Elizabeth swirled away from me, now with two others floating with her.

TWENTY

The incident with Stone was all but forgotten as Miss Mann, Johnny, and I walked down the street to meet Mother at the ferry terminal. It seemed she enjoyed seeing Johnny more, unconcerned that she might be called into child care service now that we had a nanny.

Miss Mann placed Johnny in a cart as he dawdled and stopped every few feet to stare in wonderment at trees, dogs, organ grinders, and other children. "Do you think you can spare me this evening, Mrs. Roebling?"

"Gentleman caller? Named Henri?" I smiled. It was none of my affair, of course, but I did play a hand in their romance.

"Yes, ma'am. But don't tell no one."

"Why on earth not?" My curiosity leapfrogged over my respect for her privacy. *Was Henri too old for her? Married?* The approaching ferry trilled its whistle as we reached the waterfront.

"You may call me Muriel, Mrs. Roebling."

"As soon as you call me Emily. But I'd rather you answer my question," I said with a smile, hoping to convey a kindliness behind my prying.

"You wouldn't understand."

"Why is that?" I picked up Johnny, affording him a better view of the boat being secured in the slip. "When did you become such a big, heavy boy?" I bounced to seat him more comfortably on my hip.

"Allow me." Miss Mann held out her arms for Johnny. I didn't relinquish him but tilted my head, waiting for an answer to my question.

She lowered her eyes. "We keep to ourselves, we mountain people."

We pressed up to the railing as the passengers disembarked.

"Mountain people?"

"Ramapo Mountains in New Jersey. That's where I'm from, Ringwood."

"I've been there. Lovely area."

"You haven't been to my Ringwood."

"Perhaps not. But what does this have to do with you seeing Henri?"

"You wouldn't understand."

Mother erupted from the crowd, snapping her fingers in the air, her voice ringing out above the crowd. "Porter!"

I waved, and she met my eyes, then peered behind us. "Where's your carriage?"

Miss Mann and I loaded her baggage in a teetering pile onto Johnny's wagon.

"Hardly worth the trouble for a few blocks, and I thought you'd like to stretch your legs after such a long ride."

After a couple of blocks, we stopped to rest before heading uphill, and Johnny joined some children playing hopscotch on a grid scratched into a patch of dirt. I plucked a thick volume, *Violets*, from the top of Mother's tower of luggage. No doubt she believed she'd be the first to present Carrie's newly published book. I thumbed through it without letting on that PT's gift had preceded hers.

"You can't really pay proper attention that way," Mother said.

"I'm afraid skimming is how most of my reading is accomplished these days."

"No, don't give it another thought." She snatched the book from my grasp, her lips set in a thin line of disapproval.

"What's wrong?"

"You know, Emily, it's one thing to take an interest in your husband's work and quite another to believe it your own."

"*Et tu, Mater?*" Barely a half hour into her visit, and already she had made me wince. I sighed with relief when Johnny came to my rescue.

He grabbed my hand. "Let's play, Mama."

"May I?" I asked a sweet-looking but shoeless girl in a dirty dress. She shyly handed me a small, flat stone. "Like this, Johnny." I tossed the stone and hopped to the top of the hopscotch board and back.

My lesson ended abruptly when we were stunned by an explosive blast. The children cried and held their ears as a wall of thick, heated air overwhelmed us. From the direction of the work site, a brown geyser spewed five hundred feet into the air.

Glass tinkled from shattered windows. Another thunderous roar, and rocks, dirt, and debris dropped from the sky upon us. A horse whinnied and reared up on its hind legs, then galloped away, its rider clenching its mane to hang on.

I pushed the children into a doorway. Some of them scattered, screaming. I checked those remaining for injuries, sighing with relief when I found none. Frantic mothers ran from their houses calling their children's names.

Horror hit me like a thunderclap. "Wash is down there!"

Mother sheltered Johnny with her arm. "Go."

I ran toward the river as fast as I was able, picking through debris littering the street. An old woman crawled beside her toppled cart and vegetables, and I stopped to help her to her feet. When I was nearly to the work site, I twisted my ankle and tumbled to the street, my head crashing on a stone.

Moments of blackness, the sound of horses galloping. I blinked my eyes open; two horses pulled a carriage straight toward me. The carriage halted and the driver alighted.

"Mrs. Roebling!" Dunn, bleeding from several gashes on his face and hands, knelt beside me. He lifted me under my shoulders and helped me aboard, where I found Wash. O'Brien held Wash's bandaged head in his lap. I blinked hard to clear my vision, my ankle and head throbbing.

"Out cold now, but he'll be fine soon," O'Brien said.

I picked up Wash's stiff hand, held it in mine as the carriage bumped along. My heart ached for all this to end. O'Brien explained the accident, but his words floated like jetsam on the sea. It was all meaningless, didn't he see? I was losing my husband.

Hours later, Farrington arrived at our home to check on Wash and recounted the incident. "It was what we call a blowout. We heard a deafening roar, then bricks, tools, anything unattached got sucked up the supply shaft. I hit the ground to avoid becoming a flying object, saw two workers picked up and slammed into the shaft. The limelights flickered, and some flamed out, leaving us in near darkness."

Wash groaned, lying on the settee, his arm draped across his face.

"Maybe we should leave him to rest," I said.

Wash pushed himself to sitting. "No. Need to review. Learn from it."

It didn't seem to me that Wash was learning. At least not his own limitations. Why had he stayed? He knew he couldn't tolerate being in the caisson that long, but he couldn't stop himself.

Farrington continued. "We figured out what happened. The hatch door got stuck open by a pile of bricks, and the pressure made the air rush out."

I heard but didn't listen. It seemed important for Wash and Farrington to relive the moment, to sort it out. I peeled the heavy bandage from over his left eye. The two-inch gash no longer bled, but he would have a scar.

"Young and Dunn helped us dig away bricks, debris pelting us all the while."

"That's when I got this." Wash pointed to his eye.

"Finally, the path was cleared, and the hatch slammed shut. Dunn secured the latch, and it was over," Farrington said.

"What caused it?" I asked.

"The guys up top, sending down a load of bricks, and the guys down below got their timing mixed up," Wash said. "Both hatches were open at the same time."

"So you were in the caisson much too long. What happened when you got out?" I applied a new dressing, then rolled gauze around his head to keep it in place.

"Pain seared up my legs, and they fell out from under me. What felt like fire ripped through my torso and exploded in my lungs."

The iron weight of guilt returned to the pit of my stomach. This was my responsibility. And I had failed my beloved.

⁓

Days later, Wash had grown worse. He rested in bed, pillows propping his bent and motionless limbs, knees and elbows twice their normal size, his eyes slits in his swollen and bruised face. He mumbled unrelated words from thickened lips. I held a lamp close as Dr. Smith examined him.

The doctor listened to Wash's chest with an ear horn. "His lungs are quite wet."

I bit my lips, my eyes burning with tears I wouldn't allow.

"Bring that closer." Dr. Smith indicated the lamp. He lifted each of Wash's eyelids with his thumb and inspected his vacant stare. "I consulted with a Dr. Reed at Brooklyn Hospital."

"Yes? What does he say? What can we do?"

Dr. Smith retrieved a syringe and vials of white powder and liquid from his black bag. "Mrs. Roebling—"

My vision narrowed; I saw nothing but Wash's still form on the bed.

"I don't wish to alarm you, but there's a chance he has swelling of the brain."

Alarm coursed through me despite his calm demeanor. I grasped the bedpost to steady myself, the blood running from my brain. "What does that mean?" I watched Wash's chest rise and fall, the rhythm slow but steady.

"It's impossible to say now." He mixed a potion and drew it into the syringe. "Morphine will help him rest while his body recovers."

While. Not *if.* "So he will recover? If he has this…swelling on the brain…what will happen?"

"The only thing we know for sure is that he won't be able to work for quite some time, and certainly not in the caisson. But the worst is over. Now we wait." He packed his bag. "I'll stay the night with him if you wish, but there isn't anything more I can do."

"Thank you, Doctor. I'll keep watch on my own." I rubbed Wash's puffy hand. He would want only me with him.

I lay awake next to him all night, listening to the steady rasp of his breathing. Just before dawn, his breaths slowed, then stopped. I counted. Ten seconds. Twenty. I jiggled his hand, but he remained still.

"Wash." I tapped his cheek, with no response. "Wash!" I shook his shoulder, pounded his chest. Why had I let the doctor go? My mind whirled above me, distant, useless, but my hands worked feverishly. I tore off his blankets and shook him some more. Finally, I reached under his sleep shirt, found his nipple, and twisted it, hard. He gurgled, then coughed. After a large gasp, he resumed breathing. And I fell back next to him, my body shaking, my heartbeat thundering in my ears.

At 7:00 a.m., the doctor returned. Wash slept on, having not moved a muscle all night. Dr. Smith took his temperature, then placed the ear horn on Wash's chest. "Good news. It's not pneumonia. His lungs are clearing."

"But what about...his brain?"

"Too soon to tell about that, but we have reason for optimism. I'm cutting back on his morphine. He should start to awaken."

"Will he be in terrible pain?"

"If he is, we'll give him a bit more morphine."

"What can I do?"

"Speak to him. Chat about anything, really. Make him want to wake up."

I told Wash stories about picnics and moonlit carriage rides. I spoke of our adventures in Europe and Cincinnati and Trenton. But still he slept. I spoke of the bridge, *his father's bridge*, and how they dreamed of it on a ferry. "Too bad Papa won't see it." In a moment of cruel kindness, I added, "And perhaps you won't either."

Wash moaned, his eyes slit open. He looked at me, and the tiniest smile crossed his lips.

"You're awake." I held up his head and offered him some water.

He sipped, then pushed the glass away. "My head hurts."

"You gave us quite the scare, but the doctor says you'll be fine. No more caisson for you. Martin can take over."

He pulled at his blanket and writhed as if the bed had captured him and he needed to escape.

"Wash, calm down."

"No! Never give up!" He raised a shaky fist. "We pushed the cannon up that damn hill!"

"That's over, Wash. I'm here with you."

His brilliant blue eyes widened, delirious. He focused on me with frightening intensity and clawed at the front of my dress. "You don't care... caisson...does to me."

If a horse had kicked me, it would have hurt less. Indeed, I had urged him to go to the work site but had expected he'd stay in the caisson only a short time, if at all. I remembered his hesitance the day of the blowout, how he had looked at me oddly, as if I prized work over safety, before hobbling down to the work site. But it was worse than that; he doubted my devotion to him. His eyes darted around the room, a froth on his lips as he worked to form words.

I wrung out a washrag, wiped his face and his poor wrecked body. How did those who care for invalids do this every day? The tremble of his hand, the stiffness of his arm as I lifted it, the wild roving of his eyes, all made me tremble as well. But nurses weren't wiping lips they had kissed, lips that accused, guided by a temporarily unstable mind. They weren't watching the love of their lives being torn away, bit by bit.

TWENTY-ONE

Mother stayed for many weeks during Wash's recuperation. Soon, her circle of friends visited as well, delighting in his stories of Civil War exploits. Wash was never so happy as when he had a new audience for a story. Mother, Henrietta, Carrie, and Eleanor gathered around Wash, who was propped on pillows on the long chaise in the parlor. The ladies pulled needles in and out of squares of white fabric nesting in their laps. A fire burned brightly in the fireplace, sending flashes of light and shadow across their faces.

I sat between Henrietta and Eleanor on the divan, admiring their work. Eleanor passed me a palm-full of new hairpins like a schoolgirl passing a note. I snuck a peek at them before secreting them away between the cushions. These were shaped like the others—which had rusted into uselessness—but the metal had more spring to it. Along with the tiny rounded blob of hardened glue on the tips, they were coated with bright blue paint. "Blue?" I asked in a hushed tone.

"Isn't it pretty?" she whispered back.

As Carrie stoked the fire and Mother fussed with Wash's blanket, he launched into a familiar yarn. "This reminds me of a night so dark, I saw nothing but the glowing tip of my cigar. I was all alone, deep in enemy territory—"

Having heard this story a time or two or ten, I was relieved by the knock at the door, providing the opportunity to excuse myself. I opened the door to PT, sporting a broad smile and a bottle of whiskey. Next to him was Henri, dressed for a night on the town.

Miss Mann and Henri departed, and I invited PT into the library. Maps and diagrams papered the desk and every horizontal surface; steel samples glittered on a marble-topped table. His scent of cherry tobacco and clove at once stimulated and calmed me.

"Sorry to arrive unannounced, but I've promised a progress report to the Connecticut investors."

"And I apologize for neglecting your requests."

He waved away my comment. "Your priorities are in order, my dear."

I reviewed our progress and described my meeting with Benjamin Stone. PT pretended to be Stone. He sank into Wash's leather chair and plopped his feet on the desk. Tossing a ream of paper into the air, he bellowed, "Ahhhemmm! You should be bending over backward, missy!"

I was laughing so hard, I could barely choke out, "PT, have you no respect?"

A polite cough from the doorway. Mother. Her lips were drawn tight enough to sling the arrows her eyes aimed at us.

"Oh, Mother, PT was doing the most marvelous imitation of Benjamin Stone."

"So I see. Perhaps Mr. Barnum would like to join your husband and our other guests in the parlor?"

"I'd be delighted, but please call me PT. And may I be so bold as to call you Phebe?"

"You may not," Mother said.

"We've heard those stories time and time again, Mother, and we're conducting business here." A familiar profile appeared behind Mother's head. Wonder of wonders, it was my tall, handsome brother. "GK!"

"Aha! Here you are, Little Sister! Mother, greetings."

"Oh, please come help us." I embraced his slender frame, then dragged him into the room. "This is our friend P. T. Barnum."

GK shook PT's hand. "A pleasure to meet you."

"Come, Mr. Barnum, let them have a chat," Mother said. I sensed another motive as she escorted PT from the room.

"It took a bit of searching, but it turns out I still have them." GK tapped a roll of yellowed, tattered plans against his palm.

"John's original designs?" I took the roll of papers and gingerly removed its rubber band.

"Somehow, I never got around to destroying them."

"Wise of you, considering the change in plans. Once again, the bridge committee wants to accommodate trains on the bridge." I unrolled the delicate papers and spread them across a table, using several of Wash's rock specimens as paperweights. Schooled in geology and a devoted hobbyist, he'd amassed a collection of rocks and minerals that would rival that of any museum.

"I didn't think the railroad barons would give up easily."

"That's not my battle to wage. Let's see what we have to do if the railroad wins and they come up with the money." We compared the old diagrams with the current plans, using a magnifying glass to read Papa's faded handwriting.

GK ran his hand through his dark hair, releasing the minty scent of his hair cream. He was nearly as gray as Mother. His presence brought me a sorely needed sense of calm, and my mind tumbled with the possibility of him growing more involved in the project.

"They'll win, I assure you," he said. "Why don't you ask Washington if the current infrastructure will support trains?"

I glanced toward the parlor where Wash delighted in tales of past glories.

"He always had a gift for storytelling," GK said. "Got me through many a dreary night."

"I'm afraid it would take much effort to bring his mind back to this question."

"It's that serious then?"

I nodded, avoiding his gaze. He had loved Wash like a brother since before we were married, and seeing pain in my brother's eyes would cause me to weep. "So let's see what we need to do."

We resumed comparing the two sets of plans and did some calculations on the few differences we found.

GK rolled up the old plans, tapping the end into alignment. "He hardly changed it. John, the old bastard, couldn't bring himself to do it."

"I truly worry for him." I nodded toward the laughter in the parlor.

"I worry for you."

I dismissed his comment with a wave.

"I say this because I love you." He hesitated, put his hand on my shoulder. "There's been some talk."

"Heard all the way in Iowa?"

"You must tread a fine line each day. Working among men shoulder to shoulder."

I nodded, but his words fell like rain off a duck. I'd grown too old to be lectured by my big brother.

"There can't be any hint of impropriety." He glanced toward the parlor. "I assume there is nothing but professional regard between you and Mr. Barnum. And his museum moving to Brooklyn has nothing to do with you?"

I hesitated a beat too long before blurting, "It's not—"

He held up his hand. "Remember this, dear one. You're blazing a path for all women. Don't make them pay for your mistakes."

"You'll see. You, Mother, everyone. When we finish the bridge, no one will care about any of this silliness. And you won't be the only hero in the family anymore." The words poured out, exposing a goal I didn't realize I had.

"At the rate that bridge is going up, I'm not sure either Mother or I will live to see that moment."

"How can you say such a thing?"

He tapped his chest. "People in our family are like pet goldfish. Polite enough to die before you have a chance to get tired of us."

"You're being morose. Is it your problems with the army? Have they not yet come to their senses and restored your rank?" I retrieved the papers PT had flung.

"Afraid not. Old Sheridan refuses to back down. I'm still a coward in his eyes, and Grant backs him up."

"You mustn't give up. You did the right thing and probably saved hundreds of Union soldiers."

"History will show the truth, dear."

"History? You're here, flesh and blood. You deserve recognition and honor, not living under this cloud of suspicion. It's not right."

He patted my hand as he helped square up the stack of paper. "You worry about my reputation when it is yours I came to talk about. It's enough that we and all our loved ones know what happened in the war. Focus on getting Washington well and building the bridge. That's far more important than my rank."

"Come. I'm sure Wash is eager to see you."

"There's one more thing," GK said just above a whisper, giving me a chill. "I wonder if I did the wrong thing, back in the war. For you, I mean."

"Whatever are you talking about?"

"Sometimes, I think I pushed you and Wash together. With good intentions, of course. You were a wild filly, and my instinct was to protect you. From yourself, actually."

"Don't be ridiculous."

"I thought Washington perfect for you. Strong, stable, a good influence."

"He is."

"But perhaps you belonged with someone closer to your own temperament. You might be happier if I had allowed you to find him on your own."

"Do you think someone of my temperament could be led into a marriage not of her choosing?" I took his hand, and we headed to the parlor.

"I am rather persuasive." He squeezed my hand.

"Well, you can clear your mind of this nonsense. I married the right man, for the right reasons. You simply found him before I did."

The lines in his face softened.

"My marriage is all twisted up with the bridge for now. Wash grew up in the family business, but it's new to me and rather difficult. And he's suffered so. But we love each other, and we'll overcome this."

I was glad GK couldn't see my face at that moment. If he did, he might have detected a lack of confidence in my own words. If I were to be fully truthful, PT occupied a large and growing place in my heart while Wash seemed to be pushing me away.

GK and I joined the others, now including Millie, in the parlor, pausing at the doorframe so as not to interrupt. The fire had burned down, and the timbers glowed red, the scent of smoke warm and relaxing.

"Eleanor, this is a thing of beauty." Wash must have been speaking out of politeness, for Eleanor was not the most talented seamstress. Her square was mottled with brown lumps.

"I've always thought GK was striking," Carrie said to Millie.

"Didn't he send you alone on a mission through enemy territory?" asked Henrietta.

"That he did." Wash reclined on the chaise, inspecting the women's handiwork as they filed past him, his eyes magnified by reading glasses.

"Was that before or *after* you started courting his sister?"

GK laughed, giving away our position, and the ladies beckoned us in.

"Ooh, do tell us the rest of the story," said Carrie. "It might turn up in my next book."

Wash nodded, held up his hand to shake GK's. "Just before Gettysburg, General Warren sent me home to New Jersey. My father had surveyed Pennsylvania extensively, and his maps were critical to our mission. After six straight days and nights of riding home and back to retrieve the documents, my thoughts turned to finding someplace, anyplace, to rest my weary bones." He lit his cigar and studied its smoldering tip.

"Go on!" said his admirers.

"I came upon a home along a lonely stretch of road through Pennsylvania farmland. Weeds had overgrown the walk, threaded through roses that had gone rangy. Glass from broken windows littered the front porch. I knocked but wasn't surprised when no one answered. I creaked open the door to a parlor—not dissimilar from this one, save the overturned furniture and mice scurrying about.

"I settled myself on the floor for a nap. Although it was the end of June, it was quite chilly in that old stone house, and I fumbled about for a blanket, being too lazy to return to my saddlebag.

"I lit a match and spied a cedar chest, marveling at my luck as I opened it." He struck a flame for effect in our parlor, his face eerily aglow in the dark. "But the old blanket folded on top wouldn't budge. I tugged harder, and it flew open, revealing the head of a woman."

"Eeeeeck," the ladies screamed in unison.

"So what did you do? Get back on the horse and skedaddle?" Carrie had taken out her journal and was furiously scribbling notes.

"No, I curled up with the blanket and fell blissfully to sleep, waking every so often, wondering about my dear departed companion." He caught my eye. "But I'm afraid the hour is late, and I should draw my storytelling to a close."

"Please, do go on. I love war stories," PT said.

"Very well then." Wash cast a sidelong glance at PT. "The following morning, desirous of returning the blanket to its rightful place, I creaked open the chest. But instead of a dead woman—"

PT interjected, "He found a lovely marble bust. A likeness of Martha Washington, was it not? Quite a treasure!" He laughed and slapped his thigh.

The ladies laughed too, but Wash glared at him, then at me, no doubt realizing I had shared the story with PT.

Later, PT and the ladies having departed, I tidied up and packed my work satchel. Wash, still propped on his pillows, handed me the daily journal. Unable to write, he dictated his orders. Although no longer necessary for ordinary planning, I hewed to the ritual to keep him involved.

"A productive day?" he asked.

"Somewhat." I yawned, tapping my pen on the journal.

"Phineas is helpful to you?"

"He gives good advice and provides comic relief."

Wash answered with a grunt.

"What?" I sighed.

"His humor escapes me."

I shrugged and picked up diagrams. "Have you made up your mind?"

"About what?"

"About officially turning over responsibility for the bridge."

"You seem to have things well in control." He waved at the diagrams in my hand. "Finally recognize you don't need me?"

"That's not what I meant. Martin can—"

"This is my father's bridge!" He thumped his fist on the divan.

"As you remind me every day. No one's forgetting that."

"He designed it, but he isn't here. Still, it is being built. Because *I* am here for him."

"You're here for him? You sit around drinking whiskey and telling stories while I feed the circling sharks!"

"Perhaps if you stop feeding him, he'll go away."

His face had fallen in defeat. I bit my tongue before I said something hurtful.

As I tucked the journal in my satchel, a wave of realization swept over me. Wash would neither return to work nor relinquish responsibility to another chief engineer. I was not just a messenger, filling a momentary need. Building this bridge would be my cross to bear—for him. My own goals and dreams, of nobly advancing women's causes or riding a horse through rolling hills of Kentucky, vanished like pebbles thrown into the sea.

I tossed and turned all that night. The responsibility was far too great. I had not the education nor the experience to accept it. I had to find someone else. But then I realized I wasn't alone; there were capable assistant engineers with whom to consult. Papa's design was said to be a work of genius. This was a matter of ensuring a plan was followed. Then again, how was I to know if it was?

The next morning, I went downstairs to the library to collect Papa's original plans. The room echoed with PT's laughter and GK's warnings. I smelled whiskey and tobacco, GK's hair balm, and Wash's minty liniment. I slumped into Wash's chair and closed my eyes, rubbed the walnut roundels, conjuring a genie to appear with answers. Upon opening them, there was nothing but Wash's neat rows of books. *Books.* All his texts were right here. I had perused the most basic ones in Cincinnati, but now I had more framework in which to understand them. I went to the stack labeled *Year One*, climbed the ladder, and slipped out the first of a thousand books.

TWENTY-TWO

No one wanted the Brooklyn caisson filled with concrete and sealed forever more than I. But the reports from foreman Young were worrying. While in the caisson, supervising the flowing of concrete down wooden chutes, he noticed signs of more widespread fire damage. It was a huge decision whether or not to cease the work, one that could only be done by the chief engineer.

I needed to enter the caisson to see the damage for myself, then try to get Wash to make a decision. Both were dreaded and risky tasks. Without consulting Wash, I steeled my resolve, donned my bloomer costume, and headed to the work site.

I spoke with no one, merely waved greetings at the workers on the tower top as I headed to the now unguarded hatch. Reviewing the posted safety precautions didn't dampen my resolve. After all, I had written most of them.

I opened the hatch, climbed down a few steps into the air lock chamber, then sealed the door after me. Then I stepped down the long ladder, through the narrow passageway between courses and courses of cold stone, to the lower hatch. After opening a valve to equalize the air pressure, I unlatched and pushed open the hatch door. The caisson greeted me with the rotten-egg stench of sulfur and the musk of sweat.

I heard voices in the far corner and followed them. As Wash had described, sounds transmitted in unexpected ways—the rattle of wheelbarrows and ting of hammers melded into a hodgepodge that seemed to bounce from wall to wall.

I had imagined a cave-like atmosphere, but it was more like a very large, damp cellar. Great piers of bricks stood from floor to ceiling in a grid pattern, giving a sense of stability. The limelights cast deep shadows, disguising whether an object was two or twenty feet away.

Foreman Young, his dark hair fringing from his slouchy cap, approached me. "Mrs. Roebling, I didn't expect you."

"Mr. Roebling needs his rest. I'm a trusted set of eyes and ears by now. Let me see the fire damage."

He guided me to the area of concern. "This is where the fire started."

The wood ceiling was pockmarked with concrete patches and drill holes.

I craned my neck at ceiling beams in various states of repair, some charred, other, lighter-colored ones that were replacements. "I think we need to replace this beam."

"Right. I'll see to it. But that isn't what most concerns me. Look over here." He led me another twelve feet, closer to the caisson corner.

Wispy curls of smoke emanated from the drill holes on the ceiling. My heart sank. Despite thoroughly drenching the roof structure with hoses, something in its layers was still burning.

I looked at other areas of the ceiling to see if there were other signs of smoke. But it hardly mattered. The complex roof structure was a maze of wood; flames could trickle up and down it like a game of Jacob's ladder.

"We have to flood the caisson," I said.

Young planted his hands on his hips. "By whose authority?"

"Mine."

"I disagree. We should speed up the concrete process. That will put the fire out, once and for all."

I vacillated for a moment. But if I was to be in charge, I had to make decisions, and this one was pretty clear. In fact, Wash and I had already discussed doing it if necessary. "If you want to run back and inform Mr. Roebling, by all means do so. Be certain to advise him how this was somehow overlooked." I found an iron bar and a ladder, which I dragged under one of the smoking holes. Teetering on the fourth rung, I hammered with the bar until I bashed through a good piece of patched ceiling. "Tell him the fire's not quite out and that it's been smoldering for weeks and you want a little reassurance—" I punched a hole big enough to poke my head through. "But while you're experiencing one of the world's worst tempers, I'll be here, flooding the goddamned caisson."

꩜

After evacuating all the workers from the caisson, Young and I sloshed in waist-high muck as river water gushed in through hoses.

"Should have flooded it in the first place," Young said.

I smiled to myself. One small battle won.

Creaks and squeaks filled the air, followed ominously by a loud groaning noise. Nails popped from the outer walls and sang past us. I checked a gauge. The hoses were allowing air to escape around them, and the air pressure was dropping.

"I know why you didn't. It's risky," I said.

Maintaining enough air pressure to keep the caisson from collapsing and the humans inside it alive was a delicate balance. Even a small opening, such as the ones caused by the hoses passing through, caused a vacuum effect, with the air flowing from an area of high density to lower density.

The side walls bulged. I turned a valve handle to increase the air pressure, but the needle on the gauge continued to fall. "We need more pressure! Go topside, and turn on the standby compressor," I yelled. "And turn all the water pumps full on."

"You have to come. I'm not leaving you alone down here!" Young tugged at my arm.

"I've got to open all the air valves. Go. Now!" I ordered as bricks tumbled from the piers and the walls trembled. My vision started to darken around the edges. I took several deep breaths. Thankfully, much of the caisson was filled with concrete, and it shouldn't take too long to regain pressure in the smaller open area. But I had to remain conscious. Pushing aside feelings of panic, I opened my mouth wide and breathed as deeply as I could.

The extra compressor rumbled on above; it had to be done now. I took a deep breath and held it, then dove down into the water. The cold bit into my flesh, the water turbid and grating on my eyes. Blindly, I turned the valves to raise the air pressure, their usual squeaks a hollow bellow under the water.

Coming back up for a breath, there was a welcome *whoosh* from the air supply duct. As I sucked in oxygen, the band of terror around my chest loosened. But then the waist-deep water started swirling and rising rapidly. My mind spun with an image of Elizabeth thrashing in the rippling current. The panic I had successfully tamped down returned like a lion for the kill. It wasn't too late; I could get out now. Let Young do this or someone— anyone—else. I felt myself sucked into the river, heard Elizabeth's terrified screams.

No! I fought back. Felt Wash's arms around me in France, my white dress floating in the calm river, his words caressing my ears. "*It's all right. I've got you.*" My panic subsided, and my thoughts cleared once again.

Soon, the creaking and moaning of the walls stopped. But the water was now up to my chest and advancing steadily. I spit out grit and the taste of metal. I had only a few minutes to get out.

I dove down to the exit hatch, turning the wheel for the latch as far as I could before coming up for another deep breath. Descending a second time, I turned the wheel to full open and yanked with all my strength, but the hatch door didn't budge. Another trip up for a gulp of air. I was running out of time as the water sloshed in waves against the ceiling.

I dove again, trying to force open the hatch, but the pressure of the water in the caisson was higher than the air pressure in the hatch. Bracing my legs against the sides of the hatch chute, I strained against it with all my might. The hatch cracked open but quickly slammed shut again. I pushed myself back up for air. My head bumped against the ceiling as I drew in what I feared might be my last breath. I paddled furiously to keep my head above the water, gagging and choking. My muscles were rapidly tiring, and another wave of panic clouded my thinking.

A pipe hung from the ceiling just a few feet away. I kicked and stroked my way over to it with what seemed like my last ounces of strength. I grabbed on to it and forced my mind and body to calm, taking shaky, shuddering breaths. I considered diving down again to adjust the valves letting in river water, but I wasn't sure I had the strength.

The water-muted sound of a sledgehammer clanged at the hatch. Then I heard water rushing into the air lock chamber. Mr. Young must be filling it to equalize the pressure. More creaking, valves opening. He was forcing in both air and water. Good. *Faster, faster*, I urged as the top of my head brushed the ceiling and the water reached my neck.

When I thought enough pressure had equalized to get the hatch open, I took some deep breaths and filled my lungs to capacity. Then I pushed off the ceiling and kicked down through eight feet of water. I repeated the pull and push maneuver with my legs until the door cracked open. My lungs burned as I pried open the hatch.

The sledgehammer clanged against the opposite side. A hazy shape appeared through the crack: Young, pushing the door from the air lock chamber. We overcame the pressure on the door as I pulled from my side until, at last, it swung open. Water gushed through the opening, shooting me through with it.

Young grabbed me under my arms and lifted me to the surface where I took a great gasp of air. Dark spots mottled my vision, and I worked my arm through a ladder rung to keep from slipping off.

"Have to close the hatch door!" Young dove back under the water.

I huffed breaths during the eternity that he was down there. I counted. Thirty seconds. Forty. What was taking him so long? My vision clearing, I slipped my arm from the ladder, preparing to rescue him. My arms and legs were dead weights. Did I even have the strength?

But while I tried to muster strength and courage, Young popped out of the water. He took a huge gulp of air before shouting, "We did it!"

I pulled myself up the ladder of the air lock, buoyed by relief. My clothes shed river water, its power over me diminished like a hurricane gone back to the sea.

Arriving home that evening after the tumult of the day, my muscles ached as they would after the first saddle ride in spring. I dripped up the stairs to the landing on the second floor. Wash sat at his desk at our bedroom window, reading Carrie's *Violets* with a magnifying glass. He rubbed his eyes, tossed the manuscript aside, and picked up a pair of dumbbells. Even with a body devastated by caisson disease, he affected an air of normalcy as he lifted the weights, while I affected every inch of river rat.

Not caring to explain my appearance or recount the day, I quietly slipped down the hall to the bath. I opened the hot water tap and filled the tub, allowing billows of steam into the room, then luxuriated in the big claw-footed tub. Each time the horror of being trapped underwater crept into my mind, I gripped the rolled top of the tub, took deep breaths, and forced the thoughts away.

Wash limped in and pulled up a chair. "I thought I heard you sneak in."

"You were concentrating so hard, I didn't want to disturb you. How is Johnny?" I played with the lavender-scented bubbles. *Heaven.*

"Asleep." He picked up a sponge, leaned over, and washed my back. I could only hope he didn't discover seaweed.

"I've missed yet another day with him." With horror, I realized I hadn't thought about him the entire day. "Was he a good boy?"

"As always."

I needn't have worried about Wash finding evidence of my misadventure unless the seaweed was enormous. His eyes were unfocused and jerky. A new bloomer costume embroidered with a violet hung near the window, the warm, moist air helping to smooth wrinkles.

"What? No peonies?"

"A single, lonely violet, I'm afraid. Close work is hard on my eyes." He squeezed out the sponge. "In honor of your friend's book. Have you read it?" He handed me a robe as I climbed out of the tub. I tried to catch a glimpse into his eyes, but he turned away.

"Not yet. Mother said there was a character I'd be interested in." We returned to our bedroom. I unwrapped the towel from my hair, then picked up the manuscript while Wash lifted his dumbbells. "*Violets*, by Carrie Beebe," I read aloud. "Mrs. Hamilton was a woman of indomitable energy and ambition. She was not ambitious of fame in a literary way, for her early education would hardly admit of that; and, though a professed Christian, she was not particularly 'zealous of good works.'"

He chuckled. "But in order to outshine her neighbors, especially in the matter of dress, she worked with a zest and energy worthy of a better cause."

"Do you think she's writing about me?"

"Perhaps. But I think Carrie's aim is to send all women a message."

"Who knew you were so intuitive?" I stood behind him and stroked his shoulders and arms. His muscles were as thick and smooth as ever, and he didn't flinch from my touch. "You seem to be improving."

"Now if I could get my bottom half to cooperate."

I kissed his neck and wriggled onto his lap. We kissed long and deeply as his hands found my breasts under my robe. The horror of the day faded as I let his warmth sink into me, let the power of his arms comfort me.

He whispered in my ear, "Carrie says all women should be like you."

A rush of warmth spread down my plexus. "Violets. Strong and faithful." I removed his shirt, ran my hand across the rough golden hairs of his chest. "You can trample them, but they'll find a way to spring back up." I shrugged off my robe.

He cleared his throat. "I know my flowers." He gave me a gentle nudge off his lap. "I'm sorry, dear. Another time?"

Stumbling away from him, I wrapped my robe around me, crushed worse than any violet.

"So, where are we? Progress report: is the fire damage repaired?" His eyes zigzagged.

I swallowed my disappointment and replied evenly, "In process. We found a bit more, but we're preparing to fill the rest of the caisson with concrete."

He handed me a pile of journals and a pencil. "Excellent. It should be done in a certain order. Make note of this..."

A chill began at my sodden head and worked its way down to my toes.

TWENTY-THREE

Wash was fortunate to spend much more time with Johnny, and I meant to show my son what took me away from him so frequently. We were enjoying unusually warm weather for early summer, and I chose a brilliant Sunday morning when the work site would be relatively quiet.

I was unwilling to subject Johnny to hazardous conditions or the coarse language of workers, so we boarded a huge supply barge anchored to a pier next to the tower. Here, blocks of stone created a maze in which we played hide-and-seek. The tower, now rising over twenty feet above the water, taller than most of the buildings in Brooklyn, cast its shadow on us.

After our game, I settled Johnny with a slate and piece of chalk so I could do a bit of work. I had explained to the bridge committee that since the color of the granite stones varied slightly, coming as they did from twenty different quarries, they should be mixed in their placement to lessen the chance of the tower appearing mottled when complete. This suggestion was met with enthusiasm but had the unfortunate consequence of the task falling to me to categorize the stone. I was noting the location of a particularly dark batch when I called to Johnny, "Almost done, sweetie. Such a good boy..." I turned to where I had left him, but he was gone.

"Johnny? JOHN!" I searched the barge, racing around the stacks of stones we had hidden in moments ago, then scrambled on top of a stack for a better view. My body tingled and sweated with panic. He was nowhere to be seen. Climbing back down, with panic narrowing my vision, I heard a *splash* near the side of the barge. I rushed over. Johnny was in the water, flailing his arms, his head barely afloat.

I leapt off the barge and belly-flopped the six feet down into the water. Gasping for breath, I grabbed Johnny's shirt collar as he sank beneath the surface. He lunged for me, wrapped his arms around my neck. Fighting the current and my billowing dress, I pulled and kicked through the water until at last I reached a ladder on the pier. Breathless, I gasped, "Take hold of the ladder, sweetie."

He did as he was told and scampered up the ladder, no worse for his adventure. Soon, a gaggle of children joined him. As I dragged myself and my anchor of a dress up the ladder, I felt myself once again being grabbed under the arms and hoisted aloft. I rubbed the salty sting from my eyes and saw O'Brien.

"You all right now?"

I nodded, my teeth clenched against my old adversary, the river.

His six children engaged Johnny in a rough-and-tumble game of tag. Patrick and his five younger siblings, the youngest about seven years old, were all dressed in bathing costumes and had left a trail of towels and lunch pails across the pier.

O'Brien pulled a towel from around his neck and handed it to me, but a thread caught on his silver chain and locket. It drew me awkwardly close to him for a moment. He laughed it off, then modestly pulled a shirt over his bathing costume.

"Bit of advice, ma'am. 'Tis quite dangerous to swim in full dress. Go on," he said as he waved to his children, who were clamoring to go in the water. "Your children swim?"

"Not yet. We only have the one." I shivered into the towel. Bile rising in my throat, I didn't want to talk. I wanted to close up like the wet clam I was.

A child in the river shouted a protest, eliciting a response from O'Brien. "Patrick! You'll not be dunking your brother!" He turned back to me. "Of course, wee John, nearly four years old now, isn't he? 'Bout time for another one, nah?"

I winced, although I knew he meant no harm. "Afraid not."

"Sorry, Mrs. Roebling. I wasn't meaning to…" His face reddened.

"Not to worry, Mr. O'Brien. It's lovely to watch your children play."

"We enjoy coming out here on Sundays. Don't be telling our Heavenly Father!" He raised his eyes toward the sky. "Join us with the wee bairn, won't you now?"

Johnny and I came at slack tide each Sunday thereafter for swimming lessons.

Our first lesson fell on a gloriously warm day, so I walked the half mile to the river, pulling Johnny in his wagon. It seemed every shopkeeper was out sweeping the sidewalk in front of his business. I nodded greetings and exchanged pleasantries with many.

At some point, I noticed a change. Was it my imagination, or were people turning their backs toward me? A sweet elderly Italian woman, who was always washing the windows of the family bakery, used to scurry into the shop and return with a sweet for Johnny. By July, she merely pursed her lips and slopped her rag back on the window. As the weeks passed, I was certain I was being shunned. I winced, hearing words such as *harlot* and *whore* coming from doorways of brownstones, just loud enough for me decipher.

Was it our swimming lessons with O'Brien, unchaperoned by my husband, or my audacity to work in a man's world that set their tongues wagging? It would do no good to confront them, I knew. I held my head high and proceeded with our Sunday journeys on foot. On other days of the week, I rode to save time, but I wanted Johnny to experience the neighborhood on our day together, despite our cool reception. Let them talk. Gossip has always been spread, and there is nothing to do but to live one's life as best one can.

One afternoon, we were having difficulty making our way through Brooklyn Heights. Small clumps of people blocked the sidewalk, making no allowance for my son and me. We crossed into the street, jeers and laughter following us. People poured out of residences and shops that should have been closed on Sunday in some sort of organized protest.

A neighbor with whom I had some acquaintance ambled toward me. A large man, he had a kind face and graying hair that seemed to recede from his forehead, only to slip down his neck. He was dressed in a fine black suit, no doubt having just given a sermon at Plymouth church. The preacher lifted his top hat. "A pleasure to see you, Mrs. Roebling."

"Reverend Beecher, a fine day to be out." I nodded my greeting. The dozens of people who had gathered about quieted. "It seems I'm having a bit of a problem gaining passage with so many others enjoying the fresh air."

Henry Ward Beecher was a beloved resident who had fought against slavery, not with a gun but with his eloquence, money, and influence. I greatly admired him. He was also known as quite the ladies' man, and to engage in conversation with him risked setting the gears of gossip in motion anew.

"Allow me." He gave a small bow. Addressing the throng, he bellowed in his deep, resonant voice, "Clear the way, my friends and neighbors. Let this fine woman and her child pass."

Like Moses splitting the Red Sea, he walked with me through the crowd, down the hill through the several more blocks to the water's edge. I thanked him when we reached our destination, the pier where O'Brien and his children had already gathered.

"It was my very great pleasure." He slipped a small card from his pocket. Engraved upon it was his name, and below it, *President, American Woman Suffrage Association*. "We meet at the church on Tuesday evenings. We would be honored for you to join us."

I ran my tongue along my teeth.

"Don't worry if we're not your denomination. All are welcome. Why, we have Jews and Catholics and—"

"Perhaps when I have a bit more spare time," I answered in kindness, although a closer association with Reverend Beecher would further complicate my life. I tucked the card in my canvas swim bag. "I do hope to rejoin the movement soon."

"Splendid. You'll call on me if you have any further difficulties?" He waved toward the dispersing crowd.

I nodded, and he tipped his hat before proceeding down the street with his rocking gait, stopping to converse with all on the way.

Every week, the tower grew one course of granite stones higher, and the pier offered a pleasant view. One Sunday, as the days grew shorter and cooler, slack tide arrived near dusk. O'Brien and Johnny emerged from the water, glinting in the golden light. The sight of O'Brien with my sweet son nestled in his muscled arms took my breath away.

"A regular fish, that he is!" O'Brien set Johnny down on the pier.

I swept my little boy into my arms, cool and dripping. "Mama is so proud of you!" I planted a kiss on his cool, plump cheek before he squirmed away. "Is anyone hungry?"

I offered cold chicken and biscuits, and the children swarmed like locusts. O'Brien and I carried our dinner a few steps away and sat on the pier, swinging our legs over the water.

I wrapped a napkin around the small end of a drumstick and sank my teeth into its peppery crust. "Your wife—does she not swim?"

"Died in childbirth, God bless 'er." He wiped his mouth, then kissed the locket pendant he wore around his neck.

"I'm terribly sorry. Raising six children on your own. And yet so dedicated to your work."

"Blessed to have the job, ma'am. Colonel Roebling has been very generous. Took me out of the caisson, he did. Oh, the lads tease me for that."

"You've taken care of him as well. I am grateful."

"Ah, despite everything, I'd do anything for the colonel, even if he did nearly put a bullet through my heart."

I gagged on a bite of biscuit. "Come again?"

"Maybe that's a story he hasn't told," O'Brien mumbled.

"Tell me. You can't say something like that, then leave it in the wind."

"Ah, ya got me there." He pointed at the pink and purple bands in the sky. "It was nigh about sunset, just like this. I was in your brother's division, don't you know."

I didn't know but nodded anyway.

"Had my private stripe by then, so that made me more seasoned than most." He chuckled. "I was assigned a horse and a mission to find the colonel—lieutenant back then—deep in enemy territory. I rode that horse hard, and after a day's ride, I found him near York, right where General Warren said he should be." He stopped and smiled as if the story was done. "Time to be packing up," he yelled to the children.

"Go on," I encouraged.

He folded a towel and wrapped another around his neck. "I reined my horse in when I saw the lieutenant. His mount hung its head and could barely take another step, and he himself didn't seem much better—in danger of falling asleep and sliding out of the saddle. My horse whinnied, which woke him. In a flash, he had his revolver raised and pointing squarely at me chest. I said the password, and the colonel—I mean lieutenant—holstered his sidearm." O'Brien slid the locket back and forth on its chain.

"The general was worried. Thinking Roebling was knackered from his long ride, he sent me to check on him. He had real important maps of Gettysburg. The lieutenant said he was hoping to get a night's rest, and he'd never climb in a saddle again once the war was done. 'It's only a day's ride from here, sir. You could have a rest and be there by 'morrow's eve,' I said. That would have been soon enough. But he fetched maps from his saddlebag and handed one to me. 'You take this back tonight, Private. I'll follow with the other one tomorrow. Split them up, in the event one of us manages to survive.'"

O'Brien hung his head, his eyes moist. "I gave him a telegram. It was getting dark by then, and he lit a match from his cigar to read it.

"'Congratulations. Seems like you should be smoking this,' he said and offered me his cigar." O'Brien's voice grew soft. "I told him the child would be our sixth. But my wife was having difficulty. 'Sorry to hear that,' he said. I gave him another letter, this one from the general himself. 'My orders are to continue on to New York to attend to my wife, sir. If you can spare me.'" O'Brien looped the locket from around his neck, kissed it, then handed it to me. "This was hers."

"Did you make it back in time?" I ran my finger over the locket, its monogram nearly worn smooth.

He shook his head. "He said, 'This is war, Private.'" O'Brien eyes were wet and red-rimmed; it hurt to hold his gaze. "He told me to get the map back to the general. I started to argue, but the look of him, worn down like an old shoe, I had no choice.

"I took the map and went on my way while he went into an abandoned house for a rest." O'Brien saluted the ghost of time past.

I handed back the locket. "It seems you've earned a special place in his heart."

"I wish to be treated like any other man." He yanked the towel from his neck and snapped it sharply. "See what happened when he assigned that gobshite Einar to the caisson in my stead."

With O'Brien and I engrossed in conversation, his children had snuck in one more swim. They climbed the wooden wall that surrounded the construction site and leapt into the water from it while Johnny helped me pack the basket. "Did you see her again?"

He shook his head.

"I'm so sorry." How awful Wash must have felt.

The children shouted from the water. "Da! Come see this!"

Patrick's arm dripped with dark-brown goop. We rushed over to investigate, offering a hand to help them out of the water. Each of the children had dark slime coating various appendages. They hopped about, waving their hands and holding their noses at the noxious smell. We grabbed towels and wiped the sticky substance off them. In the water next to the tower floated a viscous slick. I grabbed an empty jar from the dinner basket and collected a sample of the slimy river water.

Later that evening, Wash lathered Johnny while he played with toy sailboats in the tub. "Why, exactly, do you have one of my workers teaching Johnny to swim?"

Johnny blinked his big blue eyes, looking like an elf with a tall hat of white bubbles.

Wash's irritation puzzled me since we had been taking the lessons for several weeks. "O'Brien offered after witnessing your son's near drowning."

"For which you were totally negligent and irresponsible. Bringing a child to the work site! And a picnic with a worker and his family? Emily, you've lost the distinction between work and home life." He made a game of rinsing Johnny off, using a colander to create a rain shower.

"I most certainly have not. Anytime you choose to accompany your wife and son to work, to a picnic, to any activity at all, you are most welcome. But don't expect us to hide ourselves from society; that's *your* peculiar way." Johnny stood up in the tub, and I wrapped him in a towel. "And workers are just people like us. Sharing a meal with a lovely family should not be forbidden due to some archaic notion of class."

"It's not class. It's boundaries for those over whom you have authority. It isn't appropriate to ask special favors of them. Don't you see that?"

I sucked in my cheeks. "I suppose you're right."

"The river is not a safe place to swim. You of all people should know that. Do you think O'Brien merely happened by the day Johnny fell?"

"What are you saying?"

"Nothing. But I shall continue his lessons myself, in a more appropriate place. There's a nice lake near Trenton." He finger-combed Johnny's curls. "I can still swim, you know."

I softened my tone. "I do take your point. A lake would be better. And I do try to maintain a professional relationship with all the workers." A picture of O'Brien and Wash during the war flashed in my mind. "It seems you have some fondness for him and he for you. Did you ask him to check in on me?"

"He's a good worker. Time for a story, Johnny." He grasped our son's hand and stepped out of the room, no doubt aware of having breached the very rule he had asked me to follow.

After we put Johnny to bed, I joined Wash in the library where I had left the basket from our picnic on the pier. A waft of pungent air filled the room when I opened it. I lifted out the jar of tainted water.

"Good God, what's that smell?" Wash poured whiskey.

"I thought this strange. The children swam into it by chance, and I thought it might mean something."

He opened the jar, took a whiff, then stuck his fingers in it and rubbed them together.

"Like turpentine. Rotten turpentine," I said.

"Where was it coming from, exactly?"

"Seems to be bubbling up from the caisson."

"Burnt wood smells like this as it disintegrates." He screwed the lid back on the jar.

"But we flooded the caisson and filled every last space in the roof with concrete."

"What? I wasn't told of this flooding." He slammed the jar onto a table.

"We discussed it might be necessary. I—"

"We'll deal with that later. Our concern now is that there are burnt and rotting timbers in the caisson roof. As the wood decomposes, the wet concrete will settle into the empty spaces, causing cracking and instability in the hardened concrete. The more weight we put on it, the worse it will get."

"But doesn't all wood eventually decompose?"

"To some extent, yes. But it won't matter once the concrete is set." He went to the bookcase and, after running his hand down dozens of volumes, selected one. "It's here."

It was a text I had had considerable difficulty with, reading it at a time where very different problems were occurring. "I'm afraid I rather skimmed over that one."

"We'll correct that bad habit. From now on, you come to me with questions and take the exams at the ends of the chapters."

My spirits lifted. He wanted to tutor me. This was more interest than I had seen from him in months.

But my relief in his seeming return to the man he had been soon faded as he slammed the book shut.

"We have to chisel out every last bit of the concrete in the roof and replace the wooden beams."

"That will take months!" I cried, aghast.

"How did you let this happen? I gave specific instructions!"

"You're leaping to conclusions, Wash. Maybe we won't find more damaged beams."

"Oh, you'll find them. Or you're not looking in the right goddamn place!"

❧

As bearer of this disagreeable news to the workers, I thought it might be more palatable if I assisted in the solution. I climbed through the hatch and down the ladder into the caisson, then up through the ceiling into the roof structure where the foot-wide beams crisscrossed in a thicket. I was met by Dunn, whom I had put in charge of the concrete excavation.

His head jerked at the sight of me. "Mrs. Roebling! This is no place for a lady."

"I've been here before and survived, thank you. And by the way, my being here is not to be known outside of the workmen."

"As you wish, ma'am."

"Now, how can I help?" I held out my hands, clad in heavy work gloves.

Dunn ran his fingers through his short strawberry-blond hair. "I don't think—"

"Shall I start over there?" I picked up an ax and pointed it to an area free of workers.

"Well, if you insist, the corners are the hardest for the men to get to. Only one of them can fit in the tight spaces. Maybe you'd have better luck."

Covered in soot and breathing foul air, we crept on our bellies or lay flat on our backs, prying and chiseling out concrete and exposing charred beams. After I dug out the corners, I ferried buckets of concrete bits and burnt wood to the next worker on the chain.

Dunn brought me a canteen of water. "You're a most unusual lady."

"I'll accept that as a compliment." The water was welcome, my throat as scorched as the charred beams. "I've been impressed with your work and your loyalty."

His face lit up. "Did you know I started with the senior Mr. Roebling? I waved a signal flag from Manhattan on the very first day."

"You did? I saw it." Oh, the joy of that moment. I could see the red flag waving across the water as if it were yesterday. But then, the horror. "I do remember you visiting Mr. Roebling after the accident. You were quite concerned...for your job."

Dunn's face reddened. "You heard that?" He shook his head. "I was a foolish youngster."

"It was a difficult time."

"But still, I'm awful sorry. And to think, you and Colonel Roebling kept me on."

"There isn't one among us who hasn't said something they regret. Like a spreading fire, words, once they slip through our lips, can't be taken back. And how onerous can be the repairs."

Bumps and bruises and blistered hands proved me ill-suited for excavation work, but I was glad to have had the experience. I kept my participation a secret, not needing to read of my scandalous behavior in the newspaper.

A month later, every roof beam had been replaced and the fire damage repaired. I personally inspected it, the smell of new wood a pleasant change.

A dozen or so people gathered on top of the tower to celebrate as workers poured the last concrete down the supply shaft. C. C. Martin and Mr. Young pressed in their handprints and wrote their names in the patch, followed by the other workers. They invited me to do the same, but it didn't seem right to add my own. I still considered myself a guide, a stand-in for Wash. It was his and Papa's prints that should be there. I bit my lips to hold back tears, but the others cheered as a crane lowered a stone, sealing their handprints and the caisson forever.

The tower grew quickly after that, and for a while, my duties were limited to the aesthetics of the granite and other design elements. We ordered a supply of light-colored limestone for particular layers. This created pleasing stripes, as in Papa's Cincinnati bridge, to emphasize buttresses and add interest to long stretches of tower. By then, I was well into the third month of studying Wash's textbooks and now, with his help, I was no longer puzzled by the principles and terms of construction.

The second caisson, on the Manhattan side, was towed into position in September. We had learned so much in Brooklyn, its descent was less problematic, much to our relief. Wash was feeling much better and had mounted a campaign with Dr. Smith and me for him to return to the work site. The New York caisson was still in the early stages of its descent, so air pressures were not yet a problem, and we all agreed on his limited return.

Wash abhorred office work and left it to me. I felt rather displaced to be once again limited to the more feminine role but reminded myself to be happy with Wash's recovery. One afternoon, he surprised me, arriving in the office with a sack of fresh pretzels. "Look what I found being sold on the street."

"It seems every street vendor offers something you need."

"How can I resist urchins hawking newspapers and men selling suspenders?"

I smiled at his bright mood as he presented me with the warm treat. Its malty, yeasty aroma was cut with the taste of salt. It reminded me of Prussia, and I could see why Wash just had to buy them. "How are things progressing in Manhattan?"

"Splendid. The caisson is dropping like a cannonball down a well. Hardly a boulder to blow up, more's the pity. But I'm glad you missed the first bit. Seems that particular part of the river was a favorite dumping ground for sewage."

"I know. The stench burned noses all the way to Brooklyn."

"Happily, the stink is gone. But now we're having the opposite problem we had with the first caisson. The river silt to be evacuated is so fine that it falls right through the teeth of the digger. Sometimes the digger comes up nearly empty."

The bells on the door jingled, and Farrington entered. He removed his bowler with a gauze-wrapped hand. "Mrs. Roebling, Colonel, have you a moment?"

"What happened to your hand?" I scraped back my chair and got up to investigate.

He unwound the gauze to reveal a round, four-inch-wide red blister across his palm. "Clumsy me, I was fiddling with an air supply tube and crossed signals with the men above. They opened the seal to the tube, and my hand got sucked in."

I tilted my head in confusion.

"When they open the hatch on top, the higher pressure in the caisson causes the air to rush out through the tube."

"Does it hurt?" I asked.

Farrington rewrapped the gauze. "It'll be fine."

"Hmm." I glanced at Wash and Farrington in turn. "How strong is this effect?"

"See what happened to my hand. So powerful, it took two men to pull me away."

"Strong enough to carry silt?"

"Why yes, of course."

Wash pointed his pretzel. "What are you thinking, Em?"

"The silt is too fine for the digger, correct? Suppose you pile the silt you need to evacuate near a supply tube, open the hatch, and let air flow evacuate it from the caisson?"

Wash and Farrington looked at each other, then at me, mouths agape.

"Try it and report back to me," Wash said to him.

"Don't you want to see for yourself?"

They traded another glance. Wash pulled a pretzel from the sack, offered it to Farrington.

"Well, I'm off to test Mrs. Roebling's idea." In a sudden hurry, Farrington took his pretzel, slapped on his hat, and was out the door.

Wash studied his palms, his fingers interlaced. "I've been thinking."

"That's what you do." I winked. It was an exchange we had many times.

"Seems I'm not the thinker in the family." He leaned forward and held out his hand. "The caisson is dropping fast. We're already approaching twenty pounds of pressure."

I took his hand in mine; the dreaded tremble had returned. The blood drained from my face. *Oh no, not again. We were so careful.*

He laced his fingers back together, avoided my eyes. There was more. I wrapped my arms around myself.

"They carried me to the ferry on a stretcher. I best not return to the caisson."

My vision of Wash returning to normal faded like a dream upon awakening.

TWENTY-FOUR

1872

I resumed daily visits to the work site, checking on progress on the Brooklyn tower and making trips to the Manhattan site as well. Johnny was now four and often begged to come with me. But the horror of him falling off that barge was still too fresh for me to permit it.

My idea for evacuating the silt worked well. Too well, in fact. The silt came up with such force, it created a geyser, spraying water, silt, and pebbles for yards and causing some minor injuries.

"We have to deflect the silt," I said to Farrington.

He agreed and set up a cap of iron pipe in an elbow shape to aim the matter toward a barge alongside the work site. But the force of the spray wore through the iron in a matter of days. We changed the material to a block of granite, angled for effect. That lasted longer, and we replaced the stone as needed.

I crossed the river so often, the ferry captain gave me my own seat up front next to him, which assisted greatly with my tendency toward seasickness. The captain and I contemplated the plan to suspend the ferries when the bridge was completed. Was there not enough interest and population to support both a bridge and a ferry?

The answer to that question was both complex and disturbing. I gained some insight from PT when he dropped by the office one day. He was not a once-a-month on the third sort of visitor, more like an every-two-days to every-two-months type. This both suited my love of a pleasant surprise and disrupted my routine.

"I've been wondering how I might be of assistance in increasing the pace of construction." PT stretched out in the armchair across from my desk, fingers tented over his lap, chin resting on his chest.

"Do you have something in mind?" I closed the ledger I had been working on.

"Well, not specifically. But my interest in the project depends upon completion sometime this decade." He fetched a jelly bean from my jar, tossed it into the air, and caught it with his mouth. "I'm not alone in this. Your benefactors and supportive populace will fade away if the goal seems too remote."

I scowled. "We are making good progress. Would you risk the bridge's sound construction to save time?"

He scratched his woolly sideburn, rose from his chair, and planted a finger on the wall map. "Bridgeport, Connecticut."

I joined him at the map, the fruity jelly beans an interesting counterpoint to his spicy scent. "Your hometown."

"Exactly. And here is Castle Garden." His finger traced a path to the Battery in lower Manhattan.

"Where immigrants are processed." I shrugged. "I don't understand the connection."

"There isn't one. That's the point. Immigration follows the easiest, lowest-cost route." His finger swept out in rays from the Battery. "Extended families and new generations follow those already established."

"So?"

"To be blunt, the people of Connecticut desire to keep out the riffraff. The bridge will open all of Long Island to those with a penny in their pocket and two legs to carry them. The longer the bridge takes to build, the more poor immigrants find their way to Connecticut instead."

My gut churned. "That seems rather un-American. We're a nation of immigrants."

"And I am deeply in favor of legal and organized immigration. I could not run my businesses without the talent from abroad. But how much better to have a haven where the new arrivals can live and work among their former countrymen while they learn a new language and skills? Then, when they are ready, which may take a generation or two, let them spread out, bringing new blood and energy to the states."

"I sense a more selfish interest."

"Indeed. Tenements will significantly deflate the value of my Connecticut properties. Long Island is much better suited to that way of life, and that is an unselfish observation of fact. The faster the bridge is built, the more quickly the immigrants will discover it to be the perfect home for them."

He stabbed a finger on Connecticut. "There is more money out there. And you're in need due to all the setbacks."

"And the people of Connecticut want to invest now, because of setbacks?" I raised an eyebrow.

"Certainly. And the men injured on the job. It will create a bit of public sympathy if the investment comes to light. The papers are complaining about the slow progress as well." He tapped his fingers together. "Think of all the men you can hire with new investors."

"I agree. But an attitude of 'keeping out the riffraff' would be enticing fodder for the newspapers. And I can't bear the thought of bad publicity."

Something seemed not quite right. Were we taking advantage of the injured workers or helping them? I felt a subtle shift, as if gliding down a gentle path with nothing but quicksand at the bottom. "Shall we keep our assumed reasons for their beneficence between you and me?"

"You are learning well, my Peanut."

❧

The Brooklyn tower grew as a solid unit until it reached the openings for the roadway, where stone-laying got a bit trickier. The tower divided into three sections, each surrounded by a wooden platform, rather like a giant olive fork jutting into the air. Einar called me over one day as I inspected a new stone shipment. His face and hands were laced with scars from the fire, but he had never missed a day of work. He showed me a stone that didn't quite fit.

"No, that won't do," I said. The grandeur of the towers depended on perfect alignment. The granite was delivered already cut our specifications, but occasionally some were a bit off.

He ran his hand along the protruding side. "I can't carve that much."

"Then you'll have to remove it." I dug a fingernail into the mortar. "It's not yet set."

He waved another worker over to help him. Using great iron claws, they inched the stone out. When it was nearly free, the rough surface kept the stone wedged in place. Einar wrapped his arms around the stone block and yanked while his helper pushed, their faces red as beets, veins popping in their foreheads. They cried out as the stone broke free, and the weight of the stone and the momentum sent Einar stumbling backward. He crashed through the safety rail and fell off the tower.

"Einar!" I screamed. "Good God, no!" We peered down through the gap in the rail, fearing the worst. But a cheer arose when Einar waved up at us, having landed safely in a vat of water. The investors might look down their noses at the immigrants building our bridge, but my men were as precious and brave as any soldier. I was loyal to my troops as they were to me. The thought of losing yet another of them crushed me, and I breathed a great sigh of relief.

I rented the vacated piano store next to my office and had the blocked door between the spaces reopened. We set up a play area for Miss Mann and Johnny, and frequently, the plinking of a left-behind piano passed through the walls. I had given O'Brien clerical duties, which relieved me of much paperwork while protecting him from the dangers of the work site.

Johnny became fast friends with the O'Brien children, who joined him after school. They became the brothers and sisters he lacked. It was comforting to have Johnny close by, yet behind a closed door, so that business could be carried on uninterrupted by the squeals of children. Miss Mann taught piano lessons, and the plinking gradually progressed to recognizable tunes.

Having approved a stack of supply requests, I carried them to O'Brien for action. He arranged some personal items on his desk, moving them about like pieces on a chessboard.

"Checkmate," I said, moving a small carved horse to the center of the desk.

"Don't touch that." He scooped the horse back.

"So sorry. It didn't seem delicate."

He swept the items into a drawer.

"If you're unhappy with the change in your duties, we can see about another assignment."

"No, no, I'm thankful, Mrs. Roebling. Truly I am, especially to be close to the children. But...all these maps and pictures." He waved a hand at the cluttered walls. "And those there"—he nodded toward Wash's service revolvers and other weapons mounted above framed artwork—"they put me in another mind, someplace I don't want to be."

Several prominent artists had presented Wash and GK with lifelike portraits of battle scenes. Neither of them wanted them at home nor would give them up. Once we had additional space, hanging them in the office seemed a good compromise, and mounting the weapons in boxes served to preserve them as historic artifacts, with safety in mind as well.

"I'm sorry about that, but you'll soon forget they're there—like music in the background."

"Music? *Feckin'* music? You don't know shite about it. This here?" He plucked the wooden horse from the drawer. "The colonel carved it for me. Said they could always be replaced. This was after me own got shot out from under me."

I glanced at the children, all happily occupied at the moment, then pulled up a chair. "Tell me. Tell me the worst you're able. Then perhaps I'll have a tiny inkling of what you experienced."

"Nah. I shouldn't trouble you with this. Forgive my disrespect." He waved a dismissal, but I sat firmly in place. "All right, then, if you insist. Spotsylvania, 1864." He gazed away. "We were up on a ridge, overlooking a river. The Po, I think.

"Them rebels were just across the river, fixing their rifles on us like the deer hunters they were. A bad, bad place. So many bodies. After three days of battles, we stopped burying them. May in Virginia had heat enough to fry an egg without a fire, not that we had either one. Heat makes some real unpleasant changes to a dead body. I took off my sock and wrapped it around my nose and mouth so I could keep down my hardtack." He peered at me, reading my reaction, but I remained a neutral countenance. "What the guns didn't blow up, the heat and intestinal gas did.

"The order came to move forward. But there weren't no forward but down that hill, in full sight and range of the rebs. Oh, we tried to dodge tree to tree, climbing over bodies while blasting and reloading as fast as we could. But it was no good, no good." He buried his head in his hands.

I placed a hand on his shoulder. These were the things Wash couldn't tell me. The images were so disturbing in my own mind; how haunting they must be for the men who suffered through the war. My hand rested on a shoulder on which unimaginable burdens had lain. Wash and GK as well. I willed my strength to flow from my hand to his heart, resolved to always consider the pain that others have suffered, especially those who say the least.

Then again, there were many who were quite demonstrative about their difficulties. Unions were growing in power and encouraged their members to let their grievances be known.

Soon after my talk with O'Brien, work stopped on the Manhattan side as workers went on strike. Bedrock on the Manhattan side was much deeper and quite uneven, varying from forty to over a hundred feet below the river bed. At seventy-eight feet deep, the air pressure needed to maintain the caisson was the highest that humans had been known to survive. And some workers didn't.

They carried picket signs that read *Dangerous Work, Workers Dying*, and *We've Got the Bends, They're Giving Us the Shaft*. When two workers attempted to cross the picket line, the strikers became an angry mob. The scabs tried to escape back to the streets, but the mob chased them. They were caught, thrown to the ground, and savagely beaten.

The newspaper headlines screamed of the horror. Neighbors banged on our door, shaking the papers and demanding settlement. Our financial backing shriveled.

Shortly before the strike, workers had unearthed several human skeletal remains. Although they had probably rested under the river for decades, if not centuries, they were a grim and frightening reminder to the already skittish workers.

A critical decision needed to be made, and I had to convince Wash to visit the site. The uneven bedrock was a very different situation than what we had encountered in Brooklyn. No one wanted to take the responsibility for proceeding in conditions that had never before been faced. We would have to keep his time in the caisson very brief. Even so, I felt nauseated at the thought of exposing him to the danger once again.

The ride over on the ferry was pleasant enough, the brown river smooth and faintly smelling of fish. Waves foamed about the boat with a comforting swish. Wash asked about the welfare of the workers, especially O'Brien.

"He's not on strike. He's working in the office." I shielded my eyes from the sun with my hand in order to measure his expression. "Sad about his wife. He told me how she died."

"Did he now?" Wash said matter-of-factly.

"I must have heard that marble bust story a hundred times, but you never told me you knew O'Brien in the war."

"Did he not deliver a message from me, shortly before I returned?"

I thought back to that winter morning before we were married. "That was O'Brien?"

"The very same. He got me through times no one should have to live through. Did he tell you he replaced an orderly who had been shot through the heart by a bullet intended for me?"

"Not exactly."

"I thought not. Believe me, there are plenty of war stories you don't want to hear and I don't want to tell."

"Not only war stories. You never talk about the things that bother you most."

He tap, tap, tapped his cane, watched it land on the deck. "I rode home to get maps. Father had precisely what we needed, having surveyed most of Pennsylvania. I gave half to O'Brien. Your brother got them, and we won the battle." He faced me, his mouth drawn, his eyes wet and distant. "Is that what you wanted to know?"

The ancient Chinese practiced the "death by a thousand cuts." The phrase occurred to me as I looked at Wash and sadly wondered what had happened to our marriage. Although he was sharing, he did it under duress, creating more of a distance rather than bringing us closer. We had lost—or possibly never fully developed—a trust with our deepest thoughts and emotions. And now there was too much for us to bear, and we could no longer lay our sorrows on each other. I didn't have a clue how to change things. There was no undoing the path we had travelled, and I wasn't sure I wanted to keep treading the same way. I vowed to seek guidance from a kind and wise person. Just as soon as I had a moment to call my own.

❧

Wash, C. C. Martin, and I descended the air lock into the Manhattan caisson, the first time Wash had visited since winter. My throat tightened as my mind flashed with images of him leaving on a stretcher. But we had to make a decision regarding when to halt the descent of the caisson, and this decision was too momentous to make without him.

Having witnessed Wash's and others' attacks of the bends, each differing from the other in symptoms and severity, I tried to discern a pattern. Why were some men affected severely, some mildly, and others not at all? Wash, O'Brien, and Young, for example, had suffered greatly. They were all approximately the same age, which is to say a bit older than the average worker. But Martin was older and rarely had so much as a headache. All the men were quite fit, at least at the start, so I didn't think physical constitution played a role.

What the afflicted did have in common was a proclivity for driving themselves long and hard, making multiple trips into the caisson each day. They were hurried; perhaps they climbed out more quickly than the unaffected.

"The brighter lights and whitewashed walls are an improvement," Wash said upon entering the caisson.

"What's the strike costing us?" Martin asked.

"My sole remaining nerve," Wash responded. "The caisson needs to drop, what, another thirty, forty feet?"

"Depends on this." I picked up an iron bar and whacked at three-foot intervals across the floor. The bar thudded on ordinary ground and clanged upon hitting solid rock. "There's a ridge of bedrock here, as if on top of a mountain. To set the entire caisson on bedrock, we need to blast through this ridge."

"And there's this." Martin knelt near a two-foot-tall boulder.

Wash examined the boulder with a magnifying glass. "Sand...silt... minerals...mostly quartz and feldspar, compacted by a glacier."

Wash offered his magnifying glass, and I examined the sample. Bumpy and gray with some shiny bits. It looked like—well, a rock.

"Two strong men dug for an hour to produce this chunk," Martin said.

"Use powder to blast through both this and the bedrock ridge." Wash checked his timepiece, giving me a moment of peace, as he was keeping careful track.

"That's more money, time, and risk, and it may not be necessary," I said.

"Can we shorten the work shifts?" Martin asked. "The caisson is so deep, they're nearly all getting the bends now."

"We'll have to. Just to get them back to work," I replied.

"If there's nothing else?" Martin excused himself.

I tapped a toe against the boulder. "What's the difference between this and bedrock?"

"Origin, mostly." Wash chiseled off a chip and pocketed it.

"You said this stone was deposited by the glaciers."

He nodded. "Hardened by pressure. Quite different from the river silt above."

I put a chisel blade to the boulder and whacked off another chip. "But it's almost as hard as bedrock, rather like a natural concrete."

"Bedrock isn't glacial. It's created from the earth's mantle."

"If we go down another forty feet or so, the danger will become much higher. What if we stopped right here?"

"Give up?" he asked incredulously.

"Of course not." I whacked the boulder with the chisel, the clang ringing off the walls. "If the difference between this compressed stone and bedrock is origin, and if it's as dense and stable as concrete, does it matter if it's not bedrock?"

"We have no precedent. Concrete is stable and will support the load of the bridge. And bedrock will hold unlimited loads. But this?" He stabbed at the ground with his cane.

"May be just as strong. And the men are suffering terribly at this depth."

My gut lurched; we'd gone past five minutes. I tugged his sleeve. "We need to get you out of here."

We climbed into the exit vault. Wash turned the valves to force out air to lower the pressure to normal atmosphere.

"Wait." I rotated the valve back halfway. "Let's release slowly. Give our bodies more time to adapt."

"Don't you think we need to get out of here? This is the highest pressure I've experienced by far." He rubbed his thighs. "And my legs are tiring."

I turned the valve a little more. "Let's sit a bit. Humor me." I helped him down to the board-covered floor. After about twenty minutes of slowly decreasing the pressure, we climbed up the ladder and through the hatch at the top.

Wash gasped and bent over. Nausea rose in my stomach. A flash of pain ripped through my lungs, and strange sensations prickled up my legs and arms, like an army of ants on attack. But grace was shining down upon us that day, and we both recovered after a few minutes.

The line of strikers stretched out into the street and around several city blocks, their numbers far exceeding the actual workers. We suspected the press, the union, or both were paying sympathizers to join.

A scuffle broke out, and line-breakers were bludgeoned with picket signs. Police beat back the protesters with bobby sticks.

"Forty more feet. How many more men can we subject to this fate?" I asked.

Wash pointed his cane at the strikers. "At that depth, I'd estimate another eighty men dead or crippled from caisson disease."

"We can end the digging now. Blast what we must to get on level footing." I slipped my arm around his. "Why take the risk of sinking farther? Didn't your father lay foundation on similar ground in Cincinnati?"

"Not quite, and that was a much smaller project. We mustn't make untested comparisons. Can't risk resting this behemoth on a theory."

Two strikers carried a paralyzed victim of the bends to the line.

Wash shook his head, rested both hands on his cane, and scrutinized the river like a great opponent. "We could do some tests on the glacial bedrock."

As soon as he used that phrase, I knew his marvelous brain had worked it out, and my theory had merit. The strikers stepped aside as Wash hobbled through their line, and we safely reached our buggy, protected by my gender and his infirmity.

"We must test the glacial bedrock as you suggest. That's a brilliant idea." I took a deep breath. "It's time for an ultimatum."

"Of what sort?"

"The workers must go back or be fired. They'll return once they know we intend to replace them. We'll have Kingsley make the announcement."

Wash stopped midstep into the buggy. "Where is the sweet young woman I married?"

I squeezed the chip of glacial bedrock, cold and unforgiving, in my hand.

TWENTY-FIVE

1873

I did not think of myself as callous, and Wash's comment, though said in jest, made me bristle. In fact, I was greatly concerned with the welfare of the workers and, in concert with Dr. Smith, sought ways to prevent the injuries and ailments befalling the men, especially caisson disease.

We met in his small, cluttered office near the construction site. I had previously shared my experience with slowly releasing pressure while in the vault and that it didn't seem to be successful.

Dr. Smith scratched the top of his balding head, a fringe of hair encircling it like the laurel wreaths of the ancient Greeks. "Your symptoms were mild and resolved quickly. At that pressure, they would have been even worse if you had come up quickly." He spread a set of diagrams of a device similar to a tube-shaped coffin with gauges and air vents. "The air lock pressure can't be precisely controlled through a slow decompression. My idea is to build a chamber—something akin to a miniature caisson—but *above* ground. When workers come out of the caisson, they will rest in this chamber where air is pumped in until it matches the pressure of the caisson. Then, the air pressure would be gradually decreased."

"It seems worth a try." I handed back the drawings.

He proposed the idea to the board. His work was for naught, however, as the Manhattan caisson would be complete before we received the necessary approvals.

After laboratories performed chemical analysis, compressive strength, and other tests on samples, my theory on glacial bedrock was substantiated: the naturally formed concrete was strong enough to hold the massive tower. Accordingly, Wash agreed we would fill the caisson at seventy-eight feet of depth rather than risk more lives by digging deeper.

With both towers growing at a rapid rate, I hoped Wash would steadily improve as well. However, he rarely left the house. There were days he couldn't get out of bed, his head too painful to lift from the pillow. Dr. Smith consulted with Dr. Walter Reed, a promising young doctor at Brooklyn Hospital, who had taken an interest in caisson disease.

Dr. Reed was kind to both of us and diagnosed Wash with "contractures and neurological sequelae of the caisson disease, including headache, nystagmus, and tremor." Dr. Reed prescribed a tincture for pain and stiffness and morphine as needed. But he had no magic cure and offered few answers with regard to how long it would be before Wash could return to work or walk without a cane. We didn't ask about the marital bed situation.

Wash suffered from a range of complaints besides the headaches, limb pains, and visual disturbances, which seemed to wax and wane like phases of the moon. But something less tangible was taking hold as well: a nervous unsteadiness, vexing in its nebulous nature and persistence. He was irritable most of the time, losing interest in his pets, keeping up with the news, or even playing with Johnny. He complained of a burning feeling in his skin and couldn't tolerate being touched.

One morning in March, I woke at 4:00 a.m. to the smell of frying pork roll and an absent husband. Wash also suffered from insomnia, so this was not surprising. Inclined to provide whatever support my presence could bring, I slipped on my robe and joined him at the kitchen stove.

"Taylor ham?" I plucked a piece of the pinkish meat from the draining towel.

He playfully slapped away my thieving hand and nodded toward the small table and two stools. "Have a seat." He cut more slices from the large roll, right through the muslin casing. Chaucer, a large yellow retriever he had brought back from Trenton, licked his chops and caught tidbits Wash let drop.

"Is your headache any better?" I scraped the stool over to the cookstove and continued my uninvited intrusion. I held my hands toward the soothing heat.

He answered with a small shrug as he cut slits from the edge to near the center of the round, thin slices, using his fingers as guides.

"Can I help with that?" I was fearful his poor vision would lead to a bloody breakfast.

No answer.

"Wash, this will all be over someday. Dr. Reed says you will improve over time." The ham hissed as it met the frying pan. "Why won't you let me help you with these simple things?"

"Three slits per slice are traditional, to help it lie flat. I find that five give a more pleasant pinwheel shape."

Smoke curled from the pan, the room filling with a tangy aroma as the meat cooked. Wash placed the heaping plate on the table. I poured tea as he repositioned the stool. We ate in silence, the salty, crispy ham slices a treat, my unanswered question hanging in air.

Wash cleared his throat. "I'm going back to Trenton tomorrow."

"Oh? Getting low on precious commodities?" I held up my fork with a triangle of ham. The pressed meat was a specialty of his hometown, and he could scarcely be without it.

He cracked a smile, fumbling for his teacup. "True enough. I think being around my family will help with—well, will make me feel better. And it's time I attended to Roebling's Sons again. My brothers outvoted me. Yours truly is now president."

"I'll come with you, then. And congratulations."

"While I appreciate the offer, no thank you, dear." He dismissed me with a wave of his hand, then looped a forefinger into the ear of the cup handle. His teacup jittered against its saucer, sounding like seashells rubbing together. "You're needed here."

"I guess we can get along without each other for a few days." I rose to clear the dishes, pushing aside a pang of hurt.

"It'll be a few months at least. Perhaps a year." When I spun toward him, he held up his palm. "You can visit as you wish."

"You mean, I have no say? No discussion? When you're running back to Trenton without me?"

"Em, it's not like that. You and Martin have things well under control here, and it's better I go where I'm needed."

"What have I done to deserve this?" A mixture of hurt and rage bubbled up inside me, and I struggled to maintain a level voice. "Am I not working as hard as I can to keep your world together? What do you want from me?" I crashed a plate into the sink.

"You're taking this all out of proportion. It's merely business."

"What use is a family business if it tears a family apart?"

Wash winced at my comment. I should have known better than to question the very soul of what it meant to be a Roebling.

I forced words through clenched teeth. "Fine. Go. The bridge will be built, and we will start over. This is *not* the rest of our lives."

He tapped his spoon calmly, carefully. There had been no hesitation in his words, no glances my way as he shared his plan. Wash had thought this all through and calculated my reaction with the same skill he did trigonometry, which infuriated me all the more. I wanted to grab the spoon and hurl it at his head.

Wash's absence dragged on, but I made scant effort to visit him. It was convenient to blame the burdens of bridge supervision, running a home, and raising a son. Johnny was now five years old and desperately missed his father. He constantly begged to go to Trenton where he also had oodles of cousins to play with. But the guilty truth was that I rather despised Trenton, with its slow pace and nosy relatives. Furthermore, when I did visit, my time was spent not doing things together as a family but transcribing hundreds of pages Wash dictated, my hand cramping from the effort.

He had me write each step in the bridge-building process in excruciating detail, and after I returned to New York, he mailed the instructions for each step in the process as needed. The letters gave the appearance of him being in full control, with me by his side, even as we remained apart. While the bridge soared into the sky, our marriage was at its lowest point, glacier bedrock.

I tried to put myself in Wash's place, working to keep the family business alive for future generations. After all, the bridge would be completed one day, and I secretly hoped this would be the last Roebling bridge. Letters and the occasional telegram were no replacement for simple physical presence. Despite Wash's ailments and frailties, I missed the warmth of his body next to mine at night, the soothing sound of his voice, and the humor that would pop up at the most unexpected moment.

That summer, Wash had requested Johnny come stay with him in order to visit family, as he was too busy to come back to New York. Thus, I was stunned to receive a letter postmarked from Maine.

Dear Em,

Johnny and I are enjoying the spectacular scenery and enjoying lobster, a true delight. I can't imagine why they believe it suited only for criminals. The waves crashing on the rocks bring our son such joy! I've been dabbling in oils, trying to capture the sunlight shining through waves, but the vision proves too ephemeral for my talents. Do join us when you see fit.

W

I imagined them eating lobster and painting by the sea while I labored on alone. My arms ached to hold my son, feel the salt air against his soft cheek. I crumpled the letter and fed it to the fire.

The next morning, I awoke with my arm outstretched over the cool spot in the bed Wash had abandoned. I curled my knees to my chest and wrapped my arms around them. What else could I have done or not done?

As I dressed, I ticked off the tasks I needed to accomplish. Things to do not because of my husband's instructions but because I had determined they were necessary. I sat on my bed, wiggled my toe into a stocking, stopping midcalf. Was living happily without him simply a choice I could make? I pulled on my other stocking and my new bloomer costume, tailored by a willing seamstress.

Why should my existence, my worth, be attached to Wash?

TWENTY-SIX

1874–1875

An invitation arrived for a "Gala at the Monster Classical and Geological Hippodrome." Drawings of chariot races, dancing horses, and elegantly dressed people sipping bubbly drinks completed the oversized vellum. PT had added a note in his large, loopy handwriting: *Dear Peanut, I insist you and Mr. Roebling come, no excuses allowed!*

Wash's response came a few days later. *Please attend with my regrets, dear. You will be much more entertained by horses than would I.*

The venue was a vast outdoor space PT was leasing on Madison Avenue. It was covered by an enormous tarp, much like his first circus tents but many times larger. Chairs elevated on risers lined the perimeter around the center ring.

A waiter in white tie and tails greeted the guests at the entrance with a tray of champagne flutes. Each had a strawberry glistening with bubbles. Sipping the wine was uplifting, the first astringent note followed by a smooth and light finish. Flute in hand, I sauntered past tables laden with tea sandwiches, vegetables cut into amusing shapes, and most spectacularly, a boat carved out of ice, holding a mountain of pink shrimp. Skewering a briny morsel, I nonchalantly took notice of the other invitees: several Vanderbilts, the owners of the property; Abram Hewitt, the tall, lean gentleman I had met in Ringwood, who was now running for Congress; and a few other politicians.

The ladies' gowns, in every color imaginable, provided a peek at next year's fashions. Many featured elaborate bustles, and the shape of the skirt was decidedly slimmer than my own rather worn dress. Oceans of netting and beading and sprays of feathers to match crowned the ladies' hats. To my chagrin, tightly bound corsets were still very much in evidence. The men, in contrast, wore a uniform: black tailcoat and top hat, white shirt and tie.

Perhaps anticipating Wash's regrets and to prevent my own, PT had also graciously invited GK and Millie, and we planned to meet at the event. PT found me first, however. The picture of elegance in his crisp white tie and tails, he removed his silk top hot, spun it by its brim like a top, and greeted me with a bow. "Welcome, my dear Mrs. Roebling. I hope the refreshments are suitable?"

"Most sumptuous, Mr. Barnum."

"Excellent. I have reserved premier seats for you and your family." He waved over an usher. "Please join me after the show."

GK and Millie sat down a moment before the perimeter lamps were extinguished. As promised, we were front and center. Limelights threw the center arena into view. A spotlight shone on PT, now sporting a red-lined black cape, welcoming the audience with his commanding voice.

All eyes fixed on him. Even professional performers of Shakespeare paled in comparison. It was as if he were the Cardiff Giant brought to life, larger than mere mortal beings. But clothed, of course. Was it his words, his voice? The spotlight? Dress? Mannerisms? It was all of that, along with the grace with which he moved and the confidence that oozed from him in a clove-scented cloud.

"First, the champion chariot racers from Europe will defend their title against the Americans!" The audience whooped. PT lowered his voice so the crowd had to hush to hear the attractions. He recounted each act in the program, his voice rising with excitement, culminating with "Then, my dear friends, we will see the dancing horses, like the spectacular Lipizzans of Austria. Now, on with the show!"

My heart raced with the chariots, the pounding of their hooves reminding me of riding with youthful abandon. Exciting as the chariots were, they stirred up a dust cloud that left us brushing off our clothes and wiping our faces. GK laughed, but poor Millie was flustered. We flapped our handkerchiefs at the dirt the best we were able, but this failed to settle her, and they excused themselves.

Between acts, waiters walked down the rows, offering more champagne and bonbons. But the lingering smell of the horses, although not offensive to me, ruined my appetite for them. I scanned the tent for GK and Millie, but they were nowhere to be seen.

A sudden creak of the adjacent chair startled me as I was admiring the audience in their elegant dress.

"Are you enjoying the show?" PT mopped his brow.

"Very much so. Thank you for inviting us. Will Mrs. Barnum join us after the show?"

"You're very welcome. And no, I'm afraid she's feeling poorly." He eyed the empty seat next to him.

"Please give your wife my well wishes." I nodded toward the empty seat. "I'm afraid Millie isn't well-accustomed to horse races. Or dirt."

"My wife, the same. I thought it a feminine proclivity. But then, you disprove that; a sprinkle of earth doesn't offend you." He offered a crisp handkerchief, indicating a smudge on my face. "A wagonload, dumped at your feet, is but an opportunity to build a garden."

"Some might say I could use a bit more feminine sensibility." I showed my ankle, exposing a hem that had been repaired.

He chuckled, leaned closer, his breath on my ear giving me a shiver. "Will you allow me to send a replacement dress, as my show has undoubtedly ruined that one?"

His spicy scent was soothing, and I had an urge to run the back of my hand against his clean-shaven cheek. His attention sent a tingle through my body. Hundreds were in attendance, yet he made me feel as though I were the only one there. "No, I couldn't allow you to do that."

"Well then, I must return to my duties. The second act is about to begin."

A line of riders in dark blue uniforms stood on unsaddled white stallions. They trotted into a circle, the horses' tails held high, their manes and coats brushed until they glistened, even in the darkened arena.

"Oh, they're magnificent."

"Indeed they are. We can discuss afterward, if you desire to set up a ride."

I pictured myself riding through the countryside on a great white stallion. Oh, how I missed the freedom to do things that thrilled me. "Thank you, dear sir. What a joy that would be."

The circle of horses in the ring backed into two straight lines with the spotlight filling the space in between. A woman, standing tall in a dazzling red dress, rode into the spotlight, straddling two side-by-side horses.

"There's my cue." PT touched two fingers to his pursed lips, then bounded out of his chair, his cape floating after him.

Miss Mann—Muriel—had become indispensable to our family. As Johnny was less in need of a nanny, she had assumed the role of cook and treasured confidant to me. One especially warm evening, we thumbed through copies of *Harper's Bazaar*. Dressed in light cotton dressing gowns, we amused ourselves like schoolgirls on an overnight party, braiding our hair, playing card games, and talking about the mysteriously absent men in our lives.

"Maine of all places!" She tsked and patted Chaucer's golden head.

"Can you believe it? In fact, he once claimed that all I wanted was to ride horses in Kentucky and paint pictures in Maine." *Riding horses, yes. But when had I dreamed of painting?* The long-ago conversation—before we left for Europe—filtered into my mind. Had Wash been trying to tell me that *he* had other dreams? I quaffed the whiskey Muriel offered as I puzzled.

We scrambled for shawls to cover our thin garments at a knock on the door. PT and Henri appeared in the doorway, both surprising and pleasing me.

"Sorry for the intrusion, ladies." PT removed his hat, his eyes taking in my curious hairstyle and clothing. A crooked smile crossed his face.

"Oh my, I completely forgot!" Muriel said. As I let the two men into the room, she rushed off.

After an awkward round of drinks, with Henri abstaining and me clutching my shawl, Muriel rejoined us, now properly dressed. Henri took Muriel's arm, and they left for the evening, their laughter trailing after them. A pang of envy stirred in me, seeing the two of them go out without a chaperone. Was their culture more lenient toward courtship, or were there special considerations due to their age?

"Oh, this slipped my mind in the excitement." PT presented an elegantly wrapped box. "Cubans. Mr. Roebling will enjoy them, I'm sure." He cast about with feigned curiosity. "Is he here? I'd like to give them to him myself, perhaps share a smoke."

"You know very well he's not here. But I thank you in his stead." I led him toward the front door.

"How unfortunate. Well, I'll just secure these in his humidor."

I followed him to the library where he stowed the cigars and helped himself to another glass of whiskey. He offered me a glass as well, but I declined.

"PT, I think you best be on your way." Chaucer's ears perked up, and he headed to the door.

"Yes, yes, of course. But if you would be so kind, I have a bit of sad news, and I'm afraid old Henri is quite weary of listening to my troubles."

"What is it?" We perched on the settee. He picked up a deck of cards and shuffled and flipped them into waterfalls and sliding arcs of color. He had me so mesmerized, I barely heard his words.

"My wife, I'm afraid, is not long for this world."

Shish-shish-shish went the cards. Chaucer lay down with a grumble.

"I'm terribly sorry, PT. Is there anything I can do?"

"Give me a moment of distraction, perhaps. Do you know cribbage?" Without waiting for a response, he dealt us both a hand. His soft blue eyes welled up.

"Do you want to talk about her?" I closed my fan of cards.

"Peanut, you're endearing, but please, I'd rather have a few moments when I can give my mind a reprieve. She has been unwell for a number of years."

We played a quiet round. He gave me a small smile when I won, and I reached over to run the back of my hand across his smoothly shaven cheek. What was it about this man? We gave each other comfort, each in probably the loneliest of our days. We played hearts and poker and games he made up long past midnight. He broke down and cried, telling me of the daughter he had lost shortly before she would have turned two. He shared bits and pieces of his wife's troubles, seeming more resigned than upset. Her heart was slowly failing, and the doctors had long since given up hope.

We commiserated, telling stories of our lost loved ones, picking the best moments, the funny ones, the bittersweet ones.

"Love has no limit in time or number," PT said.

We toasted to that, pledging to cherish our memories forever.

"I shouldn't go on about my sorrows." PT refilled my tumbler of whiskey.

I shook memories away and lifted my glass to him. "To times lived and to those we have yet to live."

"And for your companionship, a bright light in my despair."

At some point, with the whiskey flowing through both our veins, it was clear he was in no condition to go home. We played ever more silly games, which he won at an impossible rate. I finally accused him of cheating. Following the hint of his eyes upon my chemise, my wrap having long since been abandoned, I found the missing three of hearts.

"How did that get there?" I demanded.

"Methinks the lady doth protest too much. I'm afraid I can't play with a cheater." He threw down his hand.

I pinched the edge of a card hidden in his sleeve. "Aha!" I laughed.

He shrugged. "I have plenty more."

I frisked him for evidence. He fell onto the floor, curled into a protective ball. His sleeves, socks, waistband, all produced playing cards. Tugging at his shirttail produced a fountain of aces. I cackled at each discovery, unmindful of his own silence. After I had found the last of the contraband, he rolled onto his back in surrender.

I plopped down next to him and fanned the cards, smooth and warm from his body heat. "Cold, hard evidence of your criminal nature. How do you plead, sir?"

"Guilty." He raised my wrists over his head, pulling me on top of him, the cards raining like confetti.

This is wrong, part of me screamed, as if alarm bells resided in my head. He let go of one of my hands and inched his own over the swell of my bottom. His other hand found my braid and followed it up to the nape of my neck. My head dipped toward him, my lips aching for his, my body tingling with want. It had been three years since Wash had shared my bed.

This is wrong, I told myself again. *But let me savor this feeling for a moment. Let me fill my flesh with the sensation of a man's touch.* I lost myself in his kiss for what seemed like an eternity and yet not long enough. His cloud of clove enveloped me, and his lips tasted of whiskey. Powerless to stop myself, my mouth, my body pleaded for him to fill my empty soul.

I tilted my head as he nuzzled my neck, but his lips faded off, hot breath taking their place.

He whispered, "It's not right. We both belong to another." But he held me still, waiting, I think, for me to overrule his objection.

But I had no strength to overrule his objection. Yes, he had a wife, and I, a husband. Our behavior could not be justified in any moral way. But my husband had all but abandoned me, and it was PT who held me now, making me feel whole and alive, giving me strength to accomplish what Wash could not or would not do on his own.

I tried to convince myself that our being together, supporting each other, was in fact what my husband wanted, needed. He left me so that I could finish his work, didn't he? I clung to PT, my cheek against his, feeling the heaving in his chest matching my own. Then I noticed his cheek was damp. I pulled back to see his eyes welled with tears.

"Tell me truly, Emily. Do you love me or the idea of me?"

Of course I loved him. But there were many sorts of love. Parental love, brotherly love, friendship. And there was passionate love, which burns brightly and swiftly, then is replaced with either the slow and steady love of lifetime partners or the ashes of boredom and regret. I tried to imagine which way my love for PT would progress and, more importantly, whether the cinders of my love for Wash had any glow left within them.

PT caressed my cheek. "You can't say it. Is that my answer then?"

The alarm bells in my head clanged once again, and I gently pushed myself back. "As you've said, there are others to consider. Until we sort that out, we have no business engaging each other like this."

My better self had pervaded me, and I blinked passion away. I rose from him and rewrapped the shawl around me.

The evening with PT confused me even more regarding my marriage and my devotion to Wash. His letter from Maine and long ago words lingered at the edges of my mind, along with the fear I had misunderstood his dreams. I had spent so much time fighting the life we were living until I gave up fighting and jumped full force into the Roebling dream.

But perhaps that wasn't what Wash wanted after all. I swallowed, bracing myself to allow a thought that had been fighting to surface: Had I missed something he was trying to tell me all along but couldn't due to family loyalty? Could it be he never really wanted the Roebling dream or me, or at least who I had become? Perhaps he had already left me. Was my marriage over, and I was the only one who wasn't aware?

It had been PT who supported me through legal battles, through self-doubt, even physical exhaustion, PT who cared enough to ensure Johnny had enough attention and encouragement from another man.

But I had never for a moment stopped loving Wash and believed he still loved me. I was standing atop two unsaddled horses that were about to gallop in different directions.

It became clear that I shouldn't be alone with PT while I was so torn, and it was impossible to discern the state of my marriage in Wash's absence. So I sent a cable to my husband:

PLEASE COME HOME

TWENTY-SEVEN

1876

T he tower on the Manhattan side grew quickly after the foundation was built and was complete in July. I had checked in frequently during the process, concerned the bedrock built by glaciers was not stable enough. But careful observation and measurements were done each step of the way. There was not an iota of settling, and there were even fewer marks of concrete crazing—the normal superficial cracking—than on the Brooklyn side, which eased all worries.

"Smooth as a baby's bottom," Martin assured me.

Little noticed but crucial to the support of the bridge were the anchorage buildings. Around eight stories high and built a half mile or so inland, their purpose was to house the anchors that would secure the main cables coming down from the towers.

On August 14, the first wire was to be strung, uniting the two towers and the anchor buildings. It was a moment I had been anticipating for months. Perhaps superstitious of me, but it seemed that a physical connection of the two sides of the bridge would give my inner being the strength to go on and a clear direction to follow, as well as an important milestone of which to be proud.

That day, a worker in Brooklyn and another in Manhattan each dropped a hemp rope from the top of the towers. A twisted steel wire, a little less than an inch in diameter, was attached to each hemp rope. Then a hoisting engine at each tower pulled the hemp ropes, then the steel wires, as they passed up and over the towers through sets of pulleys toward the land sides.

Dozens of men carried wire rope from the shore inland through their respective cities over a series of trestles between the towers and the anchor buildings. Using these trestles, men carried the rope above the rooftops, and then each wire was firmly attached to the top of an anchor building.

The next step was to connect the wires slung over each tower. A sturdy flat-bottomed boat called a scow was outfitted with a reel containing about two thousand feet of wire, threaded around a thick wooden axle. I climbed aboard the scow with Farrington and Martin.

The great port buzzed with industry; black smoke puffed from smokestacks in New Jersey, their bitter odor counterpoint to the brine of oysters harvested across the Narrows. We had to be able to see the wire, so we needed to do this during daylight hours when barges and passenger ships clogged the route. Not wishing to raise the ire of our ever-critical opponents, we decided not to request a closure of the important maritime route but instead to wait for a break in traffic.

While men scaled great heights above us, we made small talk under a blazing sun as workers fastened the scow to a tugboat. Perspiration glued my dress to my body, and I tugged it free. I set up a spotting scope as Farrington and Martin supervised the attachment of the reel wire from the scow to the wire dangling from the Brooklyn tower. The small boat rocked in the wake of the larger vessels. I was fairly bristling with excitement, but I had to sit in an unsteady boat, trying to convince my stomach to behave itself. I dangled my fingers in the cool water, smelled the salt from the sea, and listened to the cry of seagulls. Our moment of serenity in the midst of a bustling city gave no hint of the huge step about to occur: the uniting of the two towers and the anchor buildings by wire.

I manned the scope at the bow. After an hour, there was a break in marine traffic. My heart quickened; the moment was upon us. I held up a green flag to signal the tug. Martin and Farrington stood at either end of the spool, ensuring the wire unwound evenly, and would yell for me to raise a yellow or red flag to slow or stop the tug. The wire sank as it left the stern;

another tugboat was stationed behind us to keep other boats from becoming entangled in the submerged hazard.

The waves were less than a foot high, keeping my seasickness at bay. Through the scope, I saw a large, three-masted bark sailing rapidly into our path. I rang a signal bell, then waved a red flag at my spotter on the lead tug. Fighting the current and wind, our little convoy floated to a near standstill. Relief calmed my tightly strung nerves as the ship passed, not twenty feet away.

When we reached the Manhattan tower, the two wire ropes were connected as one long cable, most of it still submerged. Again, we needed a lookout so as not to slice the masts and sails off tall ships as we hoisted the cable from the river.

"Go on up there." Farrington nodded toward the top of the tower. "Great view."

"Oh no," I insisted, my gut roiling at the thought. "I wouldn't want to deprive you of such a grand moment."

He gave me a smile and mock salute as he hustled up the stairway.

Onlookers cheered as large American flags were unfurled from the tower tops. How welcome was the sound of cheering after years of suffering through the jeers! The wire rope was once again attached to a hoisting engine. Farrington gave the all clear signal from the top of the tower, a cannon fired a warning, and the engine groaned to life. The cable was wound back onto a reel, its angle of entry into the river growing higher and higher until it rose from the water, dripping and shining in the sun like a magnificent serpent.

Then the whole process was repeated as a second wire was brought across from Brooklyn, then fastened to the first, creating a continuous loop over both towers and from anchorage to anchorage. This would become one of four carrier wires from which the wires for the four cables would be brought across, one by one.

It was the breathtaking moment I had hoped for. I glanced around at many wiping their eyes, becoming misty-eyed myself.

But I was no closer to understanding my marriage or knowing my future as my heart both swelled with pride and sank with regret. Wash should have been there.

On a muggy day in late August, PT and I joined a group of fifty or so people atop the Brooklyn anchor building. In order to verify the safety of working suspended from the single wire, Farrington was to cross the loop now strung across the full length of the bridge. The *Brooklyn Eagle* had publicized the event, ensuring enthusiastic viewers on both banks and even from the water on what Wash called *those buckets of bolts*, the ferries.

Farrington climbed aboard a boatswain's chair suspended from an inch-thick cable. Benjamin Stone, PT, and I each shook his hand and wished him Godspeed.

Martin pulled the lever to start the hoisting machine that would lift Farrington to the top of the Brooklyn tower. Slowly at first, then faster with a *click, click, rumble*, the cable moved through pulleys. Farrington smiled and waved as if he were on a carnival ride. Everyone cheered as the press photographed the event. Near the top of the tower, Farrington stood in his seat, waving an arm. The crowd gasped as he took a bow, then plopped back down into the seat until he arrived at the top of the Brooklyn tower.

Farrington's journey had turned into a happy spectacle and good publicity. In a mere twenty-two minutes, he reached the Manhattan tower. A triumphant roar went up from both sides.

PT clapped and waved with enthusiasm. "Great show!"

I exhaled a great sigh of relief as if I had been on the tightrope with him. "A bit of a show-off."

"Ah, he deserves it." Martin also clapped his approval.

"No more unnecessary risks," I told Martin, taking PT's proffered arm.

There was a hint of sarcasm in Martin's voice when he responded, "That's right. The Roebling men and women abhor risk taking."

I didn't care. PT and I enjoyed a supportive and professional relationship. We had gone to the brink of something else, but we were adults in control of our impulses. I was proud of my strength and had nothing to be ashamed of. Furthermore, the state of my marriage should be of no concern to Martin or anyone else for that matter. I looked straight into Martin's beady eyes. "See that none of the workers, from the acting chief engineer on down, say or do anything that might risk their job."

"Sorry, ma'am. I didn't mean—"

The corner of my mouth tugged up at the panic contorting his face as PT wheeled me away.

Martin never did like taking risks.

A few days later, Wash came home, unannounced, after three years of almost complete absence. Curiously, he rang the bell rather than letting himself in. He stood in the doorway beaming, a large valise in each hand. "The prodigal son returns."

I blinked at this apparition. Was he home for good? He had made a few treks back and forth, mostly to pick up and deliver Johnny, never staying long enough to sort out our issues.

"Darling!" I peered behind him. "Where is Johnny?"

"He was having such a lovely summer with his cousins, we allowed him to stay on a while longer."

I bit my lips with disappointment. Sharing my feelings would only make Wash feel badly for coming at all. And I suspected ulterior motives, such as an excuse for Wash to limit his visit. Perhaps it was fortunate he hadn't brought our son. Better to make the most of this time alone together, an opportunity to give voice to our troubles.

After I helped him with his baggage, at long last, we embraced. His broad shoulders and thick arms had grown stronger, squeezing me as they had long ago. Gone was the smell of liniment, replaced with the more pleasant scent of his cinnamon chewing gum. The rub of his cotton shirt comforted me, like curling into a favorite quilt.

There was no flicker in his gaze as he held me arm's length. "You are a magnificent sight. I was lost without you."

But clearly, he had thrived.

"Chaucer!" Wash greeted the retriever that bounded into room. The dog shoved his golden head between Wash's knees and whimpered his protests at having been abandoned by his master. "That's all right, boy. Next time, you'll come with me."

My lips parted in hurt and surprise, but I let his comment hang in the air.

He led us into the library and poured a drink. "Good heavens, Emily." He held up the nearly empty decanter. His eyes fell on the ashtray, still full of thick chunks of ash and quite a few chewed cigar butts.

Good God, were they still there from PT's visit? A chill of guilt and embarrassment rippled through me. No matter now; it had been stopped in time. But I needed to fire the maid.

"Oh, that's a funny story. Henri and PT were here to pick up Muriel, and—"

"And you invited them into my library." He shook the last drops of whiskey from his glass onto his tongue. "I'm sure it's a wonderful tale. But perhaps another time." He wiped his whiskey glass dry, using a bit too much elbow grease. "I'm weary from the trip. Request permission to retire?" He gave me a peck on the cheek as he left the room, Chaucer, ever loyal, at his side.

I waited for him to glance back at me, an invitation lightening his countenance. Even a wee snuggle would have been welcome after all these months. But there was no look back as he hobbled up the stairs, leaning heavily on the banister.

I set my teeth, wanting to ask him, command him, to stop. *Stop. Let me tell you how it felt to see Farrington crossing the river on a wire. Let me tell you how alone I feel, even as I stand in a great crowd. Let me tell you I love you and that those ashes mean nothing.*

Here was the moment I had begged for, dreamed about: my beloved returning home. But anger swept through me like a brushfire, even as part of me wanted to dance with joy. I was afraid my anger would color my words, and he would mount his defenses.

Needing some fresh air, I headed out for a walk. Wandering without destination, I soon found myself at the waterfront. Three little girls were playing in the small strip of a park, laughing and kicking a rubber ball. I brushed aside some dried oak leaves and sat on a bench. To the north, the bridge towers now dominated the view. Pride in my efforts warmed my soul, but at the same time, a darker force squeezed within, anger at Wash's abandonment of both me and the bridge rising again.

It seemed I would soon need to make a choice. It was unheard of for a woman to leave her husband, but hadn't Wash left me? The knowing looks from Martin, the jabs from Mother's friends and neighbors—my predicament was well-known. I wasn't sure how much longer I could bear the long absences, broken by visits from a half stranger.

The rubber ball rolled up to my feet, a girl with blond ringlets giving chase. She reminded me of Elizabeth. I picked up the ball and handed it to her.

"Why are you so sad, missus?" asked the little girl, head cocked in concern.

"I miss someone," I replied. A gaggle of cooing pigeons strutted up to me, but I had no bread crumbs to give.

Eleanor came for a visit, and happy for an excuse for some recreation, she and I rode the streetcar to Coney Island, where lovely homes had once lined the waterfront. I was saddened to see the area was being overtaken by bathhouses, dreary hotels, and aimless characters. Nevertheless, we slipped through an alleyway to the beach and strolled along it. A strong breeze lifted our skirts, and salt air filled our lungs.

"It seems your mind is somewhere else," Eleanor said.

I nodded, wanting very much to share my concerns, but Mother had always advised against sharing domestic troubles outside the family. They would only return as unwelcome rumor. But I trusted Eleanor, so when we stopped to admire the waves crashing and the cry of the seagulls, I spoke of the changes in my marriage, hoping for some insight to my dilemma.

"My dear," Eleanor said, "you can't expect a marriage to remain as it is in the beginning. If your souls continued to burn for each other in that way, you would be cinders."

"Then what is the point? Why do we marry for life, only to see love fade away?"

"Ah, but true love doesn't fade away. It changes, deepens. It seems to disappear at times, only to come back in a different way. Think of early love like a wave in the ocean, building and building until it tumbles from its own height. Then the calm, the drawing back, only to swell and crash again. When you get past the breakers, you don't feel the crash, but the water is still lifting and falling in life's rhythm."

"Like the perpetual motion machine you made?"

"Exactly. Balance and motion, as in us and in nature. But I didn't make the machine. Mr. White made it for me." Her eyes lit up as she mentioned her late husband, now ten years gone.

I adjusted my hat to better shield my eyes from the blinding sun. "It seems I pushed through the breakers only to find my husband wasn't with me on the other side."

"Then you must swim until you find him." Eleanor kicked seaweed from the path of sandpipers, skittering from approaching foam. "Don't be tempted back into the breakers, seeking another for the journey. You may find the ocean spits you back out."

Looking at my marriage through a new lens, I strived to be more accepting of its changes. I renewed my efforts to please Wash and found he responded, perhaps not as demonstratively as I would like but the best he could. He would, for example, pull out my chair at the table as he always had, but after I was seated, he'd rest his warm hand on my shoulder for a brief moment. The tiniest of signals, but to me, it was his way of showing he was struggling back, if not to what we once were, perhaps to a different sort of intimacy.

My anger slowly faded as he made no mention of returning to Trenton. He seemed once again interested in the progress of the bridge and thanked me for my work. We avoided the topic of PT altogether. A new beginning, it seemed, as delicate as the puff of a dandelion just gone to seed.

It was difficult to appreciate the crushing weight of all Wash had been through in his adult life, the loss of his father and recently a sister, the war, and his physical destruction from the work in the caisson. Could a human being, even one as close as emotionally possible, ever totally empathize with another? A mother could, as a mother feels even more intensely the suffering of a child. But perhaps a protective barrier exists between any two adults, preventing them from being sensible to all the other's pain. To feel it all would render one useless as a support.

Confirming my enduring love for Wash did not mitigate my feelings for

PT. When I grew frustrated with Wash's unending litany of complaints, I could see PT at any number of public events to get my fill of levity. Wash was always invited and always declined. Johnny, at eight, was at a perfect age to enjoy the amusements. PT gave us tours of the animal stables, and we enjoyed concerts, art shows, and circus performances from the best seats as his guests. It certainly fulfilled the *twice as much fun* part of my pact with GK.

Perhaps Eleanor was right; the flames that rose in me in PT's presence would fade, just as they had with Wash. Perhaps his life seemed exciting and glamorous simply because it was not my own and would grow tiresome in time. And then there would be no family history to fall back on, no shared joke from long ago, no shared pride in a son well raised.

Yet it wasn't as if PT and I shared no history. And if I were to be honest with myself, my spirited nature was more similar to PT's than my own husband's. Had my marriage to Wash tamped down my exuberance, my love of adventure, my own self? Eleanor seemed to believe there was no role for friendship with men outside marriage. Maybe that was true for her, true for times gone by. But it seemed for modern women, there was room for both, if carefully managed.

~

It seemed I was not the only one debating my proclivities. GK had requested—and was given—a posting in Newport, Rhode Island, in order to be closer to family. His recent letters disturbed me, obsessed as he was with clearing his name before his death. After pages of railing about the slow-moving army, he penned his thoughts on my work: *Washington should not allow dangers unthinkable for women.*

Soon after GK's move, he visited us, presenting me with a bouquet of flowers and Wash with a package, wrapped in old newspapers. "A task from Old Useless."

Wash unwrapped the bundle and found a black felt uniform hat. The gold cord with acorns confirmed it had belonged to a general.

The men moved toward the parlor.

"I'll go put these in water." I went to the dining room to get a vase.

"What am I to do with this?" Wash asked GK.

"He wants you to sell the damn thing to Emily's circus friend for as much as you can get."

"Son of a bitch." The paneled partition between the rooms was ajar, their conversation floating through the crack.

"That's where it belongs, anyway," GK said. "A circus."

I pulled back the waxy paper around the flowers and breathed in the lovely fragrance of yellow roses.

"Speaking of Emily..."

My ears perked at GK's mention of my name as I climbed on a stool to reach the crystal vase.

Wash cut in. "You've got concerns? Do you suppose I don't? It's a bit late to be caterwauling about that now."

I shouldn't be listening. But my misbehaving half refused to move.

"Would you allow her to fight our wars?" GK asked. "You seem well enough now. Where does it stop? What kind of man puts the ones he is privileged to protect in harm's way?"

"You well know her proclivities," Wash said. "As stubborn and brave as any man."

"A dangerous combination." GK spoke in a low, resigned voice. "But that's how she was constituted from the very beginning."

"You'll broker no argument from me, sir."

"Bravery is a misunderstood thing. She has her fears, of course, but they seldom concern her own reputation," GK said. "While she was under my watch, I did that for her."

"She's a grown woman now."

"And you're not concerned with the impropriety of shirtless men in her proximity?" GK grew louder. "Or her keeping company with the likes of Barnum?"

"You had her locked up in a nunnery, but I'm a tad more lenient."

I bit my lip to suppress a laugh as GK snorted. He had, in effect, put me in a nunnery when he paid for my education at Georgetown Visitation.

"I can only trust in our vows and let the rest fall to fate." Wash's voice rose.

"Is that so? Where the hell have you been for three years?"

"I love my wife and love and respect you dearly, sir. But this matter is none of your concern."

It seemed I was wrong regarding Wash's reasoning for distancing himself from the relationship between PT and myself. His trust in me, his desire for my own free will, was greater than any need for assurance of faithfulness. Piecing together the different aspects of his love was like putting together a fretsaw puzzle with only a portrait of a cloudy sky to guide me.

I debated whether to thank Wash for defending my actions to my brother, but to do so would reveal my eavesdropping. There was nothing to gain from that. So I kept the moment tucked in memory, out of love for my protective brother and my ever-loyal husband.

⁓

With Wash seemingly at peace with my friendship with PT, I planned the long-postponed visit to his stables. Neither Wash nor Johnny showed interest, so I travelled alone by train to Bridgeport.

Connecticut was similar to upstate New York but, at the same time, more quaint. We passed farms with red barns and rolling hills, cows pleasantly chewing their cuds, in between deeply forested areas. I was met at the station by PT's carriage driver and soon arrived at his country home. I worried the strap of my day bag, not having envisioned being alone with PT so far from the public eye. Finally, we arrived at a cluster of buildings where he stood in front of a small cottage.

"It's a shame Washington was unable to join us," PT said as if sensing and trying to lessen my discomfort. "I hope you find the accommodations suitable. It's just a cabin, but I think it will provide for your needs. Your tea should be already set. The stables are just around the bend, and I shall meet you there when you are dressed for the ride."

I nodded, still taking in my circumstance. It was a sweet little cottage with just enough gingerbread ornamentation.

"Just us, then? Will we be joined by others?" I was relieved when a young lady approached. She had long blond hair, left loose around her shoulders, and seemed to be in her early twenties—a bit too young to be one of PT's daughters.

"My wife, perhaps. But she's not well-suited to a mount much larger than a pony."

"Your wife?" I tried to keep the surprise out of my voice but couldn't manage to keep my jaw in place. As far as I knew, his wife had been dead for months. "When did—"

"Ah, and here she is." The girl—or woman, that is—stood on her tiptoes to give him a peck on the cheek. "Mrs. Washington Roebling, allow me to introduce Mrs. Barnum, my wife, Nancy."

"Pleased to meet you. I'm Emily." I nodded my head, swirling as it was. PT was somewhere north of sixty. This woman would be forty years younger. No wonder he had kept her a secret.

"Four o'clock, then?" They turned toward the main house.

Dumbstruck, I waved absently. I was apparently no more to him than a momentary amusement. Despite my marriage, I wanted PT to myself. I was shocked and ashamed and disappointed, all at the same time.

After a short rest, I donned my riding clothes: calfskin breeches worn under a long jacket. If anyone recognized them as men's wear, they had been kind enough not to mention that to me. I met PT at the stables. He was elegant in his riding habit and minus the newly discovered wife.

"It was so nice to meet Mrs. Barnum." I half smiled.

"I suppose you're wondering..."

"Not at all. That is your private business."

"It isn't a marriage per se."

"Oh? I wasn't aware of per se marriages. Either you are, or you aren't."

"You may have noticed her youth."

A stable hand walked out a glorious chestnut mare, brushed to a shine. "Quite."

The assistant helped me into the saddle, adjusted the stirrups, then disappeared back into the stable.

"We have an agreement of sorts. She gets all I own at my death. Half of it if we choose to part before that."

His horse was brought out, a caramel-colored gelding. PT mounted in one swift motion, and we rode out into the August sunshine.

"Your marriage seems a financial arrangement." The *clip-clop* rhythm soothed my nerves. I relaxed into this new development, curious as to its beginnings. "What do you receive out of the bargain?"

"Do I need to explain that?" He laughed and kicked his mount into a trot.

I followed, my own horse needing little encouragement to keep pace. We raced along the open pasture, alternating leads, testing each other. It was exhilarating, the freedom of speed, the openness of the country, the smell of grass and the thud of hooves. After some time, my thighs aching, my breath coming in gasps, I was relieved when we halted near a well.

We dismounted, and he filled a trough with water for the horses and a dipper for us. I greedily drank the clear, cold water, wiping the trickle off my chin.

He removed his riding helmet and finger-raked his damp hair, then leaned against the stone of the well head, arms folded across his chest. "I hope my marriage doesn't change things. Between us, I mean."

"Why would it? We're friends, business associates, and now riding partners." I could hear the hurt in my own voice.

"Yes, but I hope for more." He caught my eye. "I am a patient man, Emily. I can wait."

"Apparently not." I leaned into my horse's firm neck, feeling its heat and strength, trying to settle my feelings.

"I'm not a saint. What would you have me do while you stay in a loveless marriage?"

"I never said it was loveless."

"He left you."

I pressed my palm against my gut, shielding it from the arrow he had slung at it. My marriage was in a phase devoid of physical love. If I could just have a warm squeeze at the end of the day, my back washed in the bath, my cheek caressed by the back of a strong hand, I would feel more satisfied, less hunger for the touch of another.

I had tried to get Wash to do these simple things, and he would, for perhaps a day. Then he would go back to his routine: a peck on the cheek for good morning and another for good night. Was this the rest of my life with him?

"He just needs time," I said, mostly to convince myself.

TWENTY-EIGHT

1877

C limbing to the top of the Brooklyn anchor building was now routine for me, but ascending the narrow footbridge leading to the top of the tower was quite another challenge. At some point, I would have to face that challenge. The open walkway, fashioned of a series of horizontal wooden planks connected by ropes and thin wire handholds, seemed insufficient for so great a height. I'd often watched the men make the climb, dread gripping me like a too-tight corset.

The four huge main cables would be galvanized steel, spun in place over the river, one thin wire at a time. Devices known as carriers, one for each cable, would run back and forth on a cable, carrying a loop with two lengths of wire on each trip. Then workers, dangling high above the river on the wooden platforms, tied these wires into bundles about three inches in diameter, creating a single strand. Nineteen strands were to be aligned in a honeycomb pattern and tied together, forming each of the great cables. The last step in creating the cables was to wrap each bundle of strands in a wire binding.

The precarious walkway, swaying in the slightest breeze, became quite the attraction, and one day, boaters reported seeing two women on it, high above the river.

The press identified them as the daughters of C. C. Martin, who faced a great deal of criticism for his lack of judgment. I was guilty of schadenfreude; it was refreshing to not be the one under scrutiny, at least from the public.

Wash and I had resumed a normal, at least for us, marriage. Sometimes, it seemed as if I had a roommate and business partner rather than a husband. He was still reclusive, refusing to see even Martin or Farrington.

He reworked the cable plan, improving on Papa's design, and was anxious for my report on whether the bundles of strands were coming together in the precise pattern he had devised.

Martin and Farrington were supervising the cabling endeavor, but when they tried to describe the progress being made, I couldn't picture it in my mind, nor could I connect their descriptions to Wash's diagrams. In addition, there were concerns regarding how to secure the saddles the cables would rest on. I would have to climb to the top of the tower to evaluate the situation.

Knowing this for quite some time, nightmares plagued me. I tried to imagine the view from the top but found myself growing more anxious rather than excited.

Wash dismissed my fears. "The view will be spectacular, Em. Think how far you'll be able to see."

"How far is that?"

"Depends on the weather, of course. You'll want to choose a clear day."

"Assuming a perfectly clear day, how far will I be able to see?"

His eyes rolled heavenward as he calculated. "About twenty miles, give or take a quarter of a mile, and the accuracy of our presumptions on the diameter of the earth."

"My goodness, that's incredible. Don't you want to come up with me? Meet with Farrington and Martin yourself?"

"No, thank you, I can see it right here." He tapped his temple.

His math was correct. I spent the better part of an afternoon studying geometry texts and encyclopedias. With pad and pencil, I had come up with the same number. It involved the height of the tower, curvature of the earth, the Pythagorean theorem, and some basic algebra. He was able to solve the problem in his head in a few seconds yet had no desire to see the spectacular answer in person. To have such a brain must be both a blessing and a curse.

I set a date for my climb up to the tower top, but as the day grew closer, the butterflies in my stomach turned to a nest of writhing snakes. Knowing Wash wouldn't come with me, I didn't bother to consult him and instead asked PT to accompany me. His ability to calm my fears was almost magical. Besides, he was certainly familiar with high-wire acts.

On the appointed June day, we had the good fortune of a cool and cloudless dawn. While riding in PT's coach, he waxed on about the spectacular view we were about to enjoy. Meanwhile, I contemplated a hundred different ways to flee. I closed my eyes and pictured GK at my side. *"You are blazing a path for all women."* There was no choice but to go forward, regardless of the opinion of my thumping heart and twirling stomach.

We met Martin and Farrington, who led us to the walkway entrance. Farrington, curiously dressed in an impeccable gray suit, went first. He scampered up the wooden steps, then loped across the narrow walkway, arms pumping at his sides. Martin followed, bracing himself with a hand on each thin rope handrail. I was next in line, with PT right behind me. I passed over the river shore, stepping carefully so as not to bounce the slender boards under my feet. It wasn't so terrible after all. About midway up to the tower, the walkway wavered and I halted. Below, the world spun into an abyss. I gripped the ropes under my white knuckles and froze in place, my face breaking out in a cold sweat, my throat closing. My heart beat so rapidly, I thought I would surely collapse.

"No. No farther. Good God, let me down." I fell to my knees and changed direction, clinging to the wobbling planks.

But PT was a considerable obstacle. He cooed reassuringly, "Come on. Only a little way to go."

A little way to go farther up, then all the way back down again. My body continued its revolt. I swallowed bile and tensed my muscles to halt their quiver.

"Don't look. Here." PT wrapped a handkerchief as a blindfold around my head.

I took a deep, shaky breath. The feel of a light breeze on my face calmed me, and the dread faded. Elizabeth had been afraid of heights, not me. Her panic on top of the cliff had led to the accident. I had been carrying her fear all these years. It was time to let go.

PT guided my hands to the ropes, and I continued, step by careful step. Soon, brilliant sunshine filtered through the blindfold as we came out of the shadow of the tower. A hand took mine—Farrington, I assumed. He led me onto the tower top. A small crowd cheered as PT ceremoniously removed my blindfold as if it were all for show. They were mostly supervisors and other workers, but I recognized a few of the more intrepid bridge committee members as well. I managed a smile and a wave, taking in the magnificent scene, 276 feet above the river. I stepped as close as I dared to the edge of the tower.

Our world spread beneath us as if in heaven. As if there were no need to breathe or stand on my own as the wind filled my lungs and the sky held me aloft. To the north, the river bent toward the sea. The island of Manhattan stretched out, a grid of dark streets lined with long rows of trees, Central Park a big, green rectangle cut into the center. To the south and east, Brooklyn and Long Island, with their mix of squatty brick houses under slate and shingled roofs, white church steeples, and the gray ocean beyond. Across the narrows, Staten Island, studded with trees, seemingly one with New Jersey to the west.

"Grand, isn't it?" PT had joined me, and I passed the field glasses to him. He scanned northeast.

"Your precious Connecticut is too far to see," I teased.

"Indeed. Another world."

Farrington showed me how the cables were coming together, the issues with some iron pulleys and fasteners that were wearing unevenly. He took some measurements, and I sketched some metal plates we would need.

Aside from acting as my chief hand-holder, PT wanted to evaluate the workers on the project. "You've stolen all the best ship riggers," he said to Martin.

"Ah, this would be the circus high-wire training program, provided to you at no extra charge. I'm sure that's why you're here," Martin said with a cynical smile.

New wires were lashed with twine at intervals to the carrier wire. Upon the wire arriving in position, the twine ties were no longer necessary and required removal before the wires could be gathered into a strand. I watched as a slender rigger on a boatswain's chair, attached by a pulley to the carrier wire, slowly descended toward us over the river from the Manhattan tower, cutting through the twine ties. One of the support wires must have snapped, as he suddenly swung erratically, barely hanging on. I held my breath. A burly rigger was his counterpart on our side, and he shoved off on another chair. He got nearly halfway across the river, close to the other rigger, when his pulley got jammed between wires. He could not reach to free himself. With the carrier cable forced to a stop, both riggers were trapped.

An audible gasp passed through the onlookers. The wind picked up, and the men swung helplessly in their chairs high over the middle of the river. Martin, Farrington, and PT consulted, their arms waving about wildly. I spotted the acrobat, Supple, whom I had borrowed from PT's circus some time ago. I waved him over and led him to the edge of the tower for a view of the trapped riggers.

Without a word, Supple swung himself onto the carrier wire, wrapped his legs around it, and pulled himself hand over hand to the trapped men. While clinging to the dangerously swaying wire with his legs, he grabbed the pulley, cut the tangled twine, and set the pulley free. Then Martin pulled the wire-hoisting lever, and all three were pulled to safety to the cheers and clapping of the crowd. PT pointed at me and led the crowd in another round of applause, which I modestly waved off. Inside, of course, I was bursting with pride.

Much as I would have preferred to end my visit to the top of the world at that moment, there were more festivities planned. As had been demonstrated, the time-consuming work of cutting the twine ties was dangerous. Nonetheless, Farrington was determined to increase the efficiency. The reason for his fancy suit became clear. He ceremoniously handed his pocket watch to Martin and climbed in a boatswain's chair hanging from the wire that stretched from the tower over a bit of river, then a half mile of the city to the Brooklyn anchorage, where another crowd had gathered.

"Give me seven minutes!" Farrington shouted to the crowd, who cheered him on. He readied his knife, the latch securing his chair was released, and he slid toward the anchorage at great speed, lashing the ties with one swoosh of his large knife, his other hand gripping the rope suspending his chair.

As the chief mechanic slid farther away, I watched him through field glasses. Halfway to the anchorage, he struggled with an especially tight tie. He lost his grip on the knife, and it tumbled to the ground. Farrington waved at us for help. Without his knife to free them, the ties impeded the progress of the pulley from which his chair hung.

Martin shook his head. He waved Supple over, surely to have him reenact his heroic rescue.

I stopped him. "No, it's too far and too dangerous over land."

"Have you gone mad? Farrington's my chief mechanic, for Christ's sake!"

"Just wait."

Farrington swung in his chair, pointing to his predicament, waving and smiling at his audience, who oohed in sympathy and worry.

Supple arrived, listened to our argument, then offered, "I can do it, ma'am."

"Thank you, Mr. Supple, but I believe he'll solve this on his own."

Farrington dangled for what seemed like an hour until he climbed onto the top of his chair. There he untied the twine, then slid to the next, making his way in increments to the anchorage, where he was greeted as a hero.

Something changed that day between Martin and me. His allegiance and trust had always belonged to Wash, as was appropriate, but that day, Martin shook PT's hand. Then, placing his hat over his heart, he gave me a small bow. I had finally gained the respect of this ornery but competent engineer.

I never had an official title. Sometimes I thought it should be *handler of all the unforeseen details*. For example, Martin came to me with a three-inch thick manual, a tremendous inventory of iron and steel parts. I recognized Wash's careful script and intricate diagrams.

"Suppliers are manufacturing the items with check marks, right on schedule." Martin turned several pages illustrating special plates, bolts, and tools necessary to put the parts in place. "Then there are the ones nobody's ever had a use for." He ran his finger down a list of parts with no name, only a diagram. "They don't exist."

One diagram showed a long metal bar, with a hole—like the eye of a needle—at each end. "I'd call this an eyebar," I said.

He penciled the word in. "So named."

Weeks later in my office, I met with a handful of suppliers who were eager for the opportunity to do business. A ruddy-faced man of about fifty showed me a sample steel fastener. "Of course, you will receive the size you specified. Now, how many of these will you need?" he asked, leaning on his fat fists halfway across my desk.

Turning my head to avoid the stench of his breath, I did some calculating. "Fifty-six. Add a few for good measure. Let's say sixty."

"Sixty!" His breath was accompanied by a spray of spittle. "Do you have any idea of the tooling for a special request such as this? We need to make thousands to make the order worthwhile."

"Just give me a price estimate." I dismissed him and his spit as I waved up the next man in line.

The bluster of Mr. Stinkbreath gave me an idea. I didn't need thousands of the same simple design; I needed few of a unique design. I remembered the *N* that Eleanor had made for me so many years ago.

I was overdue for a visit to Cold Spring anyway, so I made sure Miss Mann could stay with Johnny and made plans for a short trip by train.

Travelling north along the river, the city thinned to forest. Arriving at the tiny Cold Spring station felt like coming home and yet like entering a strange world. In contrast to the crowdedness of Grand Central, there were no more than half a dozen people milling about, including Mother and Eleanor, who had been forewarned by letter.

I was startled to see Mother limping along with a cane.

"Just a little twitch in my back." She waved away my concern.

Songs of the woodland birds I missed in Brooklyn greeted me, and I took a deep breath of the pure country air. Trees still wore the bright green leaves of early summer and cardinals and chickadees flitted in their branches. Mother, Eleanor, and I walked up the familiar street, sharing the latest town gossip. They stopped to greet each passerby, parasols bumping in neighborly greetings. With all the interruptions, we didn't get through all the juicy news in the few blocks to the house.

"So what is this proposal you've been so mysterious about?" Mother asked as I took my baggage from her wagon and bumped it up the front steps. Her housemaid arrived too late, and Mother dismissed her with a wave and roll of her eyes.

Weary from the journey, I sank into one of the double rockers on the porch. "Eleanor and I need to discuss some details regarding metalwork. You're welcome to join us, but I'm afraid it would bore you."

"Hmph. I know when I'm an outcast." Hands on hips in mock humiliation, Mother took her leave.

Eleanor sat beside me as I emptied a collection of metal screws, bolts, and plates from my bag and handed them to her.

"Junk...good...will rust in a heartbeat..." She passed judgment on each item, running her trained fingers across threads and joints, weighing their heft in an open palm.

I reviewed the exact use of the items I required, along with specifications for size and strength.

"These will be at the top of the towers?" She took a fingernail file out of her pocket and scraped the surface of a hefty bolt.

"That's right. Part of the saddle securing the cables to the tower, which sits on rollers to reduce friction as the cables are stressed. Totally exposed to the elements and under great tension."

"Hmm. What about this?" She held up a thin, irregularly shaped piece of metal.

"That needs be flexible and thin, almost painted on, and waterproof."

"Iron is no good. Galvanized steel won't give you the flexibility."

I thought of the beautiful waterproof sheathing on the *Cutty Sark*. "What about Muntz metal? An alloy of copper, zinc, and a bit of iron, melted at—"

"I know. Muntz metal would work. Problem is, it's patented and expensive."

"We don't need much. If that's what works, we'll pay the patent fees."

Eleanor pursed her lips, bending and tapping the piece of metal. "I think I can come up with something. Give me a week." She stowed the samples and diagrams in her satchel.

"How am I to pay you when you won't claim your work?" I brushed metal shavings from my lap.

"No, no, it can't be known." She grabbed my elbow. "We don't need any more controversy regarding female designers."

TWENTY-NINE

The country heaved with uprisings that summer as railroad unions went on strike and riots in Baltimore and Pittsburgh killed dozens. The year 1876 had ended with dual tragedies: the collapse of a railroad bridge in Ohio had killed ninety people a few days after fire and structural failure at the Brooklyn Theater killed 295. The theater had been built by Kingsley's construction company, a fact that gnawed at me, for he was still one of our largest contractors.

With workers motivated to keep their difficult but steady jobs, bridge construction moved at a faster pace. Four cable-spinning carriers traveled nonstop back and forth between the towers like mechanical spiders weaving a looping web, and work began on the road approaches. These were each about a quarter of a mile long in order to provide the proper incline from ground level to the top of the anchorage buildings. After clearing and preparing the site, brick and stone support structures were begun.

Compared to the grueling conditions of the caissons and towers as well as those posed by nature itself, this work progressed more quickly and with relative ease. Proper masons were in short supply, however, as tremendous construction was in progress all over the city. Being fairly simple work, the mixing and laying of bricks fell to scarcely trained but enthusiastic men.

The design for the roadway approach called for brick arches, scaled so that the arches grew larger as they neared the anchorages. I had kept O'Brien away from his true vocation of stonework for too long, and he begged me to return, especially with our current shortage of masons. His son, Patrick, was close to twenty by then and eager to learn the trade as well. Their job would be to integrate the brick and stone arches.

I beamed as Patrick followed his father's instructions, mixing mortar with a shovel. The child I had known swimming with Johnny was now grown and working alongside his father.

Workers removed wooden supports inside a recently completed arch. I spoke with O'Brien as he filled a bucket with mortar. We parted as he headed under the arch with his bucket and trowel.

"Mrs. Roebling!" Young waved me over and helped me climb to the top of the arch. What concerned him also appeared ominous to me and would have even to an untrained eye. A crack in the mortar about half an inch wide ran across the midpoint of the arch.

"That wasn't there fifteen minutes ago," Young said. He unsheathed his knife, thrust it too easily into the mortar. When he yanked it out, the knife was coated as if it had sliced into an underbaked cake. "It should be dry by now, but it's still too wet. A little too much water in the mix or maybe the humidity."

I crouched down and pinched a sample, rubbing the gritty substance between my fingers. "We better put the supports back in."

Even as we spoke, the gap widened another inch. "Get off!" we screamed simultaneously, waving the masons off the arch. Thankfully, all got off safely as the crack widened and the roadway formed a peak in the middle.

"O'Brien is under there!" I shouted to Young. He ran to where he could leap off the road, and I followed, screaming the name of my friend.

The entire arch thundered down into a cloud of dust and rubble. *Where is he?* Dread gripped me like an iron claw. *Dear God, let him be safe.*

Patrick ran up to me. "Where's my da?"

I laid my hand on the young man's shoulder but could not meet his eyes. "We'll find him."

Soon, dozens of workers and bystanders gathered at the site. Young organized them into sections, and everyone started digging with shovels, pickaxes, and bare hands. More and more people arrived, curious onlookers and helpers alike. Police placed barricades to control the crowds.

Through the afternoon, we dug. I found a wheelbarrow and carted away jumbles of debris—brick, dirt, mortar, and stone—and all the while, I hoped and prayed we would find O'Brien alive.

Exhausted, I sat on a rubble heap, watching workers leave the site as sunset streaked the sky. Young sat next to me, cradled his head in his hands. "I'm sorry, Mrs. Roebling."

"It's not your fault, Mr. Young."

"No. About this."

Young uncurled his filthy and blood-crusted fist to reveal something shining through a coat of dirt. He passed the tiny object to me, his eyes dark pools of sorrow. His arm supported me as the blood drained from my face. Without further inspection, I knew it was a silver locket. I sniffed back tears. Young's shoulders heaved as he wept in silence. He and O'Brien had worked together for nearly eight years.

I had to find Patrick. I patted Young's shoulder and left him to his grief. Soon, I found O'Brien's son. He too rested on a pile of rubble, his young face hollowed by shadows cast by a dimming sun. I sat next to him and pressed the locket into his palm, closing each of his fingers, one for each sibling, around it. He held my gaze with his for a few moments, then held me as we sobbed and sobbed as dusk turned into night.

❧

I couldn't face my husband. My heart leaden with grief, a profound sense of failure tearing me apart, I couldn't explain to him how we had lost someone we both held so dear. Martin or Young might risk Wash's wrath and notify him, but I was physically and mentally spent. I caught the ferry to Manhattan and watched the lights of the Brooklyn riverfront fading into the distance through my tears. My mind jumbled, replaying the horror.

I found PT in his downtown office, keeping his usual late hours. This office was even more ornate than the last, and his beloved monogrammed door had found its way back to Manhattan, giving me a small sense of stability in my distraught state.

He was quick to hold and comfort me, despite my dirty hands and ragged clothing.

"I don't know how I'm going to face Wash. He's so fragile these days."

"He's been through war and lost many workers on the bridge. I think he's strong enough, Emily."

"You don't understand. He'll blame me. O'Brien was special to him. To both of us."

"Yes, I know of your affection for Mr. O'Brien."

"Then you know how difficult this is."

"I am sorry for your loss. But I can't be a receptacle for all your sorrows. You yourself have insisted on a relationship that would raise no scorn."

"This moment, I am in need of a supportive friend. Wash is... He's been through so much. And now, between the two of us, we've created six orphans."

PT pulled out a handkerchief and wiped my cheek, no doubt streaked with filth and tears. "I know, and again, I am truly sorry. But here is my dilemma. I have respected your need for emotional distance during this project. Yet you come here now for comfort I would be happy to give but that is at the same time forbidden." He rounded his hands upon my shoulders. "Out of respect for me and your husband, you need to sort this out with *him*."

I was dumbstruck. I wanted him to calm me, take away some of the pain, as he had so many times before. But he was right. It was unfair for me to take advantage of his giving nature when I could not give of myself. I needed to respect the boundaries I had insisted upon.

"Go home," he added, his voice gentle. "You are stronger than you think. You and Washington will get through this." He tucked his handkerchief into my palm. "And then, dear Peanut, when this is over and you are ready to imagine another life, a life full of the sort of merriment you deserve, then I will be here for you."

I twisted the now grimy cloth, imagining Wash being assaulted with this news all alone, as surely Martin or Young would tell him. PT's words floated in air, tainted by my own selfishness.

I hurried to catch the last ferry home, then dragged myself up Columbia Heights on foot. The streetlamps threw deep shadows, profiling Wash in the middle of the street, hugging our son. Until this moment, I hadn't considered how my sweet nine-year-old would feel about the tragedy. O'Brien had been like a second father to him.

"I'm sorry, Son," Wash said. Their heads turned at the click of my heels on the cobblestones.

"I hate her, and I hate that bridge!" Johnny ran into the house.

Wash glared at me. I braced myself for the tongue-lashing I was about to receive. Willed it, almost. His words couldn't possibly make me feel worse, and perhaps their battering against me would help free my soul from its deep and lonely pain.

He squeezed my upper arms, firmly, not with affection. "I was happy to hear you were uninjured." Then his words stabbed at me like knives: "poor judgment," "careless," and, curiously, "still showing off at the dance while the soldiers lay dying."

I said little to defend myself, as he had a right to his fury. We remained in the middle of the street. Neighbors opened windows in curiosity, then slammed them shut.

He guided me back to the house, dangling his pocket watch in my face. In a low growl, he chastened, "Where have you been? Johnny has been a wreck, worried about you."

"I…"

He stopped at our front stoop, arms across his chest. "Why did I learn of this from my foreman?"

"I'm sorry. That was something I could not bring myself to do." I forced myself to meet his eyes. "It took all my strength to get through this evening. I found someone to talk to so that I could start to make sense of all this."

"Oh, indeed," Wash said, his voice bitter. "And who might this tender ear belong to?"

"P. T. Barnum."

His eyes blazed, and his jaw clenched in a flash of his father's ill temper. "So this is what I came back to." He rubbed his eyes with his fists. "I'm exhausted. I'm sure you are as well."

"Let's go in." I stepped toward the house, but Wash caught my elbow.

"I'll leave after the funeral. It's probably better for all concerned that I spend more time in Trenton." He limped into the house.

I remained for a long time gazing at the stars, bewildered and utterly alone.

Wash said little regarding the tragedy. I hoped he wanted to spare me the horror of reliving the accident. He also buried his anger at my visit to PT, another deep wound left to fester.

By the day of the funeral, I had pushed away so many feelings that I was numb inside. Wash handled the solemn ceremony with grace, reciting the words of Longfellow:

> *Lives of great men all remind us*
> *We can make our lives sublime,*
> *And, departing, leave behind us*
> *Footprints on the sands of time;*
> *Let us, then, be up and doing,*
> *With a heart for any fate;*
> *Still achieving, still pursuing,*
> *Learn to labor and to wait.*

I mourned, not only for O'Brien but for Wash and myself as well. He seemed to gather strength from the poem, although not enough to keep him home, fighting for his bridge…and for his wife.

THIRTY

1878

By springtime, the cable spinning was progressing nicely, the giant spools of wire dwindling while the four main cables grew. The workers' tasks were like clockwork: attaching individual wires to the carriers for the trip across the river, bundling hundreds of wires into each strand, then securing the strands to the anchors. Indeed, the problems we faced were more from boredom and inattention of the crew, even at the great heights at which they worked.

While walking to the work site in my bloomer costume, I counted more cheers than jeers. Johnny was ten and no longer required constant attention. Wash spent most of his time in Trenton. I spent mornings at the work site, but it was time to think of life after the bridge. In quiet moments, I imagined a life with PT. Was he waiting for me? We never again spoke of O'Brien's death, PT's promise to wait for me, or my failure to do the same. I dreamed of what my life could be after the bridge, when I could truly choose.

The only thing I was certain I wanted was to work for women's suffrage. Newspapers crackled with letters from Elizabeth Cady Stanton and Susan B. Anthony. Surely, we were now past the risk of threats from a local policeman. It was time to revisit my goal.

Mother and her women's suffrage circle had met throughout the years, but the movement progressed in fits and starts, there being no clear path forward and serious dissension within the ranks of the movement's leaders. A few years before, Susan B. Anthony had been arrested for breaking the law by voting. Many meetings were held and speeches made, but no laws changed. The movement had stalled.

My neighbor and acquaintance, Reverend Beecher, had been embroiled in an adultery scandal, the lurid headlines of lawsuits and chicanery overshadowing his leadership in suffrage. Having had my own temptations, I found it hard to judge him. I wanted to remind the naysayers of Christ's words, "Let he who is without sin cast the first stone." Still, I kept my distance from the preacher.

My mother's circle planned to travel to Manhattan to listen to Miss Anthony, who was beseeching Congress with a proposed amendment to allow women to vote. Mrs. Alva Vanderbilt was to host, and I accepted her invitation not only for the chance to hear Miss Anthony, but also to view the interior of the Vanderbilts' new Fifth Avenue mansion.

The meeting was a rather jumbled affair. Mrs. Vanderbilt had given birth twice in the last year, and the wails of both babies frequently interrupted the proceedings, despite the best efforts of two nannies. The unfinished mansion disappointed, the meeting held in one of the few completed rooms.

The women argued over whether winning the right to vote would incur military service and jury duty obligations. This led to another argument about the responsibility of women to run a home and raise children—ostensibly the most important task imaginable as one is raising the very *future* of the country. I made a few suggestions that a woman could do both but was outshouted. Having heard enough, I excused myself and wandered about the unfinished rooms, admiring the fluted columns and tall windows, until I encountered a fellow escapee.

"A frightful mess, isn't it?" A woman my mother's age, with a strong face, more handsome than lovely, held out a gloved hand. "Amelia Bloomer."

"As in bloomer costume? Pleased to meet you. I'm Emily Roebling."

"I know of you." Her eyes took in my dress, a rather frilly one I now regretted. "Yes and no. I wore the costume but didn't invent it. Somehow, my name became associated, due to my magazine, I suppose. It should have been named for Lydia Sayer Hasbrouck."

I recalled a beat too late that Mrs. Bloomer was well-known for publishing the first women's periodical, *The Lily*. I had no idea who Hasbrouck was. Mother would have been humiliated.

"I heard you wear bloomers." She crossed her arms under her considerable bosom, her gaze directed at my dress.

"Well, not on occasions such as these. As I see you agree." I nodded toward her own plain white, perfectly serviceable dress.

"We gave up wearing them when you were but a girl. Well, Lydia didn't, but she's sort of a *special case*, as they say." She rolled her eyes. "The costume does nothing but provide a distraction from the real issue of women's rights."

The statement rankled me, and her condescending tone made it worse. I held my tongue when I wanted to retort: *As if the ridiculous temperance movement, which you have interwoven with suffrage, isn't a distraction.* This sort of infighting was one of the reasons the movement was progressing so slowly. Arguing filtered in from the adjoining room. If Papa and Wash had planned bridges this way, there would be carriages swimming in rivers.

"Bloomers are practical in some workplaces." I excused myself and marched off to find Mother.

I left that day with a profound sense of unease. More and more, I was discouraged by the secretive meetings, not to mention the lack of agreement on the central issues and leadership. There had to be another way.

Believing peaceful protest to be the most successful way to effect change, I summoned the ladies' presence on a drizzly Saturday morning in April.

We met under a star—a big red star. R. H. & Macy Co. had grown to eleven buildings at Sixth Avenue and Fourteenth Street in Manhattan, so we counted on a built-in crowd of mostly women. We headed down the street wearing our finest bloomer costumes and carrying homemade signs, ignoring the heckles and stares of people on the street. Perhaps our attire was a bit of a miscalculation on my part—Amelia Bloomer might have had a point after all.

"Emily, what are you doing to us old bats? Can't we make the same statement properly dressed?" Henrietta asked as young bystanders hooted and catcalled. She gave them a fierce glare, as only Henrietta could, and the youngsters promptly hushed.

Eleanor smiled back at the crowd, deftly caught a potato launched at her, and raised it in triumph. We worked our way down the street, talking among ourselves as if we were merely out for a stroll.

"We hear such impressive things about your work with the bridge," Eleanor said.

"Mother will tell you I've been a neglectful daughter. I finally read Mrs. Beebe's book. I regret I wasn't much help."

"Oh, Emily, you were much too busy to worry about my manuscript!" assured Carrie.

"Nonetheless, I really must get something off my chest."

"What is that, dear?" Mother said, a bit of worry and a hint of warning in her voice.

A woman sweeping the sidewalk stopped, her mouth agape. Eleanor waved her over.

Henrietta was waving some papers in the air—her tax bill. "Recall the words of the Revolutionists, *Taxation without representation is tyranny*." Her voice could be heard for a block. "We have tyranny still. Women are taxed while not allowed their own vote."

The gathered cried, "Tyranny!"

"Lydia Hasbrouck went to jail for refusing to pay taxes," Henrietta said.

More cheering women gathered, encircling Henrietta, who raised her arms to the crowd, her voice growing more forceful. "Hasbrouck said: *So long as men held women as inferiors, and unworthy of citizenship, and of no account politically, save when the tax-roll was called, we should demand… to be 'let alone,' and let men pay the fiddler who gives all the golden music to them*."

The woman dropped the broom and joined us. She joined Henrietta, who used her wits and connections to build a real estate empire under her late husband's name, and Carrie, who had penned a novel that had tongues wagging all over the country. Eleanor was a genius inventor, with patents under a pseudonym.

I had failed them, my support half-hearted. So entrenched in my own world, I had failed to recognize the achievements of the women marching shoulder to shoulder with me. "I'm afraid I'm guilty of the very thing I despise. You accomplished ladies have helped me to see that."

They regarded me with raised eyebrows and small smiles.

"Don't be so mysterious, Emily. What do you mean to say?" Mother said.

By now, a larger group of women had joined the procession. I raised my voice to be heard by all. "I've long resented the barriers women face should they want a career. Denied proper education, the right to vote, even forced to wear clothing that handicaps them. Laws written by men to keep women in their place."

Pedestrians stopped and listened.

"Right to vote! Right to vote!" the women behind us chanted.

"I think we *all* share those views, dear," said Eleanor.

"Yes. I know that." I lowered my voice. "But I thought I was exceptional. That I was bright and talented and *deserved* a place working next to the men."

"While other women, like us, didn't?" Henrietta interjected without malice. We stopped walking as the ladies circled around me and the crowd chanted. Our numbers were now large enough to block street traffic. The police approached, bobby sticks at the ready. But I didn't care—they could throw me in the paddy wagon. I would run from the cause no longer.

I nodded to Henrietta. "I am guilty of underestimating my own gender, not considering how much more they were capable of. But I always thought all women should be allowed to do whatever they choose."

Mother put her arm around me. "That's all right, Em. We grow too soon old and too late smart. And you *are* exceptional. Look around you."

"Emily! Emily!" The crowd chanted as if on cue. Even though my picture had been in the newspapers several times, it startled me to be recognized. I waved in thanks, and they applauded.

Perhaps my long detour into bridge building was a journey to my true calling. The ladies wrapped their arms around me like the cloak of a queen. Mother's friends, *my* friends granting me safe passage.

I approached my work with a renewed enthusiasm. I should have liked to say that my dedication was accepted and appreciated by the scores of men with whom I worked, but that was not the case. I simply determined that their reluctance to do so was their problem, not mine.

We were entering the next critical phase of construction. The entire weight of the roadway—and anything upon it—was to be suspended on the four nearly completed cables, each about sixteen inches in diameter and about thirty-six hundred feet long. In each cable would be five thousand wires, close to seventy-eight million feet of wire rope in total.

Of course, Roebling's Sons' wire rope company produced some of the finest in the country, and the cost for transportation from Trenton would be reasonable. However, as had concerned Papa in Cincinnati, it would be unseemly to award the huge contract to the Roebling brothers, even if the deal made financial sense.

After much behind-the-scenes dealing, the Brooklyn Bridge Committee awarded the contract to a business partner of Benjamin Stone: J. Lloyd Haigh. Not only was his bid the lowest, his firm was located in Red Hook, Brooklyn, which pleased the committee.

Wash was circumspect about the decision. "So long as the wire passes all the tests, I have no issue."

Stone himself accompanied the inspectors as they tested a sample from each huge spool of wire upon arrival from the manufacturer, and he assured me the quality was as specified.

Wash wrote numerous letters and provided records to assure the committee and the public that he took no profit from the bridge, other than his salary. Although I admired his honorable ethics, the financial consequences weren't clear until one Sunday morning as he packed his bags for yet another stay in Trenton. He had been in Brooklyn for the past two months, and his palsies and headaches had resumed with ferocious intensity.

Avoiding the sight of his shaking hands as they folded shirts into neat packets, I stared out the window at the gray ribbon of river below. "Why are you are cured of your afflictions while away only for them to return when here at home?" I raised the window for some fresh air. "It seems the environments are quite similar. A city. A river. Four seasons. The only difference seems to be me."

"Come here." He sat on the bed and patted the spot next to him. "I don't know the answer to your question, but be assured, I'm not leaving to get away from you."

The springs creaked on the old bed as I joined him. I ran my hand over the quilted coverlet with its interlocking circles—the "wedding band" pattern.

He took my hand in his own, warm and trembling. "I must earn a living."

"What do you mean? The committee has continued your salary throughout."

"Ha! That salary barely covers my expenses to do the job. The travel, the lawyers, the medical bills. What do you think pays for all this?" He waved around the finely furnished room. "And Johnny's education, the help, the—"

"I see. But your inheritance. And mine. Surely—" My brow crinkled. I hadn't dwelt on our finances.

"Darling, it is all under control. But it's critical the wire business be attended to. Finding new customers, developing new products and uses." He took back his hand, stretching and clenching his fingers. "Perhaps that's part of the puzzle."

"Oh?"

"When here, I'm surrounded by reminders of all the things I can no longer do. But back home, it's all forward motion." He straightened a perfectly aligned stack of shirts. "There, I feel like a man again."

His reference to Trenton as *home* was not lost on me. I had been struggling with my love for two men but failed to consider that I might no longer fit into Wash's life. We had long since drifted apart, he to a life in Trenton, his adoring family surrounding him, and me, working hard but much preferring the grand adventures of the larger city, with its glittering lights and entertainment.

My husband had said he no longer felt like a man around me, a thought that crushed my very soul. How did one respond to that? Deny it was true? We no longer made love, and I had given up trying to entice him.

He had finally opened up, been brave enough to reveal his most vulnerable self, but I just wrung my hands. If my words didn't come out right, he'd sense my own conflict. So I did the worst thing. I pretended not to hear him.

❦

Mother's friends had hinted that they wished to take a tour of the huge cable-spinning operation. Of course, we welcomed politicians, dignitaries, and anyone with power and influence to attend carefully staged demonstrations. However, my mother and her coterie could be a bit unpredictable. After long deliberation, I decided they should have their tour, but only after I had given them a thorough lecture on safety. No bloomer costumes this time. I wanted them well-dressed, like any other important visitor. Even so, I still harbored some misgivings when Mother, Carrie, Henrietta, Eleanor, and I set out for the bridge.

The roof of the Brooklyn anchor building provided a good vantage point. Farrington gave them a brief tour of the site. "These wire strands, each three inches in diameter, are made up of a bundle of over two hundred and seventy wires." He pointed to the strands descending from the bridge tower. "Nineteen strands are being wired together to form a cable. If you studied a cross section, it would resemble a round honeycomb. That honeycomb will be wrapped like a mummy with even more wire"—he circled his finger—"giving us the four main cables that will support the roadway. The strands are attached to a chain of iron eyebars in the brick structure beneath us, then fixed to a massive iron anchor at street level."

Supple and two other workers adjusted a horseshoe-shaped iron support that clamped a taut wire strand. The iron support with the strand was lowered and disappeared into an opening leading to the anchor below. Farrington gave a signal, and workers began easing the next strand through a pulley, straining mightily against the tremendous forces as the strand tightened and the machinery took hold.

I overheard the ladies enjoying some private joke, referring to Farrington as a wire bundle. Even though I agreed it was an apt description and thought Farrington would appreciate their attentions, I kept to my script. "We are using galvanized steel wire, not iron, for an extra measure of strength and durability."

I held up a sample of the wire when—*bang!*—there was a sound akin to cannon fire as the strand snapped off the machinery. Like a steel serpent, its tail end whipped violently, first slicing across Farrington's chest and then across a worker's back, sending him flying across the anchorage. With a loud *whoosh*, the tail flew back toward us and struck Supple with such force, he vanished from the rooftop. As the terrified women and workers flattened themselves on the roof, the strand whipped, whooshing and snapping, then streaked toward the tower.

Onlookers screamed as the strand sailed over the streets, toppling trees like a giant scythe. The strand sliced the chimney off a house before sailing over the Brooklyn tower. Losing velocity, it snapped very close to a ferry boat, then crashed into the river with a huge splash.

The women huddled together, wide-eyed and shaking, in a tangle of dresses and crinolines. Farrington's injury didn't seem severe; he was shouting orders and checking others. A swarm of workers preceded me to the injured men, so I hurried to the edge of the anchor building to see if Supple had survived his fall from the building. His unnatural position, limbs splayed on concrete over eighty feet below, gave me the sad answer.

Sometimes, the mind, in times of great distress, resorts to the clinical, perhaps the most effective way of bearing with crushing sorrow. Were it not so for me, I would have sunk to the floor and wept. Instead, I puzzled: *Why did that strand snap?* The tensile strength of the many wires should have far exceeded the forces. Some wire remnants hung from a pulley. I worked the wire back and forth until it snapped. I knew the wire rope better than the texture of my own hair, and this was not what we had specified. How did it pass inspection? Had it been switched?

I grimaced at the hardening of my own heart, thinking about the wire instead of the loss of this dear man. Supple had done nothing to deserve this. In fact, he had risked his own life for others, asking nothing in return but a steady paycheck. I comforted the women, trembling in shock.

THIRTY-ONE

1879

The massive towers and anchor buildings were now connected by the graceful arcs of the cables, glinting in the sun and showing promise of the future. Contracts for the steel suspenders were opened for bids. These suspenders would hang from the cables and support the infrastructure for the roadway. Papa had specified iron, but Wash felt steel was less prone to damage from corrosion and stress.

Roebling wire had been mixed with Haigh's wire in the cables when Haigh's company couldn't keep up with the demand. The wire strand that had so violently snapped was mostly Roebling wire of good quality but had been frayed by a pulley. After repairs, I was assured it wouldn't happen again. But still, my gut twisted with the suspicion that something else was wrong. The type of wire I had recovered was unlikely to have been responsible for the accident, but its friability troubled me, and I didn't trust Haigh, the contractor who had provided it. I broke off a piece and sent it to a laboratory for testing.

The suspender wire contract was awarded to Roebling Brothers, who were not taking a profit and therefore were the lowest bidder. I was much relieved, even before we had any results of the testing.

❧

April was my favorite month. One Saturday, I took Johnny to a garden nursery, excited to see the first flowers of spring. He was now a sturdy eleven-year-old, and I piled clay pots, bags of seeds, and rooted plants into his outstretched arms until he could hold no more. After delivering them home, he begged to visit his friends. I sent him off, wistful of slowly losing my little boy.

I was planting pansies next to our front stoop when a familiar voice called my name, causing me to drop my spade. Brushing dirt from my skirt, I offered Wash my cheek. He had returned from Trenton, once again unexpectedly.

"I have a present for you." He brought his hand from behind his back, holding a three-foot-long metal bar.

"How thoughtful, as I already have plenty of flowers." I accepted the bar as if it were the king's crown. "What is it?"

"A sample of the suspender wire."

He unwound the loose end of a thin, flexible wire that wrapped a center core, which contained a bundle of thicker wires, each about the size of a pencil lead. Together, it was about two inches in diameter, a structural miniature of the great cables. The suspenders would hang vertically from the cables and connect the roadway to the cables.

"The factory is going full tilt, and the first delivery is on the way."

Soon, the suspenders were going up at a rapid rate, starting at the anchorages and spreading toward the towers on each side. Men dangling on small platforms that hung from the cables attached the suspenders—giant harp strings in the sky.

As the suspenders were placed, their bottom ends were attached to steel beams. The beams would then creep forward from both sides of the river, like the unrolling of two giant rugs, until they met in the middle. Then two layers of steel trusses with cross bracing would be added for stability, and the top layer would be yellow pine planks. A lighter-weight pedestrian walkway would be built above the roadway.

Returning home in the late afternoon on a day where much infrastructure had been laid, I found Wash at the bedroom window, examining his rock collection.

"Have you been watching?" I nodded toward his telescope.

"Is there a problem?"

"Why don't you take a peek?"

He peered through the telescope, pivoted, refocused, and in seconds was done. "All appears in order."

"In fact it is." I huffed at his nonchalance. "The suspenders and decking are in place over both land spans and started over the river span. The first order of planking has arrived and seems of uniform high quality, no knots, sap, or rot."

"Yes, as I stipulated and have seen with my own eyes." He went back to his rock collection.

"You saw all that in twenty seconds?"

"I did."

I raised an eyebrow. Had he actually spent hours watching and didn't want me to know?

"Number one, I trust Martin, Farrington, and you. Number two, my eye is trained to pick up the slightest deviance in an instant."

"As is mine." A new sensation rolled over me, as if an angel had just given me a blessing. What did it matter if Wash appreciated all I was doing? The bridge was its own reward. A graceful curve was taking shape. The roadway gradually arced up. The center of the span would be one hundred and thirty-five feet above the water. The cables, in a steeper catenary curve, came down from the towers so that at their lowest point, in the middle of the river, they would attach directly to the roadway at its highest point. Seeing plans on paper come to life was like watching an angel get her wings.

⚓

H.M.S. Pinafore was all the rage, and PT finagled tickets to not just one of the many unauthorized productions but the authentic Gilbert and Sullivan musical. We had reached an arrangement agreeable to us both. We saw each other in the company of others—our spouses on rare occasion, but more often friends or business associates. He gathered several of them in his most elegant carriage, and we ferried over to Manhattan for a Sunday matinee of song, laughter, and good spirits.

On the ride back, we sang show tunes with lively voices and improvised lyrics. When we reached my home, I departed their company in the midst of "Oh Joy, Oh Rapture Unforeseen." The harmony faded as I stepped from the carriage.

A worker sat on my stoop. He stood and removed his hat. "Sorry to bother you, ma'am. If I can have a moment of your time."

"Good afternoon, Mr. Dunn." Several years had passed, but I readily recognized the ginger-headed worker. "What brings you here on a Sunday?"

"Mr. Kingsley keeps me busy, but perhaps tomorrow would be better?"

"You're here now. What is it?" I waved an all clear to PT. "You work for Mr. Kingsley?"

Dunn worked the brim of his slouchy hat. "Yes, ma'am. Ran out of things I'm suited for on the bridge, but there's plenty of work building banks and stores and such." He scuffed his boot toe on the cobblestones. "And the Brooklyn Theater."

"You worked on that?"

"Yes, ma'am. I wasn't surprised when the balcony collapsed."

"That happens in fires."

"That's so, but nothing was done right. We were pushed, 'Get it done,' all the time. Corners cut. I know how things should be…and they weren't."

"Did you come to tell me about a fire that occurred three years ago?" I glanced up. Lamps were being lit on our second floor.

"No, ma'am. See, I needed some extra work." He flicked his eyes at me. "Gamble a little. Anyway, I was offered good money for some simple work and didn't mind seeing some of my buddies who still work the bridge."

"Many workers do that for Mr. Kingsley. It's not a problem."

"This work wasn't for Kingsley. It was for a friend of his. We loaded big spools of wire onto wagons at a warehouse in Red Hook and carted them off to another, more remote warehouse. There, we loaded up another bunch and brought those back to the first warehouse."

"They may have been replacing unsuitable wire. All the wire was inspected at the bridge site."

"Perhaps so. But it was done at midnight. And this dropped off one of the spools we moved out of Red Hook." He produced an inspection certificate from his pocket.

"I see. Tell me, Mr. Dunn, who hired you for this?"

"Don't know his name. Big fellow, nice suit. Talked all 'jolly well.'"

"Thank you. Is there anything else?"

"No, ma'am. Thought you should know. You and the colonel have been good to me."

I pressed a few coins into Dunn's hand despite his protest.

After the wire had snapped and killed Supple, I had suspected that wire had been switched. Now I ground my teeth, certain of who was behind this treacherous act.

THIRTY-TWO

1880

The newspaper headlines screamed of the certainty of Wash's removal: "Engineer Roebling to Go" and "Roebling: Mayor Proposing to Supersede Him Because He Cannot Perform His Duties." I tossed the papers in the trash bin when they appeared on my desk. At home, I hid them so Johnny wouldn't see them.

Benjamin Stone seemed to take a particular delight in presenting me with the latest diatribe. In early January, he brought a shock of cold air in the door along with his usual bluster. His puffy face was beet red, and he wiped his dripping nose with a handkerchief as he dumped three dailies on my desk. "Ahem."

"Don't want to hear it, Mr. Stone." I lifted the papers and pivoted toward the trash. Percolating in my mind was how to use the information Dunn had given me. I had not yet collected enough evidence and didn't want to tip my hand.

"You'll hear this, missy. Don't ignore what might be the last warning."

I sighed and glanced at the headlines. "Tay Bridge Disaster—Scores Dead." That got my attention. I scanned the article. A few rumors had been circulating about a bridge collapse in Scotland, but I had no idea the accident was this tragic. My cheeks burned as I read on, Stone's huffing breath above me.

"Terrible." I shook my head. "Winds over seventy miles an hour."

"You think we never experience winds like that here?" he bellowed.

"Of course that can happen anywhere, especially on a seacoast. Winds have been factored in."

"Ha. Calculated, recalculated, does anyone know anymore what that tower of ineptitude will hold?"

"Ours is a completely different design. Comparing the East River Bridge to the Tay Bridge is like comparing a steamship to a rowboat." Although my voice was measured, inside, I was plagued with doubt, remembering the brittle wire crumbling in my hand.

❧

Johnny was about to enter his teen years, and I despaired at the lack of time I had spent with him. Before long, he would be out on his own, his childhood having vanished amid the continual demands of bridge building. Wash hadn't spent much time with him either, living in Trenton more than with us. So I planned a special treat for our son. The British ship *Cutty Sark* was scheduled to arrive in New York, and as Johnny had always loved sailing ships, I arranged for us to tour the triple-masted clipper.

A few dozen people gathered to cheer as she plied up the narrows, full sails billowing in the wind. Johnny's eyes widened as she was secured to the pier, her wooden hull, painted a shiny black with golden scrollwork, gleaming in the sun. We strolled her length of over two hundred feet, her graceful shape built for speed. Johnny laughed and pointed at the figurehead, a bare-breasted woman holding what appeared to be a horse's tail.

We boarded and were treated to a full tour by the captain. I had expected to see stacks of crates of tea from China. Instead, the hold was filled with jute in various stages of manufacture into rope. Enough for every ship and circus tent in the country. Dank and earthy, the hold smelled like a circus tent as well.

"I saw her under construction," I told Johnny as we stepped back down the gangplank, then turned for a last look at the beautiful ship. "I wish you could see her hull under the waterline. It's as gold as my wedding ring."

"Mama, why did you bring me here?"

"I thought you would enjoy seeing her. You so enjoyed building models with your father."

His eyes squeezed shut as if it were a painful memory.

"Didn't you?"

His height was now equal to mine, and he opened his bright-blue eyes and looked at me intently, causing me to blink away.

"I did. Very much." He gave a goodbye wave to the crew.

"I thought it time to discuss your future studies. I... We... Your father and I don't wish to push you into the family business."

"I thought it was something else." He crossed his arms over his chest and stared at his shoes. "Are you and Pa... I mean..." He looked up, his voice just above a whisper. "I don't wish you and Pa to remain together for my sake. I'd rather you be happy."

My heart sank. Why couldn't we have one joyous day together? "We've had difficulties, Johnny, as all families do. Ours happen to be front page news. But we're as happy as we can be for the moment." I gently shook his shoulder. "Don't worry about us. Think about *your* future." I waved toward the ship. "You've always loved building things, but it doesn't need to be bridges."

He brightened. "I do prefer things that move and have power. Trains, ships. Someday, we'll have machines that fly."

"That's my boy." He allowed me to slip my arm through his as we walked down the pier.

"What about you?" he asked. "What will you do with yourself once the bridge is finished and I am released from your empire?"

"I will laze about, being fed peeled grapes while reading Shakespeare and Tolstoy and Nietzsche and Dickens and Flaubert..."

"And the week after that? What about your women's causes?"

I sighed. "When the time is right. It's hard, Johnny. It's not just social and cultural change that's needed. There are laws preventing progress on many fronts."

"Then change the laws."

"Would that I could. Hmm. Perhaps a letter-writing campaign is in my future."

"No, I mean to say change them yourself." His voice cracked as it rose with emotion.

I shook my head. "One would have to be in office, with a good under-standing of the law, to do that."

"Then attend law school." He laughed and broke away, his youthful energy held at my pace for too long.

"Well, that's one idea. Or being fed grapes."

Of course, women weren't accepted into law school. But I knew men powerful enough to change that.

I was frequently invited to the monthly board meetings held in the bridge committee boardroom to provide an update both on bridge progress and Wash's status. An impressive space: large sketches adorned the wood-paneled walls, and scale models and a cross section of cable were displayed. The usual attendees were Benjamin Stone, Kingsley, Martin, and board president Henry Murphy. Stone and I were on unfriendly footing, and I was not fond of Kingsley, whom, like Stone, I found pretentious and condescending.

Former Congressman Hewitt was sometimes present, as he had been appointed by the mayor to ensure the board remained free of corruption and undue profit taking. He had already cleared Kingsley of pocketing thousands of dollars in unexplained expenses. I noted that they frequently sat next to each other and seemed quite chummy.

I rather admired Mr. Murphy. He was an accomplished lawyer and former U.S. representative with neatly cropped gray hair, tinted here and there with its original ginger. His tailored suits complemented his spare frame. He was tough but fair, and I was ever grateful that he chaired the committee.

"I move to replace the chief engineer," said Kingsley with the same nonchalance as if remarking on the weather.

"On what grounds?" Murphy asked in his clipped, official manner.

"As is quite well known and has been the case for some time, Mr. Roebling is physically and mentally incapacitated by a nervous affliction. That the condition was brought on by his work on the bridge is unfortunate, but we must consider the consequences of allowing him to continue."

"I second the motion," Stone piped in.

Kingsley nodded.

Stone tapped his pen on the table. "Mr. Roebling is an invalid who observes the building of the bridge through a telescope. We cannot know how much his mental capacity is impaired, as he refuses to appear before us."

"We must place the safety of the people first!" Kingsley hammered the table with his meaty fist.

"We are prepared to give Mr. Roebling appropriate compensation." Stone raised his cool gaze to meet mine.

"In return for his resignation?" I shot back.

"Not entirely. He could remain on as consulting engineer. Then there's the matter of your role, Mrs. Roebling. You've presented specious qualifications. Furthermore, should we decide to delve deeper into your activities, I believe we'd find them highly illegal for a woman."

The committee murmured; some coughed to cover chuckles.

Stone rapped his pen. "Mrs. Roebling's work has never been approved by this committee and must face further scrutiny."

"While you award more contracts to your business partners?" I said.

The men stirred uneasily in their seats.

Hewitt cleared his throat. "Gentlemen, I believe Mr. Stone is leading us down a rabbit hole. The legality of women's work is not an argument appropriate for our agenda."

I glanced toward the aging iron baron and politician, but he studied his fingertips. I had thought him to be aligned with Stone. Wash had no use for Hewitt, going back to the curious meeting with his father in Ringwood. "Hewitt cannot be trusted," Wash had written to Murphy. "He is ambitious beyond all measure and wields his power by extracting a hefty fee from those his power can assist." He was referring to the Brooklyn firm that won the wire award—Stone's business partner, Haigh.

"No good will come of challenging him. That is not our affair," Wash had told me.

But I could no longer allow the practice of awarding contracts and receiving bribes to go unchallenged. In my lap beneath the table, I twisted the piece of wire I had collected from the anchor building the day Supple was killed.

"If there is blame to be had, perhaps you should look no further than this room." I threw my evidence onto the long, polished table, let it skitter across, about as welcome as a dead fish. "The entire project was put at risk so that a few could extract unseemly profits." After making sure they were all watching, I picked up the wire and pinched it between my fingers, bending until it snapped—much too easily.

"How dare you make such accusations!" Stone bellowed.

"Would you care to explain, Mr. Stone, how a company in which you have considerable financial interest won the steel contract? Perhaps you can enlighten the committee on how inferior wire was switched for the wire we ordered?"

"You tell me, Mrs. Roebling. The wire that failed at the anchorage building was Roebling wire."

A rumble spread through the room.

"That is so. But that defect was found to have been caused by a faulty pulley, which sheared the wire. The important thing is that it led to the discovery of this wire, which has been mixed with the Roebling wire." I held up the piece of cable wire I had collected.

Wash was right. This was a serious accusation to level at anyone, and the meeting disintegrated into discordant shouting until Murphy banged his gavel to restore order.

Stone's threats, demands, and unceasing doubt over the past years boiled inside me. I used the ensuing silence to continue my attack. "Explain to us why your profits are more important than the safety of the millions of people who will pass over this bridge."

"I demand this woman be removed from the meeting immediately!" Stone thundered.

"I would remind the board that this meeting concerns the role of Mr. Roebling," Murphy said.

"Mr. Roebling's position is that if you have lost faith in him, he will step down entirely," I said.

"As he wishes." Stone chortled, followed by the laughter of his cohorts.

Murphy banged his gavel. "Mr. Stone, you are out of order. The board will render its decision shortly on the chief engineer. As his wife is but an advisor and messenger, I see no reason to examine her qualifications, and Mr. Hewitt's comments are valid." He wrote a note and passed it to the recorder. "A full investigation on the wire contracts will begin immediately. All in favor?"

All but Stone, who crossed his arms over his ample chest and glared at me, raised their hands.

THIRTY-THREE

1881

My frustration mounted at the board's sluggish investigation of the wire scandal, but at least the construction proceeded on schedule. No guilty parties had been identified, but a message from the board arrived, authorizing all future wire to be purchased from Roebling's Sons. With a combination of relief and concern, I read the rather hasty addendum: *We, the East River Bridge Committee, wish to express our ongoing faith in the chief engineer.* My own doubts would never be shared.

Wash wrote from Trenton, lifting my spirits and giving me hope: *Once again, I must thank you, my love, for having come to the rescue. Without your brave protest, I despair to think of the result, not only for the margin of safety for the bridge but our family business as a whole. We are all deeply in your debt.*

❧

Construction reached a milestone in December: the completion of the understructure of the roadway across the river. Workers had laid enough wooden planks across its length to create a walkway, and a celebratory walk from Brooklyn to Manhattan over the East River was planned.

I was to lead the small delegation. Climbing the roadway approach to the Brooklyn tower was familiar, yet this time excitement lifted my steps as if I were dancing.

Although not nearly as high as the tower top, the openness of the roadway support structure made my head spin as I watched chunks of ice pass over one hundred feet below. As workers placed the last planks in the walkway, I pressed my lips together, steeling myself for the walk across.

The mayor of Brooklyn, other dignitaries, and I would meet the mayor of New York and his entourage in the middle. Then, we were to share glasses of champagne. But it seemed sipping bubbly on an open walkway a hundred feet over the East River on a blustery day had little appeal. Instead, as a small crowd watched, I led a group of top-hatted men all the way across the bridge, and we toasted each other on the Manhattan side.

I thought it best not to invite PT to this ceremony, desiring to create at least the perception of a respectable distance. Never one to be slighted or ignored, he arranged for a big basket of flowers and scrumptious treats to be awaiting our arrival in Manhattan. The unmistakable red-and-white-striped cartons of peanuts and yellow ribbons emblazoned with *Greatest Show on Earth* foiled my plan.

It took two more years to sort out the web of deceit, theft, and corruption surrounding the wire fiasco. As Wash suspected, the contract had been awarded to J. Lloyd Haigh, a known crook, for political and financial gain. Haigh's wire was then switched for an even poorer grade. How much faulty wire had been woven into the cables was unknown. Blended as it was with thousands of miles of good wire, the inferior wire was impossible to remove.

I pored over the inspection records and did as much testing as possible on the few areas where the cable wire was still accessible. Wash and I exchanged many letters concerning practical ways to ensure the load-bearing strength. We came up with a solution: additional diagonal suspender wires, or stays, were to be attached directly from the towers to the roadway, as well as additional vertical suspenders from the four main cables. We calculated that the bridge was still four times stronger than necessary.

Roebling's Sons hummed along, and Wash returned to Brooklyn, but he scarcely left the house. His nervous condition had shown little improvement, requiring quiet at all times. Visitors were out of the question, and I fielded questions from reporters and politicians myself.

I had mixed emotions upon his return. I was happy to have him with me, of course, and hoped we could resume some sort of agreeable marriage. At the same time, I resented the loss of freedom as pangs of guilt engulfed me whenever I left him alone.

However, my presence no longer seemed to comfort to him. While helping him unpack his trunk, my hand crossed his arm as we reached for the same set of trousers. He jerked his arm back, as if sparked by electricity. I blinked at his reaction. I had assumed this ailment had resolved long before, as it didn't appear on the long list of complaints in his letters.

He brushed the matter aside, mumbling, "My skin is a bit sensitive these days."

THIRTY-FOUR

1882

On a steamy August afternoon, I traveled up to Cold Spring to celebrate the publication of Carrie Beebe's second book with her friends. Mother, ever the gracious hostess, served tea and sandwiches as we perused copies spread across the dining room table. Being a rather ungracious guest desperate to cool off, I slipped slices of cucumber off of a tray and onto my sweaty forehead, then shrugged my shoulders at the women's giggles.

The women were curious about the wire scandal, having witnessed the deadly consequences firsthand, and I had brought along samples of both the inferior wire and the wire we had specified.

"Using inferior wire. When John Roebling invented proper wire himself." Mother shook her head as she passed the samples to Carrie.

"The committee made the decision on the supplier. We had to abide by it, Mother."

"Frightful. Switching good wire for bad in the dark of the night and risking the whole project." Carrie shook her head as she bent the wires one by one.

"Thankfully, John's design has a huge margin of safety, and Roebling wire was used for all the suspenders. Nevertheless, I must apologize again for subjecting you ladies to that terrible sight."

"No, we should apologize to you," Eleanor said.

She was always so sweet, I half expected the other ladies to roll their eyes at this ridiculous reversal of culpability—after all, I was in charge. But instead, they exchanged glances and nodded in agreement.

"I don't understand." I said. The room was stifling. I fanned myself with Carrie's book.

"It should not have taken that gruesome event for us to act," Eleanor said as if this clarified matters, but I was still in the dark.

"Quite so." Until now, Henrietta had busied herself in Carrie's book, no doubt seeking references to herself.

"Mother, what are they talking about?"

Henrietta answered for her, removing her reading glasses from her beaky nose. "Don't be naive, dear. How do you suppose those contracts were switched to Roebling's Sons?"

"Politicians have their price," Mother added as she refilled teacups. The ladies fanned themselves and the teacups.

"I thought they were the lowest bidder. No? Who convinced the committee to change the award?"

They smiled smugly back at me.

"You did? But you don't even have a vote!"

Carrie, her soft voice barely audible, said, "There is something even more powerful than votes to a politician."

"Money," Mother, Henrietta, and Eleanor answered in unison, laughing.

"Still, some people should be in jail." Henrietta bobbed her head decisively, her unruly nest of gray hair adding emphasis.

"It's a filthy scandal that should see the light of day," Mother agreed. Her housemaid brought out a chunk of ice from the icebox. Mother took the ice pick from the maid and stabbed at the ice herself.

"Ah, but there are also scandals that *shouldn't* see the light of day," Henrietta added with a conspiratorial grin. She plunked a shard of ice into her tea.

Eleanor jabbed an elbow into Henrietta's ribs.

"Is there something else I should know about?" I asked, mulling over their casual indifference to the use of political coercion.

Chip, chip, chip. Mother hacked at the ice, her lips pursed with words she held back.

"Henrietta, I'm tired of your gossiping." Eleanor sipped her tea with her pinky pointed skyward.

"Why, I didn't—"

"What Henrietta is alluding to but in typical fashion isn't coming right out and saying plainly is the matter of Emily's relationship with Mr. Barnum."

"*Now* who's the gossip, Eleanor?" Henrietta rubbed her bodice where Eleanor had poked her.

I sighed. I thought we had gotten past this nonsense. "What are people saying?"

"It's nothing. A bunch of jealous old women entertaining themselves at the expense of a true heroine." Eleanor smiled, trying to smooth over her indiscretion, but it was as if a skunk had snuck into the garden.

Chip, chip, chip. The ice chunk finally gave way, and we each grabbed a shard to rub on our hot skin.

Later, after the ladies had departed, Mother dismissed the help, and we washed the dishes ourselves. She trusted no outsider with the delicate family heirlooms.

"You can tell me. I won't judge." She handed me a saucer to dry. "Mind the gold verge."

I dabbed at the delicate china with a white cotton cloth. "It's rather complex."

"Marriage always is. Do you love him?"

I set my lips. It was unlike Mother to pry like this, preferring to meddle in more subtle ways. "I love Washington, of course."

She stacked dry dishes into the cupboard with a clatter. "Do you love another?"

"You mean PT?" I rubbed my temples.

She affirmed with a glance. I considered reminding her my marriage was none of her business, wrestled with the desire to declare my adult status once again. But for all her pushing and prodding, I knew she always had my best interests in mind. The crinkles around her eyes deepened in concern. I wanted to answer the question I was still asking myself.

"Afraid so." I lowered my eyes. "If I could bind the best of them together, I'd have one perfect man."

She folded and refolded the drying towels, hand pressing their wrinkles. "Of all my children, you're the only one who finds herself in these predicaments. And do you know why?" She rested her hand on my shoulder and waited until our eyes met. "Because enough is never enough for you."

"You promised not to judge."

"I'm not the judge you should be worried about. Notoriety is not your friend right now. And I can't keep this out of the papers forever."

"What do you mean?"

"What do you think?"

Of course, being well respected and moderately wealthy, my mother wielded some power and influence. It had never occurred to me that she had been using it. There were a number of gossip rag newspapers that obtained a significant share of their revenue from keep-quiet payments. I wasn't sure if Mother's involvement in this was right or wrong and was still digesting the revelation when a knock at the door broke the tension. I practically skipped over to answer.

A messenger in a blue uniform, bearing a telegram, greeted me and caused me to gasp. Messengers were rarely a good omen. My mind raced back to Rhode Island, where Wash and Johnny were. *Good God, let them be all right.* But the telegram was addressed to Mother. She came, drying her hands on a dish towel, and I offered her the pale yellow envelope. She nodded for me to open it.

Sorry to inform you...death...Gouverneur were the only words I saw. "Mother, I'm afraid it's GK—we've lost him."

Mother grabbed the note, read it, then fell to her knees clutching the piece of paper bearing news of her son. I helped her to the settee. As we sat there in shock, I wept over the brother who'd been my keeper, in jagged breaths agonizing about how I'd wasted precious time being upset with him. My sweet, kind GK, always concerned with everyone else. A vision: him tapping his heart, something about a goldfish. My God, why didn't I pay more attention?

Cause of death, liver failure.

"What, what did he—?" Mother choked on the words.

"He died of a broken heart," I said.

I felt as if my own heart had been torn from my body. I raged at the army, especially General Sheridan. Despite the lives my brother saved through caution and foresight, he was unjustly accused of apathy, relieved of duty, and demoted. Although he went on, building bridges in the west, his boundless enthusiasm never returned.

We traveled to Newport, Rhode Island, GK's last duty station, to lay him to rest. This made little sense to me; he would have had an honorable resting place on either side of the Hudson River, so central to our lives.

Perhaps it was due to bitterness that he did not wish to be buried at West Point, his alma mater, but certainly he bore no ill will toward Cold Spring, the idyllic village of our birth. No, he wanted to be buried in plain clothes, with no military honors, near the beach. I had to laugh at his sense of fun and final jab at expectations.

As I sprinkled a handful of the sandy soil onto his casket, I mourned not only for the loss of my beloved brother and protector but for the cruel waste of so much of his career. One wrongful act had spoiled his reputation, leading GK to spend his remaining years battling the very army he had adored.

I committed myself to restoring his legacy as I rode home from the cemetery that solemn August evening. I would commission the finest artists to create life-size sculptures to remind future generations of his importance and create scholarships for future engineers and other bright students, as he had always supported my education. Despite his attempts to the contrary, I was determined that his bravery, patriotism, and sacrifice would never be forgotten.

GK died not knowing if his reputation would be restored. President Hayes convened a special panel that completely exonerated GK. It came three months and an eternity too late.

THIRTY-FIVE

1883

The first months of the year I was to turn forty were spent supervising the completion of the roadway, painting, and other finishing touches on the bridge. With the reinforcements we had added, Wash harbored no doubts regarding soundness but worried that pedestrians would be unnerved by vibration as horses galloped across it. He urged me to drive a buggy across at the earliest opportunity and report back to him.

The press caught wind of this, and my test turned into a publicity stunt. So we borrowed two fine horses and a coach with a folding roof for the journey, although not one emblazoned with *Barnum's Circus and Museum*, much to PT's disappointment. I chose a sumptuous blue silk dress for the occasion and had C. C. Martin stand by to detect any movement of the bridge.

I was to meet Franklin Edson, the mayor of New York, and his entourage on the other side. Good manners dictated a gift for His Honor, so I had the driver stop at one of the Chinese markets on the way. I rushed into the shop where the owner greeted me with a pleasant smile. We had a bit of a language barrier but had always managed to communicate.

"Rooster," I said.

He pointed to the plucked birds hanging in nooses in the window.

I shook my head, stuck my thumbs in my armpits, and flapped my elbows. "Er-ah er-ah roooo."

"Ah." He nodded and waved me to a back room, where chickens cackled and the air was thick with the odor of their droppings. He picked up a hatchet.

"No." I pushed down his hatchet and selected a fine white rooster from the dozens of caged, raucous birds. "A symbol of good luck and the victory of light over darkness."

The shop owner tilted his head in confusion.

"From the Bible? Never mind." I offered a handful of coins to pay for the rooster and cage.

He picked up a newspaper and pointed to a story on my bridge ride. "No charge." He waved my hand away. "Good luck."

Outside, the driver paced in front of the carriage.

"Will you put the roof down, please?" I asked. "The rooster would like to see the view."

The driver's eyes widened, but he did as I asked.

The cock crowed all the way to the river, entertaining the crowds that had gathered in the streets. We rode up the long approach with the police clearing the way. After clearing the construction barrier, the horses stepped gingerly onto the roadway. Patches of open water could be seen through the boards of the incomplete flooring. I fought the urge to grab the reins myself, not knowing how well the driver would react if the horses panicked. If I was sweating, the horses were surely uneasy as well.

But the driver proved competent and the horses steady. I relaxed back into the seat. In the middle of the bridge, at the bottom of the catenary curve of the giant cables, I had the driver stop. It was eerily quiet, save the sputtering of the horses. Even the rooster had hushed.

A light wind blew upriver, and I sat still to detect any sway. Then I stepped out ahead of the carriage and had the coachman drive past me. The bridge remained steady; nary a vibration touched my feet. I spun, seeing the whole of the East River Bridge. The grandeur of the towers, the grace of the cables, the harp strings of the suspenders took my breath away. I paused facing our home where I suspected Wash was watching through his telescope. I lifted my arm to him. *I hope you are happy, my love.*

Soon, too soon, the driver turned to me. "Ma'am?"

The New York entourage had gathered at the other side.

"Thank you. I'm ready."

◦❧

Shaking the hand of the mayor of the greatest city on earth paled in comparison to the transcendent wonder of standing alone in the center of the bridge. Mayor Edson wrinkled his brow at the gift of the crowing rooster, but it certainly added a joyful noise to the festivities.

Later, I reassured Wash that the bridge felt as steady as the street outside our door.

"I'm so glad you were the first, my dear." He smiled as he patted Chaucer's broad head.

A warm feeling filled me within. I had been the first person to both walk and ride across the bridge, and Wash had orchestrated both events. He had allowed those moments of triumph to be mine. Despite all my mistakes and setbacks, our misunderstandings and arguments, he did appreciate what I had done.

"Thank you," I said.

"Well deserved."

I kissed him tenderly, combing my fingers through his graying hair. "I love you."

He nodded and didn't flinch at my touch. For a moment, the brilliance returned to his eyes, and the pain receded from his face. What sad irony, for a man who had taken such comfort in physical contact to have become unable to bear it. I hoped that time was healing this as well.

◦❧

In April, crowds gathered daily at both ends of the bridge. By early May, people were sneaking onto the entire span. Additional police were retained to man barricades while the roadways were prepared for traffic, electric lights installed, and tracks laid for trains.

On a sultry evening, I was in a hurry to get home and grew annoyed by the loitering throngs. I stepped down a stone alley to a hidden passageway. Little girls gathered flowers that had sprung up under the protective shield of the bridge—daisies with bright yellow faces straining toward the sun.

One of the girls rubbed the top of her head and tilted her face up to the bridge. The other children stopped playing, watching in amazement as coins and other small objects fell around them. A parasol tumbled from the side of the bridge. We would have to expand safety measures, request even more police. *Probably not a safe place to play anymore.* I shooed the children away, then hurried home.

Wash was examining his rock collection in the parlor. I picked up the *Brooklyn Eagle* and scanned the front page.

"Nice to note your fondness and loyalty to my fashion design." He nodded at my shabby bloomer costume. I had refused the sewing of any more for some time. "Now that the bridge is nearly finished, perhaps I should turn my talents to dressmaking. I believe I'm ready to conquer the bustle."

"I'll be sad to give up my bloomer costume, but I'll return to proper dress soon, dearest, not to worry." Although a slight improvement over the voluminous dresses of the '70s, the bustle was quite a ridiculous contraption.

"That will be a welcome sight to my poor eyes."

The iceberg had been melting since the night I first rode across the bridge. "Thank you for the bloomer costumes. I'm not sure I ever told you that."

"Hell, making them is the most fun thing I've done in thirteen years."

"That's sad. Perhaps if I didn't fight it so hard, I could have enjoyed sewing."

"No, you were completely hopeless at it. This"—he tapped the newspaper in my hand—"*this* is what you were meant to do."

His words washed over me like a fresh breeze on a hot day. I cocked my head, craving to hear more.

"What do the papers say?" he asked.

Though his mind was already occupied with the news, I smiled inwardly. His simple comment was an enormous compliment.

Reading remained difficult for him, and he relied on me or Johnny for his news. I helped him to the divan. Several dailies and monthlies were neatly stacked on a table beside it.

"This is all about the bridge." I showed him a wonderful photograph on the front page of *Harper's* accompanied by a lengthy article with striking photographs of both Papa and Wash. "The *Brooklyn Eagle* says 'Great anticipation for the grand opening next week' and mentions problems keeping people off the bridge until then."

"I'm sure the novelty will pass."

"Don't be. We need more police. People are coming from as far away as Chicago to see your bridge."

"Brooklyn's bridge, dear. And your photograph should be in this article."

"You nearly lost your life."

"Ah, but here I am, still above ground."

I gave him a kiss and sat next to him. "Thank God. But I'll never forgive myself for letting you back in that caisson."

He patted my hand. "We've been through a great deal, my darling. I look forward to less adventurous years to come."

"A goal anyone would envy." Was it possible we'd get through this happy, whole, and together? I dared to hope. And I dared to approach him with an adventure he probably wasn't anticipating. "Wash, I've been thinking I want to study law."

"Have you now. For what purpose?"

"For the women's movement. We need women trained in the law so that we may have a say in changing them."

"Your first hurdle would be to gain acceptance." He rubbed his beard, a smile peeking from behind his whiskers. "But I have no doubt you could convince a school to accept you."

"Do you really think so? Is it not too late for me?"

"If not you, then who? You have proven yourself quite a capable woman."

My spirits rose with fresh dreams. I planted a big kiss on his bristly cheek just as a knock at the door interrupted our discussion.

"I hope it's not reporters again," I sighed.

"Comes with the territory, I'm afraid."

I answered the door. PT and Martin rushed inside without exchanging pleasantries.

"Gentlemen?" I trailed after them.

"Huge problem at the bridge. A panic. People getting crushed. A nightmare," blurted Martin.

PT remained calm. "We have a coach ready for you should you wish a ride," he said as serenely as if he were offering a trip to the park.

Wash, unable to rise unaided from the low sofa, gestured for Martin to help him get to the window.

PT took my elbow and led me to the foyer. His sanguine demeanor had disappeared, possibly an act for Wash's benefit. "I'm so sorry, Emily."

"What caused the panic?"

"That's not clear at the moment. Some sort of protest going on. Perhaps someone started pushing or some demolition explosions went off in a nearby construction site. Many people were on the bridge."

I called to Martin and Wash. "Are you coming? Wash, let's go!"

"Perhaps it's better for me to hold the fort here."

PT caught my arm as I grabbed my hat. "I should warn you," he said.

"I've seen horrible accidents and, yes, death before, PT."

"Of course. But prepare yourself—some are placing the blame on you."

THIRTY-SIX

The horses struggled to draw PT's coach through streets surging with people, some pushing toward the bridge, others fleeing. I feared the horses or carriage wheels would crush anyone who stumbled to the ground in their path. Hordes were shoving and hurtling over the bridge barricades. Some who fell were trampled by others. Men and women staggered by, streaks of blood on their faces, arms held against chests, eyes wild with fright.

Silhouettes of bodies appeared against the darkening sky as they chose to jump or fell into the river. *Oh no, oh no.* A sea of thrashing bodies filled one of the entrances, a narrow stone stairwell. They climbed over each other to escape while more tumbled upon them from above. Two legs kicked inside an overturned hoop skirt like an upside-down parasol.

Siren bells pierced through the screaming of the mob, and police with shields and bobby sticks beat back the throngs. Along the edges of the crowd, protesters held signs declaring *Bridge Unsafe! Built on Sand! Built by Imposter!*

The carriage stopped, the crowd too dense for us to proceed any farther. PT climbed out and whacked a path with his walking stick to get closer to the bridge. I followed with Martin, my heart hammering in my chest, fearing for our safety. Soon, PT was overpowered and in danger of being trampled. We linked arms and threaded our way back to the carriage.

When the chaos subsided, Martin stepped out to speak to some police officers, and I pushed against the tide of escapers toward the bridge. It had no apparent impairment. *What had caused the pandemonium?* I tried to detain several of the fleeing pedestrians for an explanation, but they shook me off in their haste. At last, one disheveled woman, stopping to catch her breath, answered me.

"I was up top, near the barricade. There were hundreds, maybe thousands of people on the bridge." She took a deep, shuddering breath. "Everything was fine, then we heard screams. We got pushed first from the New York side, then from the Brooklyn. People were falling."

"Were you injured?"

She shook her head. "I tried to stop and help, but they all kept on trampling them."

"But why?" I walked beside her.

"Bridge isn't safe. Best to get out of here 'less you want to get trampled as well." She hustled away.

I whirled around, hoping to find another person willing to talk, when a large woman ran smack into me. She gripped the hand of a little girl who held a small sign.

"Mama, it's her." She pointed squarely at me.

The mother glared at me, then spat. She tugged the little girl after her and they fled, but not before I saw a likeness of my face on the sign.

Working my way back to the carriage, I received little more information. With its gaudy gold lettering illuminated by the glare of the new streetlamps, the coach was hard to miss. PT offered a hand to help me into the coach. Across from me, Martin examined a poster, another copy of the one the little girl had held. He took a quick glance, then crumpled it, his face contorted in anger.

I took the wadded paper from his hand, flattened the wrinkles, and held it toward the gas lamp. It featured a large likeness of me and the words: *IMPOSTER, BRIDGE UNSAFE, BUILT ON SAND, WOMAN TO BLAME*, and *WIRE SCANDAL!*

I handed PT the poster. The carriage rocked as the crowd tried to push against it, their hands thundering on the sides. We all cried out as the carriage tilted. PT rang a signal bell and banged on the roof with his palm. The horses pulled, and we crept forward.

The scene repeated against my closed eyelids, my cheeks flaming with humiliation and horror. PT laid a comforting arm across my shoulder. I opened my eyes; Martin stared hot daggers at me, then at PT. The screams and sirens assaulted our ears like gunfire. Crimson splatters marked each of our clothes from contact with the fleeing crowd. A wave of nausea hit me at the warm, musky smell of blood.

❧

Well into the next morning, I remained curled up in bed. Grief, the elephant on my chest, wouldn't allow the stretching of arm or leg or even a deep sigh of resignation. Stubborn determination had led me into this state of horror, but no will of my own could lead me out.

Wash sat at his desk under the window, writing bank checks and peering through his telescope at the bridge. One of the checks no doubt would be addressed to Patrick O'Brien. The thought of his father's death made me want to curl tighter, the quilt my protective shell.

"No workers on the bridge. Not even guards. Strange." Wash licked a stamp.

"Our world is collapsing, and you're worried about guards?"

"Our *world* isn't collapsing. This is just a temporary setback." He organized envelopes into a neat stack.

"Twelve people crushed to death is hardly a minor setback."

"Many factors were involved, none which were under our control. The bridge is sound."

His unflappable attitude made me shudder. "Not true. My involvement was totally under our control."

He spun around in his wheeled chair and faced me. "You need to get out of bed."

"No." I was done taking his orders.

"I'll make you."

I appraised him in his chair, gave a cruel laugh. "You can't." I wished him to go away and stay away this time. Guilt from my own thoughts punched my gut.

"I will."

"Ha!"

"Come on. Get up. We've a life to live."

"What life? You're a wreck. I'm a disgrace. I'm almost glad GK didn't live to see this."

He hobbled to the bed. Yanked away my quilt. "That's an awful thing to say."

Although my recalcitrant body flopped like a dead fish, he pulled me up. I was surprised by his strength as he held me firmly but not without affection.

"You would use your last ounce of strength to remove your wife from your bed?"

"There's more work to be done."

"So that's the extent of wallowing allowed in the Roebling household." I reached for the quilt. "For me of course. Present company excluded."

"Em, it's by your strength alone we have gotten this far. We're so close to the finish. Now you need to get up, move on, and be the heroine that I know you are."

So like the bridge, with iron determination and heart of stone, he confounded my efforts to escape his will.

Wash was correct: our work remained unfinished. PT was helpful during those difficult days, bringing bits of news to us—good or bad—so we might concentrate on our next steps. Late one afternoon, soon after the panic, he brought a newspaper with the bold headline: "Bridge Closed! Questions of Competence Create Panic." Below it was the same photograph of me featured on those awful posters.

"Godforsaken papers, promoting mass hysteria," Wash grumbled. "Let's throw the blame squarely where it should lie."

"They're right. I had no business—"

"Blame, blame. Who's to blame?" PT said. "Stop beating yourself about the head. Not enough police for the size of the crowd. That's it. Nothing else."

"There's more involved." I waved PT over and pointed to a picture of Stone in the newspaper. "I fell into his trap like everyone else."

"Whose trap?" Wash asked.

"Benjamin Stone. He had something to do with it."

PT gave me a consoling pat on the shoulder. Wash glared at him.

"I have an idea," I said. "We could hold a demonstration to generate public attention while at the same time prove the bridge's strength."

"Ooh." PT perked up. "Now you are smack in *my* bailiwick."

He put a hand on my sleeve as he showed me his pocket watch—we had an appointment soon. I was to deliver yet another speech to the bridge board that evening.

"Would you mind stepping away from my wife?" Wash said.

"Pardon?" PT asked. "Emily, it's almost time to go. We can talk about your idea on the way."

"Are you deaf? Get away from my wife!"

My jaw dropped at Wash's sudden anger.

"Now, now, we're all a bit on edge," PT crooned as he helped me with my wrap.

Wash was out of his chair, his face apoplectic with fury and...what? Jealousy? He shoved PT in the chest. I blinked with disbelief. *Men!* I headed for the door, relieved that it was time to leave.

"Come along, PT."

But PT stood his ground, smirking. "Hmm. Someone has found his manhood."

Wash landed a fist on his nose.

"Mr. Roebling!" I shouted.

PT staggered back, his face bloodied. I offered my handkerchief, but he straight-armed me away, his other hand cupping his nose. While nudging him toward the door, I glanced back at my husband. He patted the whimpering dog, which seemed more upset about the event than did Wash. He consoled his best friend as I did mine.

It was probably not the best decision to leave with PT at that particular moment, but I wasn't sure it was a decision at all. We were late, PT needed a talking-to, and I needed his support before a critical appearance before the board. I was carrying on with business, whatever the detritus left behind.

THIRTY-SEVEN

P T held a handkerchief to his swollen nose, and I attempted to study my speech notes, but the bumpy carriage ride and my mental distraction prevented much progress. Although speaking to the bridge committee had become almost routine, I still didn't enjoy public appearances.

Adding to my worries, it seemed Wash suspected my friendship with PT had developed into something else. Why couldn't Wash understand that I needed the showman's exuberance? And why couldn't PT be more compassionate regarding Wash's limitations?

PT pulled up my fallen wrap, leaving his arm resting on my shoulder. We needed to discuss his altercation with Wash and more, but my immediate task was more pressing.

"You're shaking. From cold or nerves?" he asked.

"Both, I suppose."

"Do you want to rehearse your speech again?"

"Was it worth it?" I whispered to him, to myself, to heaven above.

"Pardon?"

"Lord, give me your guidance and the strength. First Papa, then GK, now Wash. They've gone and left me alone."

"Don't go down that road." PT cupped my chin and eyed me with tenderness. "Buck up, Peanut. Say a prayer if you like, but I'm right here."

I patted his hand, the knots in my neck softening in the sweet comfort of his presence.

The carriage stopped in front of the brownstone office building. Twilight was giving way, and new electric streetlamps buzzed to life, casting the street in a yellow haze.

PT glanced at his timepiece. "We're a bit early, so let's do your exercises. Close your eyes."

By now, my pre-speech routine was instinctual. I closed my eyes and exhaled slowly, letting my body relax and my mind drift.

"Think of a happy memory." PT's hand warmed mine, but in my mind, it was Wash's as we danced at our wedding. The music was lovely, and PT's voice, smooth as silk, weaved through my reverie. "Where are you?"

"I'm dancing."

"Good, we're dancing."

I opened one eye. His were closed, lost in his own dream. I had worked hard at suppressing my feelings toward him and was proud of my ability to retain his friendship. Yet there was still something magical about him, as if he could wave away my troubles with sleight of hand. Sitting next to him, my feet didn't quite meet ground. I closed my eyes and floated in the ballroom.

The bridge committee gathered in the boardroom, the various maps and diagrams on the walls now yellowed and curled with age. PT sat next to C. C. Martin as the meeting was gaveled to order.

"Our first order of business is of utmost importance as we evaluate the safety of the bridge," Chairman Murphy declared. "I call on Assistant Engineer Martin for his statement."

Martin stood, his suit resting on his spare frame as though the garment were still on the hanger. He cleared his throat, then proceeded in his even way. "Gentlemen. After a thorough review by the chief engineer, his staff, and consulting engineers, our opinion remains unchanged. There is no correlation between the unfortunate panic on the bridge and the safety of the bridge itself."

Benjamin Stone shook his head and folded his arms across his chest. "Then how do you account for the loss of twelve lives and the serious injury of hundreds more? Your affirmation of the bridge's soundness means nothing, especially to the families of the deceased." He rose from his seat like a bear rising on its hind legs. "The people of New York and Brooklyn deserve answers!" Stone hammered his fist on the table, causing pens to jump, then threw his arms heavenward, straining the seams of his jacket.

PT rolled his eyes and cast a conspiratorial glance at me. *Amateur.*

I must have sighed or rolled my eyes as well, because Stone turned on me sharply and bellowed, "Mrs. Roebling, do you have something to add?"

"I do."

Stone had ceased to intimidate me long ago. Thanks to PT, I knew a show when I saw one and could give one of my own. I stood and made eye contact with each person in the room.

"Gentlemen, thank you for this opportunity to speak before you. When my father-in-law dreamt of this bridge over thirty years ago, he knew there would be risks. Certainly, lives would be lost in the construction of it, lives would be lost in the usage of it, and we would face unforeseen challenges and disasters simply because a public entity exists where there once was none." I held Chairman Murphy's gaze until heads bobbed in agreement.

"But he knew—and the wise men in power knew—that the bridge had to be built if this great city and nation were to grow and prosper. We could not wait until we had acquired the perfect knowledge and technology and materials, for they may never come.

"We blazed new trails by ceaselessly studying, assessing, and, in some cases, inventing what did not exist, for that, indeed, is how progress is made."

There were shouts of protest.

I held up a hand. "Given the magnitude, obstacles, and inherent dangers of the project, we are fortunate that more lives were not lost.

"The panic on the bridge had nothing to do with the competency of its builders or integrity of design. The loss of lives stemmed from fear and paranoia, fueled by irresponsible journalism and the agenda of enemies within whose motivations I cannot begin to fathom."

Several board members turned toward Stone, who fiddled with his pocket watch.

All eyes widened as Wash entered the room, leaning heavily on his cane, perspiration beading his forehead. I cupped my hand to my mouth. How hard it must have been for him to make the trip. Buoyed by his presence, I went on with renewed vigor.

"Much was said about my role, for I am but the engineer's wife with no formal training or degree. However, I would remind those assembled that the great engineer Eads also had no formal training. Nevertheless, the bridge over the Mississippi is testament to his competence as designer and builder."

Wash caught my eye with a nod. "The education and competence of women is a debate we must save for another day," Wash said as he limped the length of the long table until he was directly behind me. His hands warmed my shoulders. "There is no question concerning the strength of the bridge. Indeed, there was not a hint of trouble, even with thousands stampeding its span. But there *is* a question concerning the management of its use."

Side conversations bubbled up as the men conferred with one another. I put up my arm to hush them. I took a deep breath, concentrated on using my diaphragm muscle to strengthen my voice. "We must learn and move on, putting this incident far behind us. The people have demanded this, paid for this. Some paid with their lives." I paused, wanting my final words to echo in their ears. "It is your *duty*, your *honor*. You must open this bridge!"

One by one, the committee stood and applauded, all except Stone. Then, with a great scrape of his chair, he grudgingly joined the others.

Chairman Murphy banged his gavel. "The committee will consider all factors and will vote at the next meeting. The bridge will remain closed, gated, and padlocked until that time."

Wash and I accepted handshakes and reassurances from the board after the meeting adjourned. I walked out with Wash's arm across my back, lifted with happiness and pride for all we had done. I wanted to thank PT for all his support and patience with me, but he had managed to leave unnoticed ahead of us.

It had rained while we were in the meeting, and the wet cobbles reflected white in the streetlamps or disappeared in dark shadows. The portly figure of Stone shuffled down the checkerboarded street, using an umbrella as a walking stick.

I excused myself from Wash and caught up with Stone. "You despicable man," I seethed. "Your actions should be reported to the police."

"You know nothing would come of that," he replied quietly. "But I do owe you an apology." His shoulders slumped; he seemed six inches shorter. "Do you remember the terrible accident in England I told you of, when the bridge gave way?"

I thought this a strange apology. "And that gives you license to persecute us and sabotage this bridge?"

"I lost my wife and daughter. You resemble—" He paused, his face pained.

The portrait in his office came to mind. "I resemble your late wife?"

He nodded. "In several ways."

"Then why on earth have you been hampering me at every turn?"

"It's not what you think."

"Then please enlighten me."

"You probably think I was motivated by profits."

"Partially. I understand you have emotional involvement."

"I can't deny profit was a consideration. But it wasn't the only one."

Wash was waiting for me. "Please, walk with me," I said, trying to steer him back toward Wash. But that was like turning around a steamship. "Go on." He might as well get it all out now.

"Ever since I laid eyes on you, I knew you were someone special."

"Oh? When was that?"

"As an adult, when you were giving a talk about the grand bridge to be built at the home of your mother."

"A rather amateur performance, I'm afraid."

"Oh, you were so young and untainted. I imagined you were much like my daughter would have been. In fact, I allowed that fantasy to grow beyond all reason."

My heart remained hardened even as he took a handkerchief to his eyes.

"I felt the need to protect you, as I so miserably failed to protect my wife and our sweet little girl."

"I'm sorry for your terrible loss, Mr. Stone."

"And I am sorry for yours."

"My loss?"

"I knew your father. He told me of the terrible tragedy of your sister after my own daughter drowned. I came to this country having left England and everyone I knew behind."

I cringed at the memory of my lost father and sister.

Perhaps aware of inflicting more pain, his voice softened. "We were soul mates of suffering. After he was gone, I watched out for you."

"I wish I had known I was a bit of a surrogate daughter to you. Perhaps things would have been different between us. But still, I fail to understand how you dreamed you were protecting me or anybody with your actions."

"I believed our wire was as good as the approved wire. I don't want to bore you with the technicalities, but I did some testing on my own and—"

"But there was no report, no scientific data to support that. Hardly seems to be something to keep secret."

"Well, you see…" He smoothed the closed umbrella, cleared his throat. "I knew the wire substitution would eventually be discovered."

"I'm afraid you've lost me. If not for profit, then why did you make the switch, especially knowing it would be discovered?"

He stared at his shoes and tapped his umbrella on the cobblestones.

Then it came to me. I was stunned by the awfulness of it. "The panic. You wanted to create a panic."

I could read the pain in his eyes but felt no sympathy for this monster. "Good God, why? You knew the limitations of the exit passageways. You had to have known the tragic consequences of a mass of hysterical people. You set them up to die for your own distorted cause." I took a step closer, glared into his watery eyes. "You're tilting at windmills, but instead of slaying imaginary giants, you've killed real people."

"I never wanted anyone to get hurt," he whispered.

Down the street, Martin was having words with Wash. He seemed angry, waving his arms for emphasis. I needed to sort out the matter, but I was determined to get a full explanation for Mr. Stone's reprehensible behavior. I contemplated the charges we could level against Stone while watching Martin and Wash out of the corner of my eye. Martin jabbed a finger toward PT, who stood across the street, looking the other way. Bewildered with that sideshow, I turned back to Stone.

"It was always about the *trains*," he said. "Trains weren't in the original plan we approved. As you might expect, I am exceedingly averse to the notion of trains going over bridges. I thought that if it should turn out that there was a perception—a *perception*, mind you—that we didn't have a comfortable margin of safety designed into the bridge, then the addition of a train track would be scuttled."

"But the bridge *was* determined safe for trains, despite the faulty wire." His motive was becoming clearer.

"A mistake, I assure you. There was quite a lot of politicking involved in that decision. You should investigate who owns the trains. I think you'll be surprised."

"Don't evade the issue here."

"Henry Murphy for one," he offered, doing my assigned research for me. "One of your favorites, no?"

But I wasn't to be sidetracked.

He answered my glare. "Yes, I may have had some influence on the development of a panic. You must find some way to get those trains off that bridge!"

"You are a shortsighted and dangerous man."

"I don't deny it. But I'm not the only one who should pay for the greedy and callous decisions that put so many in danger." He handed me a sealed envelope. "Take this. Please read it tomorrow."

"I have to go."

"I never wanted anyone to get hurt!" he repeated to my back, but I had heard enough.

I reached Wash as Martin left his side.

"I've uncovered some ugly truths," I said to Wash. "About the panic—"

PT joined us. "I should like to offer you both a ride as soon as I locate my carriage." He scanned the streets.

"Thank you, Mr. Barnum, but I shall provide a ride for my wife." Despite his polite words, judging from the intensity in Wash's eyes, his earlier anger had not abated. Yet he clasped my hand and squeezed it.

Wash was within his rights to throw a punch earlier, as PT had some difficulties with boundaries. But considering the good reception we had received at the meeting and that PT was trying to correct his faux pas, Wash could be more gracious. I scolded myself. This evening would have been very difficult for him, and yet he came to support me.

"You're not going to believe what Stone admitted."

I was burning to tell Wash what I had learned, but he tapped his cane impatiently. Beads of sweat collected on his brow, and his face flushed, even on this cool evening. What had Martin told him?

Wash pulled my hand. "Come, Emily, our ride is waiting."

"Thank you for all your help, PT."

Wash led me to a horse hitched to a post—Theo, one of our carriage horses. I greeted him, and he nuzzled me. A large and strong stallion, saddling him would have been a challenge. "How did—"

"I thought this would be more romantic." He unhitched the horse. "'Bout time I saddled up. You still enjoy riding, don't you?"

"Wash!" He had stunned me three times this evening. "You haven't ridden a horse since—"

"The war. And I swore I'd never get on one again." He mounted, then offered me a hand to lift me astride in front of him. The stretch of my legs and the smooth leather of the saddle filled me with the delight of my younger days.

"I have a confession to make." He replaced the wrap on my shoulder. "I released Barnum's horses."

"You what? Why?"

"Churlish of me, but there you have it." He handed me the reins and circled his arms around my waist. "He's all yours."

It had been some time, and Theo was prone to jigging, but my skills returned naturally as I guided the horse down the street. "What convinced you to come tonight?"

"I was thinking about the war. That damn cannon. Pushing it up that blasted hill." He raised his voice over the *clip-clop* of the horse's hooves.

"What hill?"

It grew quieter, having passed the congestion of the main street.

"Little Round Top." He leaned closer to my ear. "Your brother made us push a cannon up a wooded hill, over boulders and felled trees. You've heard about the courageous fight for that hill. Perhaps a turning point of the war."

We came to a corner. I guided the horse left toward home. Wash took hold of my hands over the reins and pulled them right. The confused horse stopped and sputtered.

"No. We're going to the bridge," Wash whispered in a tone that raised the hairs on the back of my neck.

We turned right, but unsure of what he had in mind, I held the horse to a slow walk.

"Do you know why we fought so hard for Little Round Top?" Wash's breath warmed my ear, his arms tightening around my waist. "Not because it was the general's strategy but because it was so damn hard to push that cannon up there. We weren't giving up. It was our turf."

The night of his delirious ranting about cannons, all mixed up with caissons, came back to me. "I'm glad you're finally ready to talk about it. But why now? Does this have something to do with the board meeting?"

"Of course. I want to hear all about it from your perspective. Martin has already given me an earful."

"Oh? What did he say?"

"He thought the board was putty in your hands."

"I wish I were so sure. There are still many things they could throw at us before they'll open the bridge. It could take years." But that didn't seem to be what sparked Wash's anger earlier in the evening.

We left the lighted street and climbed the approach to the deserted bridge. A full moon shone in the clearing sky as if to make up for the absence of lights on the bridge. Theo hesitated as his eyes adjusted to the darkness, then we crept up the familiar incline.

"I've been thinking," Wash said.

"That's what you do." I laughed, but he didn't join me.

"I will move back to New Jersey permanently."

I swallowed. Trenton represented home to him. But my roots were planted in New York. "What do you mean, 'I'?"

We had arrived at the Brooklyn tower, where the roadway was blocked by a barrier. The wind whipped around us, carrying scents of coal fires and horse droppings. *Why has he brought us up here?*

He dismounted, then helped me down. After handing me his cane so he could tether the horse, he led me to the barricade. A sign read: *By order of the Brooklyn Police, DO NOT ENTER.*

"I don't want to be selfish about this." Wash opened a padlock on the gate and pushed through the barrier.

"About what?" Perspiration dampened my dress even as the cool sea wind blew.

He beckoned me to follow him onto the bridge. "Come."

We stepped over the creamy yellow wood planks in silence. The lights of Manhattan sparkled across the way, their reflections stretching in the water.

The moon slipped behind a cloud, cloaking us in surreal emptiness. When we reached the middle of the bridge, it was as if we were all alone in a dark space between two worlds.

Wash hooked his cane on the handrail, gripped the rail in both hands, and focused downriver. I bit my lips in the awkward silence and rested my back on the rail next to him.

"You do as you wish. As when you got on that ship. Knowing full well that our child was on the way." He glanced at me. "On the way but not in the way, as long as I didn't interfere."

"Not my best moment. But I paid for my mistake." The sad memory rose to the surface, but I tamped it back down. I thought instead of our healthy baby boy, now nearly grown. Chilled by the damp air, I tugged my wrap closer.

"*We* paid. Or am I the only one who wanted more children?" he said.

"You know that's not so. Why are you bringing this up now? You want to discuss what happened sixteen years ago?"

"No. I want to discuss what happened eighteen years ago. You might recall that event."

Finally, the moon emerged from the cloud, and I could more clearly see his face, creased and weary, strands in his beard shining silver in the light.

"Our wedding? I know we haven't properly celebrated our anniversaries, but—"

"Not the wedding. Our marriage."

The dread building in the pit of my stomach deepened.

"My vision may be weak, but I'm not blind. And of course there's talk."

"Good heavens, you know better than to listen to gossip. Especially if it concerns me—an irresistible target."

"Perhaps. But there's truth to it. We've been torn apart."

"And whose fault is that?"

Wash shook his head. "I never had the brain my father expected of me. I lost my soul in the war. My body has been broken building this bridge. But I know this much. I still love you too much to hold you against your will... as if I or anyone could do that."

"I never left you. Quite the opposite." *What did Martin tell him?* I was about to ask.

"I'm not the man I was eighteen years ago, it's true, so you have some reason to find another. But if I am to preserve what is left of my heart and my dignity, you must choose. I cannot—I *will* not—have a wife who seeks another man's affections."

Oh God. Martin's whispered confidences with eyes flicking toward me. The discussion in the street, pointing to PT. I blinked as it all clicked into place. Martin, that bastard.

"Nothing happened." I spun to peer with him into the dark water far below. He still cringed at an unexpected touch, but I took a risk and gently placed my hand over his.

He slid his cane back and forth along the railing, knocking my hand loose. "I disagree."

I tried to catch his eye. "Wash, there isn't—"

"You remember when the workers were striking, and you offered an ultimatum?"

"Of course, but—"

"They were to report to work or walk away." He grimaced with a mixture of anger and sadness. "Well, this is my ultimatum. It shouldn't be difficult to decide. You have always known what you wanted."

"Wash—" I pushed against his shoulder to turn him to me. "Listen to me."

"No, you listen." He stepped away, pointed his cane toward Manhattan. "Come with me to Trenton and never see *him* again."

"Wash, you don't mean this. I don't think you understand."

"Or leave me." The moon shone behind him, lighting his profile but shrouding his face in darkness.

I froze in place, my tongue and lips refusing to form words. A gust of wind blew my dress, and it glowed strangely in the eerie light. Tendrils of my hair broke free and whipped at my face. I no longer knew the man standing a few steps away. *Does he not love me anymore? Is this his way of telling me to go?* For once in my life, I had absolutely nothing to say. I held my hands out to him in a silent plea.

"But a soldier fights fiercest for his own turf. And I am not ready to give up the fight." He threw down his cane, his face tight, arms up as if to strike. He crushed me to him, nearly taking my breath. "God help me, I love you." His eyes shone with tears and moonlight, and his wet cheek against mine told me all I needed to know. He kissed me passionately, and I dissolved into him, lost in the warmth of his arms. Overwhelmed by his kisses, I was barely aware of him lifting my dress.

I believe we unintentionally made history when we made love in the middle of that moonlit bridge.

THIRTY-EIGHT

The note Stone had given me seemed some type of joke, as in it, he requested I search for yet another note on the bridge. So the next day I went back, this time with Johnny. He was old enough to understand more things now, and I felt it important to prepare him for the changes ahead. We watched workers repairing damage from the panic and ignored the passersby as they stared, pointed, and shook their heads at us.

Johnny seemed oblivious to all this, being consumed with self-interest like most fifteen-year-olds. "So I'm definitely thinking of attending Rensselaer."

"Son, you shouldn't feel obliged. If anything, all this should scare you away."

"No, I want to. And I have the grades, at least so far."

I dodged the spit of a passerby. Johnny lunged toward him, but I grabbed his arm. "No question you're capable, Johnny, but your father and I agree, it is better to follow your own heart. We'll send you anywhere you want to go. Besides, I'm not sure I could endure another generation of this life."

"Mother." His newly deepened voice still startled me. "This is who I am. John, not Johnny anymore."

We arrived at the blockade that Wash had relocked the night before. I searched for Stone's note.

"Come on. Let's go on the bridge anyway." He rattled against the barrier.

"No, John."

"Then why did we come here? So you could torture yourself? And me?"

306 TRACEY ENERSON WOOD

"You'll survive."

"How would you know?" he asked in that churlish manner of a boy not yet a man.

"Because I raised you to be strong and independent."

"You raised me? Ha!"

"Well, it was a community effort." I could admit that much. I searched the area. "His note said he'd leave something for me here. Strange man. Help me find it."

"Raising a child, caring for Pa, and building the bridge must have been difficult. Is that…is that why I'm an only child?"

"Not exactly."

He cocked his head.

"We were blessed with only one child. I'm not sure knowing any more would interest you."

"I'm grown now."

"So you are," I said, admiring my tall, dark-haired son with Wash's blue eyes and earnest face. I wanted that moment back. That moment in the nursery, bouncing the ball with him, perfect in his innocence. I wanted back all the moments that I didn't have with him. The hours I spent at the work site instead of helping him with his homework, going to the park or the zoo, watching him delight in the animals.

I wanted both worlds and to show that women could do it all. But maybe we had to choose a slice of this and a slice of that. My choices kept me from having another child and from a good part of raising the one I had.

"Childbirth can be dangerous, Son." Perhaps American doctors couldn't have done any better, but Wash would never forgive me anyway.

But John was already back to the task at hand, searching for the note. "What's this?" He found a very tattered and faded rag doll, tucked behind the *Do Not Enter* sign. He handed me the rag doll. "What happened when I was born?"

I pressed my lips together; it wasn't fair to burden him with that newly raw wound.

John's eyes softened. "It doesn't matter. I love you, Mama." He draped an arm across my shoulder. "And the bridge is beautiful."

"I love you too, Son. It is beautiful, isn't it?" My brow furrowed. I had to break the news to him that we might be moving and he would have to change schools. "But now that it's nearly done, our lives will change."

I turned over the old rag doll and found an envelope pinned to its back. In faded ink, I could just make out an 1847 English postmark and the addressee: *Mr. Benjamin Stone*. Scrawled over that were chilling words: *We shall be together in the cold depths, our fates forever entwined.*

Stone had told me to be there. Was he waiting for me? My mind raced, and I looked past the barrier to see if anyone was on the bridge. Sure enough, a figure in dark clothing was leaning over the guardrail. It seemed he was talking to someone who had gone over the side. Panic rose within me. Whose fate was to be sealed with his? What about Wash's strange behavior?

"Good God, Johnny, they're going to jump!"

Johnny hurdled over the barrier and ran full speed. I fumbled with the key in the padlock, my hands shaking. At last, the lock opened, and I hurried after Johnny.

I reached the middle of the bridge in time to see a figure hanging on the outside of the safety railing. As I rushed toward it, the hands gave way, and the figure disappeared. I whirled. Where was Johnny? The memory of him falling off the barge as a toddler flashed through my mind. Surely, he wouldn't jump from that great height to save someone? Unless it was his father. I screamed, "Johnny!"

We stayed long enough to see the police pull Stone's body into a boat, then call off the search. We returned home shaken but unharmed. Johnny had scrambled up the cable for a better view, and I was too relieved to scold him.

The tattered old rag doll and Stone's note found its way back with us as well. My instinct had been to toss it in the water, but his curious postscript prevented me: *Say goodbye to Gertrude for me.* My fingers tracing the doll's face, I pictured the little girl who had once done the same. Perhaps I should have shared the story with Wash. Instead, I tossed the doll into the fireplace and let the flames lick away the pain.

In the library, a police officer was on his way out. Wash poured whiskey in the far corner.

"Like a glass?" he offered, his eyes flitting to my tear-stained face and disheveled hair. "Don't cry for him. His soul is finally at peace."

He handed me the glass, and I allowed the liquid to burn sense into my throat.

"And *your* soul?"

"Unlike Stone, the problem is not mine to solve." He circled the whiskey in his glass.

"So it's all my fault." The bridge closure, the suicide, or PT? I wasn't sure which problem he was referring to, only that he blamed me.

"*I* wasn't cavorting with other women."

Oh, that one. "That was never a problem."

"Not possible, you mean." Clearly, he had no intention of soothing my rattled nerves from the horror his son and I had witnessed. Of course, he had no idea of the anxious moments I had spent, wondering if he had also plunged out of my life forever.

"Wash, last night—"

"What? Surprised I still can?"

"Only when you're angry. Not exactly the best timing."

"Blame me for things I can't help." He slammed his glass onto the table.

"I understand your condition. For thirteen years, I've seen you able to walk one day and confined to bed the next."

"Hard to live with, I know. So you have a choice."

"Wash, I do love you."

"That isn't the question."

"It's not your condition I find unbearable."

"Just me."

I winced. "You know that's not so."

"Then you love PT in the way you don't love me anymore."

"No!"

"You deny loving him?"

"No. I don't deny that." I drained my glass. "God, this is difficult."

Wash folded his arms across his chest, self-defense of the heart. "Tell me."

"I'm not a man, so perhaps I don't understand some things."

He put his palms up as if to say *What?*

"You left me. Abandoned me when things changed in our bed."

"Good God."

"I don't mean only physically."

"How can I not turn away when you get what you need somewhere else?" He scrunched a fistful of his hair. "How much do you wish me to suffer?"

A terrible realization washed over me. "You still think I'm having an affair."

A slight nod.

Why didn't he believe me? Damn that Martin!

"I've told you nothing happened. How long have you felt this way?" I gently palmed his cheek and held his face toward me. There was to be no escaping into his shell. But the pained squint in his eyes said *A very long time*.

"Dear Lord, Wash!"

"Am I wrong?" Finally, he held my gaze, but the mix of anger, hurt, and resignation caused me to wince.

"A supportive ear? Yes! I'm guilty of finding that outside our marriage. But I never shared his bed!"

"Do you want to?"

I crossed my arms and regarded my toes.

"Well, there we have it."

"I'm being honest. Have you never wanted another woman? What matters is whether you act on it."

"It's not the same. Clearly, he's in love with you and you love him. This isn't a matter of mere lust."

"No. It's about sharing a life."

"You're blaming me again."

"No, I'm trying to understand you."

He sighed. "A faulty, broken man." He opened the humidor, releasing the sweet scent of Cuban cigars, selected one, put it in the chopper, and guillotined off its head.

"You used to confide in me." I tried not to sound accusing.

"Emily, I've always wanted—"

I held up a finger, then lowered it, my anger fading to sadness and guilt. "Maybe at some point, I stopped listening." My own admission stung.

"I am afraid of losing you. At the same time, I should set you free." He sank into his favorite armchair, calmly lighting his cigar as if this were a business meeting.

"Ugh! Set me free, as if I am a caged bird?" This argument was not over, despite his retreating to his place of comfort. But now, wiser from experience, I wouldn't turn away. I would dig deeper until I brought out the truth, however ugly and uncomfortable it might be.

"Oh, dear Em. You know better than that. Have you already forgotten who sewed all those bloomer costumes?" Chaucer brushed by me, sat at Wash's feet, and rested his graying muzzle on his lap.

I sank down in my usual chair. Whiskey dulled my senses, and exhaustion set in. It would be easier to accept our situation. Why dredge up these buried emotions? *Move on*, my weary soul told me. But complacence had only led to distance.

"Why do you fear losing me?" I asked.

He held his cigar aloft and gazed into the curling smoke. "This business with Stone reminded me of something I hadn't thought about for years. Perhaps it affected my judgment."

I held out two fingers for a taste of his cigar.

"Some time ago—over twenty years now—there was one who loved me before you. A college friend." He patted the dog's head and smiled. "We had great fun and were very close."

"I didn't expect I was the first."

His smile faded. "It was an unrequited love. And it ended badly."

"Those things usually do." I was beginning to regret my vow to be a better listener. "What does this have to do with us?"

"Well, he died it seems..."

"He?"

"By his own hand." He took back the cigar and pulled from it. "I tried to be kind in my rejection but in fact could never love him in that way, and thus he killed himself. It's nothing to do with you, I know here." He pointed to his head. "But it has everything to do with you"—he pointed to his heart—"here."

"Wash, you never told me—"

"Do you think for one moment I didn't want you? But you can't hold on to something not yours. I've never forgotten you were the belle of the ball. That you could have any man with the crook of a finger. Men enjoy your company"—his eyes flashed at me—"and you theirs. This is not to say that's your fault. But I lived in constant fear of losing you, perhaps not in the extreme measure of my classmate but overwhelming all the same."

The deep, wounded appearance returned to his eyes, as after the war. Chaucer seemed to sense Wash's pain, looking at me to take it away. "I gave you more freedom than most in an effort to make up for...uh...shall we say, my deficiencies, and see how you repay me."

My head jerked in surprise. It had never crossed my mind that he was knowingly sacrificing a good measure of pride, allowing me my flirtations and apparently considerably more. In fact, it wasn't the *more* that so greatly troubled him. Rather, it seemed it was the affection and emotional bond I shared with PT that he found intolerable.

I squeezed my eyes shut, trying to stop the spinning in my mind. So many years, he knew—or thought he knew—yet said nothing. "Why now, Wash?"

He shrugged. "You asked."

"Why? Why would you suffer in silence, believing yourself cuckolded?"

"I told you why."

"There's something else. I know you too well."

He sighed, tapped his cigar on the ash tray. "Do you really want me to say it?"

Yes, damn it, I thought. *Admit your motivation for accepting an unfaithful wife had more to do with a certain engineering project and less to do with guilt from a distant unrequited love.* But before I could form the words in a somewhat less offensive manner or decide if they even needed saying, he turned away, the shell closing around him to protect his tender soul.

I wondered if it were possible to continue to love this man. There was, after all, another man—a friend who loved me and had waited for me while my own husband had been willing to trade my fidelity for his own damned project.

Things remained strained in our household. Wash's ultimatum and startling revelations hung over my head, but the parade of journalists, politicians, and investors through our home prevented resolution.

One Sunday evening, we attempted a normal family dinner. That was until Johnny asked about PT's bandaged nose.

"So you clobbered him?" Johnny punched the air, delighting in his father's somewhat edited recounting of that awful evening.

I glared at Wash in warning.

"Not proud of it," he lied, "but yes, I did."

"Can't wait to tell my friends," Johnny said, stabbing at his meatball.

"You'll do nothing of the sort." I twirled pasta onto my fork. "This family has had quite enough publicity. And don't talk with your mouth full."

"You listen to your mama now, Mr. Johnny." Muriel appeared in the dining room doorway. Her hair now dusted with gray, she was considerably slower-moving these days. "Mr. Roebling, you have a guest."

Standing next to her, C. C. Martin was smiling, a rare event.

"Sorry to disturb you, but I thought you would want to know right away." He handed documents to Wash, who riffled through them.

"The bridge has been thoroughly inspected. The board and city have declared it safe." The normally stoic Martin cheered. He nodded toward me. "Mrs. Roebling's performance won them over."

I was on my feet in an instant, hugging Wash, Johnny, Muriel, and even Martin. "Hooray! Hooray!" *Pop* went the cork from a champagne bottle Muriel opened, and we laughed at the geyser it produced.

Wash remained calm, barely cracking a smile. "Of course the bridge is safe. When will it open?"

There was one more obstacle, at least as far as the bridge was concerned. We calculated that if crowds were allowed unlimited access to the bridge, it was possible to exceed its weight limit. Wash dictated a note to the board:

I will not be responsible for the consequences if people are allowed to crowd on as they like. It would be possible for one hundred thousand people to crowd the main span of the bridge and cover every available foot of space, cables, and tops of trusses. This would make a load three times greater than the live load calculated for. In addition, the stairway from the footpaths on both sides— Brooklyn and Manhattan—are not wide enough to accommodate more than a few pedestrians at a time. Accordingly, provisions for orderly access and egress must be implemented immediately.

The trustees, for once, were quick to act. Proper crowd control was implemented, with a system of tickets for the event set up. Finally, we could be assured that another crowding disaster would not occur.

THIRTY-NINE

W e planned to host a large reception to celebrate the completion of the bridge, and invited the mayors of New York and
Brooklyn, the bridge committee, family, friends, and some
influential guests. Rumors circulated that the president of the United States
might attend.

Thrown into the unfamiliar role of grand hostess, the first thing I did
was to consult Mother. She was in her glory as she and her circle advised
me concerning invitations, refreshments, and music. For weeks, they delved
into planning the party as their raison d'être.

My relationship with PT had yet to be sorted out, but I decided to invite
him to the event, as I longed to see him. The risk of another altercation at
so public an event seemed slight, and the number of guests ensured he and
Wash need not run into each other.

Banners, flags, and coats of arms of both cities adorned the front of our
home. The streets leading up to it were lined with elaborate posters and
banners.

Bronze likenesses of both Papa and Wash were delivered and set up on
pedestals in our parlor. The sculptor had done a fine job, capturing much of
Papa's intensity in the cold, hard metal. Wash's likeness was stunning. Even
in sculpture, his handsome features showed strength and compassion. Wash
shook his head at these, mortified. All the attention rather embarrassed
him, but I was proud.

Finally, the day of the reception arrived. Wash was having a particularly difficult time with his suit buttons and bow tie. As I retied the knot, I was suddenly taken aback by the crinkles around his eyes. Though only in his midforties, he had aged tremendously in the last decade, his once deep-golden hair now faded. The pine scent of his shaving soap stirred long-buried feelings of walks in the woods and of dancing three feet off the ground.

"You smell nice," he said as if reading my thoughts. His hands on my waist, it seemed he wanted a kiss.

"Thank you. I better get downstairs."

I gathered with Mother, Henrietta, Eleanor, and Carrie in our formal gowns for photographs. My favorite dressmaker had created a gorgeous black silk gown. When it arrived, I discovered the ladies had added a little detail. Fastened to the waist was a cluster of silk violets. A small thing, perhaps, but to me, it symbolized my acceptance into their world just as I was.

"We have another little surprise for you." Mother took my hand, and her friends followed us into the library. It had become a staging area for the event, with caterer's supplies, flower cuttings, boxes, and crates everywhere. "Close your eyes."

I did as she asked, there was a rustle of boxes and paper, and in a moment, she said, "Now open them."

Henrietta and Eleanor held aloft a quilt. A very special quilt.

"Oh my word!" My hand clapped to my mouth. The quilt was composed of many squares, each with brown or blue or gray embroidery. The squares pieced together to create a beautiful image of the bridge.

Mother rested her arm on my shoulder. "I used a drawing John Senior gave me long ago to make a pattern for each square, and we all worked on it."

"Me as well." Johnny entered the room, kissed my cheek. "Here's the best square of all." He pointed to a spot toward the bottom. It pictured a sailing ship.

"The *Cutty Sark*. Thank you, John." My whole body warmed with love and joy. "Thank you all. I will treasure this always."

"Pa did the border." The quilt was framed in golden-yellow fabric, and violets were sewn within it. "He told me violets mean 'forever faithful.'"

My heart skipped a beat, and I searched his eyes for any hint of scorn but found none.

Mother patted my hand. "Thank *you*, my dear. But speaking of Washington, you better see if he's ready. It's almost time."

I hurried upstairs where Wash waited for me at our bedroom door, elegant in his black coattails, white shirt, and bow tie.

"There you are, my lovely. I have a little something for you." He presented me with a small velvet box.

"Oh my, another present? I'm overwhelmed by the quilt, Wash. How did you keep that a secret?"

"We're devious." He tapped the velvet box in my hand. "It's more of a peace offering than a present. Open it."

I opened the box, expecting a bracelet that I had longed for at Tiffany's. But inside were cameo earrings. The same pair he had given to me after our wedding so long ago. My breath caught.

His eyes flicked from the earrings to me. "Do you remember?"

"From the war…you gave them to me on the train" was all I was able to say through the lump in my throat.

"You never wore them. I found them in a box in the attic years ago and wondered why you didn't like them. Then I realized that *I* wasn't ready for them. You were right to tuck them away." He lifted my chin, met my eyes with his, focused and tender. "You saved me. Twice."

I touched the delicate white silhouettes against the coral background. I had long since forgotten about them. "They weren't taken off some dead person, were they?"

He smiled and shook his head.

It warmed my heart that he understood the reason I never wore them. "Are you ready for them now?"

"I am." He clipped them on my earlobes. "Do you have a hug left for an old bridge builder?"

I held out my arms, and he hugged me, hard and steady, as if he never wanted to let go.

He spoke softly in my ear. "I'm sorry for these long years of putting up with me and my dreams, and I promise to make it up to you. Will you take one more train ride to Trenton with me?"

I was still angry with him, but the power of his physical presence was making me melt once again. I pushed my palm against his chest. "Let's get through tonight. Our guests await."

He opened our bedroom door for me, and below us was a ten-piece band. The dark-blue uniforms, gold braids, and gleaming instruments were a breathtaking sight. Simultaneously, they lifted their instruments, our appearance apparently their cue. We stood at the top of the staircase, admiring the gathering. The band played a rousing Sousa march, and the crowd cheered as we descended, hand in hand.

The panels between the parlor and dining room were folded away and most of the furniture removed, creating a grand space. Flower arrangements perfumed the room. Several were displayed on stands and connected with white ribbons to delineate the dance floor.

President Arthur was indeed coming. One of the many assistants who suddenly materialized instructed us to stand inside our front door at the appointed time. After the shootings of Presidents Lincoln and Garfield, men were dispatched ahead of time to orchestrate the exact movements of all who would come into contact with the president.

We welcomed the many more guests lining the walk and all the way down the street. It seemed our home would never contain them all.

The band played "Hail to the Chief," and the guests cheered. They parted for the entrance of President Arthur, Governor Cleveland, and their entourages. The president shook Wash's hand and gave him a hearty pat on the shoulder. The photographs I had seen in the newspapers showed a robust, even portly man, but in person, he was drawn and sallow. He took my hand in both of his with a firm grip, his rough skin rasping against my glove. "Thank you, Mrs. Roebling. I understand we would not be here today if it weren't for your tremendous efforts."

"I'm happy to have helped."

President Arthur stayed for about an hour, shaking hands and thrilling the guests with his attention, then slipping out a side door without much fanfare. "The party is not in our honor but yours," he said as he more or less pushed three hundred pounds of Governor Cleveland out the door ahead of him.

Poor Wash was already tired and uncomfortable by that point. He settled on a divan in a quiet corner.

I flitted like a bumblebee between the guests (even the naysayers were now effusive with praise for the bridge), the wait staff, and Wash. I was on my way to check on the band, which had taken a long pause, when I ran, quite literally, into PT at the edge of the dance floor.

"Congratulations, my dear." He took my hand much more gently than the president had, pressing his lips to my glove. "You look stunning tonight."

The band started up again, playing a waltz.

"Shall we dance?" He offered his arm, then swirled me around with his hand on the small of my back. Noting the bouquet at my waistband, he said, "I see the violets have progressed to your formal wear."

"Thank you, Mr. Barnum." I hesitated. I had so much to tell him, but this was neither the time nor the place. "We're so grateful for your assistance. I'm not sure we could have gotten through this without you."

"We're back to Mr. Barnum, are we? Ah yes, you do have a bit of company." He was an exquisite dancer, light on his feet and able to lead me effortlessly through the crowd to a more open space. He leaned close and lowered his voice. "Now that the bridge is finally open, I'm curious where that leaves us."

I touched his slightly crooked nose. "You deserved this, you know."

He shrugged. "Surely, you know my feelings."

"About me? Oh, PT." I laughed derisively. "I'm an old married woman. And although it seems to be a well-kept secret, you are a married man."

He glanced around to see if anyone was watching, then his cheek grazed mine, sending a tingle down my spine.

The band finished the piece, and I backed away. "I really must get back."

"The party awaits its gracious hostess." He bowed and blew a kiss as I broke away.

I nervously cast about and was relieved to see Johnny conferring with the conductor of the band. Wash had left his corner, working his way through the crowd toward me with his short, halting steps. As he reached me, a pianist began the lush opening notes of Liszt's "Liebestraum No. 3 (Love's Dream)," the song we danced to on the night we met.

I glanced toward the piano. Johnny answered my suspicion with a big grin as he played it himself.

"Little plotter." I laughed, accepting Wash's hand, imagining the ball so long ago, the crowd younger, my burdens lighter, the same crystal-blue eyes gazing at me. Only now they reflected not only the trauma of the war he had kept hidden from me then and physical pain he had suffered since but also the hurt I had caused him as well.

Wash pulled me close. The crowd cheered and cleared space for us.

"Your ultimatum?" I said.

"Still flapping in the breeze like so much laundry."

"I chose you eighteen years ago, now and forever. I am even more flawed than I was when you met me, with a need for companionship that you can't meet. Can you live with that?"

"I have no issue with you seeking female companionship." He nodded toward the hundred or so women in the room.

"I should be able to commiserate with anyone I choose. You have to trust me. I shouldn't have to limit friendship to women."

He stopped dancing. "You push boundaries by nature, I understand that. If that were not so, you couldn't have accomplished all that you have." He led me away from the dance floor. "I love you, Emily. That will never change. But while you can spread your affection like morning dew on grass, I have no such ability."

"I don't ask that of you."

"No, you are strong of heart. But you must consider the wreckage in the hearts you leave behind." Wash was clear in his ultimatum: himself or PT, with none of the middle ground I sought.

He hobbled away, leaving me alone in the crowded room.

FORTY

H enri let me into the museum. It was after hours, but I knew PT would still be in his office.

"How are things with Miss Mann?" I asked.

"Just fine, Mrs. Roebling, just fine." He escorted me past the Cardiff Giant to the office door. "Turns out her family wasn't upset with her leaving the mountain for good. Got you to thank for that."

I smiled and patted his hand. At least there was one thing I managed not to destroy.

PT was on the floor, playing with a monkey. The familiar spicy aroma mixed with animal musk filled the air. He greeted me with his usual gusto, and we settled in to discuss our project at hand.

"Have you had time to complete the plan?" I asked.

"My dear, for you, I have planned a most spectacular event." He picked up a schedule from his desk. "What you are experiencing is something we in the business refer to as a *public relations* problem. And the cure for *that* is to create excitement!"

"Haven't we had quite enough of that?" I reconsidered the wisdom of requesting his services for this particular project.

"We'll provide a distraction from what the people believe—or have been falsely led to believe—they should be worried about." He handed me the schedule. Using his ringleader voice, he called out, "Put on a show! An exhibition at the bridge, a grand parade! Entertainers, bands, horses with grand carriages! Acrobats, cannons!" He paced the room, pumping his arms with each attraction.

I ran my finger down the detailed schedule. "Marvelous. An event families will enjoy on the promenade."

"Oh no, not the promenade." He flipped to the next page in my hand. "Right down the roadway."

"We would have to close the bridge."

"Exactly. Serving to underscore its necessity."

"Seems a bit contrived."

"I haven't told you the best part. You've heard of Jumbo?"

"Of course."

"Jumbo, the greatest elephant on earth, is at my disposal."

"An elephant?"

"A score of them."

"A herd of elephants stampeding the bridge." I chortled. "John Roebling will be rolling over in his grave."

"A magnificent parade with you in the lead. Then Jumbo and twenty more elephants thundering across the bridge! Crowds will love it!" He returned to his desk throne.

"A larger scale than I envisioned, but I think it will work." I was already picturing the spectacle.

"It will *work*? It's pure genius! With all that weight, there will be no doubt about the strength of the bridge. And everyone knows an elephant won't step where it's not safe."

"Then they have more brains than I."

He laughed and shook his head.

"And what do you expect from this?"

"My outrageous fee, you mean?"

"That is what I have learned to expect."

"Quite so." He lit a cigar, his cheeks sucking in, then puffing out a cloud of smoke. "Did I mention that I would love for you to lead the parade?"

"I gather as part of your scheme to rehabilitate my reputation—"

"Why not? Make an exuberant appearance. Defy the scuttlebutt."

"While that's tempting, I plan to fade from the spotlight and enjoy a more conventional life. You haven't answered my question."

He leaned forward. "I have never given up on a certain quest. As dear as he is, I'm sure Mr. Roebling's...*condition* presents some limitations."

"Certainly none of your concern."

He touched his nose as if it were still sore. "I beg your pardon. That was boorish and not even the point."

"Apology accepted. And although I tremble to hear it, what is your quest?"

"You want me to spell it out. As you wish. Peanut, I am offering my heart. Tell me, what are you going to do with it?" He put down his cigar. "Shall we remain supportive friends, or is there something else in our future?"

The power he had over me had returned. I could be sucked into his world like a wave pulled back to the sea. My spirits lifted with the possibility of a carefree life, filled with travel, laughter, fun, companionship...and more. I took a deep breath, clenched my fists. "No. This has to stop."

He eyed me intently; he was gifted at reading a face. My innermost feelings seemed naked under his scrutiny.

"My foolish heart." He sighed.

"I am not without my own temptations."

"But I am rejected nonetheless."

"Afraid so. If I were—"

"It doesn't matter." He closed his books, and I felt a part of me close as well.

"I have leaned on you for so long, PT, and now I've hurt you. I'm sorry."

"A foolish pursuit. How many years?"

I swallowed. This was the worst part. "I'm afraid we have to end our friendship."

After a long, uncomfortable pause, he said, "Is that what you want?"

Having no fair way to answer that, I bit my lip and averted my gaze.

"I understand. But the parade should proceed as planned." The showman was gone; the businessman appeared. "A parade for you and for the bridge." He scribbled something in a notebook, then snapped it shut.

"You don't have to do this."

"Good publicity. A show on the greatest bridge on earth. Despite my wrong-headed intentions, it's still a grand idea." He opened his top desk drawer and slipped something out. "Besides, you've already paid the fee." He fanned the tattered bills I gave him years ago.

My heart was breaking as I turned away.

"Goodbye, my Peanut."

I pulled open that heavy door for the last time.

⁓

I wanted to curl up and lick my wounds before I told Wash. Of course, that would serve no purpose, and I wanted to clear the air before the official bridge opening. My marriage, as always, was intertwined with the bridge, something I had long since learned to accept. But that project was ending, and our future paths needed to be charted, whether together or divided. He deserved to know my decision before his big day, but first, I had an ultimatum of my own.

I found him on the rooftop that balmy evening, sitting on a bench, enjoying the view of city lights in a light breeze. He slid over to make room for me.

"Wash, do you remember when I mentioned going to law school?"

"Yes, some time ago. Thought you had lost interest."

"No, just otherwise occupied." I caught his eye.

"Have you found a school—one that will accept—"

"Not yet. But I think we have enough influence here that an exception can be made for me."

"I see. So you're staying in New York." His gaze fell to his lap where his hands rested, palms to the sky.

"No, dear. I couldn't trust all those Roeblings to give you any peace without my interference. I think we want a rather grand house in Trenton for family get-togethers and perhaps grandchildren visiting someday."

He looked up, a smile creeping across his face.

"However," I said.

He shook his head. "There's always 'however.'"

"I want you to promise I can come back to New York to study law. Maybe once Johnny is off to university." I waited for him to look at me directly, wanting him to fully understand my position. "Promise me that I don't have to give up all my dreams."

He reached out, touched the cameo on my earlobe. "It seems a fine plan. I not only agree, I may insist upon it." He traced a finger along my jaw. "But Phineas? I won't change my mind about him."

I took a breath to steady my voice. "That has been settled."

He responded simply, "Then we are agreed."

I laid my head in his lap, contemplating all I had lost and all that I would soon give up. Perhaps I would learn to love living in Trenton, but that seemed a distant possibility. And would visits to New York be the same without the company of my dear friend?

I allowed a tear to flow across my face and fall on his trousers. It was as Eleanor had described; we had gone through the breakers and found each other on the other side. No city lights, no racing horses in the countryside could replace the oneness Wash and I shared, the deep love that comes from having sacrificed everything for each other. And perhaps more importantly, he knew me as no other, understood my passion to overcome barriers for women, supported it even. He was my ally for life.

The night was dark and clear; the Milky Way shone like a moonlit cloud. Millions of stars, all those worlds, and we were mere specks huddled together on one tiny planet, lifting and falling in life's rhythm.

Wash bent to kiss me, absently fingering my curls. "Look. A falling star." He began to sing softly, sweetly:

"The Star that watched you in your sleep
Has just put out his light.
'Good-day, to you on earth,' he said,
'Is here in heaven Good-night.'"

FORTY-ONE

The morning of May 24, 1883, I was up at dawn. Out our bedroom window, the bridge stood out in silhouette against a lightening sky with only a few clouds. This should be a perfect day, I thought, as Wash began to rustle.

Too nervous to eat, I spent the early hours reading and catching up on correspondence. My excitement grew as I sorted through the heaps of letters of congratulation. Wash sat at the window, watching the fabulous shadows move across the bridge in the sun and listening as I read some of the notes out loud.

When it was time to get ready, I sorted through my dresses. "I don't know. Which one do you think, Wash?"

"Just pick one," he said rather irritably.

"Aren't you excited?" He made no move to get dressed. "Please don't say you're going to watch from your window."

"My job is done. I don't have any need for spectacle. You know I can barely handle a single visitor, never mind a crowd." He struggled up from his chair and sorted through the dresses I had tossed on the bed.

"This one." He handed me a lovely cream-colored dress I hadn't worn in some time. *Does it have sentimental value?* I wondered, until he added, "It'll be warm out there."

"But it's going to be glorious!" I said as I slipped into the dress. "You will be honored as a hero."

He opened an old textbook and slipped out the tattered drawing of the bridge made by his father on the ferry. Long ago, Wash had written upon it in his tiny, neat script: *We don't fight the river. We rise above it.*

"It is done, Papa." He glanced at the framed portrait of Papa he kept on his desk. "What do you think he would do?"

I held up my hair so he could button the back of my dress. "This would be your father's proudest day. He wouldn't miss the ceremony."

Having finished my buttons, he turned me to him. "Go. Enjoy, my love." He nodded toward Papa's portrait. "We'll watch from here."

Johnny sat with me, leading a grand carriage parade of family and friends from our home to the bridge, followed by dozens more carriages. The celebrating crowds were so thick, the horses struggled to move forward. People leaned out windows and waved at our cavalcade from rooftops, dropping confetti. I couldn't imagine a more joyful day.

American flags and red, white, and blue bunting adorned the bridge, the colors vibrant against the stone. We stepped out of our carriages under the arch of the Brooklyn tower and continued on foot, walking across the river to the cheers of thousands.

Church bells rang. Steam whistles blew from every factory, train engine, and boat for miles. Artillery on each shoreline boomed. So many boats clogged the river, it seemed you could walk across the river on them. Some sprayed huge plumes of water.

As we made our way to the bridge on the Brooklyn side, another parade approached from Manhattan. Leading this was President Arthur, Governor Cleveland, and Mayor Edson in an open carriage. The Seventh Regiment Army Band followed them, playing patriotic songs.

We met them as they reached the New York tower. A soldier commanded, "Present arms," and an honor guard snapped their rifles smartly. The president waved and tipped his hat to the crowd, then stepped down from the carriage and shook my hand. Together, we walked across the bridge with the band and the rest of the parade following.

Having concluded my part of the ceremony, I joined Mother and Johnny in the grandstand to listen to speeches and watch the rest of the parade. As the various mayors and dignitaries waxed eloquent about the bridge representing a magnificent testament to man's ingenuity and determination, I wondered where they had hidden their enthusiasm during the dark days of doubt.

Papa's former business associate, Congressman Abram Hewitt, surprised me when he waved toward me while reciting a list of accomplishments of the ancient Greeks.

"It is thus an everlasting monument to the self-sacrificing devotion of a woman and of her capacity for that higher education from which she has been too long debarred."

The subject of this unexpected soliloquy, I peered over my shoulder—the audience fastened its attention on me. One by one, they stood, and men took off their hats and held them high. Hewitt concluded by saying, "The name of Mrs. Emily Warren Roebling will thus be inseparably associated with all that is admirable in human nature and with all that is wonderful in the constructive world of art."

It was a moment I shall never forget. To be publicly recognized and applauded was a great honor, of course. I stood and waved as I sniffed back tears. Tears of happiness, not only that my efforts had been acknowledged but that a man in Hewitt's position recognized the importance of higher education for women. He would surely be an ace in my pocket when the time came to apply to law school.

"On with the parade!" Mayor Edson proclaimed, and there was a huge cheer for PT, who led acrobats, clowns, jugglers, chimpanzees, and camels. A flush of purple graced his lapel—he wore a boutonniere of violets.

The processional paused. Then a baby elephant scampered across the bridge. And another and another. The crowd cheered wildly. The elephants grew larger and larger, until finally, Jumbo, festooned in a scarlet and gold headdress, made his entrance. I cheered as he lumbered across, each step assured, his head held high.

As the parade ended, a jubilant crowd filled both decks of the bridge, making toasts and singing songs. As excited as they were, their feelings could only be a mere fraction of the joy and relief that enveloped me. It was as if I had become an entirely new person, and each stone, each wire represented an achievement I had watched and guided and protected.

At dusk, the bridge was cleared, and a stunning fireworks display exploded from the towers, the center of the bridge, and from boats on the river. The colorful extravaganza could be seen for miles across the newly united cities.

And so, I had my part in the building of the great bridge. Wash thought the parade too extravagant, but the people loved it, and PT was in his glory. When the elephants strutted by, it seemed as if they knew—knew that the people had their bridge, and Papa and Wash had kept their promises and fulfilled their dreams. They would always be honored for their brilliance and perseverance. But the circus parade? Oh, the parade was for me.

EPILOGUE

1884

At night, I stand alone on the grand expanse. The moonlight alternates an eerie glow with ribbed shadows on the giant steel cables, hurtling down toward me from the Brooklyn tower, running beside me for a bit, then arching back up to the other tower and on to Manhattan.

My hand grips a cold, wet railing as I peer skyward at clouds playing hide-and-seek with the moon. Ghosts of riggers sit on platforms high above, sharing a joke and a ham sandwich as they attach jail bars of suspension cables two hundred feet over the water. The wind howls and whips my dress against me, but there is no tremble in the steel beams underneath. Papa would be pleased.

The Great Bridge, they call it. A monument, a fortress, a miracle. Perhaps only I know its complete story, the struggle to build it, the sacrifices better left unknown. In a hundred years, there may be nothing here but a giant pile of stone, hardly a testament to the immense task—connecting a city ripped in two by a churning river. Then again, maybe the bridge will still be standing proud, towers in the mist, travelers crossing by the thousands.

There is one thing left to do before leaving. The little girls have given me a ring of flowers, a chain of daisies they picked from the little spot of undisturbed earth beneath the bridge. I finger the twists of the slim green stems, the velvety white petals. Children watched as their homes were destroyed, watched as workers retched and collapsed. Maybe some of them lost their own fathers. Yet they give me flowers in thanks. They humble me.

An image: Elizabeth and me, picking dandelions and daisies, tiny bouquets for our mother in our little fists. "I forgive you," she says. She holds out her bouquet to me, her other hand brushing aside her golden curls.

"For the fight? For pushing you?"

She smiles, shakes her head, her eyes matching the sky. I'm five years old, running along the riverbank, panting, knees bobbing up and down, gravel crunching under my wet shoes. Tall grasses whip me. I push, push through along the river. Up ahead, a dark form. It climbs out of the water. A baby bear. No. It crawls on hands and knees, dripping, its head sagging, lower. It collapses, flattens onto the shore. I run, closer now. Not a bear. A brown shirt. Dark hair. I reach him, throw myself onto him.

It is my brother who survived.

And I am glad it's him.

My sister's gentle voice: "I forgive you." She presses the blossoms into my hand. "Forgive yourself."

The daisy chain is soft and fresh and sweet when I press my nose into it.

Forgiveness seeps into my healing heart.

I toss the flower ring into the abyss.

AFTERWORD

I n my opinion, the point of historical fiction is to learn about an interesting time in a more entertaining manner than reading the unembellished truth. The very things that make a story come to life, such as the emotions and personal dialogue, are frequently undocumented and therefore have no place in nonfiction. The challenge for the author is to strike a balance between fact and fiction, sometimes bending the truth in order to better tell a story.

In this story, I hoped to shed light on a time very different from the present, though its results are still very much in evidence. The Brooklyn Bridge is an icon, a symbol not only of New York City but a monument of American style and ingenuity known worldwide. Indeed, I rarely spend a day without seeing an image of it in the media.

I hope the reader will view the Brooklyn Bridge with increased insight after reading *The Engineer's Wife* and that the very real sacrifices of its builders will never be forgotten. Although the exact toll is unknown, of the more than six hundred workers, at least twenty lost their lives, and scores if not hundreds more suffered severe injuries.

In addition, I wished to shed light on the astounding limitations faced by women of that era, the very long route of suffrage that finally enabled American women to vote nationally in 1920. Women's fashions of the 1800s, which severely hampered their activities, always interested me, along with the consequences for those who challenged the norm.

For the reader who wishes a bit of a guideline to which story elements are factual, I offer the following:

The timeline of the main characters' lives and bridge construction are mostly factual, with some exceptions. Emily's mother, Phebe, died in late 1870. The incident of John and Washington on the trapped ferry, the impetus for John's idea to build the bridge, reportedly happened in 1853, not 1848 as in the story.

The timeline of the repair work, flooding, and concrete filling of the Brooklyn caisson, as well as other small details, have been altered to better suit the pace of narration. The deadly panic on the bridge actually occurred a week after the official opening, not before.

The *Cutty Sark* was built in 1869, a bit too late for Washington and Emily to have seen it under construction. However, it is quite logical that they would have visited ships under construction in order to learn about building caissons. I chose the *Cutty Sark* because she visited New York City in the time frame in the story, she is a fabulous example of the shipbuilding techniques of the era, and because she is now stunningly showcased in a museum in Greenwich, England. One can also visit the nearby Royal Observatory.

Washington and Emily initially lived on Hicks Street in Brooklyn before purchasing the home on Columbia Heights. John Roebling died in the Hicks Street home.

The following characters are, although used fictitiously, based on actual persons and served in more or less the same capacity as in the story: Emily, Washington, John, John Roebling II, Phebe Warren, G. K. Warren, Abram Hewitt, Henry Ward Beecher, Edmond Farrington, C. C. Martin, William Kingsley, Charles Young, Amelia Bloomer, Alva Vanderbilt, and Henry Murphy.

The good-night poem recited by Wash at his son's bedside is "The Baby's Star" by John Banister Tabb (1845–1909), a Confederate prisoner of war. It is of some personal significance to me as I found the poem in an old schoolbook, one of my late mother's few possessions.

There are several collections of Roebling letters, open to the public for research purposes, in various universities (Rutgers, Rensselaer Polytechnic, Princeton) and museums and collections (the Roebling Museum in New Jersey, the Brooklyn Historical Society). Letters in the novel are a combination of their actual writings, interpretations of such, and entirely imagined missives.

The bridge collapse and train wreck on the River Dee are historical, although the characters and details are imagined.

Benjamin Stone and his family are fictitious characters but are compilations of actual persons. Carrie Beebe did indeed write *Violets* at about this time (first known publishing in 1873) in New York State, but her character is otherwise fictional. The connection was inspired by the violets Emily was reported to have worn at the celebratory party and the curious passage that seemed to echo beliefs about women's place in the era, especially women who dared to be different.

John Roebling engineered the Cincinnati bridge over the Ohio River, which stands today, and of course also designed the Brooklyn Bridge. His unfortunate accident and resultant death from tetanus are historical.

P. T. Barnum was, of course, a real person, but his role in the building of the bridge and relationship with Emily are entirely imagined. However, there are several parallels to the Roeblings that indicate there could indeed have been a relationship between them.

Barnum was one of the most wealthy and influential men in New York City at the time, and it is entirely possible that he had some role in the financing and planning for the bridge. It is accurate that Barnum had several museums in New York that burned and were eventually replaced and another opened in Brooklyn. However, the exact timeline of his various enterprises, his first wife's death, and his second marriage have been altered to better fit the pace of the story. Barnum also leased the space for his popular hippodrome, the former train station that later became the first Madison Square Garden. He was one of the first to popularize peanuts as a snack fit for humans.

His museum did display a hat that belonged to Ulysses S. Grant, but the way he obtained it in this story is imagined. General Warren's contempt for Grant was widely known, and such a donation could have happened. It is also true that Barnum planned a parade, featuring twenty-four elephants, including Jumbo, across the bridge for the opening ceremonies. However, his proposal was rejected, then revived a year later to show the safety of the bridge, as in the story.

There is also the commonality of employing ship riggers for the circus and bridge building. Barnum did live in Connecticut with his large family, but his opinions on immigration patterns are imagined.

Emily did indeed come from a Cold Spring family of twelve children, five of whom were lost in childhood, although the story of Elizabeth's death is fictitious.

The Civil War stories were inspired by historical events or in some cases, such as the head in the chest tale, were oft-told family tales of questionable verity. O'Brien is a fictitious character, although the death of a worker in the arch collapse, leaving six children fatherless, is factual. General G. K. Warren and Washington Roebling were indeed at Little Round Top at the Battle of Gettysburg. Warren was demoted and then cleared of wrongdoing as in the story.

Emily and Washington met at a military ball while Washington was serving as G. K. Warren's aide, as in the story. That Washington had a pet water snake that frequently escaped is documented. Its appearance in Emily's bathtub is thankfully imagined.

The loss of Washington's college roommate to suicide, following a confession of romantic love, is true. Although his inner turmoil can only be guessed at, it seems to have been significant, as it was not until several years after the incident that he entered into a romantic relationship.

Muriel Mann and Henri are fictitious, but the history and culture of the Mountain People are not. The Borough of Ringwood was not incorporated until 1918. The area went by various names before that, and I used the current official name for simplicity.

Washington's partial blindness, nervous condition, and general infirmity as a result of caisson disease and his extended absences from the work site are well documented. His sexual dysfunction is undocumented, at least as far as I could research, but is a very common occurrence in the disease, especially at the severity he experienced. Dr. Andrew Smith did not become the site physician until 1872. My research did not reveal who tended Wash's caisson disease before then.

Emily's role in the construction was considerable, including design of certain metal parts, as surviving letters attest. Her work began as a messenger for Washington and evolved as she learned more and more. Indeed, there is a plaque on the bridge that honors her efforts, along with her husband and father-in-law. However, her adventures in the caisson and atop the towers are imagined, as I did not find documentation confirming that she visited these areas.

Washington recovered from his injuries and was well enough to run the family wire business in Trenton well into his old age. The stress of the bridge and caring for him seemed to have taken a toll on Emily, as she was fifty-nine when she died in 1903 of stomach cancer. Washington outlived Emily by twenty-three years. Although he remarried late in life, Washington and Emily rest side by side in the Cold Spring cemetery.

For those seeking additional reading, David McCullough's *The Great Bridge: The Epic Story of the Building of the Brooklyn Bridge* is a thoroughly researched book, as is Marilyn Weigold's *Silent Builder: Emily Warren Roebling and the Brooklyn Bridge*, the only biography written on Emily Warren Roebling of which I am aware. In addition, Ken Burns did an Academy Award–nominated documentary titled *Brooklyn Bridge* in 1981.

Other than these researchable elements, the characters, actions, and events are fictitious.

READING GROUP GUIDE

1. Before accepting Wash's proposal, Emily worries about losing a sense of herself. How would you characterize the changes Emily undergoes during her marriage? Were any of these changes negative?

2. Wash returns from the war a different man, with what today would be diagnosed as PTSD. Discuss the ways you think his time in the war affected him long-term. How did his behavior change? How did he change emotionally?

3. Emily juggles working at the bridge and managing office work while taking care of a young child. Discuss the difficulties of being a working mother. What kinds of challenges does Emily face? How do they differ from challenges modern working mothers face?

4. Building the Brooklyn Bridge was a dangerous process—working in the caisson results in multiple deaths and injuries, and men like O'Brien and Supple die during construction. Do you think sacrifices like these were/are justified, then or now? Do losses undermine or enhance the image of the bridge?

5. Emily is forced to choose between continuing her work with the bridge—thereby fulfilling Wash's dreams—and being a part of the suffragist movement. Did she make the right choice? Put yourself in

her shoes. What would you do? Do you think Wash was right to make her choose in the first place?

6. PT asks Emily if she loves him or the idea of him. What does he mean by this, and which is true?

7. Emily admits to underestimating the women around her. Discuss the effects of this internalized misogyny. How do you think this affects her relationships with other women?

8. As Emily rises to the occasion and does the job of the chief engineer, Wash becomes listless and reclusive. Why do you think this is? Is he threatened by Emily? Discuss how masculinity was perceived at the time.

9. How do both Wash and PT help Emily take risks and become the person she was meant to be?

10. Though they can't vote, the group of suffragettes finds ways of being influential behind the scenes. Discuss the ways that women have enacted change while avoiding the public eye throughout history.

11. Emily becomes frustrated with the suffragist meetings because of the infighting and the lack of agreement on central issues. Can you think of other movements that have suffered in this way? In what ways were they still successful?

12. Throughout the course of the book, Emily and Wash lose many people they love—siblings, friends, and parents. How do you think they each cope with grief differently? Which character's loss did you grieve the most?

13. Emily is in a difficult position: she is married to Wash but also loves PT. How do you feel about Wash's ultimatum to Emily? What would

you do if you were given a similar choice? Whom did you think she should have chosen?

14.   Which of Emily's traits are your favorite? Do you relate to her?

15.   Emily has a lifelong habit of breaking societal rules and conventions. How do the important people in her life—her mother, GK, Wash, and PT—either encourage or try to limit this?

16.   After twelve people die from the panic on the bridge, Emily almost loses her will to continue working on the project. Have you ever faced a crossroads like this? What did you do to keep going?

A CONVERSATION
WITH THE AUTHOR

How did you first learn about Emily Warren Roebling? What inspired you to write her story?

I was doing research for a play, which was to center on multiple generations of a family who were involved in the same dangerous occupation. I wanted to explore the family dynamics of such a situation: the conflict between sharing a passion and livelihood while at the same time subjecting loved ones to danger. In my research, I discovered the Roebling family and was immediately captivated by them, especially Emily.

I grew up in northern New Jersey, and my father had a penchant for taking my siblings and me for climbs to the top of everything. Hills, cliffs, buildings, monuments, whatever—if we could get to the top of it, we did. We also walked across long and high bridges. I remember how startling and frightening it was to be in the middle of the George Washington Bridge and feeling it sway in the wind.

When I discovered that Emily's story had never been novelized, I knew it had to be and that I was the person to do it.

The Engineer's Wife relies on a great deal of research. What was that process like?

I am lucky in that the construction of the bridge is well documented. Between purchasing several excellent texts, borrowing library books, and internet searches, I found the answers to all my questions. The more difficult part was digesting the scientific information and writing it in a way that readers would understand it and not get bored. Therefore, many of the most complicated processes are simplified or left out of the story.

I am also fortunate that a large number of personal papers and correspondence has been preserved, shedding light on the central characters.

As you were writing the book, did the story unfold basically as you had expected? Were there any surprises along the way or places where your research took you in a different direction from what you had initially envisioned?

Oh my yes. I created fictional secondary characters to serve particular functions; for example, Phebe's circle of friends was intended to reflect on the expected roles of women at the time. But as their characters developed in the story, they took on other duties in subplots: suffrage, parenting, supporters, and naysayers.

PT was to have been a financial advisor and supporter and somehow became much more as I delved into Emily's predicament as she was left behind by her husband.

Sometimes, research would reveal an enticing detail that I enjoyed working into the story, such as Washington's pet snakes, a fire in the caisson, and glacial bedrock.

Emily and Washington's love story is a complicated one. Did you find it challenging to portray the dynamics of their relationship?

I found the relationship fascinating and enjoyed sussing out the very complicated nature of what they had to accomplish together, the numerous obstacles they faced, and how that would affect their marriage. They were both incredibly intelligent people, so getting into how their minds might have worked was a challenge!

Which character, if any, from the book did you relate to the most?

Mostly Emily, for her slightly rebellious yet loving and dedicated nature, but also Eleanor, for her levelheaded wisdom. Not that I have that, but it's something I aspire to.

Have you always enjoyed science yourself, or was writing about engineering and bridge building a whole new world for you?

Science was always my favorite subject, but I gravitated to the life sciences. I certainly wish I had studied the physical sciences more, as I had quite the learning curve.

Who are some of your favorite authors, and why?

I enjoy reading Ann Hood, both her novels and memoirs, due to the lovely flow of her words and the ease with which she shows her characters' emotions. Kristin Hannah is another favorite, as she has a way of making history relevant and personal. Going back a ways, Herman Wouk's historical fiction is what turned me on to the genre, and I enjoy early dystopians, such as Aldous Huxley and George Orwell. They were way ahead of their times.

What are you working on now?

Currently, I'm drafting a historical novel starring another heroine who did amazing things yet is obscure in history. Julia Stimson was an American nurse who recruited, trained, and led a group of nurses to serve in France during World War I before U.S. troops even arrived. She went on to lead all the nurses in the theater, then later headed the Army Nurse Corps, being the first woman to attain the rank of major.

ACKNOWLEDGMENTS

There is a saying that the zest in life is the journey, not the destination. So true for the writing of this book. This was a surprise, as my initial goal was only to put this fabulous story into words. I didn't foresee the enormous adventure ahead and all the people I would meet and learn from along the way.

First, I must thank my ever-patient family, especially my husband, Dave, who stood by me through every triumph, disappointment, and long hours when my focus was 150 years in the past.

Next, my writers' groups, from which many participants have become dear friends. The Eckerd College Olli Writers' Circle, led by the dedicated Pat Brown, was the first to read pages from early drafts and provided excellent feedback and support. To Jami Deise, Tom Cuba, and all the fabulous writers at the St. Pete Meetup, I miss you, and thank you forever. The biographers and historians whose hard work was the focus of my research are too numerous to list, but they have my gratitude as well.

Another organization I was privileged to be part of, Pitch Wars class of 2015 and Pitch Wars Mentors class of 2017, proved a giant step forward in the editing and publication process. Thank you to all these fabulous writers who continue to support one another in numerous ways. A special thanks to my mentor, Alex White, and Brenda Drake for creating these groups that have benefitted so many.

I am fortunate to have attended a number of conferences where I was able to workshop my manuscripts and improve my craft, such as Writers in Paradise, where I learned from the best: John Searles, Andre Dubus III, Lori

Roy, and Laura Lippman; the Surrey International Writers' Conference, where I had the pleasure of a session with Diana Gabaldon; and the Salt Cay Retreat, where I received critical advice from David Ebershoff.

Another important lesson is that it is difficult to judge when your own prose misses the mark. It is essential to have sharp-eyed readers to help you. Thank you to my many critique partners, who spent countless hours on the many manuscript drafts or assisted in research. This list is not complete, but I would like to personally thank Carol Van Drie, Stephen Maher, Anne Lipton, Joan Lander, and Sue Wolfrom.

Finally, my eternal gratitude to my agent, Lucy Cleland; editor, Anna Michels; and the entire Sourcebooks team, who made my impossible dream come true.

ABOUT THE AUTHOR

Tracey Enerson Wood has always had a writing bug. While working as a registered nurse, starting an interior design company, raising two children, and bouncing around the world as a military wife, she indulged in her passion as a playwright, screenwriter, and short story writer. She has authored magazine columns and other nonfiction and written and directed plays of all lengths, including *Grits*, *Fleas and Carrots*, *Rocks and Other Hard Places*, *Alone*, and *Fog*. Her screenplays include *Strike Three* and *Roebling's Bridge*. *The Engineer's Wife* is her first published novel.

A New Jersey native, Tracey now lives with her family in Florida. Follow her @traceyenerson.

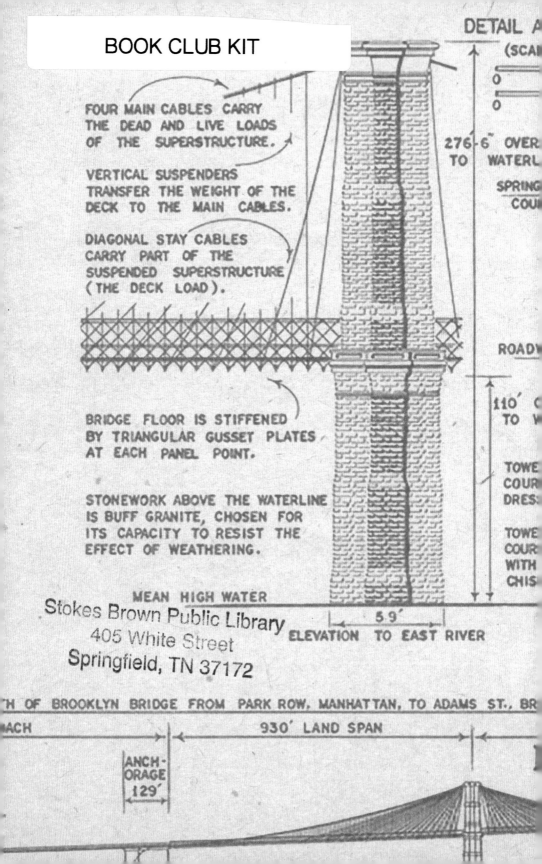

DETAIL A
(SCA

O

O

276-6" OVER
TO WATERL

SPRING
COU

FOUR MAIN CABLES CARRY
THE DEAD AND LIVE LOADS
OF THE SUPERSTRUCTURE.

VERTICAL SUSPENDERS
TRANSFER THE WEIGHT OF THE
DECK TO THE MAIN CABLES.

DIAGONAL STAY CABLES
CARRY PART OF THE
SUSPENDED SUPERSTRUCTURE
(THE DECK LOAD).

ROADW

110' C
TO W

BRIDGE FLOOR IS STIFFENED
BY TRIANGULAR GUSSET PLATES
AT EACH PANEL POINT.

TOWE
COUR
DRES

STONEWORK ABOVE THE WATERLINE
IS BUFF GRANITE, CHOSEN FOR
ITS CAPACITY TO RESIST THE
EFFECT OF WEATHERING.

TOWE
COUR
WITH
CHIS

MEAN HIGH WATER

5.9'

ELEVATION TO EAST RIVER

'H OF BROOKLYN BRIDGE FROM PARK ROW, MANHATTAN, TO ADAMS ST., BR

ACH

930' LAND SPAN

ANCH-
ORAGE
129'